Praise for the novels of Debbie Macomber

"Macomber's assured storytelling and affirming narrative is as welcoming as your favorite easy chair."

—*Publishers Weekly* on *Twenty Wishes*

"It's impossible not to cheer for Macomber's characters.... When it comes to creating a special place and memorable, honorable characters, nobody does it better than Macomber."

—*BookPage* on *Twenty Wishes*

"It's clear that Debbie Macomber cares deeply about her fully realized characters and their family, friends and loves, along with their hopes and dreams. She also makes her readers care about them."

—*Bookreporter.com* on *Susannah's Garden*

"Macomber is a master storyteller."

—*RT Book Reviews*

"Macomber spins another pure-from-the-heart romance giddy with love and warm laughter."

—*BookPage* on *The Snow Bride*

"Popular romance author Debbie Macomber has a gift for evoking the emotions that are at the heart of the genre's popularity."

—*Publishers Weekly*

Debbie Macomber is a number one *New York Times* and *USA TODAY* bestselling author. Her books include *1225 Christmas Tree Lane, 1105 Yakima Street, A Turn in the Road, Hannah's List* and *Debbie Macomber's Christmas Cookbook*, as well as *Twenty Wishes, Summer on Blossom Street* and *Call Me Mrs. Miracle.* She has become a leading voice in women's fiction worldwide and her work has appeared on every major bestseller list, including those of the *New York Times, USA TODAY, Publishers Weekly* and *Entertainment Weekly.* She is a multiple award winner, and won the 2005 Quill Award for Best Romance. There are more than one hundred million copies of her books in print. Two of her MIRA Books Christmas titles have been made into Hallmark Channel Original Movies, and the Hallmark Channel has launched a series based on her bestselling Cedar Cove series. For more information on Debbie and her books, visit her website, debbiemacomber.com.

#1 *New York Times* Bestselling Author

Debbie Macomber

Right Next Door

ISBN-13: 978-0-373-40103-1

Recycling programs for this product may not exist in your area.

Right Next Door

This edition published by arrangement with Harlequin Books S.A.

For questions and comments about the quality of this book, please contact us at CustomerService@Harlequin.com.

Printed in U.S.A.

CONTENTS

FATHER'S DAY 7

THE COURTSHIP OF CAROL SOMMARS 187

FATHER'S DAY

For Lois and Bill Hoskins,
living proof that love is
better the second time around

Chapter 1

"I can't believe I'm doing this," Robin Masterson muttered as she crawled into the makeshift tent, which was pitched over the clothesline in the backyard of her new home.

"Come on, Mom," ten-year-old Jeff urged, shifting to make room for her. "It's nice and warm in here."

Down on all fours, a flashlight in one hand, Robin squeezed her way inside. Jeff had constructed the flimsy tent using clothespegs to hold up the blankets and rocks to secure the base. The space was tight, but she managed to maneuver into her sleeping bag.

"Isn't this great?" Jeff asked. He stuck his head out of the front opening and gazed at the dark sky and the spattering of stars that winked back at them. On second thought, Robin decided they were laughing at her, those stars. And with good reason. There probably wasn't another thirty-year-old woman in the entire state of California who would've agreed to this craziness.

It was the first night in their new house and Robin was exhausted. They'd started moving out of the apartment before five that morning and she'd just finished unpacking the last box. The beds were assembled, but Jeff wouldn't hear of doing anything as mundane as sleeping on a real mattress. After waiting years to camp out in his own backyard, her son wasn't about to delay the adventure by even one night.

Robin couldn't let him sleep outside alone and, since he hadn't met any neighbors yet, there was only one option left. Surely there'd be a Mother of the Year award in this for her.

"You want to hear a joke?" Jeff asked, rolling on to his back and nudging her.

"Sure." She swallowed a yawn, hoping she could stay awake long enough to laugh at the appropriate time. She needn't have worried.

For the next half hour, Robin was entertained with a series of riddles, nonsense rhymes and off-key renditions of Jeff's favourite songs from summer camp.

"Knock knock," she said when it appeared her son had run through his repertoire.

"Who's there?"

"Wanda."

"Wanda who?"

"Wanda who thinks up these silly jokes?"

Jeff laughed as though she'd come up with the funniest line ever devised. Her son's enthusiasm couldn't help but rub off on Robin and some of her weariness eased. Camping was fun—sort of. But it'd been years since she'd slept on the ground and, frankly, she couldn't remember it being quite this hard.

"Do you think we'll be warm enough?" she teased. Jeff had used every blanket they owned, first to construct the tent and then to pad it. To be on the safe side, two or three more were piled on top of their sleeping bags on the off-chance an arctic frost descended upon them. It was spring, but a San Francisco spring could be chilly.

"Sure," he answered, missing the kidding note in her voice. "But if you get cold, you can have one of mine."

"I'm fine," she assured him.

"You hungry?"

Now that she thought about it, she was. "Sure. Whatcha got?"

Jeff disappeared into his sleeping bag and returned a moment later with a limp package of licorice, a small plastic bag full of squashed marshmallows and a flattened box of raisins. Robin declined the snack.

"When are we going to buy me my dog?" Jeff asked, chewing loudly on the raisins.

Robin listened to the sound and said nothing.

"Mom…the dog?" he repeated after a few minutes.

Robin had been dreading that question most of the day. She'd managed to forestall Jeff for the past month by telling him they'd discuss getting a dog after they were settled in their house.

"I thought we'd start looking for ads in the paper first thing tomorrow," Jeff said, still munching.

"I'm not sure when we'll start the search for the right dog." She was a coward, Robin freely admitted it, but she hated to disappoint Jeff. He had his heart set on a dog. How like his father he was, in his love for animals.

"I want a big one, you know. None of those fancy little poodles or anything."

"A golden retriever would be nice, don't you think?"

"Or a German shepherd," Jeff said.

"Your father loved dogs," she whispered, although she'd told Jeff that countless times. Lenny had been gone for so many years, she had trouble remembering what their life together had been like. They'd been crazy in love with each other and married shortly after their high-school graduation. A year later, Robin became pregnant. Jeff had been barely six months old when Lenny was killed in a freak car accident on his way home from work. In the span of mere moments, Robin's comfortable world had been sent into a tailspin, and ten years later it was still whirling.

With her family's help, she'd gone back to school and obtained her degree. She was now a certified public accountant working for a large San Francisco insurance firm. Over the years she'd dated a number of men, but none she'd seriously consider marrying. Her life was far more complicated now than it had been as a young bride. The thought of falling in love again terrified her.

"What kind of dog did Dad have when he was a kid?" Jeff asked.

"I don't think Rover was any particular breed," Robin answered, then paused to recall exactly what Lenny's childhood dog had looked like. "I think he was mostly… Labrador."

"Was he black?"

"And brown."

"Did Dad have any other animals?"

Robin smiled at her warm memories of her late husband. She enjoyed the way Jeff loved hearing stories about his father—no matter how many times he'd already heard them. "He collected three more pets the first year we were married. It seemed he was always bringing home a stray cat or lost dog. We couldn't keep them, of course, because we weren't allowed pets in the apartment complex. We went to great lengths to hide them for a few days until we could locate their owners or find them a good home. For our first wedding anniversary, he bought me a goldfish. Your father really loved animals."

Jeff beamed and planted his chin on his folded arms.

"We dreamed of buying a small farm someday and raising chickens and goats and maybe a cow or two. Your father wanted to buy you a pony, too." Hard as she tried, she couldn't quite hide the pain in her voice. Even after all these years, the memory of Lenny's sudden death still hurt. Looking at her son, so eager for a dog of his own, Robin missed her husband more than ever.

"You and Dad were going to buy a farm?" Jeff cried, his voice ebullient. "You never told me that before." He paused. "A pony for me? Really? Do you think we'll ever be able to afford one? Look how long it took to save for the house."

Robin smiled. "I think we'll have to give up on the idea of you and me owning a farm, at least in the near future."

When they were first married, Robin and Lenny had talked for hours about their dreams. They'd charted their lives, confident that nothing would ever separate them. Their love had been too strong. It was true that she'd never told Jeff about buying a farm, nor had she told him how they'd planned to name it Paradise. Paradise, because that was what the farm would be to them.

In retrospect, not telling Jeff was a way of protecting him. He'd lost so much—not only the guidance and love of his father but all the things they could have had as a family. She'd never mentioned the pony before, or the fact that Lenny had always longed for a horse....

Jeff yawned loudly and Robin marvelled at his endurance. He'd carried in as many boxes as the movers had, racing up and down the stairs with an energy Robin envied. He'd unpacked the upstairs bathroom, as well as his own bedroom and had helped her organize the kitchen.

"I can hardly wait to get my dog," Jeff said, his voice fading. Within minutes he was sound asleep.

"A dog," Robin said softly as her eyes closed. She didn't know how she was going to break the bad news to Jeff. They couldn't get a dog—at least not right away. She was unwilling to leave a large dog locked indoors all day while she went off to work and Jeff was in school. Tying one up in the backyard was equally unfair, and she couldn't afford to build a fence. Not this year, anyway. Then there was the cost of feeding a dog and paying the vet's bills. With this new home, Robin's budget was already stretched to the limit.

Robin awoke feeling chilled and warm at the same time. In the gray dawn, she glanced at her watch. Six-thirty. At some point during the night, the old sleeping bag that dated back to her high-school days had come unzipped and the cool morning air had chilled her arms and legs. Yet her back was warm and cozy. Jeff had probably snuggled up to her during the night. She sighed, determined to sleep for another half hour or so. With that idea in mind, she reached for a blanket to wrap around her shoulders and met with some resistance. She tugged and pulled, to no avail. It was then that she felt something wet and warm close to her neck. Her eyes shot open. Very slowly, she turned her head until she came eyeball to eyeball with a big black dog.

Robin gasped loudly and struggled into a sitting position, which was difficult with the sleeping bag and several blankets wrapped around her legs, imprisoning her.

"Where did you come from?" she demanded, edging away from the dog. The Labrador had eased himself between her and Jeff and made himself right at home. His head rested on his paws and he looked perfectly content, if a bit disgruntled about having his nap interrupted. He didn't seem at all interested in vacating the premises.

Jeff rolled over and opened his eyes. Immediately he bolted upright. "Mom," he cried excitedly. "You got me a dog!"

"No—he isn't ours. I don't know who he belongs to."

"Me!" Jeff's voice was triumphant. "He belongs to me." His thin arms hugged the animal's neck. "You really got me a dog! It was supposed to be a surprise, wasn't it?"

"Jeff," she said firmly. "I don't know where this animal came from, but he isn't ours."

"He isn't?" His voice sagged in disappointment. "But who owns him, then? And how did he get inside the tent with us?"

"Heavens, I don't know." Robin rubbed the sleep from her eyes while she attempted to put her garbled thoughts in order. "He looks too well fed and groomed to be a stray. He must belong to someone in the neighborhood. Maybe he—"

"Blackie!" As if in response, she was interrupted by a crisp male voice. "Blackie. Here, boy."

The Labrador lifted his head, but stayed where he was. Robin didn't blame him. Jeff was stroking his back with one hand and rubbing his ears with the other, all the while crooning to him softly.

With some effort, Robin managed to divest herself of the sleeping bag. She reached for her tennis shoes and crawled out of the tent. No sooner was she on her feet than she turned to find a lanky man standing a few yards from her, just on the other side of the three-foot hedge that separated the two properties. Obviously he was her neighbor. Robin smiled, but the friendly gesture was not returned. In fact, the man looked downright *un*friendly.

Her neighbor was also an imposing man, at least six feet tall. Since Robin was only five-three, he towered head and shoulders above her. Instinctively, she stiffened her back, meeting his dark eyes. "Good morning," she said coolly.

He barely glanced in her direction, and when he did, he dismissed her with little more than a nod. After a night on the ground, with her son and a dog for bedmates, Robin realized she wasn't looking her best, but she resented the way his eyes flicked disinterestedly over her.

Robin usually gave people the benefit of the doubt, but toward this man, she felt an immediate antipathy. His face was completely emotionless, which lent him an intimidating air. He was clearly aware of that and used it to his advantage.

"Good morning," she said again, clasping her hands

tightly. She drew herself to her full height and raised her chin. "I believe your dog is in the tent with my son."

Her news appeared to surprise him; his expression softened. Robin was struck by the change. When his face relaxed, he was actually a very attractive man. For the most part, Robin hardly noticed how good-looking a man was or wasn't, but this time…she noticed. Perhaps because of the contrast with his forbidding demeanor of a moment before.

"Blackie knows better than to leave the yard. Here, boy!" He shouted for the Labrador again, this time including a sharp whistle loud enough to pierce Robin's eardrums. The dog emerged from the tent and approached the hedge, slowly wagging his tail.

"Is that your dog?" Jeff asked, dashing out behind Blackie. "He's great. How long have you had him?"

"I'll make sure he doesn't bother you again," the man said, ignoring Jeff's question. Robin supposed his words were meant to be an apology. "He's well trained—he's never left my yard before. I'll make sure it doesn't happen again."

"Blackie wasn't any bother," Jeff hurried to explain, racing forward. "He crawled into the tent with us and made himself at home, which was all right with us, wasn't it, Mom?"

"Sure," Robin answered, flipping her shoulder-length auburn hair away from her face. She'd had it tied back when she'd gone to bed, but it had pulled free during the night. Robin could well imagine how it looked now. Most mornings it tended to resemble foam on a newly poured mug of beer.

"We're friends, aren't we, Blackie?" Jeff knelt, and

without hesitation the dog came to him, eagerly licking his face.

The man's eyes revealed astonishment, however fleeting, and his dark brows drew together over his high-bridged nose. "Blackie," he snapped. "Come."

The Labrador squeezed between two overgrown laurel bushes and returned to his master, who didn't look any too pleased at his dog's affection for Jeff.

"My son has a way with animals," Robin said.

"Do you live here?" Jeff asked next. He seemed completely unaware of their new neighbor's unfriendliness.

"Next door."

"Oh, good." Jeff grinned widely and placed his right hand on his chest. "I'm Jeff Masterson and this is my mom, Robin. We moved in yesterday."

"I'm Cole Camden. Welcome to the neighborhood."

Although his words were cordial, his tone wasn't. Robin felt about as welcome as a punk-rock band at a retirees' picnic.

"I'm getting a dog myself," Jeff went on affably. "That's why we moved out of the apartment building—I couldn't have a pet there except for my goldfish."

Cole nodded without comment.

Oh, great, Robin thought. After years of scrimping and saving to buy a house, they were going to be stuck with an ill-tempered next-door neighbor. His house was older than the others on the block. Much bigger, too. Robin guessed that his home, a sprawling three-story structure, had been built in the early thirties. She knew that at one time this neighborhood had been filled with large opulent homes like Cole Camden's. Gradually, over the years, the older places had been torn down and a series of two-story houses and trendy ramblers built in their place. Her neighbor's house was the last vestige of an era long past.

"Have you got any kids?" Jeff could hardly keep the eagerness out of his voice. In the apartment complex there'd always been plenty of playmates, and he was eager to make new friends, especially before he started classes in an unfamiliar school on Monday morning.

Cole's face hardened and Robin could have sworn the question had angered him. An uncomfortable moment passed before he answered. "No, I don't have any kids." His voice held a rough undertone, and for a split second Robin was sure she saw a flash of pain in his eyes.

"Would it be okay if I played with Blackie sometimes? Just until I get my own dog?"

"No." Cole's response was sharp, but, when Jeff flinched at his vehemence, Cole appeared to regret his harsh tone. "I don't mean to be rude, but it'd probably be best if you stayed in your own yard."

"That's all right," Jeff said. "You can send Blackie over here to visit anytime you want. I like dogs."

"I can see that." A hint of a smile lifted the corners of his mouth. Then his cool gaze moved from Jeff to Robin, his face again expressionless, but she sensed that he'd made up his mind about them, categorized them and come to his own conclusions.

If Cole Camden thought he could intimidate her, Robin had news for him. He'd broadcast his message loud and clear. He didn't want to be bothered by her or her son, and in exchange he'd stay out of her way. That was fine with her. Terrific, in fact. She didn't have time for humoring grouches.

Without another word, Cole turned and strode toward his house with Blackie at his heels.

"Goodbye, Mr. Camden," Jeff called, raising his hand.

Robin wasn't surprised when their neighbor didn't give them the courtesy of a reply.

In an effort to distract Jeff from Cole Camden's unfriendliness, she said brightly, "Hey, I'm starving. How about you?"

Jeff didn't answer right away. "Do you think he'll let me play with Blackie?"

Robin sighed, considering the dilemma that faced her. She didn't want Cole to hurt Jeff's feelings, but it wasn't likely their neighbor would appreciate her son's affinity with his Labrador. By the same token, a neighbor's dog, even one that belonged to a grouch, would ease her guilt over not being able to provide Jeff with the dog she'd promised him.

"What do you think, Mom?" Jeff prompted. "He'll probably let me play with Blackie sometimes, don't you think?"

"I don't know, honey," she whispered. "I just don't know."

Later the same day, after buying groceries to stock their bare kitchen shelves and picking up other necessities, Robin counted the change at the bottom of her purse. She needed to be sure she had money for the subway on Monday morning. Luckily she had enough spare change for BART—Bay Area Rapid Transit—to last the week, but it was packed lunches for her and Jeff until her next payday, which was in two weeks.

Her finances would've been in better shape if she'd waited another year to move out of the apartment. But interest rates were at a two-year low and she'd decided soon after the first of the year that if they were ever going to move out of the apartment this was the time.

"Mom!" Jeff crashed through the back door, breathless. "We're in trouble."

"Oh?" Robin glanced up from the salad she was mixing. A completely disgusted look on his face, her son flung himself into a chair and propped his elbows on the table. Then he let out a forceful sigh.

"What's wrong, Jeff?"

"I'm afraid we made a bad mistake."

"How's that?"

"There's nothing but girls in this neighborhood." He made it sound as though they'd unexpectedly landed in enemy territory. "I rode my bike up and down the street and all I saw were *girls*." He wrinkled his nose.

"Don't worry, you'll be meeting lots of boys in school on Monday."

"You aren't taking this seriously!" Jeff cried. "I don't think you understand what this means. There are seven houses on this block. Six of them have kids and only one has a boy, and that's me. I'm surrounded by women!"

"How'd you find all this out?"

"I asked, of course." He sighed again. "What are you going to do about it, Mom?"

"Me?" Robin asked. "Are you suggesting we move back to the apartment?"

Jeff considered this for only a moment. "I'd think we should if it wasn't for two things. We can't have a dog there. And I found a fort."

"A fort?"

"Yes," he said solemnly. "It's hidden way back in Mr. Camden's yard and covered by a bunch of brush. It's real neat there. I don't think he knows about it, because the word on the street is he doesn't like kids. Someone must've built it and I'm going to find out who. If there's a club going, I want in. I've got the right—I live closer to Mr. Camden than anyone else does."

"Agreed." Robin munched on a slice of green pepper and handed one to Jeff. "So you think it'd be all right if we stayed?"

"I guess so," Jeff conceded, "at least until I find out more about the fort."

Robin was about to say something else when the doorbell chimed.

Jeff's blue eyes met hers. "I bet it's one of those pesky girls," he said in disgust.

"Do you want me to get rid of her?"

Jeff nodded emphatically.

Robin was smiling when she answered the front door. Jeff was right; it was a girl, one who seemed to be a couple of years younger than her son. She hadn't come alone, though. Standing with the youngster was an adult.

"Hi," the woman said cheerfully, flashing Robin a warm smile. "I know you've hardly had a chance to get settled, but I wanted to introduce myself. I'm Heather Lawrence and this is my daughter, Kelly. We live next door, and we'd like to welcome you to the neighborhood."

Robin introduced herself as she opened the door and invited them in. Heather was cute and perky. Her hair was cut in a short bob that bounced when she spoke. Robin knew right away that she was going to like these neighbors. Heather's warm reception was a pleasant change from the way Cole Camden had greeted her.

"Would you like some coffee?" Robin asked.

"If you're sure I'm not interrupting anything."

"I'm sure." Robin led her into the kitchen, where Jeff sat waiting. He cast her a look that suggested she should be shot for treason, then muttered something about forgetting that mothers were really *girls* in disguise. Then he headed out the front door.

Robin reached for two matching ceramic mugs and poured coffee for herself and her new friend. She offered Kelly a glass of juice, then slid into a chair across the table from the girl and her mother. "I'm sorry about Jeff." She felt obliged to apologize. "He's at the age where he thinks girls are a plague to society."

"Don't worry about it," Heather said, smiling. "Kelly isn't keen on boys herself."

"They're creeps. I'd rather ride my bicycle than play with a boy," the girl announced. "But Mom wanted me to come over with her so she didn't look like a busybody. Right, Mom?"

Heather blushed and threw her daughter a murderous glance.

Robin laughed. "I thought it would take several weeks to get to know my neighbors and I've met two in one day."

"Someone else has already been over?"

"Cole Camden introduced himself this morning," she explained, keeping her eyes averted to hide the resentment she felt toward her unfriendly neighbor. Even now, hours later, she couldn't help thinking about the way he'd reacted to her and Jeff.

"Cole Camden introduced himself?" Heather repeated, sounding shocked. She frowned, staring into space as though digesting the fact.

"To be honest, I think he would've preferred to avoid me, but his dog wanted to make friends with Jeff."

Heather's mouth opened and closed twice. "Blackie did?"

"Is there something strange about that?"

"Frankly, yes. To say Cole keeps to himself is an understatement. I don't think he's said more than a handful of words to me in the entire two years since Kelly and I moved here. I don't know why he stays in the neighborhood." She paused to respond to her daughter, who was asking permission to go home. "Thank Robin for the juice, honey. Anyway," she went on, turning back to Robin when her daughter had skipped out the door, "he's all alone in that huge house and it's ridiculous, really. Can you imagine what his heating bills must be? Although, personally, I don't think money is much of a problem for him. But I've never heard any details."

It didn't surprise Robin to learn Cole lived alone. She'd barely met the man, but guessed that life held little joy for him. It was as though love, warmth and friendship had all been found lacking and had therefore been systematically dismissed.

"Apparently, he was married once, but he was divorced long before I came here."

Robin had dealt with unfriendly men before, but something about Cole struck her hard and deep, and she wasn't sure what it was or why he evoked such a strong feeling within her.

"He and his dog are inseparable," Heather added.

Robin nodded, hardly listening. He'd intimidated her at first, but when she'd pulled herself together and faced him squarely he'd loosened up a bit and, later, even seemed amused. But then Jeff had asked him about children, and Robin had seen the pain in his eyes.

As if by magic, her son's face appeared around the door. When he saw that Kelly was gone, he walked into the room, hands in his back pockets.

"Do you have a dog?" he asked Heather.

"Unfortunately, no. Kelly's allergic."

Jeff nodded as though to say that was exactly the kind of thing he expected from a girl. "We're getting a German shepherd soon, aren't we, Mom?"

"Soon," Robin responded, feeling wretched. After Heather left, she was going to tell Jeff the truth. She fully intended to let him have his dog, but he'd have to wait a while. She'd been practicing what to say. She'd even come up with a compromise. They could get a cat. Cats didn't seem to mind being left on their own, and they didn't need to be walked. Although she wasn't happy about keeping a litter box in the house, Robin was willing to put up with that inconvenience. Then, when she could afford to have a fence built, they'd get a dog. She planned to be positive and direct with Jeff. He'd understand. At least she hoped he would.

Heather stayed only a few more minutes. The visit had been a fruitful one. Robin had learned that Heather was divorced, worked mornings in an office and provided after-school day care in an effort to spend more time with Kelly. This information was good news to Robin, and the two women agreed that Jeff would go to the Lawrence house before and after school, instead of the community center several blocks away. The arrangement suited them both; even Jeff shrugged in agreement.

Robin would've liked to ask her new friend more

about Cole, but his name didn't come up again, and she didn't want to seem too curious about him.

After Heather left, Robin braced herself for the talk with Jeff about getting a dog. Unfortunately, it didn't go well. It seemed that after waiting nearly ten years, a few more months was completely unacceptable.

"You promised!" he shouted. "You said I could have a dog when we moved into the house!"

"You can, sweetheart, but not right away."

Unusual for Jeff, tears gathered in his eyes, and he struggled to hold them back. Soon Robin felt moisture filling her own eyes. She hated disappointing Jeff more than anything. His heart was set on getting a dog right away, and he considered the offer of a cat a poor substitute.

He left the house soon afterward. In an effort to soothe his hurt feelings, Robin cooked her son's favorite meal—macaroni and cheese with sliced sausage and lots of ketchup.

She didn't see him on the pavement or the street when she went to check half an hour later. She stood on the porch, wondering where he'd gone. His bike was inside the garage, and he'd already aired his views about playing with any of the girls in the neighborhood.

It would be just like him to storm into his room in a fit of indignation and promptly fall asleep. Robin hurried upstairs to his bedroom, which was across the hall from her own.

His bed was made and his clothes hung neatly in the closet. Robin decided that in another day or two, everything would be back to normal.

It wasn't until she turned to leave that she saw the

note on his desk. Picking it up, Robin read the first line and felt a swirling sense of panic.

Dear Mom,
You broke your promise. You said I could have a dog and now you say I have to wait. If I can't have a dog, then I don't want to live with you anymore. This is goodbye forever.
Love, Jeff

Chapter 2

For a moment, Robin was too stunned to react. Her heart was pounding so hard it echoed in her ears like thunder, so loud it seemed to knock her off balance.

Rushing down the stairs, she stood on the porch, cupped her hands over her mouth and screamed frantically. "Jeff! Jeffy!"

Cole Camden was standing on his front porch, too. He released a shrill whistle and stood waiting expectantly. When nothing happened, he called, "Blackie!"

"Jeff!" Robin tried again.

"Blackie!"

Robin called for Jeff once more, but her voice cracked as the panic engulfed her. She paused, placed her hand over her mouth and closed her eyes, trying to regain her composure.

"Blackie!" Cole yelled. He looked furious about his dog's disappearance.

It took Robin only a moment to put two and two together. "Cole," she cried, running across the lawn toward him. "I think Jeff and Blackie might have run away together."

Cole looked at her as if she was deranged, and Robin couldn't blame him. "Jeff left me a note. He wants a dog so badly and we can't get one right now because... well, because we can't, and I had to tell him, and he was terribly disappointed and he decided to run away."

Cole's mouth thinned. "The whole idea is ridiculous. Even if Jeff did run away, Blackie would never go with him."

"Do you honestly think I'd make this up?" she shrieked. "The last time I saw Jeff was around four-thirty, and I'd bet cold cash that's about the same time Blackie disappeared."

Cole's gaze narrowed. "Then where are they?"

"If I knew that, do you think I'd be standing around here arguing with you?"

"Listen, lady, I don't know your son, but I know my dog and– "

"My name's not lady," Robin flared, clenching her hands at her sides. He was looking at her as though she were a madwoman on the loose –which she was where her son was concerned. "I'm sorry to have troubled you. When I find Jeff, I'll make sure your dog gets home."

Cole's eyes shot sparks in her direction, but she ignored them. Turning abruptly, she ran back to her own house. Halfway there, she stopped dead and whirled around to face Cole again. "The fort."

"What fort?" Cole demanded.

"The one that's in the back of your yard. It's covered with brush.... Jeff found it earlier today. He wouldn't know anywhere else to go and that would be the perfect hiding place."

"No one's been there in years," Cole said, discounting her suggestion.

"The least we can do is look."

Cole's nod was reluctant. He led the way to his backyard, which was much larger than hers. There was a small grove of oak trees at the rear of the property and beyond that a high fence. Apparently the fort was situated between the trees and the fence. A few minutes later, in the most remote corner of the yard, nestled between two trees, Robin saw the small wooden structure. It blended into the terrain, and if she hadn't been looking for the hideaway, she would never have seen it.

It was obvious when they neared the space that someone had taken up residence. Cole lowered himself down to all fours, peered inside, then looked back at Robin with a nod. He breathed in sharply, apparently irritated by this turn of events, and crawled through the narrow entrance.

Not about to be left standing by herself, Robin got down on her knees and followed him in.

Just as she'd suspected, Jeff and Blackie were huddled together in a corner. Jeff was fast asleep and Blackie was curled up by his side, guarding him. When Cole and Robin entered, the Labrador lifted his head and wagged his tail in greeting.

The fort wasn't much bigger than the tent Jeff had constructed the night before, and Robin was forced to pull her knees close and loop her arms around them. Cole's larger body seemed to fill every available bit of space.

Jeff must have sensed that his newfound home had

been invaded because his eyes fluttered open and he gazed at Robin, then turned his head to stare at Cole.

"Hi, Mom," he said sheepishly. "I bet I'm in trouble, aren't I?"

Robin was so grateful to find him that all she could do was nod. If she'd tried to speak, her voice would've been shaking with emotion, which would only have embarrassed them both.

"So, Jeff," Cole said sternly. "You were going to run away from home. I see you brought everything you needed." He pushed the frying pan and atlas into the middle of their cramped quarters. "What I want to know is how you convinced Blackie to join you."

"He came on his own," Jeff murmured, but his eyes avoided Cole's. "I wouldn't have taken him on purpose—he's your dog."

"I'm glad you didn't…coerce him."

"All you took was a frying pan and an atlas!" Robin cried, staring at the cast-iron skillet and the atlas with its dog-eared pages.

Cole and Jeff both ignored her outburst.

"I take it you don't like living here?" Cole asked.

Jeff stiffened, then shook his head vigorously. "Mom told me that when we moved I could have a dog and now I can't. And…and she dragged me into a neighborhood filled with girls. That might've been okay if I had a dog, but then she broke her promise. A promise is a promise and it's sacred. A guy would never do that."

"So you can't have a dog until later?"

"All because of a stupid fence."

Cole nodded. "Fences are important, you know. And you know what else? Your mom was worried about you."

Jeff looked at Robin, who was blinking furiously to keep the tears from dripping down her face. The upheaval and stress of the move had drained her emotionally and she was an unmitigated mess. Normally, she was a calm, controlled person, but this whole drama with Jeff was her undoing. That and the fact she'd hardly slept the night before in his makeshift tent.

"Mom," Jeff said, studying her anxiously, "are you all right?"

She covered her face with both hands. "I slept with a dog and you ran away and all you took was a frying pan and an atlas." That made no sense whatsoever, but she couldn't help it, and once the tears started they wouldn't stop.

"I'm sorry, Mom," Jeff said softly. "I didn't mean to make you cry."

"I know," she whimpered. "I want you to have a dog, I really do, but we can't keep one locked up in the house all day and we don't have a fence and...and the way you just looked at me, I swear it was Lenny all over again."

"Who's Lenny?" Cole cocked his head toward Jeff, speaking in a whisper.

"Lenny was my dad. He died when I was real little. I don't even remember him."

Cole shared a knowing look with her son. "It might be a good idea if we got your mother back inside the house."

"You think I'm getting hysterical, don't you?" Robin burst out. "I want you both to know I'm in perfect control. A woman can cry every now and then if she wants. Venting your emotions is healthy—all the books say so."

"Right, Mom." Jeff gently patted her shoulder, then

crawled out of the fort. He waited for Robin, who emerged after him, and offered her a hand. Cole and Blackie followed.

Jeff took Robin's arm, holding her elbow as he led her to the back door of their house, as if he suspected she couldn't find her way without his guidance.

Once inside, Robin grabbed a tissue and loudly blew her nose. Her composure was shaky, but when she turned to Cole, she intended to be as reasonable as a judge. As polite as a preacher.

"Have you got any aspirin?" Cole asked Jeff.

Jeff nodded, and dashed up the stairs to the bathroom, returning in thirty seconds flat with the bottle. Cole filled a glass with water and delivered both to Robin. How he knew she had a fierce headache she could only guess.

"Why don't you lie down for a few minutes? I'm sure you'll feel better."

"I feel just fine, thank you," she snapped, more angry with herself for overreacting than with him for taking charge.

"Do you have family close by?" Again Cole directed the question to Jeff, which served to further infuriate Robin. Jeff was ten years old! She, on the other hand, was an adult. If this man had questions they should be directed to her, not her son.

"Not anymore," Jeff answered in an anxious whisper. "Grandma and Grandpa moved to Arizona last year, and my uncle lives in L.A."

"I don't need to lie down," Robin said forcefully. "I'm perfectly fine."

"Mom," Jeff countered, his voice troubled, "you don't look so good."

"You were talking about frying pans and sleeping with dogs in the same breath," Cole elaborated, his eyebrows raised.

"I think Mr. Camden's right," Jeff said. "You need rest—lots of rest."

Her own son had turned traitor on her. Robin was shocked. Jeff took her hand and led her into the family room, which was off the kitchen. He patted the quilted pillow on the sofa, wordlessly suggesting she place her head there. When she resisted, he pulled the afghan from the chair and draped it around her, tucking the ends behind her shoulders.

Robin couldn't believe she was allowing herself to be led around like a…like a puppy. As if reading her thoughts, Blackie wandered over to her side and lowered his bulk onto the carpet beside the sofa.

"That's a neat fort you've got there," Jeff told Cole once he'd finished tucking in the blanket. Robin watched him hurry back to the kitchen, grab a plate, then load it with macaroni and cheese and hand it to Cole, apparently wanting to share his favorite meal with their neighbor.

Cole set the plate on the counter. "Thanks anyway, Jeff, but I've got to get back to the house. In the future, if you're thinking about running away—don't."

"Yeah, I guess you're right," Jeff said with a mildly guilty look. "My mom turned into a basket case."

Cole smiled—at least, it was as close to a smile as Robin had seen. "You're both going to be fine. She intends to get you that dog, you know. Just hang on. It'll be sooner than you think."

Jeff walked to the sliding glass door with Cole. "Mr. Camden, can I ask you something important?"

"Sure."

"Is anyone using the fort?"

"Not that I know of."

Jeff's expression was hopeful. "It didn't look like anyone had been inside for a long time."

"Six years," Cole murmured absently.

"That long? How come?" Jeff asked. "It's a *great* fort. If it's all right with you I'd like to go over there sometimes. I promise not to walk in any flowerbeds or anything, and I won't leave a mess. I'll take real good care of everything."

Cole hesitated for a moment. He looked at Jeff, and Robin held her breath. Then he shook his head. "Maybe sometime in the future, but not now."

Jeff's deep blue eyes brightened; apparently the refusal didn't trouble him. "Okay. When I can use the fort, would it be all right if I took Blackie with me? He followed me today, you know. I didn't have to do anything to get him to tag along." Jeff paused and lowered his eyes. "Well, hardly anything."

"I thought as much. As your mom said, you have a way with animals."

"My dad did, too. If he hadn't died he would've gotten me a pony and everything."

There was such pride in Jeff's voice that Robin bit her bottom lip to keep from crying all over again. Jeff and Lenny were so much alike. What she'd told her son earlier was true. More and more, Jeff was starting to take on his father's looks and personality.

Cole gazed down at Jeff, and an emotion flashed in his eyes, so transient Robin couldn't recognize it. He laid his hand on Jeff's shoulder. "Since your mother explained there's going to be a delay in getting you a dog, it'd be okay with me if you borrowed Blackie every now and then. You have to stay in your own yard, though. I don't want him running in the neighborhood unless he's on a leash."

"Do you mean it? Thanks, Mr. Camden! I'll do everything you ask."

Robin had the feeling Jeff would've agreed to just about any terms as long as he could see Blackie. It wasn't a dog of his own, but it was as close as he was going to get for the next few months.

Once Cole had left, Jeff joined her on the sofa, his hands folded on his lap. "I'm sorry, Mom," he muttered, his chin buried in his chest. "I promise I'll never run away again."

"I should hope not," she said. Wrapping her arms around him, she hugged him close, kissing his cheek.

"Gee whiz," Jeff grumbled, rubbing his face. "I'd never have apologized if I'd known you were going to kiss me."

A week passed. Jeff liked his new school and, as Robin had predicted, found his class contained an equal number of boys and girls. With his outgoing personality, he quickly collected new friends.

On Sunday afternoon, Robin was in the family room reading the paper when Jeff ambled in and sat down across from her. He took the baseball cap from his head and studied it for a moment.

"Something bothering you?" she asked, lowering the paper to get a better view of her son.

He shrugged. "Did you know Mr. Camden used to be married?"

"That's what I heard," Robin said absently. But other

than Heather's remarks the previous week, she hadn't heard anything else. In fact, she'd spoken to her neighbor only when she'd gone to pick up Jeff every afternoon. The child-care arrangement with Heather was working beautifully, but there'd been little opportunity to chat.

As for Cole, Robin hadn't seen him at all. Since he'd been so kind and helpful in the situation with Jeff, Robin had revised her opinion of him. He liked his privacy and that was fine by her; she had no intention of interrupting his serene existence. The memory of their first meeting still rankled, but she was willing to overlook that shaky beginning.

"Mr. Camden had a son who died."

Robin's heart constricted. It made sense: the pain she'd seen when Jeff had asked him about children, the word on the street that Cole didn't like kids, the abandoned fort. "I… How did you find that out?"

"Jimmy Wallach. He lives two streets over and has an older brother who used to play with Bobby Camden. Jimmy told me about him."

"I didn't know," Robin murmured, saddened by the information. She couldn't imagine her life without Jeff—the mere thought of losing him was enough to tear her apart.

"Mrs. Wallach heard Jimmy talking about Bobby Camden, and she said Mr. Camden got divorced and it was real bad, and then a year later Bobby died. She said Mr. Camden's never been the same since."

Robin ached for Cole, and she regretted all the uncharitable thoughts she'd had that first morning.

"I feel sad," Jeff whispered, frowning. His face was as intent as she'd ever seen it.

"I do, too," Robin returned softly.

"Mrs. Wallach seemed real surprised when I told her Mr. Camden said I could play in Bobby's fort someday. Ever since his son died, he hasn't let any kids in the yard or anything. She said he hardly talks to anyone in the neighborhood anymore."

Heather Lawrence had said basically the same thing, but hadn't explained the reason for it. Probably because she didn't know.

"Are you still going to barbecue hamburgers for dinner tonight?"

Robin nodded, surprised by the abrupt way Jeff had changed the subject. "If you want." Next to macaroni and cheese, grilled burgers were Jeff's all-time favorite food.

"Can I invite Mr. Camden over to eat with us?"

Robin hated to refuse her son, but she wasn't sure a dinner invitation was a good idea. She didn't know Cole very well, but she'd already learned he wasn't one to socialize with the neighbors. In addition, Jeff might blurt out questions about Cole's dead son that would be terribly painful for him.

"Mom," Jeff pleaded, "I bet no one ever invites him to dinner and he's all alone."

"Sweetheart, I don't know if that would be the right thing to do."

"But we *owe* him, Mom," Jeff implored. "He let me throw sticks for Blackie twice this week."

"I don't think Mr. Camden's home," Robin said, picking up the newspaper while she weighed the pros and cons of Jeff's suggestion. Since last Sunday, Robin hadn't spoken to Cole once, and she wasn't eager to initiate a conversation. He might read something into it.

"I'll go and see if he's home." Before she could react, Jeff was out the front door, letting the screen door slam in his wake.

He returned a couple of minutes later breathless and excited. "Mr. Camden's home and he said he appreciates the invitation, but he has other plans for tonight."

"That's too bad," Robin said, hoping she sounded sincere.

"I told him we were having strawberry shortcake for dessert and he said that's his favorite."

Robin didn't want to admit it, but she was relieved Cole wouldn't be showing up for dinner. The man made her feel nervous and uncertain. She didn't know why that should be, only that it was a new and unfamiliar sensation.

"Thanks, Mom."

Robin jerked her head up from the paper. "Thanks for what?" She hadn't read a word in five minutes. Her thoughts had been on her neighbor.

Jeff rolled his eyes. "For letting me take a piece of strawberry shortcake over to Mr. Camden."

"I said you could do that?"

"Just now." He walked over to her and playfully tested her forehead with the back of his hand. "You don't feel hot, but then, with brain fever you never know."

Robin swatted playfully at her son's backside.

Laughing, Jeff raced outdoors, where his bicycle was waiting. A half hour later, he was back in the house. "Mom! Mom!" he cried, racing into the kitchen. "Did you know Mr. Camden owns a black Porsche?"

"I can't say I did." She was more interested in peeling potatoes for the salad than discussing fancy cars.

She didn't know enough about sports cars to get excited about them.

Jeff jerked open the bottom drawer and rooted through the rag bag until he found what he was looking for. He pulled out a large square that had once been part of his flannel pyjamas, then started back outside. "He has another car, too, an SUV."

"Just where are you going, young man?" Robin demanded.

"Mr. Camden's waxing his car and I'm gonna help him."

"Did he ask for your help?"

"No," Jeff said impatiently.

"He may not want you to."

"Mom!" Jeff rolled his eyes as if to suggest she was overdoing this mothering thing. "Can I go now?"

"Ah…I suppose," she agreed, but her heart was in her throat. She moved into the living room and watched as Jeff strolled across the lawn to the driveway next door, where Cole was busy rubbing liquid wax on the gleaming surface of his Porsche. Without a word, Jeff started polishing the dried wax with his rag. Cole straightened and stopped smearing on the wax, obviously surprised to see Jeff. Robin bit her lip, not knowing how her neighbor would react to Jeff's willingness to help. Apparently he said something, because Jeff nodded, then walked over and sat cross-legged on the lawn. They didn't seem to be carrying on a conversation and Robin wondered what Cole had said to her son.

Robin returned to the kitchen, grateful that Cole's rejection had been gentle. At least he hadn't sent Jeff away. She peeled another potato, then walked back to the living room and glanced out the window again. This time she saw Jeff standing beside Cole, who was, it seemed, demonstrating the correct way to polish a car. He made wide circular motions with his arms, after which he stepped aside to let Jeff tackle the Porsche again. Cole smiled, then patted him on the head before walking around to the other side of the car.

Once the salad was ready, Robin ventured outside.

Jeff waved enthusiastically when he caught sight of her on the porch. "Isn't she a beaut?" he yelled.

It looked like an ordinary car to Robin, but she nodded enthusiastically. "Wonderful," she answered. "Afternoon, Cole."

"Robin." He returned her greeting absently.

He wore a sleeveless gray sweatshirt and she was surprised by how muscular and tanned his arms were. From a recent conversation with Heather Lawrence, Robin had learned Cole was a prominent attorney. And he seemed to fit the lawyer image to a T. Not anymore. The lawyer was gone and the *man* was there, bold as could be. Her awareness of him as an attractive virile male was shockingly intense.

The problem, she decided, lay in the fact that she hadn't expected Cole to look so…fit. The sight of all that lean muscle came as a pleasant surprise. Cole's aggressive, unfriendly expression had been softened as he bantered with Jeff.

Blackie ambled to her side and Robin leaned over to scratch the dog's ears while she continued to study his master. Cole's hair was dark and grew away from his brow, but a single lock flopped stubbornly over his forehead and he had to toss it back from his face every once in a while. It was funny how she'd never noticed that about him until now.

Jeff must've made some humorous remark because Cole threw back his head and chuckled loudly. It was the first time she'd ever heard him laugh. She suspected he didn't often give in to the impulse. A smile crowded Robin's face as Jeff started laughing, too.

In that moment the oddest thing happened. Robin felt something catch in her heart. The tug was almost physical, and she experienced a completely unfamiliar feeling of vulnerability....

"Do you need me to roll out the barbecue for you?" Jeff shouted when he saw that she was still on the porch. He'd turned his baseball cap around so the bill faced backward. While he spoke, his arm continued to work feverishly as he buffed the passenger door with his rag.

"Not...yet."

"Good, 'cause Mr. Camden needs me to finish up this side for him. We're on a tight schedule here, and I don't have time. Cole's got a dinner date at five-thirty."

"I see." Standing on the porch, dressed in her old faded jeans, with a mustard-spotted terrycloth hand towel tucked in the waistband, Robin felt as appealing as Ma Kettle. "Any time you're finished is fine."

So Cole Camden's got a date, Robin mused. *Of course he's got a date,* she told herself. Why should she care? And if watching Jeff and Cole together was going to affect her like this, it would be best to go back inside the house now.

Over dinner, all Jeff could talk about was Cole Camden. Every other sentence was Cole this and Cole that, until Robin was ready to slam her fist on the table and demand Jeff never mention their neighbor's name again.

"And the best part is, he *paid* me for helping him wax

his car," Jeff continued, then stuffed the hamburger into his mouth, chewing rapidly in his enthusiasm.

"That was generous of him."

Jeff nodded happily. "Be sure and save some shortcake for him. He said not to bring it over 'cause he didn't know exactly when he'd get home. He'll stop by, he said."

"I will." But Robin doubted her neighbor would. Jeff seemed to be under the impression that Cole would show up at any time; Robin knew better. If Cole had a dinner date, he wasn't going to rush back just to taste her dessert, although she did make an excellent shortcake.

As she suspected, Cole didn't come over. Jeff grumbled about it the next morning. He was convinced Cole would've dropped by if Robin hadn't insisted Jeff go to bed at his regular time.

"I'll make shortcake again soon," Robin promised, hurrying to pack their lunches. "And when I do, you can take a piece over to him."

"All right," Jeff muttered.

That evening, when Robin returned home from work, she found Jeff playing with Blackie in Cole's backyard.

"Jeff," she cried, alarmed that Cole might discover her son on his property. He'd made it clear Jeff wasn't to go into his yard. "What are you doing at Mr. Camden's? And why aren't you at Heather's?" She walked over to the hedge and placed her hands on her hips in frustration.

"Blackie's chain got all tangled up," Jeff said, looking sheepish. "He needed my help. I told Heather it would be okay with you and..." His voice trailed off.

"He's untangled now," Robin pointed out.

"I know, but since I was here it seemed like a good time for the two of us to—"

"Play," Robin completed for him.

"Yeah," her son said, nodding eagerly. Jeff was well aware he'd done something wrong, but had difficulty admitting it.

"Mr. Camden doesn't want you in his yard, and we both know it." Standing next to the laurel hedge, Robin watched with dismay as Cole opened his back door and stepped outside. Blackie barked in greeting, and his tail swung with enough force to knock Jeff off balance.

When Cole saw Jeff in his yard, he frowned and cast an accusing glare in Robin's direction.

"Jeff said Blackie's chain was tangled," she rushed to explain.

"How'd you get over here?" Cole asked her son, and although he didn't raise his voice it was clear he was displeased. "The gate's locked and the hedge is too high for him to jump over."

Jeff stared down at the lawn. "I came through the gap in the hedge—the same one Blackie uses. I crawled through it."

"Was his chain really tangled?"

"No, sir," Jeff said in a voice so low Robin had to strain to hear him. "At least not much… I just thought, you know, that maybe he'd like company."

"I see."

"He was all alone and so was I." Jeff lifted his eyes defiantly to his mother's, as if to suggest the fault was entirely hers. "I go to Mrs. Lawrence's after school, but it's all girls there."

"Don't you remember what I said about coming into my yard?" Cole asked him.

Jeff's nod was sluggish. "Yeah. You said maybe I could sometime, but not now. I thought…I hoped that since you let me help you wax your car, you wouldn't mind."

"I mind," Cole said flatly.

"He won't do it again," Robin promised. "Will you, Jeff?"

"No," he murmured. "I'm sorry, Mr. Camden."

For a whole week Jeff kept his word. The following Monday, however, when Robin came home from the BART station, Heather told her Jeff had mysteriously disappeared about a half hour earlier. She assumed he'd gone home; he'd said something about expecting a call.

Unfortunately, Robin knew exactly where to look for him, and it wasn't at home. Even more unfortunate was the fact that Cole's car pulled into the driveway just as she was opening her door. Throwing aside her briefcase and purse, she rushed through the house, jerked open the sliding glass door at the back and raced across her yard.

Her son was nowhere to be seen, but she immediately realized he'd been with Blackie. The dog wasn't in evidence, either, and she could see Jeff's favorite baseball cap on the lawn.

"Jeff," she called, afraid to raise her voice. She sounded as though she was suffering from a bad case of laryngitis.

Neither boy nor dog appeared.

She tried again, taking the risk of shouting for Jeff in a normal tone, praying it wouldn't attract Cole's attention. No response. Since Jeff and Blackie didn't seem to be within earshot, she guessed they were in the fort. There was no help for it; she'd have to go after him herself. Her only hope was that she could hurry over to the fort, get Jeff and return to her own yard, all without being detected by Cole.

Finding the hole in the laurel proved difficult enough. The space was little more than a narrow gap between two thick plants, and for a distressing moment, Robin doubted she was slim enough to squeeze through. Finally, she lowered herself to the ground, hunched her shoulders and managed to push her way between the shrubs. Her head had just emerged when she noticed a pair of polished men's shoes on the other side. Slowly, reluctantly, she glanced up to find Cole towering above her, eyes narrowed with suspicion.

"Oh, hi," she said, striving to sound as though it was perfectly normal for her to be crawling into his yard on her hands and knees. "I suppose you're wondering what I'm doing here…."

"The question did cross my mind."

Chapter 3

"It was the most embarrassing moment of my entire life," Robin repeated for the third time. She was sitting at the kitchen table, resisting the urge to hide her face in her hands and weep.

"You've already said that," Jeff grumbled.

"What possessed you to even *think* about going into Mr. Camden's yard again? Honestly, Jeff, you've been warned at least half a dozen times. What do I have to do? String barbed wire between our yards?"

Although he'd thoroughly disgraced himself, Jeff casually rotated the rim of his baseball cap between his fingers. "I said I was sorry."

A mere apology didn't begin to compensate for the humiliation Robin had suffered when Cole found her on all fours, crawling through his laurel hedge. If she lived to be an old woman, she'd never forget the look on his face.

"You put me on TV, computer and phone restriction already," her son reminded her.

That punishment could be another mistake to add to her growing list. At times like this, she wished Lenny were there to advise her. She needed him, and even after all these years, still missed him. Often, when there was no one else around, Robin found herself talking to Lenny. She wondered if she'd made the right decision, wondered what her husband would have done. Without television, computer or phone, the most attractive form of entertainment left open to her son was playing with Blackie, which was exactly what had gotten him into trouble in the first place.

"Blackie belongs to Mr. Camden," Robin felt obliged to tell him. Again.

"I know," Jeff said, "but he likes me. When I come home from school, he goes crazy. He's real glad to see me, Mom, and since there aren't very many boys in this neighborhood—" he paused as if she was to blame for that "—Blackie and I have an understanding. We're buds."

"That's all fine and dandy, but you seem to be forgetting that Blackie doesn't belong to you." Robin stood and opened the refrigerator, taking out a package of chicken breasts.

"I wish he was my dog," Jeff grumbled. In an apparent effort to make peace, he walked over to the cupboard, removed two plates and proceeded to set the table.

After dinner, while Robin was dealing with the dishes, the doorbell chimed. Jeff raced down the hallway to answer it, returning a moment later with Cole Camden at his side.

Her neighbor was the last person Robin had expected to see—and the last person she *wanted* to see.

"Mom," Jeff said, nodding toward Cole, "it's Mr. Camden."

"Hello, again," she managed, striving for a light tone, and realizing even as she spoke that she'd failed. "Would you like a cup of coffee?"

"No, thanks. I'd like to talk to both of you about—"

Not giving him the opportunity to continue, Robin nodded so hard she nearly dislocated her neck. "I really am sorry about what happened. I've had a good long talk with Jeff and, frankly, I understand why you're upset and I don't blame you. You've been very kind about this whole episode and I want you to know there won't be a repeat performance."

"From either of you?"

"Absolutely," she said, knowing her cheeks were as red as her nail polish. Did he have to remind her of the humiliating position he'd found her in earlier?

"Mom put me on TV, computer and phone restriction for an entire week," Jeff explained earnestly. "I promise not to go into your fort again, Mr. Camden. And I promise not to go in my backyard after school, either, because Blackie sees me and gets all happy and excited—and I guess I get all happy and excited, too—and that's when I do stuff I'm not supposed to."

"I see." Cole smiled down at Jeff. Robin thought it was a rather unusual smile. It didn't come from his lips as much as his eyes. Once more she witnessed a flash of pain, and another emotion she could only describe as longing. Slowly his gaze drifted to Robin. When his dark eyes met hers, she suddenly found herself short of breath.

"Actually I didn't come here to talk to you about what happened this afternoon," Cole said. "I'm going to be out of town for the next couple of days, and since Jeff and Blackie seem to get along so well I thought Jeff might be willing to look after him. That way I won't have to put him in the kennel. Naturally I'm prepared to pay your son for his time. If he agrees, I'll let him play in the fort while I'm away, as well."

Jeff's eyes grew rounder than Robin had ever seen them. "You want me to watch Blackie?" he asked, his voice incredulous. "And you're going to *pay* me? Can Blackie spend the night here? Please?"

"I guess that answers your question," Robin said, smiling.

"Blackie can stay here if it's okay with your mom," Cole told Jeff. Then he turned to her. "Would that create a problem for you?"

Once more his eyes held hers, and once more she experienced that odd breathless sensation.

"I... No problem whatsoever."

Cole smiled then, and this time it was a smile so potent, so compelling, that it sailed straight through Robin's heart.

"Mom," Jeff hollered as he burst through the front door late Thursday afternoon. "Kelly and Blackie and I are going to the fort."

"Kelly? Surely this isn't the *girl* named Kelly, is it? Not the one who lives next door?" Robin couldn't resist teasing her son. Apparently Jeff was willing to have a "pesky" girl for a friend, after all.

Jeff shrugged as he opened the cookie jar and groped inside. He frowned, not finding any cookies and removed his hand, his fingertips covered with crumbs that he promptly licked off. “I decided Kelly isn’t so bad.”

“Have you got Blackie’s leash?”

“We aren’t going to need it. We’re playing Sam Houston and Daniel Boone, and the Mexican army is attacking. I’m going to smuggle Blackie out and go for help. I can’t use a leash for that.”

“All right. Just don’t go any farther than the Alamo and be back by dinnertime.”

“But that’s less than an hour!” Jeff protested.

Robin gave him one of her don’t-argue-with-me looks.

“But I’m not hungry and—”

“Jeff,” Robin said softly, widening her eyes just a bit, increasing the intensity of her look.

“You know, Mom,” Jeff said with a cry of undisguised disgust, “you don’t fight fair.” He hurried out the front door with Blackie trotting faithfully behind.

Smiling to herself, Robin placed the meat loaf in the oven and carried her coffee into the backyard. The early evening air was filled with the scent of spring flowers. A gentle breeze wafted over the budding trees. How peaceful it seemed. How serene. All the years of pinching pennies to save for a house of their own seemed worth it now.

Her gaze wandered toward Cole Camden’s yard. Jeff, Kelly and Blackie were inside the fort, and she could hear their raised voices every once in a while.

Cole had been on her mind a great deal during the past couple of days; she’d spent far too much time dwelling on her neighbor, thinking about his reputation in the neighborhood and the son he’d lost.

The tranquillity of the moment was shattered by the

insistent ringing of the phone. Robin walked briskly to the kitchen, set her coffee on the counter and picked up the receiver.

"Hello."

"Robin, it's Angela. I'm not catching you at a bad time, am I?"

"No," Robin assured her. Angela worked in the same department as Robin, and over the years they'd become good friends. "What can I do for you?" she asked, as if she didn't already know.

"I'm calling to invite you to dinner—"

"On Saturday so I can meet your cousin Frank," Robin finished, rolling her eyes. Years before, Angela had taken on the task of finding Robin a husband. Never mind that Robin wasn't interested in meeting strangers! Angela couldn't seem to bear the thought of anyone spending her life alone and had appointed herself Robin's personal matchmaker.

"Frank's a really nice guy," Angela insisted. "I wouldn't steer you wrong, you know I wouldn't."

Robin restrained herself from reminding her friend of the disastrous date she'd arranged several weeks earlier.

"I've known Frank all my life," Angela said. "He's decent and nice."

Decent and *nice* were two words Robin had come to hate. Every man she'd ever met in this kind of arrangement was either decent or nice. Or both. Robin had come to think the two words were synonymous with dull, unattractive and emotionally manipulative. Generally these were recently divorced men who'd willingly placed themselves in the hands of family and friends to get them back into circulation.

"Didn't you tell me that Frank just got divorced?" Robin asked.

"Yes, about six months ago."

"Not interested."

"What do you mean you're not interested?" Angela demanded.

"I don't want to meet him. Angela, I know you mean well, and I apologize if I sound like a spoilsport, but I can't tell you the number of times I've had to nurse the fragile egos of recently divorced men. Most of the time they're emotional wrecks."

"But Frank's divorce was final months ago."

"If you still want me to meet him in a year, I'll be more than happy to have you arrange a dinner date."

Angela released a ragged sigh. "You're sure?"

"Positive."

There was a short disappointed silence. "Fine," Angela said in obvious frustration. "I'll see you in the morning."

"Right." Because she felt guilty, Robin added, "I'll bring the coffee."

"Okay."

Robin lingered in the kitchen, frowning. She hated it when her friends put her on the spot like this. It was difficult enough to say no, but knowing that Angela's intentions were genuine made it even worse. Just as she was struggling with another attack of guilt, the phone rang again. Angela! Her friend must have suspected that Robin's offer to buy the coffee was a sign that she was weakening.

Gathering her fortitude, Robin seized the receiver and said firmly, "I'm not interested in dating Frank. I don't want to be rude, but that's final!"

Her abrupt words were followed by a brief shocked silence, and then, "Robin, hello, this is Cole Camden."

"Cole," she gasped, closing her eyes. "Uh, I'm sorry, I thought you were someone else. A friend." She slumped against the wall and covered her face with one hand. "I have this friend who's always trying to arrange dates for me, and she doesn't take no for an answer," Robin quickly explained. "I suppose you have friends wanting to arrange dates for you, too."

"Actually, I don't."

Of course he didn't. No doubt there were women all over San Francisco who longed to go out with Cole. He didn't require a personal matchmaker. All someone like him had to do was look interested and women would flock to his side.

Her hand tightened around the receiver and a sick weightless feeling attacked the pit of her stomach. "I apologize. I didn't mean to shout in your ear."

"You didn't."

"I suppose you called to talk to Jeff," she said. "He's with Blackie and Kelly—Kelly Lawrence, the little girl who lives on the other side of us."

"I see."

"He'll be back in a few minutes, if you'd like to call then. Or if you prefer, I could run and get him, but he said something about sneaking out and going for help and—"

"I beg your pardon? What's Jeff doing?"

"Oh, they're playing in the fort, pretending they're Houston and Daniel Boone. The fort is now the Alamo."

He chuckled. "I see. No, don't worry about chasing after him. I'd hate to see you waylaid by the Mexican army."

"I don't think I'd care for that myself."

"How's everything going?"

"Fine," she assured him.

She must have sounded rushed because he said, "You're sure this isn't a bad time? If you have company…"

"No, I'm here alone."

Another short silence, which was broken by Cole. "So everything's okay with Blackie? He isn't causing you any problems, is he?"

"Oh, no, everything's great. Jeff lavishes him with attention. The two of them are together practically every minute. Blackie even sleeps beside his bed."

"As you said, Jeff has a way with animals," Cole murmured.

His laugh, so tender and warm, was enough to jolt her. She had to pinch herself to remember that Cole was a prominent attorney, wealthy and respected. She was an accountant. A junior accountant at that.

The only thing they had in common was the fact that they lived next door to each other and her son was crazy about his dog.

The silence returned, only this time it had a relaxed, almost comfortable quality, as though neither wanted the conversation to end.

"Since Jeff isn't around," Cole said reluctantly, "I'll let you go."

"I'll tell him you phoned."

"It wasn't anything important," Cole said. "Just wanted to let you know when I'll be back—late Friday afternoon. Will you be home?"

"Of course."

"You never know, your friend might talk you into going out with Fred after all."

"It's Frank, and there isn't a snowball's chance in hell."

"Famous last words!"

"See you Friday," she said with a short laugh.

"Right. Goodbye, Robin."

"Goodbye, Cole."

Long after the call had ended, Robin stood with her hand on the receiver, a smile touching her eyes and her heart.

"Mom, I need my lunch money," Jeff yelled from the bottom of the stairs.

"I'll be down in a minute," she said. Mornings were hectic. In order to get to the Glen Park BART station on time, Robin had to leave the house half an hour before Jeff left for school.

"What did you have for breakfast?" she hollered as she put the finishing touches on her makeup.

"Frozen waffles," Jeff shouted back. "And don't worry, I didn't drown them in syrup and I rinsed off the plate before I put it in the dishwasher."

"Rinsed it off or let Blackie lick it for you?" she asked, as she hurried down the stairs. Her son was busy at the sink and didn't turn around to look at her.

"Blackie, honestly, is that maple syrup on your nose?"

At the sound of his name, the Labrador trotted over to her. Robin took a moment to stroke his thick fur before fumbling for her wallet to give Jeff his lunch money.

"Hey, Mom, you look nice."

"Don't act so surprised," she grumbled. "I'm leaving now."

"Okay," Jeff said without the slightest bit of concern. "You won't be late tonight, will you? Remember Mr. Camden's coming back."

"I remember, and no, I won't be late." She grabbed her purse and her packed lunch, putting it in her briefcase, and headed for the front door.

Even before Robin arrived at the subway station, she knew the day would drag. Fridays always did.

She was right. At six, when the subway pulled into the station, Robin felt as though she'd been away forty hours instead of the usual nine. She found herself hurrying and didn't fully understand why. Cole was scheduled to return, but that didn't have anything to do with her, did it? His homecoming wasn't anything to feel nervous about, nor any reason to be pleased. He was her neighbor, and more Jeff's friend than hers.

The first thing Robin noticed when she arrived on Orchard Street was Cole's Porsche parked in the driveway of his house.

"Hi, Mom," Jeff called as he raced across the lawn between the two houses. "Mr. Camden's back!"

"So I see." She removed her keys from her purse and opened the front door.

Jeff followed her inside. "He said he'd square up with me later. I wanted to invite him to dinner, but I didn't think I should without asking you first."

"That was smart," she said, depositing her jacket in the closet on her way to the kitchen. She opened the refrigerator and took out the thawed hamburger and salad makings.

"How was your day?" she asked.

Jeff sat down at the table and propped his elbows on it. "All right, I guess. What are you making for dinner?"

"Taco salad."

"How about just tacos? I don't get why you want to ruin a perfectly good dinner by putting green stuff in it."

Robin paused. "I thought you liked my taco salad."

Jeff shrugged. "It's all right, but I'd rather have just tacos." Once that was made clear, he cupped his chin in his hands. "Can we rent a movie tonight?"

"I suppose," Robin returned absently as she added the meat to the onions browning in the skillet.

"But I get to choose this time," Jeff insisted. "Last week you picked a musical." He wrinkled his nose as if to suggest that being forced to watch men and women sing and dance was the most disgusting thing he'd ever had to endure.

"Perhaps we can find a compromise," she said.

Jeff nodded. "As long as it doesn't have a silly love story in it."

"Okay," Robin said, doing her best not to betray her amusement. Their difference in taste when it came to movies was legendary. Jeff's favorite was an older kids' film, *Scooby Doo,* that he watched over and over, which Robin found boring, to say the least. Unfortunately, her son was equally put off by the sight of men and women staring longingly into each other's eyes.

The meat was simmering in the skillet when Robin glanced up and noted that her son was looking surprisingly thoughtful. "Is something troubling you?" she asked, and popped a thin tomato slice into her mouth.

"Have you ever noticed that Mr. Camden never mentions he had a son?"

Robin set the paring knife on the cutting board. "It's probably painful for him to talk about."

Jeff nodded, and, with the innocent wisdom of youth, he whispered, "That man needs someone."

The meal was finished, and Robin was standing in front of the sink rinsing off the dinner plates when the doorbell rang. Robin knew it had to be Cole.

"I'll get it," Jeff cried as he raced past her at breakneck speed. He threw open the door. "Hi, Mr. Camden!" he said eagerly.

By this time Robin had smoothed her peach-colored sweater over her hips and placed a friendly—but not too friendly—smile on her face. At the last second, she ran her fingers through her hair, striving for the casual I-didn't-go-to-any-trouble look, then wondered at her irrational behavior. Cole wasn't coming over to see *her.*

Robin could hear Jeff chatting away at ninety miles an hour, telling Cole they were renting a movie and how Robin insisted that every show he saw had to have the proper rating, which he claimed was totally ridiculous. He went on to explain that she considered choosing the film a mother's job and apparently a mere kid didn't have rights. When there was a pause in the conversation, she could envision Jeff rolling his eyes dramatically.

Taking a deep breath, she stepped into the entryway and smiled. "Hello, Cole."

"Robin."

Their eyes met instantly. Robin's first coherent thought was that a woman could get lost in eyes that dark and not even care. She swallowed and lowered her gaze.

"Would you like a cup of coffee?" she asked, having difficulty dragging the words out of her mouth.

"If it isn't too much trouble."

"It isn't." Or it wouldn't be if she could stop her heart from pounding so furiously.

"Where's Blackie?" Jeff asked, opening the screen door and glancing outside.

"I didn't bring him over. I thought you'd be tired of him by now."

"Tired of Blackie?" Jeff cried. "You've got to be kidding!"

"I guess I should've known better," Cole teased.

Robin returned to the kitchen and took mugs from the cupboard, using these few minutes to compose herself.

The screen door slammed, and a moment later Cole appeared in her kitchen. "Jeff went to my house to get Blackie."

She smiled and nodded. "Do you take cream or sugar?" she asked over her shoulder.

"Just black, thanks."

Robin normally drank hers the same way. But for some reason she couldn't begin to fathom, she added a generous teaspoonful of sugar to her own, stirring briskly as though she feared it wouldn't dissolve.

"I hope your trip went well," she said, carrying both mugs into the family room, where Cole had chosen to sit.

"Very well."

"Good." She sat a safe distance from him, across the room in a wooden rocker, and balanced her mug on her knee. "Everything around here went without a hitch, but I'm afraid Jeff may have spoiled Blackie a bit."

"From what he said, they did everything but attend school together."

"Having the dog has been wonderful for him. I appreciate your giving Jeff this opportunity. Not only does it satisfy his need for a dog, but it's taught him about responsibility."

The front door opened and the canine subject of their conversation shot into the room, followed by Jeff, who was grinning from ear to ear. "Mom, could Mr. Camden stay and watch the movie with us?"

"Ah..." Caught off guard, Robin didn't know what to say. After being away from home for several days, watching a movie with his neighbors probably held a low position on Cole's list of priorities.

To Robin's astonishment, Cole's eyes searched hers as though seeking her approval.

"You'd be welcome...I mean, you can stay if you'd like, unless...unless there's something else you'd rather do," she stammered. "I mean, I'd...we'd like it if you did, but..." She let whatever else she might have said fade away. She was making a mess of this, and every time she tried to smooth it over, she only stuck her foot further down her throat.

"What movie did you rent?"

"We haven't yet," Jeff explained. "Mom and me had to come to an understanding first. She likes mushy stuff and gets all bent out of shape if there's an explosion or anything. You wouldn't believe the love story she made me watch last Friday night." His voice dripped with renewed disgust.

"How about if you and I go rent the movie while your mother and Blackie make the popcorn?"

Jeff's blue eyes brightened immediately. "That'd be great, wouldn't it, Mom?"

"Sure," she agreed, and was rewarded by Jeff's smile.

Jeff and Cole left a few minutes later. It was on the

tip of her tongue to give Cole instructions on the type of movie appropriate for a ten-year-old boy, but she swallowed her concerns, willing to trust his judgment. Standing on the porch, she watched as they climbed inside Cole's expensive sports car. She pressed her hand to her throat, grateful when Cole leaned over the front seat and snapped Jeff's seat belt snugly in place. Suddenly Cole looked at her; she raised her hand in farewell, and he did the same. It was a simple gesture, yet Robin felt as if they'd communicated so much more.

"Come on, Blackie," Robin said, "let's go start the popcorn." The Lab trailed behind her as she returned to the kitchen. She placed a packet of popcorn in the microwave. It was while she was waiting for the kernels to start popping that the words slipped from her mouth.

"Well, Lenny, what do you think?" Talking to her dead husband came without conscious thought. It certainly wasn't that she expected him to answer. Whenever she spoke to him, the words came spontaneously from the deep well of love they'd once shared. She supposed she should feel foolish doing it, but so many times over the long years since his death she'd felt his presence. Robin assumed that the reason she talked to him came from her need to discuss things with the one other person who'd loved her son as much as she did. In the beginning she was sure she needed to visit a psychiatrist or arrange for grief counseling, but later she convinced herself that every widow went through this in one form or another.

"He's grown so much in the past year, hasn't he?" she asked, and smiled. "Meeting Cole has been good for Jeff. He lost a child, you know, and I suppose having Jeff move in next door answers a need for him, too."

About ten minutes later, she'd transferred the popcorn to a bowl and set out drinks. Jeff and Cole came back with a movie that turned out to be an excellent compromise—a teen comedy that was surprisingly witty and entertaining.

Jeff sprawled on the carpet munching popcorn with Blackie by his side. Cole sat on the sofa and Robin chose the rocking chair. She removed her shoes and tucked her feet beneath her. She was enjoying the movie; in fact, several times she found herself laughing out loud.

Cole and Jeff laughed, too. The sounds were contrasting—one deep and masculine, the other young and pleasantly boyish—yet they harmonized, blending with perfect naturalness.

Soon Robin found herself watching Jeff and Cole more than the movie. The two…no, the three of them had grown comfortable together. Robin didn't try to read any significance into that. Doing so could prove emotionally dangerous, but the thought flew into her mind and refused to leave.

The credits were rolling when Cole pointed to Jeff, whose head was resting on his arms, his eyes closed.

"He's asleep," Cole said softly.

Robin smiled and nodded. She got up to bring the empty popcorn bowl into the kitchen. Cole stood, too, taking their glasses to the sink, then returned to the family room to remove the DVD.

"Do you want me to carry him upstairs for you?" he asked, glancing down at the slumbering Jeff.

"No," she whispered. "When he wakes up in the morning, he'll think you treated him like a little kid. Egos are fragile at ten."

"I suppose you're right."

The silence seemed to resound. Without Jeff, awake and chattering, as a buffer between them, Robin felt clumsy and self-conscious around Cole.

"It was nice of you to stay," she said, more to fill the silence than because she had anything important to communicate. "It meant a lot to Jeff."

Jeff had told her Cole had an active social life. Heather Lawrence had confirmed it by casually letting it drop that Cole was often away on weekends. Robin wasn't entirely sure what to think about it all. But if there was a woman in his life, that was his business, not hers.

"It meant a lot to me, too," he said, returning the DVD to its case.

The kitchen and family room, actually quite spacious, felt close and intimate with Cole standing only a few feet away.

Robin's fingers were shaking as she placed the bowls and soda glasses in the dishwasher. She tried to come up with some bright and witty comment, but her mind was blank.

"I should be going."

Was that reluctance she heard in his voice? Somehow Robin doubted it; probably wishful thinking on her part. Half of her wanted to push him out the door and the other half didn't want him to leave at all. But there really wasn't any reason for him to stay. "I'll walk you to the door."

"Blackie." Cole called for his dog. "It's time to go."

The Lab didn't look pleased. He took his own sweet time lumbering to his feet and stretching before trotting to Cole's side.

Robin was about to open the door when she realized she hadn't thanked Cole for getting the movie. She turned, and his dark eyes delved into hers. Whatever thoughts had been taking shape fled like leaves scattering in the wind. She tried to smile, however weakly, but it was difficult when he was looking at her so intently. His gaze slipped to her mouth, and in a nervous movement, she moistened her lips. Before she was fully aware of how it had happened, Cole's fingers were in her hair and he was urging her mouth to meet his.

His eyes held hers, as if he expected her to stop him, then they slowly closed and their lips touched. Robin's eyes drifted shut, but that was the only response she made.

He kissed her again, even more gently than the first time. Robin moaned softly, not in protest, but in wonder and surprise. It had been so long since a man had kissed her like this. So long that she'd forgotten the wealth of sensations a mere kiss could evoke. Her hands crept to his chest, and her fingers curled into the soft wool of his sweater. Hesitantly, timidly, her lips trembled beneath his. Cole sighed and took full possession of her mouth.

Robin sighed, too. The tears that welled in her eyes were a shock. She was at a loss to explain them. They slipped down her face, and it wasn't until then that she realized she was crying.

Cole must have felt her tears at the same moment, because he abruptly broke off the kiss and raised his head. His eyes searched hers as his thumb brushed the moisture from her cheek.

"Did I hurt you?" The question was whispered.

She shook her head vehemently.

"Then why…?"

"I don't know." She couldn't explain something she didn't understand herself. Rubbing her eyes, she attempted to wipe away the evidence. She forced a smile. "I'm nothing if not novel," she said with brittle cheerfulness. "I don't imagine many women break into tears when you kiss them."

Cole looked as confused as Robin felt.

"Don't worry about it. I'm fine." She wanted to reassure him, but was having too much trouble analyzing her own reactions.

"Let's sit down and talk about this."

"No," she said quietly. Adamantly. That was the last thing she wanted. "I'm sorry, Cole. I really am. This has never happened before and I don't understand it either."

"But…"

"The best thing we can do is chalk it up to a long workweek."

"It's not that simple."

"Probably, but I'd prefer to just forget it. Please?"

"Are you all right?"

"Emotionally or physically?" She tried to joke, but didn't succeed.

"Both."

He was so serious, so concerned, that it was all Robin could do not to dissolve into fresh tears. She'd made a world-class fool of herself with this man, not once but twice.

This man, who had suffered such a tremendous loss himself, was so gentle with her, and instead of helping, that only made matters worse. "I'm sorry, really I am," she said raggedly, "but perhaps you should go home now."

Chapter 4

"You know what I'm in the mood for?" Angela Lansky said as she sat on the edge of Robin's desk early Monday afternoon.

"I certainly hope you're going to say food," Robin teased. They had shared the same lunch hour and were celebrating a cost-of-living raise by eating out.

"A shrimp salad," Angela elaborated. "Heaped six inches high with big fresh shrimp."

"I was thinking Chinese food myself," Robin said, "but, now that you mention it, shrimp salad sounds good." She opened her bottom drawer and took out her purse.

Angela was short and enviably thin with thick brown hair that fell in natural waves over her shoulders. She used clips to hold the abundant curls away from her face and looked closer to twenty than the thirty-five Robin knew her to be.

"I know just the place," Angela was saying. "The Blue Crab. It's on the wharf and worth the trouble of getting there."

"I'm game," Robin said.

They stopped at the bank, then headed for the restaurant. They decided to catch the Market Street cable car to Fisherman's Wharf and joined the quickly growing line.

"So how's the kid doing?" Angela asked. She and her salesman husband didn't plan to have children themselves, but Angela enjoyed hearing about Jeff.

"He signed up for baseball through the park program and starts practice this week. I think it'll be good for him. He was lonely this weekend now that Blackie's back with Cole."

"But isn't Blackie over at your place as much as before?" Angela asked.

Robin shook her head. "Cole left early Saturday morning and took the dog with him. Jeff moped around for most of the weekend."

"Where'd your handsome neighbor go?"

"How am I supposed to know?" Robin asked with a soft laugh, hiding her disappointment at his disappearance. "Cole doesn't clear his schedule with me."

The way he'd left—without a word of farewell or explanation—still hurt. It was the kind of hurt that came from realizing what a complete fool she'd made of herself with this worldly, sophisticated man. He'd kissed her and she'd started crying. Good grief, he was probably doing backflips in order to avoid seeing her again.

"Do you think Cole was with a woman?"

"That's none of my business!"

"But I thought your neighbor said Cole spent his weekends with a woman."

Robin didn't remember mentioning that to Angela, but she obviously had, along with practically everything else. Robin had tried to convince herself that confiding in Angela about Cole was a clever way of thwarting her friend's matchmaking efforts. Unfortunately, the whole thing had backfired in her face. In the end, the last person she wanted to talk about was Cole, but of course Angela persisted in questioning her.

"Well?" Angela demanded. "Did he spend his weekend with a woman or not?"

"What he does with his time is his business, not mine," Robin reiterated. She pretended not to care. But she did. Too much. She'd promised herself she wasn't going to put any stock in the kiss or the powerful attraction she felt for Cole. Within the space of one evening, she'd wiped out every pledge she'd made to herself. She hadn't said anything to Jeff—how could she?—but she was just as disappointed as he was that Cole had left for the weekend.

"I was hoping something might develop between the two of you," Angela murmured. "Since you're obviously not interested in meeting Frank, it would be great if you got something going with your neighbor."

Robin cast her a plaintive look that suggested otherwise. "Cole Camden lives in the fanciest house in the neighborhood. He's a partner in the law firm of Blackwell, Burns and Dailey, which we both know is one of the most prestigious in San Francisco. And he drives a car with a name I can barely pronounce. Now, what would someone like that see in me?"

"Lots of things," Angela said.

Robin snickered. "I hate to disillusion you, my friend, but the only thing Cole Camden and I have in common is the fact that my small yard borders his massive one."

"Maybe," Angela agreed, raising her eyebrows. "But I could tell you were intrigued by him the very first time you mentioned his name."

"That's ridiculous!"

"It isn't," Angela insisted. "I've watched you with other men over the past few years. A guy will show some interest, and at first everything looks peachy-keen. You'll go out with him a couple of times, maybe even more, but before anything serious can develop you've broken off the relationship without really giving it a chance."

Robin didn't have much of an argument, since that was true, but she made a token protest just the same. "I can't help it if I have high standards."

"High standards!" Angela choked back a laugh. "That's got to be the understatement of the century. You'd find fault with Prince Charming."

Robin rolled her eyes, but couldn't hold back a smile. Angela was right, although that certainly hadn't slowed her matchmaking efforts.

"From the time you started talking about your neighbor," Angela went on, "I noticed something different about you, and frankly I'm thrilled. In all the years we've known each other, this is the first time I can remember you giving a man this much attention. Until now, it's always been the other way around."

"I'm not interested in Cole," she mumbled. "Oh, honestly, Angela, I can't imagine where you come up with these ideas. I think you've been reading too many romance novels."

Angela waved her index finger under Robin's nose. "Listen, I'm on to you. You're not going to divert me with humor, or weasel your way out of admitting it. You can't fool me—you're attracted to this guy and it's scaring you to death. Right?"

The two women gazed solemnly at each other, both too stubborn to admit defeat. Under the force of her friend's unyielding determination, Robin was the one who finally gave in.

"All right!" she cried, causing the other people waiting for the cable car to turn and stare. "All right," she repeated in a whisper. "I like Cole, but I don't understand it."

Angela's winged brows arched speculatively. "He's attractive and wealthy, crazy about your son, generous and kind, and you haven't figured it out yet?"

"He's also way out of my league."

"I wish you'd quit categorizing yourself. You make it sound as though you aren't good enough for him, and that's not true."

Robin just sighed.

The cable car appeared then, its bell clanging as it drew to a stop. Robin and Angela boarded and held on tight.

Jeff loved hearing about the history of the cable cars, and Robin loved telling him the story. Andrew Hallidie had designed them because of his deep love for horses. Day after day, Hallidie had watched them struggling up and down the treacherous hills of the city, dragging heavy burdens. Prompted by his concern for the animals, he'd invented the cable cars that are pulled by a continuously moving underground cable. To Jeff and to many others, Andrew Hallidie was a hero.

Robin and Angela were immediately caught up in the festive atmosphere of Fisherman's Wharf. The rows of fishing boats along the dock bobbed gently with the tide, and although Robin had never been to the Mediterranean the view reminded her of pictures she'd seen of French and Italian harbors.

The day was beautiful, the sky blue and cloudless, the ocean sparkling the way it did on a summer day. This spring had been exceptionally warm. It wasn't uncommon for Robin to wear a winter coat in the middle of July, especially in the mornings, when there was often a heavy fog accompanied by a cool mist from the Bay. But this spring, they'd experienced some lovely weather, including today's.

"Let's eat outside," Angela suggested, pointing at a free table on the patio.

"Sure," Robin agreed cheerfully. The Blue Crab was a popular restaurant and one of several that lined the wharf. More elegant dining took place inside, but the pavement was crowded with diners interested in a less formal meal.

Once they were seated, Robin and Angela were waited on quickly and ordered their shrimp salads.

"So," Angela said, spreading out her napkin while closely studying Robin. "Tell me more about your neighbor."

Robin froze. "I thought we were finished with this subject. In case you hadn't noticed, I'd prefer not to discuss Cole."

"I noticed, but unfortunately I was just getting started. It's unusual for you to be so keen on a man, and I know hardly anything about him. It's time, Robin Masterson, to tell all."

"There's nothing to tell. I already told you everything I care to," Robin said crossly. She briefly wondered if Angela had guessed that Cole had kissed her. At the rate things were going, she'd probably end up admitting it before lunch was over. Robin wished she could think of some surefire way to change the subject.

Tall glasses of iced tea arrived and Robin was reaching for a packet of sugar when she heard a masculine chuckle that reminded her instantly of Cole. She paused, savoring the husky sound. Without really meaning to, she found herself scanning the tables, certain Cole was seated a short distance away.

"He's here," she whispered before she could guard her tongue.

"Who?"

"Cole. I just heard him laugh."

Pushing back her chair in order to get a fuller view of the inside dining area, Robin searched through a sea of faces, but didn't find her neighbor's.

"What's he look like?" Angela whispered.

Ten different ways to describe him shot through her mind. To say he had brown hair, neatly trimmed, coffee-colored eyes and was about six foot two seemed inadequate. To add that he was strikingly attractive further complicated the problem.

"Tell me what to look for," Angela insisted. "Come on, Robin, this is a golden opportunity. I want to check this guy out. I'm not letting a chance like this slip through my fingers. I'll bet he's gorgeous."

Reluctantly, Robin continued to scan the diners, but she didn't see anyone who remotely resembled Cole. Even if she did see him, she wasn't sure she'd point him out to Angela, although she hated to lie. Perhaps she wouldn't have to. Perhaps she'd imagined the whole thing. It would've been easy enough to do. Angela's questions had brought Cole to the forefront of her mind; they'd just been discussing him and it was only natural for her to—

Her heart pounded against her rib cage as Cole walked out of the restaurant foyer. He wasn't alone. A tall, slender woman with legs that seemed to go all the way up to her neck and a figure as shapely and athletic as a dancer's was walking beside him. She was blond and, in a word, gorgeous. Robin felt as appealing as milkweed in comparison. The woman's arm was delicately tucked in Cole's, and she was smiling up at him with eyes big and blue enough to turn heads.

Robin's stomach tightened into a hard knot.

"Robin," Angela said anxiously, leaning toward her, "what is it?"

Cole was strolling past them, and in an effort not to be seen, Robin stuck her head under the table pretending to search for her purse.

"Robin," Angela muttered, lowering her own head and peeking under the linen tablecloth, "what's the matter with you?"

"Nothing." Other than the fact that she was going to be ill. Other than the fact that she'd never been more outclassed in her life. "I'm fine, really." A smile trembled on her pale lips.

"Then what are you doing with your head under the table?"

"I don't suppose you'd believe my napkin fell off my lap?"

"No."

A pair of shiny black shoes appeared. Slowly, Robin

twisted her head and glanced upward, squinting at the flash of sunlight that nearly blinded her. It was their waiter. Heaving a giant sigh of relief, Robin straightened. The first thing she noticed was that Cole had left.

The huge shrimp salads were all but forgotten as Angela, eyes narrowed and elbows braced on the table, confronted her. "You saw him, didn't you?"

There was no point in pretending otherwise, so Robin nodded.

"He was with someone?"

"Not just someone! The most beautiful woman in the world was draped all over his arm."

"That doesn't mean anything," Angela said. "Don't you think you're jumping to conclusions? Honestly, she could've been anyone."

"Uh-huh." Any fight left in Robin had long since evaporated. There was nothing like seeing Cole with another woman to bring her firmly back to earth—which was right where she belonged.

"She could've been a client."

"She probably was," Robin concurred, reaching for her fork. She didn't know how she was going to manage one shrimp, let alone a whole plate of them. Heaving another huge sigh, she plowed her fork into the heap of plump pink darlings. It was then that she happened to glance across the street. Cole and Ms. Gorgeous were walking along the sidewalk, engrossed in their conversation. For some reason, known only to the fates, Cole looked across the street at that very moment. His gaze instantly narrowed on her. He stopped midstride as though shocked to have seen her.

Doing her best to pretend she hadn't seen *him,* Robin

took another bite of her salad and chewed vigorously. When she glanced up again, Cole was gone.

"Mom, I need someone to practice with," Jeff pleaded. He stood forlornly in front of her, a baseball mitt in one hand, a ball in the other.

"I thought Jimmy was practicing with you."

"He had to go home and then Kelly threw me a few pitches, but she had to go home, too. Besides, she's a girl."

"And what am I?" Robin muttered.

"You're a mom," Jeff answered, clearly not understanding her question. "Don't you see? I've got a chance of making pitcher for our team if I can get someone to practice with me."

"All right," Robin agreed, grumbling a bit. She set aside her knitting and followed her son into the backyard. He handed her his old catcher's mitt, which barely fit her hand, and positioned her with her back to Cole's yard.

Robin hadn't been able to completely avoid her neighbor in the past week, but she'd succeeded in keeping her distance. For that matter, he didn't seem all that eager to run into her, either. Just as well, she supposed.

He stayed on his side of the hedge. She stayed on hers.

If he passed her on his way to work, he gave an absent wave. She returned the gesture.

If they happened to be outside at the same time, they exchanged smiles and a polite greeting, but nothing more. It seemed, although Robin couldn't be sure, that Cole spent less time outside than usual. So did she.

"Okay," Jeff called, running to the end of their yard. "Squat down."

"I beg your pardon?" Robin shouted indignantly. "I agreed to play catch with you. You didn't say anything about having to squat!"

"Mom," Jeff said impatiently, "think about it. If I'm going to be the pitcher, you've got to be the catcher, and catchers have to be low to the ground."

Complaining under her breath, Robin sank to her knees, worried the grass would stain her jeans.

Jeff tossed his arms into the air in frustration. "Not like that!" He said something else that Robin couldn't quite make out—something about why couldn't moms be guys.

Reluctantly, Robin assumed the posture he wanted, but she didn't know how long her knees would hold out. Jeff wound up his arm and let loose with a fastball. Robin closed her eyes, stuck out the mitt and was so shocked when she caught the ball that she toppled backward into the wet grass.

"You all right?" Jeff yelled, racing toward her.

"I'm fine, I'm fine," she shouted back, discounting his concern as she brushed the dampness from the seat of her jeans. She righted herself, assumed the position and waited for the second ball.

Jeff ran back to his mock pitcher's mound, gripped both hands behind his back and stepped forward. Robin closed her eyes again. Nothing happened. She opened her eyes cautiously, puzzled about the delay. Then she recalled the hand movements she'd seen pitchers make and flexed her fingers a few times.

Jeff straightened, placed his hand on his hip and stared at her. "What was that for?"

"It's a signal…I think. I've seen catchers do it on TV."

"Mom, leave that kind of stuff to the real ballplayers. All I want you to do is catch my pitches and throw them back. It might help if you kept your eyes open, too."

"I'll try."

"Thank you."

Robin suspected she heard a tinge of sarcasm in her son's voice. She didn't know what he was getting so riled up about; she was doing her best. It was at times like these that she most longed for Lenny. When her parents had still lived in the area, her dad had stepped in whenever her son needed a father's guiding hand, but they'd moved to Arizona a couple of years ago. Lenny's family had been in Texas since before his death. Robin hadn't seen them since the funeral, although Lenny's mother faithfully sent Jeff birthday and Christmas gifts.

"You ready?" Jeff asked.

"Ready." Squinting, Robin stuck out the mitt, prepared to do her best to catch the stupid ball, since it seemed so important to her son. Once more he swung his arms behind him and stepped forward. Then he stood there, poised to throw, for what seemed an eternity. Her knees were beginning to ache.

"Are you going to throw the ball, or are you going to stare at me all night?" she asked after a long moment had passed.

"That does it!" Jeff tossed his mitt to the ground. "You just broke my concentration."

"Well, for crying out loud, what's there to concentrate on?" Robin grimaced, rising awkwardly to her feet. Her legs had started to lose feeling.

"This isn't working," Jeff cried, stalking toward her.

"Kelly's only in third grade and she does a better job than you do."

Robin decided to ignore that comment. She pressed her hand to the small of her back, hoping to ease the ache she'd begun to feel.

"Hello, Robin. Jeff."

Cole's voice came at her like a hangman's noose. She straightened abruptly and winced at the sharp pain shooting through her back.

"Hi, Mr. Camden!" Jeff shouted as though Cole was a conquering hero returned from the war. He dashed across the yard, past Robin and straight to the hedge. "Where have you been all week?"

"I've been busy." He might've been talking to Jeff, but his eyes were holding Robin's. She tried to look away—but she couldn't.

His eyes told her she was avoiding him.

Hers answered that he'd been avoiding *her.*

"I guess you *have* been busy," Jeff was saying. "I haven't seen you in days and days and days." Blackie squeezed through the hedge and Jeff fell to his knees, his arms circling the dog's neck.

"So how's the baseball going?" Cole asked.

Jeff sent his mother a disgusted look, then shrugged. "All right, I guess."

"What position are you playing?"

"Probably outfield. I had a chance to make pitcher, but I can't seem to get anyone who knows how to catch a ball to practice with me. Kelly tries, but she's a girl and I hate to say it, but my mother's worthless."

"I did my best," Robin protested.

"She catches with her eyes closed," Jeff said.

"How about if you toss a few balls at me?" Cole offered.

Jeff blinked as if he thought he'd misunderstood. "You want me to throw you a few pitches? You're sure?"

"Positive."

The look on her son's face defied description as Cole jumped over the hedge. Jeff's smile stretched from one side of his face to the other as he tore to the opposite end of the yard, unwilling to question Cole's generosity a second time.

For an awkward moment, Robin stayed where she was, not knowing what to say. She looked up at Cole, her emotions soaring—and tangling like kites in a brisk wind. She was deeply grateful for his offer, but also confused. Thrilled by his presence, but also frightened.

"Mom?" Jeff muttered. "In case you hadn't noticed, you're in the way."

"Are you going to make coffee and invite me in for a chat later?" Cole asked quietly.

Her heart sank. "I have some things that need to be done, and…and…"

"Mom?" Jeff shouted.

"I think it's time you and I talked," Cole said, staring straight into her eyes.

"Mom, are you moving or not?"

Robin looked frantically over her shoulder. "Oh… oh, sorry," she whispered, blushing. She hurried away, then stood on the patio watching as the ball flew across the yard.

After catching a dozen of Jeff's pitches, Cole got up and walked over to her son. They spoke for several minutes. Reluctantly, Robin decided it was time to go back in.

She busied herself wiping kitchen counters that were already perfectly clean and tried to stop thinking about the beautiful woman she'd seen with Cole on the Wharf.

Jeff stormed into the house. "Mom, would it be okay if Mr. Camden strings up an old tire from the apple tree?"

"I suppose. Why?"

"He said I can use it to practice pitching, and I wouldn't have to bother you or Kelly."

"I don't think I have an old tire."

"Don't worry, Mr. Camden has one." He ran outside again before she could comment.

Jeff was back in the yard with Cole a few minutes later, far too soon to suit Robin. She forced a weak smile. That other woman was a perfect damsel to his knight in shining armor, she thought wryly. Robin, on the other hand, considered herself more of a court jester.

Her musings were abruptly halted when Cole walked into the kitchen, trailed by her son.

"Isn't it time for your bath, Jeff?" Cole asked pointedly.

It looked for a minute as though the boy was going to argue. For the first time in recent memory, Robin would've welcomed some resistance from him.

"I guess," he said. Bathing was about as popular as homework.

"I didn't make any coffee," Robin said in a small voice. She simply couldn't look at Cole and not see the beautiful blonde on his arm.

"That's fine. I'm more interested in talking, anyway," he said. He walked purposefully to the table and pulled out a chair, then gestured for her to sit down.

Robin didn't. Instead, she frowned at her watch. "My goodness, will you look at the time?"

"No." Cole headed toward her, and Robin backed slowly into the counter.

"We're going talk about that kiss," Cole warned her.

"Please don't," she whispered. "It meant nothing! We'd both had a hectic week. We were tired.... I wasn't myself."

Cole's eyes burned into hers. "Then why did you cry?"

"I...don't know. Believe me, if I knew I'd tell you, but I don't. Can't we just forget it ever happened?"

His shoulders rose in a sigh as he threaded his long fingers through his hair. "That's exactly what I've tried to do all week. Unfortunately it didn't work."

Chapter 5

"I've put it completely out of my mind," Robin said, resuming her string of untruths. "I wish you'd do the same."

"I can't. Trust me, I've tried," Cole told her softly. He smiled and his sensuous mouth widened as his eyes continued to hold hers. The messages were back. Less than subtle messages. *You can't fool me,* they said, and *I didn't want to admit it either.*

"I…"

The sense of expectancy was written across his face. For the life of her, Robin couldn't tear her eyes from him.

She didn't remember stepping into his arms, but suddenly she was there, encompassed by his warmth, feeling more sheltered and protected than she had since her husband's death. This comforting sensation spun itself around her as he wove his fingers into her hair, cradling her head. He hadn't kissed her yet, but Robin felt the promise of it in every part of her.

Deny it though she might, she knew in her heart how badly she wanted Cole to hold her, to kiss her. He must have read the longing in her eyes, because he lowered his mouth to hers, stopping a fraction of an inch from her parted lips. She could feel warm moist breath, could feel a desire so powerful that she wanted to drown in his kiss.

From a reservoir of strength she didn't know she possessed, Robin managed to shake her head. "No… please."

"Yes…please," he whispered just before his mouth settled firmly over hers.

His kiss was the same as it had been before, only more intense. More potent. Robin felt rocked to the very core of her being. Against her will, she felt herself surrendering to him. She felt herself forgetting to breathe. She felt herself weakening.

His mouth moved to her jaw, dropping small, soft kisses there. She sighed. She couldn't help it. Cole's touch was magic. Unable to stop herself, she turned her head, yearning for him to trace a row of kisses on the other side, as well. He complied.

Robin sighed again, her mind filled with dangerous, sensuous thoughts. It felt so good in his arms, so warm and safe…but she knew the feeling was deceptive. She'd seen him with another woman, one far more suited to him than she could ever be. For days she'd been tormented by the realization that the woman in the restaurant was probably the one he spent his weekends with.

"No, please don't." Once more she pleaded, but even to her own ears the words held little conviction.

In response, Cole brought a long slow series of feather-light kisses to her lips, effectively silencing any protest. Robin trembled, breathless.

"Why are you fighting me so hard?" he whispered. His hands framed her face, his thumbs stroking her cheeks. They were damp and she hadn't even known she was crying.

Suddenly she heard footsteps bounding down the stairs. At the thought of Jeff finding her in Cole's arms, she abruptly broke away and turned to stare out the darkened window, hoping for a moment to compose herself.

Jeff burst into the room. "Did you kiss her yet?" he demanded. Not waiting for an answer, Jeff ran toward Robin and grabbed her by the hand. "Well, Mom, what do you think?"

"About…what?"

"Mr. Camden kissing you. He did, didn't he?"

It was on the tip of her tongue to deny the whole thing, but she decided to brazen it out. "You want me to rate him? Like on a scale of one to ten?"

Jeff blinked, uncertain. His questioning glance flew to Cole.

"She was a ten," Cole said, grinning.

"A…high seven," Robin returned.

"A high seven!" Jeff cried, casting her a disparaging look. He shook his head and walked over to Cole. "She's out of practice," he said confidingly. "Doesn't know how to rate guys. Give her a little time and she'll come around."

"Jeff," Robin gasped, astounded to be having this

kind of discussion with her son, let alone Cole, who was looking all too smug.

"She hardly goes out at all," Jeff added. "My mom's got this friend who arranges dates for her, and you wouldn't believe some of the guys she's been stuck with. One of them came to the door—"

"Jeff," Robin said sharply, "that's enough!"

"But one of us needs to tell him!"

"Mr. Camden was just leaving," Robin said, glaring at her neighbor, daring him to contradict her.

"I was? Oh, yeah. Your mom was about to walk me to the door, isn't that right, Robin?"

She gaped at Cole as he reached for her hand and gently led her in the direction of the front door. Meekly she submitted, but not before she saw Jeff give Cole a thumbs-up.

"Now," Cole said, standing in the entryway, his hands heavy on her shoulders. "I want to know what's wrong."

"Wrong? Nothing's wrong."

"It's because of Victoria, isn't it?"

"Victoria?" she asked, already knowing that had to be the woman with him the day she'd seen him at the restaurant.

"Yes. Victoria. I saw you practically hiding under your table, pretending you didn't notice me."

"I… Why should I care?" She hated the way her voice shook.

"Yes, why should you?"

She didn't answer him. Couldn't answer him. She told herself it didn't matter that he was with another woman. Then again, it mattered more than she dared admit.

"Tell me," he insisted.

Robin lowered her gaze. If only he'd stop holding her, stop touching her. Then she might be able to think clearly. "You looked right together. She was a perfect complement to you. She's tall and blond and—"

"Cold as an iceberg. Victoria's a business associate—we had lunch together. Nothing more. I find her as appealing as...as dirty laundry."

"Please, don't explain. It's none of my business who you have lunch with or who you date or where you go every weekend or who you're with. Really. I shouldn't have said anything. I don't know why I did. It was wrong of me—very wrong. I can't believe we're even talking about this."

Jeff poked his head out from the kitchen. "How are things going in here?"

"Good," Robin said. "I was just telling Cole how much we both appreciated his help with your pitching."

"I was having real problems until Cole came along," Jeff confirmed. "Girls are okay for some things, but serious baseball isn't one of them."

Robin opened the front door. "Thanks," she whispered, her eyes avoiding Cole's, "for everything."

"Everything?"

She blushed, remembering the kisses they'd shared. But before she could think of a witty reply, Cole brushed his lips across hers.

"Hey, Cole," Jeff said, hurrying to the front door. "I've got a baseball game Thursday night. Can you come?"

"I'd love to," Cole answered, his eyes holding Robin's. Then he turned abruptly and strode out the door.

"Jeff, we're going to be late for the game if we don't leave now."

"But Cole isn't home yet," Jeff protested. "He said he'd be here."

"There's probably a very good explanation," Robin said calmly, although she was as disappointed as Jeff. "He could be tied up in traffic, or delayed at the office, or any one of a thousand other things. He wouldn't purposely not come."

"Do you think he forgot?"

"I'm sure he didn't. Come on, sweetheart, let's get a move on. You've got a game to pitch." The emphasis came on the last word. The first game of the season and Jeff had won the coveted position of first-string pitcher. Whether it was true or not, Jeff believed Cole's tutoring had given him an advantage over the competition. Jeff hadn't told him the news yet, keeping it a surprise for today.

"When you do see Cole, don't say anything, all right?" Jeff pleaded as they headed toward the car. "I want to be the one who tells him."

"My lips are sealed," she said, holding up her hand. For good measure, she pantomimed zipping her mouth closed. She slid into the car and started the engine, but glanced in the rearview mirror several times, hoping Cole would somehow miraculously appear.

He didn't.

The game was scheduled for the baseball diamond in Balboa Park, less than two miles from Robin's house. A set of bleachers had been arranged around the diamonds, and Robin climbed to the top. It gave her an excellent view of the field—and of the parking area.

Cole knew the game was at Balboa Park, but he didn't know which diamond and there were several. Depending on how late he was, he could waste valuable time looking for the proper field.

The second inning had just begun when Heather Lawrence joined Robin. Robin smiled at her.

"Hi," Heather said. "What's the score?"

"Nothing nothing. It's the top of the second inning."

"How's the neighborhood Randy Johnson doing?"

"Jeff's doing great. He managed to keep his cool when the first batter got a hit off his second pitch. I think I took it worse than Jeff did."

Heather grinned and nodded. "It's the same with me. Kelly played goalie for her soccer team last year, and every time the opposing team scored on her I took it like a bullet to the chest."

"Where's Kelly now?"

Heather motioned toward the other side of the field. The eight-year-old was leaning casually against a tall fir tree. "She didn't want Jeff to know she'd come to watch him. Her game was over a few minutes ago. They lost, but this is her first year and just about everyone else's, too. The game was more a comedy of errors than anything."

Robin laughed. It was thoughtful of Heather to stop by and see how Jeff's team was doing.

Heather laced her fingers over her knees. "Jeff's been talking quite a bit about Cole Camden." She made the statement sound more like a question and kept her gaze focused on the playing field.

"Oh?" Robin wasn't sure how to answer. "Cole was kind enough to give Jeff a few pointers about pitching techniques."

"Speaking of pitching techniques, you two certainly seem to be hitting it off."

Heather was beginning to sound a lot like Angela,

who drilled her daily about her relationship with Cole, offering advice and unsolicited suggestions.

"I can't tell you how surprised I am at the changes I've seen in Cole since you two moved in. Kelly's been wanting to play in that fort from the moment she heard about it, but it's only since Jeff came here that she was even allowed in Cole's yard."

"He's been good for Jeff," Robin said, training her eyes on the game. Cole's relationship with her son forced Robin to examine his motives. He'd lost a son, and there was bound to be a gaping hole in his heart. At first he hadn't allowed Jeff in his yard or approved of Blackie and Jeff's becoming friends. But without anything ever being said, all that had fallen to the wayside. Jeff played in Cole's yard almost every day, and with their neighbor's blessing. Jeff now had free access to the fort and often brought other neighborhood kids along. Apparently Cole had given permission. Did he consider Jeff a sort of substitute son? Robin shook off the thought.

"Jeff talks about Cole constantly," Heather said. "In fact, he told me this morning that Cole was coming to see him pitch. What happened? Did he get hung up at the office?"

"I don't know. He must've been delayed, but—"

"There he is! Over there." Heather broke in excitedly. "You know, in the two years we've lived on Orchard Street, I can only recall talking to Cole a few times. He was always so standoffish. Except when we were both doing yard work, I never saw him, and if we did happen to meet we said hello and that was about it. The other day we bumped into each other at the grocery store and he actually smiled at me. I was stunned. I swear that's the first time I've seen that man smile. I honestly think you and Jeff are responsible for the change in him."

"And I think you're crediting me with more than my due," Robin said, craning her head to look for Cole.

"No, I'm not," Heather argued. "You can't see the difference in him because you're new to the neighborhood, but everyone who's known him for any length of time will tell you he's like a different person."

Jeff was sitting on the bench while his team was up at bat. Suddenly he leapt to his feet and waved energetically, as though he was flagging down a rescue vehicle. His face broke into a wide, eager smile. His coach must have said something to him because Jeff nodded and took off running toward the parking area.

Robin's gaze followed her son. Cole had indeed arrived. The tension eased out of her in a single breath. She hadn't realized how edgy she'd been. In her heart she knew Cole would never purposely disappoint Jeff, but her son's anxiety had been as acute as her own.

"Listen," Heather said, standing, "I'll talk to you later."

"Thanks for stopping by."

"Glad to." Heather climbed down the bleachers. She paused when she got to the ground and wiggled her eyebrows expressively, then laughed merrily at Robin's frown.

Heather must have passed Cole on her way out, but Robin lost sight of them as Jeff raced on to the pitcher's mound for the bottom of the second inning. Even from this distance Robin could see that his eyes were full of happy excitement. He discreetly shot her a look and Robin made a V-for-victory sign, smiling broadly.

Cole vaulted up the bleachers and sat down beside

her. "Sorry I'm late. I was trapped in a meeting, and by the time I could get out to phone you I knew you'd already left for the field. I would've called your cell," he added, "but I didn't have the number."

"Jeff and I figured it had to be something like that."

"So he's pitching!" Cole's voice rang with pride.

"He claims it's all thanks to you."

"I'll let him believe that," Cole said, grinning, "but he's a natural athlete. All I did was teach him a little discipline and give him a means of practicing on his own."

"Well, according to Jeff you taught him everything he knows."

He shook his head. "I'm glad I didn't miss the whole game."

"There'll be others," she said, but she was grateful he'd come when he had. From the time they'd left the house, Robin had been tense and guarded. Cole could stand *her* up for any date, but disappointing Jeff was more than she could bear. Rarely had she felt this emotionally unsettled. And all because Cole had been late for a Balboa Park Baseball League game. It frightened her to realize how much Jeff was beginning to depend on him. And not just Jeff, either....

"This is important to Jeff," Cole said as if reading her mind, "and I couldn't disappoint him. If it had been anyone else it wouldn't have been as important. But Jeff matters—" his eyes locked with hers "—and so do you."

Robin felt giddy with relief. For the first time since Lenny's tragic death, she understood how carefully, how completely, she'd anesthetized her life, refusing to let in anyone or anything that might cause her or Jeff more pain. For years she'd been drifting in a haze of denial and grief, refusing to acknowledge or deal with either. What Angela had said was true. Robin had dated infrequently and haphazardly, and kept any suitors at a safe distance.

For some reason, she hadn't been able to do that with Cole. Robin couldn't understand what was different or why; all she knew was that she was in serious danger of falling for this man, and falling hard. It terrified her....

"Have you and Jeff had dinner?" Cole asked.

Robin turned to face him, but it was a long moment before she grasped that he'd asked her a question. He repeated it and she shook her head. "Jeff was too excited to eat."

"Good. There's an excellent Chinese restaurant close by. The three of us can celebrate after the game."

"That'd be nice," she whispered, thinking she should make some excuse to avoid this, and accepting almost immediately that she didn't want to avoid it at all.

"Can I have some more pork-fried rice?" Jeff asked.

Cole passed him the dish and Robin watched as her son heaped his plate high with a third helping.

"You won," she said wistfully.

"Mom, I wish you'd stop saying that. It's the fourth time you've said it. I *know* we won," Jeff muttered, glancing at Cole as if to beg forgiveness for his mother, who was obviously suffering from an overdose of maternal pride.

"But Jeff, you were fantastic," she couldn't resist telling him.

"The whole team was fantastic." Jeff reached for what was left of the egg rolls and added a dollop of plum sauce to his plate.

"I had no idea you were such a good hitter," Robin

said, still impressed with her son's athletic ability. "I knew you could pitch—but two home runs! Oh, Jeff, I'm so proud of you—and everyone else." It was difficult to remember that Jeff was only one member of a team, and that his success was part of a larger effort.

"I wanted to make sure I played well, especially 'cause you were there, Cole." Jeff stretched his arm across the table again, this time reaching for the nearly empty platter of almond chicken.

As for herself, Robin couldn't down another bite. Cole had said the food at the Golden Wok was good, and he hadn't exaggerated. It was probably the best Chinese meal she'd ever tasted. Jeff apparently thought so, too. The boy couldn't seem to stop eating.

It was while they were laughing over their fortune cookies that Robin heard bits and pieces of the conversation from the booth behind them.

"I bet they're celebrating something special," an elderly gentleman remarked.

"I think their little boy must have done well at the baseball game," his wife said.

Their little boy, Robin mused. The older couple dining directly behind them thought Cole and Jeff were father and son.

Robin's eyes flew to Cole, but if he had heard the comment he didn't give any sign.

"His mother and father are certainly proud of him."

"It's such a delight to see these young people so happy. A family should spend time together."

A family. The three of them looked like a family.

Once more Robin turned to Cole, but once more he seemed not to hear the comments. Or if he had, he ignored them.

But Cole must have sensed her scrutiny because his gaze found hers just then. Their eyes lingered without a hint of the awkwardness Robin had felt so often before.

Jeff chatted constantly on the ride home with Robin. Since she and Cole had both brought their cars, they drove home separately. They exchanged good-nights in the driveway and entered their own houses.

Jeff had some homework to finish and Robin ran a load of clothes through the washing machine. An hour later, after a little television and quick baths, they were both ready for bed. Robin tucked the blankets around Jeff's shoulders, although he protested that he was much too old for her to do that. But he didn't complain too loudly or too long.

"Night, Jeff."

"Night, Mom. Don't let the bedbugs bite."

"Don't go all sentimental on me, okay?" she teased as she turned off his light. He seemed to fall asleep the instant she left the room. She went downstairs to secure the house for the night, then headed up to her own bedroom. Once upstairs, she paused in her son's doorway and smiled gently. They'd both had quite a day.

At about ten o'clock, she was sitting up in bed reading a mystery when the phone rang. She answered quickly, always anxious about late calls. "Hello."

"You're still awake." It was Cole, and his voice affected her like a surge of electricity.

"I…was reading," she said.

"It suddenly occurred to me that we never had the chance to finish our conversation the other night."

"What conversation?" Robin asked.

"The one at the front door…that Jeff interrupted. Remind me to give that boy lessons in timing, by the way."

"I don't even remember what we were talking about." She settled back against the pillows, savoring the sound of his voice, enjoying the small intimacy of lying in bed, listening to him. Her eyes drifted shut.

"As I recall, you'd just said something about how it isn't any of your business who I lunch with or spend my weekends with. I assume you think I'm with a woman."

Robin's eyes shot open. "I can assure you, I don't think anything of the sort."

"I guess I should explain about the weekends."

"No. I mean, Cole, it really isn't my business. It doesn't matter. Really."

"I have some property north of here, about forty acres," he said gently, despite her protests. "The land once belonged to my grandfather, and he willed it to me when he passed away a couple of years back. This house was part of the estate, as well. My father was born and raised here. I've been spending a lot of my free time remodeling the old farmhouse. Sometime in the future I might move out there."

"I see." She didn't want to think about Cole leaving the neighborhood, ever.

"The place still needs a lot of work, and I've enjoyed doing it on my own. It's coming along well."

She nodded and a second later realized he couldn't see her action. "It sounds lovely."

"Are there any other questions you'd like to ask me?" His voice was low and teasing.

"Of course not," she denied immediately.

"Then would you be willing to admit you enjoy it when I kiss you? A high seven? Really? I think Jeff's right—we need more practice."

"Uh..." Robin didn't know how to answer that.

"I'm willing," he said, and she could almost hear him smile.

Robin lifted the hair from her forehead with one hand. "I can't believe we're having this discussion."

"Would it help if I told you how much I enjoy kissing you?"

"Please…don't," she whispered. She didn't want him to tell her that. Every time he kissed her, it confused her more. Despite the sheltered feeling she experienced in his arms, something deep and fundamental inside her was afraid of loving again. No, terrified. She was terrified of falling in love with Cole. Terrified of what the future might hold.

"The first time shook me more than I care to admit," he said. "Remember that Friday night we rented the movie?"

"I remember."

"I tried to stay away from you afterward. For an entire week I avoided you."

Robin didn't answer. She couldn't. Lying back against the pillows, she stared at the ceiling as a sense of warmth enveloped her. A feeling of comfort…of happiness.

There was a short silence, and in an effort to bring their discussion back to a less intimate—less risky—level, she said, "Thank you for dinner. Jeff had the time of his life." She had, too, but she couldn't find the courage to acknowledge it.

"You're welcome."

"Are you going away this weekend to work on the property?"

She had no right to ask him that, and was shocked at how easily the question emerged.

"I don't think so." After another brief pause, he murmured, "When's the last time you went on a picnic and flew a kite?"

"I don't recall."

"Would you consider going with me on Saturday afternoon? You and Jeff. The three of us together."

"Yes…Jeff would love it."

"How about you? Would you love it?"

"Yes," she whispered.

There didn't seem to be anything more to say, and Robin ended the conversation. "I'll tell Jeff in the morning. He'll be thrilled. Thank you."

"I'll talk to you tomorrow, then."

"Yes. Tomorrow."

"Good night, Robin."

She smiled softly. He said her name the way she'd always dreamed a man would, softly, with a mixture of excitement and need. "Good night, Cole."

For a long time after they'd hung up Robin lay staring at her bedroom walls. When she did flick off her light, she fell asleep as quickly as Jeff seemed to have. She woke about midnight, surprised to find the sheets all twisted as if she'd tossed and turned frantically. The bedspread had slipped onto the floor, and the top sheet was wound around her legs, trapping her.

Sitting up, she untangled her legs and brushed the curls from her face, wondering what had caused her restlessness. She didn't usually wake abruptly like this.

She slid off the bed, found her slippers and went downstairs for a glass of milk.

It was while she was sitting at the table that it came to her. Her hand stilled. Her heartbeat accelerated. The couple in the Chinese restaurant. Robin had overheard them and she was certain Cole had, too.

Their little boy. A family.

Cole had lost a son. From the little Robin had learned, Cole's son had been about the same age Jeff was now when he'd died. First divorce, and then death.

Suddenly it all made sense. A painful kind of sense. A panicky kind of sense. The common ground between them wasn't their backyards, but the fact that they were both victims.

Cole was trying to replace the family that had been so cruelly taken from him.

Robin was just as guilty. She'd been so caught up in the tide of emotion and attraction that she'd refused to recognize what was staring her in the face. She'd ignored her own suspicions and fears, shoving them aside.

She and Cole were both hurting, needy people.

But once the hurt was assuaged, once the need had been satisfied, Cole would discover what Robin had known from the beginning. They were completely different people with little, if anything, in common.

Chapter 6

"What do you mean you want to meet my cousin?" Angela demanded, glancing up from her desk, a shocked look on her face.

"You've been after me for weeks to go out with Fred."

"Frank. Yes, I have, but that was B.C."

"B.C.?"

"Before Cole. What happened with you two?"

"Nothing!"

"And pigs have wings," Angela said with more than a trace of sarcasm. She stood up and walked around to the front of her desk, leaning against one corner while she folded her arms and stared unblinkingly at Robin.

Robin knew it would do little good to try to disguise her feelings. She'd had a restless night and was convinced it showed. No doubt her eyes were glazed; they ached. Her bones ached. But mostly her heart ached.

Arranging a date with Angela's cousin was a sure indication of her distress.

"The last thing I heard, Cole was supposed to attend Jeff's baseball game with you."

"He did." Robin walked to her own desk and reached for the cup of coffee she'd brought upstairs with her. Peeling off the plastic lid, she cautiously took a sip.

"And?"

"Jeff pitched and he played a fabulous game," Robin said, hoping her friend wouldn't question her further.

Angela continued to stare at Robin. Good grief, Robin thought, the woman had eyes that could cut through solid rock.

"What?" Robin snapped when she couldn't stand her friend's scrutiny any longer. She took another sip of her coffee and nearly scalded her lips. If the rest of her day followed the pattern set that morning, she might as well go home now. The temptation to climb back into bed and hide her head under the pillow was growing stronger every minute.

"Tell me what happened with Cole," Angela said again.

"Nothing. I already told you he was at Jeff's baseball game. What more do you want?"

"The least you can do is tell me what went on last night," Angela said slowly, carefully enunciating each word as though speaking to someone who was hard of hearing.

"Before or after Jeff's game?" Robin pulled out her chair and sat down.

"Both."

Robin gave up. Gesturing weakly with her hands, she shrugged, took a deep breath and poured out the whole story in one huge rush. "Cole was held up at the office in a meeting, so we didn't meet at the house the way we'd planned. Naturally Jeff was disappointed, but we decided that whatever was keeping Cole wasn't his fault, and we left for Balboa Park without him. Cole arrived at the bottom of the second inning, just as Jeff was ready to pitch. Jeff only allowed three hits the entire game, and scored two home runs himself. Afterward Cole took us all out for Chinese food at a fabulous restaurant I've never heard of but one you and I will have to try sometime. Our next raise, okay? Later Cole phoned and asked to take Jeff and me on a picnic Saturday. I think we're going to Golden Gate Park because he also talked about flying kites." She paused, dragged in a fresh gulp of air and gave Angela a look that said "make something out of that if you can!"

"I see," Angela said after a lengthy pause.

"Good."

Robin wasn't up to explaining things, so if Angela really *didn't* understand, that was just too bad. She only knew that she was dangerously close to letting her emotions take charge of her life. She was becoming increasingly attracted to a man who could well be trying to replace the son he'd lost. Robin needed to find a way to keep from following her heart, which was moving at breakneck speed straight into Cole's arms.

"Will you introduce me to Frank or not?" she asked a second time, strengthening her voice and her conviction.

Angela was still watching her with those diamond-cutting eyes. "I'm not sure yet."

"You're not sure!" Robin echoed, dismayed. "For weeks you've been spouting his virtues. According to you, this cousin is as close to a god as a human being can get. He works hard, buys municipal bonds, goes to church regularly and flosses his teeth."

"I said all that?"

"Just about," Robin muttered. "I made up the part about flossing his teeth. Yet when I ask to meet this paragon of limitless virtue, you say you're not sure you want to introduce me. I would've thought you'd be pleased."

"I am pleased," Angela said, frowning, "but I'm also concerned."

"It's not your job to be concerned. All you have to do is call Fred and let him know I'm available Saturday evening for drinks or dinner or a movie or whatever. I'll let him decide what he's most comfortable with."

"It's Frank, and I thought you said you were going on a picnic with Cole on Saturday."

Robin turned on her computer, prepared to check several columns of figures. If she looked busy and suitably nonchalant, it might prompt Angela to agree. "Jeff and I will be with Cole earlier in the day. I'll simply make sure we're back before late afternoon, so there's no reason to worry."

Robin's forehead puckered. "I *am* worried. I can't help being worried. Honestly, Robin, I've never seen you like this. You're so…so determined."

"I've always been determined," Robin countered, glancing up from the computer.

"Oh, I agree one hundred percent," Angela said with a heavy sigh, "but not when it comes to anything that has to do with men. My thirteen-year-old niece has more savvy with the opposite sex than you do!"

"Mom, look how high my kite is," Jeff hollered as his box kite soared toward the heavens.

"It's touching the sky!" Robin shouted, and laughed with her son as he tugged and twisted the string. Despite all her misgivings about her relationship with Cole, she was thoroughly enjoying the afternoon. At first, she'd been positive the day would turn into a disaster. She was sure Cole would take one look at her and know she was going out with another man that evening. She was equally sure she'd blurt it out if he didn't immediately guess.

Cole had been as excited as Jeff about the picnic and kite-flying expedition. The two of them had been fussing with the kites for hours—buying, building and now flying them. For her part, Robin was content to soak up the sunshine.

The weather couldn't have been more cooperative. The sky was a brilliant blue and the wind was perfect. Sailboats scudding on the choppy green waters added dashes of bright color.

In contrast to all the beauty surrounding her, Robin's heart was troubled. Watching Cole, so patient and gentle with her son, filled her with contradictory emotions. Part of her wanted to thank him. Thank him for the smile that lit up Jeff's face. Thank him for throwing open the shades and easing her toward the light. And part of her wanted to shut her eyes and run for cover.

"Mom, look!" Jeff cried as the kite whipped and kicked in the wind. Blackie raced at his side as the sleek red-and-blue kite sliced through the sky, then dipped sharply and crashed toward the ground at heart-stopping speed, only to be caught at the last second and lifted higher and higher.

"I'm looking, I'm looking!" Robin shouted back. She'd never seen Jeff happier. Pride and joy shone from his face, and Robin was moved almost to tears.

Cole stood behind Jeff, watching the kite. One hand rested on the boy's shoulder, the other shaded his eyes as he gazed up at the sky. They laughed, and once more Robin was struck by the mingling of their voices. One mature and measured, the other young and excited. Both happy.

A few minutes later, Cole jogged over to Robin's blanket and sat down beside her. He did nothing more than smile at her, but she felt an actual jolt.

Cole stretched out and leaned back on his elbows, grinning at the sun. "I can't remember the last time I laughed so much."

"You two seem to be enjoying this," Robin said.

If Cole noticed anything awry, he didn't comment. She'd managed not to tell him about the date with Angela's cousin; she certainly didn't want him to think she was trying to make him jealous. That wasn't the evening's purpose at all. Actually she wasn't sure *what* she hoped to accomplish by dating Fred…Frank. She mentally shouted the name five times. Why did she keep calling him Fred? She didn't know that any more than she knew why she was going out with him. On the morning she'd talked Angela into making the arrangements for her, it had seemed a matter of life and death. Now she only felt confused and regretful.

"Jeff says you've got a date this evening."

So much for her worry that she might blurt it out herself, Robin thought. She glanced at Cole. He might've been referring to the weather for all the emotion revealed in his voice.

"A cousin of a good friend. She's been after me for months to meet Frank—we're having dinner."

"Could this be the Frank you weren't going out with and that was final?"

Robin stared at him blankly.

"You answered the phone with that when I called to inquire about Blackie. Remember?"

"Oh, yes…" Suddenly she felt an intense need to justify her actions. "It's just that Angela's been talking about him for so long and it seemed like the right thing to do. He's apparently very nice and Angela's been telling me he's a lot of fun and I didn't think it would hurt to meet him…." Once she got started, Robin couldn't seem to stop explaining.

"Robin," Cole said, his eyes tender. "You don't owe me any explanations."

She instantly grew silent. He was right, she knew that, yet she couldn't help feeling guilty. She was making a terrible mess of this.

"I'm not the jealous type," Cole informed her matter-of-factly.

"I'm not trying to make you jealous," she returned stiffly.

"Good," Cole said and shrugged. His gaze moved from her to Jeff, who was jogging across the grass. Blackie was beside him, barking excitedly.

He hadn't asked, but she felt obliged to explain who'd be looking after her son while she was out. "Jeff's going to the movies with Heather and Kelly Lawrence while I'm out."

Cole didn't say anything. All he did was smile. It was the same smile he'd flashed at her earlier. The same devastating, wickedly charming smile.

He seemed to be telling her she could dine with a thousand different men and it wouldn't disturb him in the least. As he'd said, he wasn't the jealous type. Great. This was exactly the way she'd wanted him to respond, wasn't it? She could date a thousand different men, because Cole didn't care about her. He cared about her son.

"Let me know when you want to leave," he said with infuriating self-assurance. "I wouldn't want you to be late."

On that cue, Robin checked her watch and was surprised to note that it was well past four. They'd been having so much fun, the day had simply slipped away. When she looked up, she found Cole studying her expectantly. "It's… I'm not meeting Frank until later," she said, answering his unspoken question evasively while she gathered up the remains of their picnic.

An hour later, they decided to leave Golden Gate Park. Jeff and Cole loaded up the kites, as well as the picnic cooler, in the back of Cole's car. It took them another hour to get back to Glen Park because of the traffic, which made Robin's schedule even tighter. But that was hardly Cole's fault—it wasn't as if he'd *arranged* for an accident on the freeway.

Cole and Jeff chatted easily for most of the ride home. When they finally arrived at the house, both Robin and Jeff helped Cole unload the car. Blackie's barking only added to the confusion.

"I suppose I'd better get inside," Robin said, her eyes briefly meeting Cole's. She felt awkward all of a sudden, wishing Jeff was standing there as a barrier, instead of busily carrying things onto Cole's porch.

"We had a great time," she added self-consciously. She couldn't really blame her nervousness on Cole; he'd been the perfect companion all day. "Thank you for the picnic."

Jeff joined them, his eyes narrowing as he looked at Cole. "Are you gonna let her do it?"

"Do what?" Robin asked.

"Go out with that other man," Jeff said righteously, inviting Cole to leap into the argument. "I can't believe you're letting her get away with this."

"Jeff. This isn't something we should be discussing with Mr. Camden."

"All right," he murmured with a sigh. "But I think you're making a mistake." He cast a speculative glance in Cole's direction. "Both of you," he mumbled under his breath and headed for the house.

"Thanks for the wonderful afternoon, Cole," Robin said again.

"No problem," he responded, hands in his pockets, his stance relaxed. "Have a good time with Frank."

"Thanks, I will," she said, squinting at him suspiciously just before she turned toward the house. Darn it, she actually felt guilty! There wasn't a single solitary reason she should feel guilty for agreeing to this dinner date with Angela's cousin, yet she did. Cole must've known it, too, otherwise he wouldn't have made that remark about having a good time. Oh, he knew all right.

As Robin was running the bath, Jeff raced up the stairs. "Mom, I need money for the movie." He thrust her purse into her hands. "How much are you giving me for goodies?"

"Goodies?"

"You know, popcorn, pop, a couple of candy bars. I'm starving."

"Jeff, you haven't stopped eating all day. What about the two hot dogs I just fixed you?"

"I ate them, but that was fifteen minutes ago. I'm hungry again."

stand, his wife left him and sometime later his son died."

"That's tough," Frank said, picking up his coffee. "But that was years ago, wasn't it?"

"I...don't know. Cole's never told me these things himself. In fact, he's never mentioned either his wife or his son."

"He's *never* mentioned them?"

"Never," she confirmed. "I heard it from a neighbor."

"That's what's bothering you, isn't it?"

The question was sobering. Subconsciously, from the moment Robin had learned of Cole's loss, she'd been waiting for him to tell her. Waiting for him to trust her enough.

Frank and Robin lingered over coffee, chatting about politics and the economy and a number of other stimulating topics. But the question about Cole refused to fade from her mind.

They parted outside the restaurant and Frank kissed her cheek, but they were both well aware they wouldn't be seeing each other again. Their time together had been a brief respite. It had helped Frank deal with his loneliness and helped Robin understand what was troubling her about Cole.

The first thing Robin noticed when she pulled into her driveway was that Cole's house was dark. Dark and silent. Lonely. So much of her life had been like that—before she'd met him.

She needed to talk to him. She wanted to ask about his phone call. She wanted to ask about his wife and the son he'd lost. But the timing was all wrong.

For a long moment Robin sat alone in her car, feeling both sad and disappointed.

Heather greeted her with a smile and a finger pressed to her lips. "Both kids were exhausted. They fell asleep in the living room almost as soon as we got back."

After Jeff's busy day, she could hardly believe he'd lasted through the movie. "I hope he wasn't cranky."

"Not in the least," Heather assured her.

Robin yawned, completely exhausted. She wanted nothing more than to escape to her room and sleep until noon the following day.

"Would you like a cup of coffee before you go?" Heather asked.

"No, thanks." Robin had been blessed with good neighbors. Heather on her right and Cole on her left....

Together Robin and Heather woke Jeff, who grumbled about his mother being late. He was too drowsy to realize it was only nine-thirty or that she'd returned ahead of schedule.

After telling Heather a little about her evening, Robin guided her son across the yard and into the house. She walked upstairs with him and answered the slurred questions he struggled to ask between wide, mouth-stretching yawns.

Tugging back his quilt, Robin urged him into his bed. Jeff kicked off his shoes and reached for the quilt. It wasn't the first time he'd slept in his clothes and it probably wouldn't be the last.

Smiling to herself, Robin moved quietly down the stairs.

On impulse, she paused in the kitchen and picked up the phone. When Cole answered on the first ring, she swallowed a gasp of surprise.

"Hello," he said a second time.

"What did you lie about?" she asked softly.

"Where are you?"

"Home."

"I'll be right there." Without a further word, he hung up.

A minute later, Cole was standing at her front door, hands in his back pockets. He stared at her as if it had been months since they'd seen each other.

"You win," he said, edging his way in.

"Win what? The door prize?" she asked, controlling her amusement with difficulty.

Not bothering to answer her, Cole stalked to the kitchen, where he sank down in one of the pine chairs. "Did you have a good time?"

She sat down across from him. "I really did. Frank's a very pleasant, very caring man. We met at the Higher Ground—that's a cute little restaurant close to the BART station and—"

"I know where it is."

"About your phone call earlier. You said—"

"What's he like?"

"Who? Frank?"

Cole gave her a look that suggested she have her intelligence tested.

"Like I said, he's very pleasant. Divorced and lonely."

"What's he do for a living?"

"He works for the city, I think. We didn't get around to talking about our careers." No doubt Cole would be shocked if he knew she'd spent the greater part of the evening discussing her relationship with *him!*

"What did you talk about, then?"

"Cole, honestly, I don't think we should discuss my evening with Frank. Would you like some coffee? I'll make decaf."

"Are you going to see him again?"

Robin ignored the question. Instead she left the table and began to make coffee. She was concentrating so carefully on her task that she didn't notice Cole was directly behind her. She turned—and found herself gazing into the darkest, most confused and frustrated pair of eyes she'd ever seen.

"Oh," she said, startled. "I didn't realize you were so close."

His hands gripped her shoulders. "Why did you go out with him?"

Surely that wasn't distress she heard in Cole's voice? Not after all that casual indifference this afternoon. She frowned, bewildered by the pain she saw in his eyes. And she finally understood. Contrary to everything he'd claimed, Cole was jealous. Really and truly jealous.

"Did he kiss you?" he asked with an urgency, an intensity, she'd never heard in his voice before.

Robin stared, frozen by the stark need she read in him.

Cole's finger rested on her mouth. "Did Frank kiss you?" he repeated.

She shook her head and the motion brushed his finger across her bottom lip.

"He wanted to, though, didn't he?" Cole asked with a brooding frown.

"He didn't kiss me." She was finally able to say the words. She couldn't kiss Frank or anyone else. The only man she wanted to kiss and be kissed by was the man looking down at her now. The man whose lips were descending on hers….

Chapter 7

"So, did you like this guy you had dinner with last night?" Jeff asked, keeping his eyes on his bowl of cold cereal.

"He was nice," Robin answered, pouring herself a cup of coffee and joining him at the table. They'd slept late and were spending a lazy Sunday morning enjoying their breakfast before going to the eleven o'clock service at church.

Jeff hesitated, his spoon poised in front of him. "Is he nicer than Cole?"

"Cole's...nicer," Robin admitted reluctantly. *Nice* and *nicer* weren't terms she would've used to describe the differences between Frank and Cole, but in her son's ten-year-old mind they made perfect sense.

A smile quivered at the edges of Jeff's mouth. "I saw you two smooching last night," he said, grinning broadly.

"When?" Robin demanded—a ridiculous question. It could only have happened when Cole had come over to talk to her. He'd confessed how jealous he'd been of Frank and how he'd struggled with the emotion and felt like a fool. Robin had been convinced she was the one who'd behaved like an idiot. Before either of them could prevent it, they were in each other's arms, seeking and granting reassurance.

"You thought I was asleep, but I heard Cole talking and I wanted to ask him what he was gonna do about you and this other guy, so I came downstairs and saw you two with your faces stuck together."

The boy certainly had a way with words.

"You didn't look like you minded, either. Cole and me talked about girls once, and he said they aren't much when they're ten, but they get a whole lot more interesting later on. He said girls are like green apples. At first they're all sour and make your lips pucker, but a little while later they're real good."

"I see," Robin muttered, not at all sure she liked being compared to an apple.

"But when I got downstairs I didn't say anything," Jeff said, "because, well, you know."

Robin nodded and sipped her coffee in an effort to hide her discomfort.

Jeff picked up his cereal bowl and drank the remainder of the milk in loud gulps. He wiped the back of his hand across his lips. "I suppose this means you're going to have a baby now."

Robin was too horrified to speak. The swallow of coffee got stuck in her throat and she started choking. Trying to help her breathe, Jeff pounded her back with his fist, which only added to her misery.

By the time she caught her breath, tears were streaking down her face.

"You all right, Mom?" Jeff asked, his eyes wide with concern. He rushed into the bathroom and returned with a wad of tissue.

"Thanks," she whispered, wiping her face. It took her a moment or two to regain her composure. This was a talk she'd planned on having with him soon—but not quite yet. "Jeff, listen…kissing doesn't make babies."

"It doesn't? But I thought… I hoped… You mean you won't be having a baby?"

"I… Not from kissing," she whispered, taking in deep breaths to stabilize her pulse.

"I suppose the next thing you're gonna tell me is we'll have to save up for a baby the way we did for the house and now the fence before we get me a dog."

This conversation was getting too complicated. "No, we wouldn't have to save for a baby."

"Then what's the holdup?" her son demanded. "I like the idea of being a big brother. I didn't think much about it until we moved here. Then when we were having dinner at the Chinese restaurant I heard this grandma and grandpa in the booth next to us talking, and they were saying neat things about us being a family. That's when I started thinking about babies and stuff."

"Jeff," Robin said, rubbing her hands together as she collected her thoughts. "There's more to it than that. Before there's a baby, there should be a husband."

"Well, of course," Jeff returned, looking at her as if she'd insulted his intelligence. "You'd have to marry Cole first, but that'd be all right with me. You like him, don't you? You must like him or you wouldn't be kissing him that way."

Robin sighed. Of course she *liked* Cole, but it wasn't that simple. Unfortunately she wasn't sure she could explain it in terms a ten-year-old could understand. "I—"

"I can't remember ever seeing you kiss a guy like that. You looked real serious. And when I was sneaking back up the stairs, I heard him ask you to have dinner alone with him tonight and that seemed like a real good sign."

The next time Cole kissed her, Robin thought wryly, they'd have to scurry into a closet. The things that child came up with…

"You *are* going to dinner with him, aren't you?"

"Yes, but—"

"Then what's the problem? I'll ask him to marry you if you want."

"Jeff!" she cried, leaping to her feet. "Absolutely not! That's between Cole and me, and neither of us would appreciate any assistance from you. Is that clearly understood?"

"All right," he sighed, but he didn't look too pleased. He reached for a piece of toast, shredding it into thirds. "But you're going to marry him, aren't you?"

"I don't know."

"Why not? Cole's the best thing that's ever happened to us."

Her son was staring at her intently, his baseball cap twisted around to the back of his head. Now that she had his full attention, Robin couldn't find the words to explain. "It's more complicated than you realize, sweetie." She made a show of glancing at the clock. "Anyway, it's time to change and get ready for church."

Jeff nodded and rushed up the stairs. Robin followed

at a much slower pace, grateful to put an end to this difficult and embarrassing subject.

The minute they were home from the service, Jeff grabbed his baseball mitt. "Jimmy Wallach and I are going to the school yard to practice hitting balls. Okay?"

"Okay," Robin said absently. "How long will you be gone?"

"An hour."

"I'm going grocery shopping, so if I'm not home when you get back you know what to do?"

"Of course," he muttered.

"You're Robin Masterson, aren't you?" a tall middle-aged woman asked as she maneuvered her grocery cart alongside Robin's.

"Yes," Robin said. The other woman's eyes were warm and her smile friendly.

"I thought you must be—I've seen you from a distance. I'm Joyce Wallach. Jimmy and Jeff have become good friends. In fact, they're at the school yard now."

"Of course," Robin said, pleased to make the other woman's acquaintance. They'd talked on the phone several times, and she'd met Joyce's husband once, when Jimmy had spent the night. The boys had wanted to play on the same baseball team and were disappointed when they'd been assigned to different teams. It had been Jimmy who'd told Jeff about the death of Cole's son.

"I've been meaning to invite you to the house for coffee," Joyce went on to say, "but I started working part-time and I can't seem to get myself organized."

"I know what you mean." Working full-time, keeping up with Jeff and her home was about all Robin could manage herself. She didn't know how other mothers were able to accomplish so much.

"There's a place to sit down here," Joyce said, and her eyes brightened at the idea. "Do you have time to chat now?"

Robin nodded. "Sure. I've been wanting to meet you, too." The Wallachs lived two streets over, and Robin fully approved of Jimmy as a friend for Jeff. He and Kelly had become friends, too, but her ten-year-old son wasn't as eager to admit being buddies with a girl. Kelly was still a green apple in Jeff's eye, but the time would come when he'd appreciate having her next door.

"I understand Jeff's quite the baseball player," Joyce said at the self-service counter.

Robin smiled. She poured herself a plastic cup of iced tea and paid for it. "Jeff really loves baseball. He was disappointed he couldn't play with Jimmy."

"They separate the teams according to the kid's year of birth. Jimmy's birthday is in January so he's with another group." She frowned. "That doesn't really make much sense, does it?" She chuckled, and Robin couldn't help responding to the soft infectious sound of Joyce's laughter. She found herself laughing, too.

They pulled out chairs at one of the small tables in the supermarket's deli section.

"I feel like throwing my arms around you," Joyce said with a grin. "I saw Cole Camden at Balboa Park the other day and I couldn't believe my eyes. It was like seeing him ten years ago, the way he used to be." She glanced at Robin. "Jeff was with him."

"Cole came to his first game."

"Ah." She nodded slowly, as if that explained it. "I don't know if anyone's told you, but there's been a marked difference in Cole lately. I can't tell you how happy I am to see it. Cole's gone through so much heartache."

"Cole's been wonderful for Jeff," Robin said, then swallowed hard. She felt a renewed stab of fear that Cole was more interested in the idea of having a son than he was in a relationship with her.

"I have the feeling you've *both* been wonderful for him," Joyce added.

Robin's smile was losing its conviction. She lowered her eyes and studied the lemon slice floating in her tea.

"My husband and I knew Cole quite well before the divorce," Joyce went on to say. "Larry, that's my husband, and Cole played golf every Saturday afternoon. Then Jennifer decided she wanted out of the marriage, left him and took Bobby. Cole really tried to save that marriage, but the relationship had been in trouble for a long time. Cole doted on his son, though— he would've done anything to spare Bobby the trauma of a divorce. Jennifer, however—" Joyce halted abruptly, apparently realizing how much she'd said. "I didn't mean to launch into all of this—it's ancient history. I just wanted you to know how pleased I am to meet you."

Since Cole had told her shockingly little of his past, Robin had to bite her tongue not to plead with Joyce to continue. Instead, she bowed her head and said, "I'm pleased to meet you, too."

Then she looked up with a smile as Joyce said, "Jimmy's finally got the friend he's always wanted. There are so few boys his age around here. I swear my son was ready to set off fireworks the day Jeff registered at the school and he learned you lived only two blocks away."

"Jeff claimed he couldn't live in a house that's surrounded by girls." Robin shook her head with a mock grimace. "If he hadn't met Jimmy, I might've had a mutiny on my hands."

Joyce's face relaxed into another warm smile. She was energetic and animated, gesturing freely with her hands as she spoke. Robin felt as if she'd known and liked Jimmy's mother for years.

"There hasn't been much turnover in this neighborhood. We're a close-knit group, as I'm sure you've discovered. Heather Lawrence is a real sweetie. I wish I had more time to get to know her. And Cole, well… I realize that huge house has been in his family forever, but I half expected him to move out after Jennifer and Bobby were killed."

The silence that followed was punctuated by Robin's soft, involuntary gasp. "What did you just say?"

"That I couldn't understand why Cole's still living in the house on Orchard Street. Is that what you mean?"

"No, after that—about Jennifer and Bobby." It was difficult for Robin to speak. Each word felt as if it had been scraped from the roof of her mouth.

"I assumed you knew they'd both been killed," Joyce said, her eyes full of concern. "I mean, I thought for sure that Cole had told you."

"I knew about Bobby. Jimmy said something to Jeff, who told me, but I didn't have any idea that Jennifer had died, too. Heather Lawrence told me about the divorce, but she didn't say anything about Cole's wife dying…."

"I don't think Heather knows. She moved into the neighborhood long after the divorce, and Cole's pretty close-mouthed about it."

"When did all this happen?"

"Five or six years ago now. It was terribly tragic,"

Joyce said. "Just thinking about it makes my heart ache all over again. I don't mean to be telling tales, but if there's any blame to be placed I'm afraid it would fall on Jennifer. She wasn't the kind of woman who's easy to know or like. I shouldn't speak ill of the dead, and I don't mean to be catty, but Jen did Cole a favor when she left him. Naturally, he didn't see it that way—he was in love with his wife and crazy about his son. Frankly, I think Cole turned a blind eye to his wife's faults because of Bobby."

"What happened?" Perhaps having a neighbor fill in the details of Cole's life was the wrong thing to do; Robin no longer knew. Cole had never said a word to her about Jennifer or Bobby, and she didn't know if he ever would.

"Jen was never satisfied with Cole's position as a city attorney," Joyce explained. "We'd have coffee together every now and then, and all she'd do was complain how Cole was wasting his talents and that he could be making big money and wasn't. She had grander plans for him. But Cole loved his job and felt an obligation to follow through with his commitments. Jennifer never understood that. She didn't even try to sympathize with Cole's point of view. She constantly wanted more, better, newer things. She didn't work herself, so it was all up to Cole." Joyce shrugged sadly.

"Jen was never happy, never satisfied," she went on. "She hated the house and the neighborhood, but figured out that all the whining and manipulating in the world wasn't going to do one bit of good. Cole intended to finish out his responsibilities to the city, so she played her ace. She left him, taking Bobby with her."

"But didn't Cole try to gain custody of Bobby?"

"Of course. He knew, and so did everyone else, that Jennifer was using their son as a pawn. She was never the motherly type, if you know what I mean. If you want the truth, she was an alcoholic. There were several times I dropped Bobby off at the house and suspected Jen had been drinking heavily. I was willing to testify on Cole's behalf, and I told him so. He was grateful, but then the accident happened and it was too late."

"The accident?" A heaviness settled in her chest. Each breath pained her and brought with it the memories she longed to forget, memories of another accident—the one that had taken her husband.

"It was Jennifer's fault—the accident, I mean. She'd been drinking and should never have been behind the wheel. The day before, Cole had been to see his attorneys, pleading with them to move quickly because he was afraid Jennifer was becoming more and more irresponsible. But it wasn't until after she'd moved out that Cole realized how sick she'd become, how dependent she was on alcohol to make it through the day."

"Oh, no," Robin whispered. "Cole must've felt so guilty."

"It was terrible," Joyce returned, her voice quavering. "I didn't know if Cole would survive that first year. He hid inside the house and severed relationships with everyone in the neighborhood. He was consumed by his grief. Later he seemed to come out of it a little, but he's never been the same.

"The irony of all this is that eventually Jen would've gotten exactly what she wanted if she'd been more patient. A couple of years ago, Cole accepted a partnership in one of the most important law firms in the city. He's made a real name for himself, but money and position don't seem to mean much to him—they never have. I wouldn't be surprised if he walked away from the whole thing someday."

"I think you're right. Cole told me not long ago that he has some property north of here that he inherited from his grandfather. He's restoring the house, and he said something about moving there. It's where he spends most of his weekends."

"I wondered if that was it," Joyce said, nodding. "There were rumors floating around the neighborhood that he spent his weekends with a woman. Anyone who knew Cole would realize what a crock that is. Cole isn't the type to have a secret affair."

Robin felt ashamed, remembering how she'd been tempted to believe the rumor herself.

"For a long time," Joyce murmured, "I wondered if Cole was ever going to recover from Jennifer's and Bobby's deaths, but now I believe he has. I can't help thinking you and Jeff had a lot to do with that."

"I...think he would gradually have come out of his shell."

"Perhaps, but the changes in him lately have been the most encouraging things so far. I don't know how you feel about Cole or if there's anything between you, but you couldn't find a better man."

"I...I'm falling in love with him," Robin whispered, voicing her feelings for the first time. The words hung there, and it was too late to take them back.

"I think that's absolutely wonderful, I really do!" Joyce said enthusiastically.

"I don't." Now that the shock had worn off, Robin was forced to confront her anger. Cole had told her none of this. Not a single word. That hurt. Hurt more than she would've expected. But the ache she felt was nothing compared to the grief Cole must face each morning, the pain that weighed down his life.

"Oh, dear," Joyce said. "I've really done it now, haven't I? I knew I should've kept my mouth shut. You're upset and it's my fault."

"Nonsense," Robin whispered, making an effort to bring a smile to her dry lips and not succeeding. "I'm grateful we met, and more than grateful you told me about Jennifer, and about Cole's son." The knowledge produced a dull ache in Robin's heart. She felt grief for Cole and a less worthy emotion, too—a sense of being slighted by his lack of trust in her.

She was so distressed on the short drive home that she missed the turn and had to take a side street and double back to Orchard Street.

As she neared the house, she saw that Cole was outside watering his lawn. He waved, but she pretended not to see him and pulled into her driveway. Desperate for some time alone before facing Cole, Robin did her best to ignore him as she climbed out of the car. She needed a few more minutes to gather her thoughts and control her emotions.

She was almost safe, almost at the house, when Cole stopped her.

"Robin," he called, jogging toward her. "Hold on a minute, would you?"

She managed to compose herself, squaring her shoulders and drawing on her dignity.

His wonderful eyes were smiling as he hurried over. Obviously he hadn't noticed there was anything wrong. "Did Jeff happen to say anything about seeing us kiss last night?" he asked.

Her mouth was still so dry she had to swallow a couple of times before she could utter a single syllable. "Yes, but don't worry, I think I've got him squared away."

"Drat!" he teased, snapping his fingers. "I suppose this means I don't have to go through with the shotgun wedding?"

She nodded, keeping her eyes lowered, fearing he'd be able to read all the emotion churning inside her.

"You have nothing to fear but fear itself," she said, forcing a lightness into her tone.

"Robin?" He made her name a question and a caress. "Is something wrong?"

She shook her head, shifting the bag of groceries from one arm to the other. "Of course not," she said with the same feigned cheerfulness.

Cole took the bag from her arms. Robin knew she should have resisted, but she couldn't; she felt drained of strength. She headed for the house, knowing Cole would follow her inside.

"What's wrong?" he asked a second time, setting the groceries on the kitchen counter.

It was difficult to speak and even more difficult, more exhausting, to find the words that would explain what she'd learned.

"Nothing. It's just that I've got a lot to do if we're going out for dinner tonight."

"Wear something fancy. I'm taking you to a four-star restaurant."

"Something fancy?" Mentally she reviewed the contents of her closet, which was rather lacking in anything fancy.

"I'm not about to be outclassed by Frank," Cole said

with a laugh. "I'm going to wine and dine you and turn your head with sweet nothings."

He didn't need to do any of those things to turn her head. She was already dangerously close to being in love with him, so close that she'd blurted it out to a woman she'd known for a total of twelve minutes.

Abruptly switching her attention to the bag of groceries, Robin set several packages on the counter. When Cole's hands clasped her shoulders, her eyes drifted shut. "It isn't necessary," she whispered.

Cole turned her around to face him. "What isn't?"

"The dinner, the wine, the…sweet nothings."

Their eyes held. As if choreographed, they moved into each other's arms. With a groan that came from deep in his throat, Cole kissed her. His hands tangled in the auburn thickness of her hair. His lips settled on hers with fierce protectiveness.

Robin curled her arms tightly around his neck as her own world started to dip and spin and whirl. She was standing on tiptoe, her heart in her throat, when she heard the front door open.

Moaning, she dragged her mouth from Cole's and broke away just as her son strolled into the kitchen.

Jeff stopped, his brow furrowed, when he saw the two of them in what surely looked like suspicious circumstances.

"Hi, Mom. Hi, Cole." He went casually to the refrigerator and yanked open the door. "Anything decent to drink around this place?"

"Water?" Robin suggested.

Jeff rolled his eyes. "Funny, Mom."

"There are a few more sacks of groceries in the car. Would you get them for me?" He threw her a disgruntled look, until Robin added, "You'll find a six-pack of soda in there."

"Okay." He raced out of the house and returned a minute later, carrying one sack and sorting through its contents as he walked into the kitchen.

"I'll help you," Cole said, placing his hand on Jeff's shoulder. He glanced at Robin and his eyes told her they'd continue their discussion at a more opportune moment.

Robin started emptying the sacks, hardly paying attention as Jeff and Cole brought in the last couple of bags. Cole told her he'd pick her up at six, then left.

"Can I play with Blackie for a while?" Jeff asked her, a can of cold soda clenched in his hand.

"Sure," Robin answered, grateful to have a few minutes alone.

Robin cleared the counters and made Jeff a sandwich for his lunch. He must've become involved in his game with Cole's dog because he didn't rush in announcing he was hungry.

She went outside to stand on her small front porch and smiled as she watched Jeff and Blackie. Her son really had a way with animals—like his father. Every time Robin saw him play with Cole's Labrador, she marveled at how attuned they were to each other.

She smiled when she realized Cole was outside, too; he'd just finished watering his lawn.

"Jeff, I made a sandwich for you," she called.

"In a minute. Hey, Mom, watch," he yelled as he tossed a ball across the lawn. Blackie chased after it, skidding to a stop as he caught the bright red ball.

"Come on, Blackie," Jeff urged. "Throw me the ball."

"He can't do that," Robin said in astonishment.

"Sure, he can. Watch."

And just as Jeff had claimed, Blackie leapt into the air, tossed his head and sent the ball shooting into the street.

"I'll get it," Jeff hollered.

It was Cole's reaction that Robin noticed first. A horrified look came over his face and he threw down the hose. He was shouting even as he ran.

Like her son, Robin had been so caught up in Blackie's antics that she hadn't seen the car barreling down the street, directly in Jeff's path.

Chapter 8

"Jeff!" Robin screamed, fear and panic choking her. Her hands flew to her mouth in relief as Cole grabbed Jeff around the waist and swept him out of the path of the speeding car. Together they fell backward onto the wet grass. Robin ran over to them.

"Jeff, how many times have I told you to look before you run into the street? How many times?" Her voice was high and hysterical. "You deserve the spanking of your life for that stunt!"

"I saw the car," Jeff protested loudly. "I did! I was going to wait for it. Honest." He struggled to his feet, looking insulted at what he obviously considered an over-reaction.

"Get into the house," Robin demanded, pointing furiously. She was trembling so badly she could barely speak.

Jeff brushed the grass from his jeans and raised his

head to a dignified angle, then walked toward the house. Not understanding, Blackie followed him, the ball in his mouth, wanting to resume their play.

"I can't, boy," Jeff mumbled just loudly enough for her to hear. "My mother had some kind of anxiety attack that I'm gonna get punished for."

Cole's recovery was slower than Jeff's. He sat up and rubbed a hand across his eyes. His face was ashen, his expression stark with terror.

"Everything's all right. Jeff isn't hurt," Robin assured him. She slipped to her knees in front of him.

Cole nodded without looking at her. His eyes went blank and he shook his head, as if to clear his mind.

"Cole," Robin said softly, "are you okay?"

"I… I don't know." He gave her a faint smile, but his eyes remained glazed and distant. He placed one hand over his heart and shook his head again. "For a minute there I thought Jeff hadn't seen that car and…I don't know… If that boy had been hurt…"

"Thank you for acting so quickly," Robin whispered, gratitude filling her heart. She ran her hands down the sides of his face, needing to touch him, seeking a way to comfort him, although her heart ached at his words. So many times over the past few weeks, she'd suspected—and feared—that Cole's feelings had more to do with replacing the family he'd lost than love for her and Jeff.

With a shudder, Cole locked his arms around her waist and pulled her close, burying his face in the curve of her neck as he dragged deep gulps of air into his lungs.

"Come inside and I'll get us some coffee," Robin suggested.

Cole murmured agreement, but he didn't seem in any

hurry to release her. Nor she him. Her hands were in his hair and she rested her cheek against his, savoring these moments of closeness now that the panic was gone.

"I lost my son," Cole whispered and the words seemed to be wrenched from the deepest part of his soul. His voice held an agony only those who had suffered such a loss could understand. "In a car accident six years ago."

Robin kissed the crown of his head. "I know."

Cole broke away from her, slowly raising his eyes to meet hers. Mingled with profound grief was confusion. "Who told you?"

"Joyce Wallach."

Cole closed his eyes. "I could use that coffee."

They both stood, and when Cole wrapped his arm around her waist Robin couldn't be sure if it was to lend support or to offer it.

Inside the house, Jeff was sitting at the bottom of the stairs, his knees under his chin. Ever loyal, Blackie lay beside him.

Jeff looked up when Robin opened the front door. "I saw the car," he repeated. "You're getting upset over nothing. I hope you realize that. Hey, what's wrong with Cole?" he asked abruptly. He glanced from Robin to their neighbor and then back to his mother. "He looks like he's seen a ghost."

In some way, Robin supposed, he had.

"You all right, sport?" Cole asked. "I didn't hurt you when we fell, did I?"

"Nah." He bit his lip, eyes lowered.

Cole frowned. "You don't sound all that certain. Are you sure you're okay?"

Jeff nodded reluctantly. "I will be once I find out

what my mother plans to do to me. I really was gonna stop at the curb. Honest."

The kid would make an excellent attorney, Robin thought wryly.

"I think I might've overreacted," Cole said. He held open his arms and Jeff flew into them without a second's hesitation. Briefly Cole closed his eyes, as though in silent thanksgiving for Jeff's safety.

"I didn't mean to scare you," Jeff murmured. "I would've stopped."

"I know."

"I promise to be more careful."

"I certainly hope so," Robin said.

Cole released Jeff and sighed deeply, then looked at Robin. "You said something about coffee?"

She smiled and nodded. "I'll get it in a minute. Jeff, you can go outside, but from now on if you're playing ball with Blackie, do it in the backyard. Understand?"

"Sure, Mom," her son said eagerly. "But—" he paused "—you mean that's it? You aren't going to ground me or anything? I mean, of course you're not because I did everything I was supposed to—well, almost everything. Thanks, Mom." He tossed the red ball in the air and caught it deftly with one hand. "Come on, Blackie, we just got a pardon from the governor."

Robin followed the pair into the kitchen and watched as Jeff opened the sliding glass door and raced into the backyard with Blackie in hot pursuit. Reassured, she poured two mugs of coffee while Cole pulled out one of the kitchen chairs. She carried the mugs to the table, then sat down across from him.

Cole reached for her hand, lacing her fingers with

his own. He focused his concentration on their linked hands. "Bobby was my son. He died when he was ten."

"Jeff's age," Robin said as a chill surrounded her heart.

"Bobby was so full of life and laughter I couldn't be around him and not smile."

Talking about Bobby was clearly difficult for Cole, and Robin longed to do or say something that would help. But she could think of nothing to ease the agony etched so deeply on his face.

"He was the kind of boy every father dreams of having. Inquisitive, sensitive, full of mischief. Gifted with a vivid imagination."

"A lot like Jeff," she said, and her hands tightened around the mug.

Cole nodded. "Bobby used to tell me I shouldn't worry about Jennifer—she was my ex-wife—because *he,* my ten-year-old son, was taking care of her."

Robin held her breath as she watched the fierce pain in his eyes. "You don't need to tell me this." Not if it was going to rip open wounds that weren't properly healed.

"I should've told you before this," he said, frowning slightly. "It's just that even now, after all this time, it's difficult to talk about my son. For a good many years, I felt as though part of me had died with Bobby. The very best part of me. I don't believe that anymore."

"Jeff reminds you a lot of Bobby, doesn't he?" Robin doubted Cole fully grasped that he was transferring his love from one boy to the other.

A smile tugged at the corners of his mouth. "Bobby had a huskier build and was taller than Jeff. His sport was basketball, but he was more of a spectator than a participant. His real love was computers. Had he lived,

I think Bobby would have gone into that field. Jen never understood that. She wanted him to be more athletic, and he tried to please her." Cole's gaze dropped to his hands. "Jennifer and I were divorced before the accident. She died with him. If there's anything to be grateful for in their deaths, it's the knowledge that they both went instantly. I couldn't have stood knowing they'd suffered." He paused long enough to take a sip of the coffee, and grimaced once. "You added sugar?"

"I thought you might need it."

He chuckled. "I have so much to thank you for."

"Me?"

"Do you remember the afternoon Jeff ran away?"

She wasn't likely to forget it. With Jeff around, Robin always figured she didn't need exercise to keep her heart in shape. Her son managed to do it with his antics.

"I left on a business trip to Seattle soon afterward," he reminded her.

She nodded. That was when Jeff had looked after Blackie for him.

"Late one afternoon, when the meeting was over and dinner wasn't scheduled for another couple of hours, I went for a stroll," Cole said. "It was still light and I found myself on the waterfront. The sky was a vivid blue and the waters green and clear. It's funny I'd remember that, but it's all so distinct in my memory. I stood alone on the pier and watched as a ferry headed for one of the islands, cutting a path through the waves. Something brought Bobby to my mind, although he's never far from my thoughts, even now. The most amazing thing happened that afternoon. It's difficult to find the words to explain." He hesitated, as though searching for a way to make Robin understand. Then apparently he gave up the effort and shook his head.

"Tell me about it," Robin said in a quiet voice.

"Well, standing there at the end of the pier...I don't know. For the first time since I lost my son, I felt his presence more than I did his absence. It was as if he was there at my side, pointing out the Olympic Mountains and asking questions. Bobby was always full of questions. My heart felt lighter than it had in years—as though the burden of pain and grief had been lifted from my shoulders. For no reason whatsoever, I started to smile. I think I've been smiling ever since. And laughing. And feeling.

"When I got back to the hotel, I had the sudden urge to hear your voice. I didn't have any excuse to call you, so I phoned on the pretense of talking to Jeff and checking up on Blackie. But it was your voice I wanted to hear."

Robin smiled through the unexpected rush of tears, wondering if Cole realized what he was saying. It might've been her voice he *thought* he wanted to hear, but it was Jeff he'd called.

"I discovered a new freedom on that Seattle pier. It was as if, in that moment, I was released from the past. I can't say exactly what changed. Meeting you and Jeff played a big role in it, I recognize that much, but it was more than that. It was as if something deep inside me was willing to admit that it was finally time to let go."

"I'm glad for you," Robin whispered.

"The problem is, I never allowed myself to grieve properly or deal with the anger I felt toward Jennifer. She was driving at the time and the accident was her fault. Yet deep in my heart I know she'd never purposely have done anything to hurt Bobby. She loved him as much as I did. He was her son, too.

"It wasn't until I met you that I knew I had to forgive her. I was never the kind of husband she needed and I'm afraid I was a disappointment to her. Only in the last few years of our marriage was I willing to accept that she suffered from a serious emotional and mental illness. Her addiction to alcohol was as much a disease as cancer. I didn't understand her illness, and because of that we all suffered."

"You're being too hard on yourself," Robin said, but she doubted Cole even heard her.

"After the accident, the anger and the grief were a constant gnawing pain. I refused to acknowledge or deal with either emotion. Over the years, instead of healing, I let the agony of my loss grow more intense. I closed myself off from friends and colleagues and threw myself into work, spending far more time in the office than I did at home. Blackie was virtually my only companion. And then a few years ago I started working on my place in the country. But the pleasure that gave me came from hard physical work, the kind that leaves you too tired to think." His features softened and he smiled at her. "I'd forgotten what it was like to fly a kite or laze in the sunshine."

"That's why you suggested the picnic with Jeff and me?"

He grinned and his dark eyes seemed almost boyish. "The last time I was in Golden Gate Park was with Bobby, shortly before the accident. Deciding to have a picnic there was a giant step for me. I half expected to feel pangs of grief, if not a full-blown assault. Instead I experienced joy—and appreciation for the renewal I felt. Laughter is a gift I'd forgotten. You and Jeff helped me see that, as well."

Everything Cole was saying confirmed her worst fears.

"Mom!" Jeff roared into the kitchen with Blackie at his heels. "Is there anything to eat? Are you guys still going out to dinner? I don't suppose you'd bring me, would you?"

Cole chuckled, then leapt to his feet to playfully muss Jeff's hair. "Not this time, sport. Tonight's for your mother and me."

Two hours later, as Robin stood in front of the bathroom mirror, she had her reservations about this dinner date. She was falling in love with a man who hadn't fully dealt with the pain of losing his wife and his son. Perhaps she recognized it in Cole because she saw the same thing in herself. She loved Lenny and always would. He'd died years ago, and she still found herself talking to him, refusing to involve herself in another relationship. A part of her continued to grieve and she suspected it always would.

Examining herself in the mirror, Robin surveyed her calf-length skirt of soft blue velvet and white silk blouse with a pearl necklace.

She was fussing with her hair, pinning one side back with combs and studying the effect, when Jeff wandered in. He leaned casually against the doorway, a bag of potato chips in his hand.

"Hey, you look nice."

"Don't sound so surprised." She decided she'd spent enough time on her hair and fastened her pearl earrings. Jeff was disappointed about not joining them, but he'd been a good sport—especially after Cole promised him lunch at a fish-and-chip place on the Wharf the following Saturday.

"You're wearing your pearls," Jeff mumbled, his mouth full.

"Yes," Robin said, turning to face him. "Do they look all right?"

Jeff's halfhearted shrug didn't do a lot to boost Robin's confidence. "I suppose. I don't know about stuff like that. Mrs. Lawrence could probably tell you." He popped another potato chip in his mouth and crunched loudly. "My dad gave you those earrings, didn't he? And the necklace?"

"For our first wedding anniversary."

Jeff nodded. "I thought so." His look grew reflective. "When I grow up and get married, will I do mushy stuff like that?"

"Probably," Robin said, not bothering to disguise her amusement. "And lots of other things, too. Like taking your wife out to dinner and telling her how beautiful she is and how much you love her."

"Yuck!" Jeff wrinkled his nose. "You really know how to ruin a guy's appetite." With that he turned to march down the stairs, taking his potato chips with him.

Robin stood at the top of the staircase. "Cole will be here any minute, so you can go over to Kelly's now," she called down.

"Okay. I put my plate in the dishwasher. Is there anything you want me to tell Kelly's mom?"

"Just that I won't be too late."

"You're sure I can't come with you?" Jeff tried one more time.

Robin didn't give him an answer, knowing he didn't

really expect one. After a moment, Jeff grumbled, more for show than anything, then went out the front door to their neighbor's.

Robin returned to the bathroom and smiled into the mirror, picturing Jeff several years into the future and seeing Lenny's handsome face smiling back at her. She was warmed by the image, certain that her son would grow into as fine a young man as his father had been.

"You don't mind that I'm wearing the pearls for Cole, do you?" she asked her dead husband, although she knew he wouldn't have objected. She ran the tips of her fingers over the earrings, feeling reassured.

The doorbell chimed just as Robin was dabbing perfume on her wrists. She drew in a calming breath, glanced quickly at her reflection one last time, then walked down the stairs to answer the door.

Cole was dressed in a black pin-striped suit and looked so handsome that her breath caught. He smiled as she let him in, but for the life of her she couldn't think of a thing to say.

His eyes held hers as he reached for her hands. Slowly he lowered his gaze, taking in the way she'd styled her hair, the pearl necklace and the outfit she'd chosen with such care.

"You are so beautiful," he said.

"I was just thinking the same about you," she confessed.

His mouth tilted in a grin. "If I kiss you, will it ruin your lipstick?"

"Probably."

"I'm going to kiss you, anyway," he said in a husky murmur. Tenderly he fit his mouth to hers, slipping his fingers through her hair. The kiss was gentle and thorough and slow. A single kiss, and she was like clay ready to be molded. The realization struck her hard—when Cole touched her, Robin felt alive all the way to the soles of her feet. *Alive.* Healthy. A red-blooded woman. He released her, and she was shocked to find she was trembling. From the inside out.

"I've mussed your hair," he apologized. His hands slid under the soft cloud of hair to her nape.

"And you've got lipstick on your mouth," she said with a quaver, reaching up to wipe it away. "There. It'll only take me a moment to fix my hair," she said, picking up her purse and moving to the hallway mirror.

He stood behind her, hands on her shoulders as she brushed her hair, then carefully tucked the loose curls back into place with the tortoiseshell combs.

"Are you ready?" he asked when she'd finished.

Robin nodded, unable to speak.

Cole led her outside to his car and held the passenger door. He dropped a quick kiss on her unsuspecting lips, then hurried around the car, his movements lighthearted, and got into the driver's seat.

"You didn't tell me where we're having dinner."

"I told Heather Lawrence in case she needs to get hold of you, but otherwise it's a surprise."

Robin wasn't sure what to think. A number of San Francisco's restaurants were internationally famous, but her knowledge of fancy dining places was limited. She assumed this one was somewhere in the heart of the city, until he exited from the freeway heading south along Highway 101 toward the ocean.

"Cole?" she asked hesitantly.

"Don't worry," he said, casting her a swift glance that

didn't conceal the mischievous twinkle in his eyes. "I promise you dinner will be worth the drive."

The restaurant sat high on a cliff, with a stunning view of the surf battering the jagged rocks below.

Cole parked the Porsche, then came around to help her out, taking the opportunity to steal another kiss. It was with obvious reluctance that he let her go. His arm around her waist, he directed her toward the doors leading into the elegant restaurant. The maître d' escorted them to a table that overlooked the water and with a flourish presented them with elaborate menus.

Robin scanned the entrées, impressed with the interesting variations on basic themes. She was less impressed with the prices—a single dinner cost as much as an entire week's worth of lunches. For her *and* Jeff.

"When you said fancy you weren't joking, were you?" she whispered, biting her lip.

Cole lowered his menu and sent her a vibrant smile. "Tonight is special," he said simply.

"You're telling me. If I wasn't having dinner with you, I'd probably have eaten a toasted cheese sandwich and a bowl of tomato soup with Jeff."

Their waiter appeared and they ordered wine—a bottle of sauvignon blanc. Then they each chose the restaurant's specialty—a scallop and shrimp sauté—which proved as succulent and spicy as the menu had promised.

They talked through dinner and afterward, over steaming cups of Irish coffee. It astonished Robin that they had so much to say to each other, although they hadn't touched on the issue closest to her heart. But she hesitated to broach the subject of Cole's relationship with Jeff. She didn't want to risk the delightful camaraderie they were sharing tonight. Their conversation could have gone on for hours and in fact did. They talked about books they'd read, recent movies they'd seen, music they liked. It came as a pleasant surprise to discover that their tastes were similar.

All evening they laughed, they argued, they talked, as if they'd been friends most of their lives. Cole grinned so often, it was hard for Robin to remember that at one time she'd actually wondered if the man ever smiled.

Robin told Cole about her job and how much she enjoyed accounting. She voiced her fears about not being the kind of mother she wanted to be for Jeff. "There are so many things I want to share with him that I don't have time for. There just aren't enough hours in a day."

Cole talked about his career goals and his dreams. He spoke of the forty acres willed to him by his grandfather and how he'd once hoped to close himself off from the world by moving there.

"But you aren't going to now?" Robin asked.

"No. I no longer have any reason to hide. The house is nearly finished and I may still move there, but I'll maintain my work schedule." He stared down into his coffee. "I was approached last week about running for the state senate."

Robin's heart swelled with pride. "Are you going to do it?"

"No. I'm not the right man for politics. I'll support someone else, but a political career doesn't interest me. It never has, although I'll admit I'm flattered."

A band started playing then, and several couples took to the dance floor.

"Shall we?" Cole asked, nodding in that direction.

"Oh, Cole, I don't know. The last time I danced was

at my cousin's wedding ten years ago. I'm afraid I'll step all over your feet."

"I'm game if you are."

She was reluctant but agreed to try. They stood, and she moved naturally into his embrace, as if they'd been partners for years. Robin's eyes slowly closed when Cole folded her in his arms, and in that moment she experienced a surge of joy that startled her with its intensity.

The dance ended, but they didn't leave the floor.

"Have I told you how lovely you are?" Cole asked, his mouth close to her ear.

Grinning, Robin nodded. "Twice. Once when you picked me up at the house and once during the meal. I know you're exaggerating, but..." She shrugged, then added, "When I'm with you, I feel beautiful."

"I don't think a woman's ever paid me a higher compliment."

She raised her eyes and was shocked by the powerful emotions in his.

"Do you mind if we leave now?" he asked suddenly.

"No, of course not, if that's what you want."

He frowned. "If it was up to me I'd spend the rest of the night here with you in my arms, but I have this sudden need to kiss you, and if I do it here and do it properly we're going to attract a lot of attention."

Cole quickly paid the bill and he hurried Robin to the car. The minute they were settled inside, he reached for her. He did as he'd promised, kissing her until she was breathless. Her arms clung to him as his mouth sought hers once more.

"At least I'm not making you cry this time," he said softly.

"That still embarrasses me," she told him. "It's never happened before. I still don't understand it. I don't know if I ever will."

"I don't think I'll ever forget it."

"Please do."

"No," he said, shaking his head. "It touched me in a way I can't explain. It helped me realize I was going to love you. After Jennifer and Bobby, I doubted there was any love left in me. You taught me otherwise. Jeff taught me otherwise. My heart is full and has been almost from the time we met." He took her hand and pressed her palm to his heart. "Do you feel it?"

Robin nodded. "It's beating so hard," she whispered.

"That's because I'm nervous."

"Nervous? About what?"

Cole slid a hand into his pocket and brought out a small black velvet box.

Robin's heart started to pound in double time. "Cole?" she said anxiously, not sure what she should think or how she should act.

"I love you, Robin." His voice was hoarse. "I knew it the moment I heard your voice when I called from Seattle. And every moment since has convinced me how right this is." He opened the box and revealed the largest diamond Robin had ever seen. Slowly he raised his eyes to hers. "I'm asking you to be my wife."

Chapter 9

"You mean this whole evening…you arranged this whole evening because you intended to ask me to marry you?" Robin asked, pressing the tips of her fingers to her trembling lips. Despite her fears a gentle gladness suffused her heart.

"Surely it isn't that much of a surprise?" he said. "I've never made an effort to hide how I feel about you or how much I enjoy Jeff."

Contrary to what Cole might think, his proposal *did* come as a surprise. "I…I don't know what to say."

"A simple yes would suit me," Cole urged warmly.

"But… Oh, Cole, it would be so easy to marry you, so easy to join my life and Jeff's to yours and never look back. But I don't know if it would be right for us or for you. There's so much to consider, so many factors to weigh, in a decision this important. I'd like nothing better than to just say yes, but I can't."

"Are you asking for time?" Cole's eyes seemed to penetrate hers, even in the dark.

"Please." For now, that seemed the simplest thing to say, although her hesitation was based on something much deeper. Cole had rediscovered a peace within himself since meeting her and Jeff; he'd told her so that very afternoon. She was tempted to say yes, to turn away from her doubts and agree to marry him. Cole had been so good for Jeff, so wonderful to her.

"I hate to disappoint you," she murmured sadly.

"I know exactly what you're thinking, exactly how you're feeling."

"You do?" Somehow she doubted it. But knowing she couldn't delay it any longer, she jumped in with both feet. "I was…just thinking about what you told me this afternoon. How you'd recently dealt with the loss of Jennifer and Bobby. While you were talking, I couldn't help feeling your exhilaration. You've obviously found a newborn sense of freedom. I think the question you need to ask yourself is if this rebirth you've experienced is what prompted the idea of marrying again."

"No," he said flatly. "Falling in love with you did."

"Oh, Cole," she whispered. "It must seem like fate to have Jeff and me move in next door, and it gets more complicated with Jeff being the same age as Bobby…."

"Maybe it does all appear too convenient, but if I was just looking for a woman and a child, then Heather Lawrence would've filled the bill. It's you I fell in love with."

"But how can you be so sure?" she countered quickly. "We barely know each other."

Cole smiled at her doubts. "The first time we kissed was enough to convince me I was going to love you. It was the Friday night after I returned from Seattle, remember?"

Robin nodded, wincing a little.

"I was so stunned by the effect that kiss had on me, I avoided you for an entire week afterward. If you want the truth, I was terrified. You'll have to remember, up until that time I was convinced I was incapable of ever falling in love again. One kiss, and I felt jolted to the core. You hit me hard, Robin, and I needed time to step back and analyze what was happening. That's the reason I don't have any qualms about giving you however long you need to sort out what you're feeling. I want you to be very sure."

Robin released a pent-up sigh. Cole folded her in his arms and his chin brushed against her hair while his hands roved in wide circles across her back. The action was soothing and gentle. She was beginning to feel more confident in his love, but she had to be careful. She *wanted* him to love her, because she was so much in love with him.

Cole tucked a finger under her chin and lifted her face to his. As their eyes met, he slanted his mouth over hers in a wildly possessive kiss, a kiss filled with undisguised need.

When he broke away, Robin was trembling. She buried her face in his neck and drew several deep breaths.

"If you're going to take some time to think about things," Cole whispered against her hair, "then I wanted to give you something else to think about."

"Have you had a chance to check those figures on—" Angela began, then stopped abruptly, waving her hand in front of Robin's face.

"A chance to check what figures?" Robin asked, making a determined effort to focus. She knew she'd been acting like a sleepwalker most of the morning, but she couldn't stop thinking about Cole's proposal.

"What's with you today?" Angela demanded. "Every time I look over here, I find you staring into space with this perplexed expression on your face."

"I was…just thinking," Robin muttered.

"About what?"

"Nothing."

"Come on, girl, you know better than that. You can't fool me." Angela leaned against the edge of Robin's desk and crossed her arms, taking her usual aggressive stance. "I've known you far too long. From everything you *haven't* said, I'd guess your handsome neighbor's involved. What's he done now?"

"Cole? What makes you ask anything so ridiculous?"

Angela frowned, shaking her head. Then she stretched out her hands and made a come-hither motion. "Tell Mama everything," she intoned. "You might as well get it over with and tell me now, because you know that sooner or later I'm going to drag it out of you. What kind of friend would I be if I didn't extract your deepest, darkest secrets?"

"He took me to dinner," Robin admitted, knowing that Angela was right. Sooner or later, she'd wheedle it out of her.

"Where'd he take you?"

She shrugged, wanting to keep that to herself. "It was outside the city."

"*Where* outside the city?" Angela pressed.

"Heavens, I don't know. Somewhere along the coast on Highway 101."

Angela uncrossed her arms and started pacing. "It wasn't the Cliffhouse, was it?"

"I…I think it might have been," Robin murmured, concentrating on the task in front of her. The one she should've finished hours earlier. The one she couldn't seem to focus on, even now.

"Aha!" Angela cried, pointing her index finger at the ceiling, like a detective in a comic spoof.

"What?" Robin cried.

"If Cole took you to the Cliffhouse, he did it for a reason."

"Of course he did. The food was fabulous. By the way, you were right about Frank, he's exceptionally nice," Robin said in an effort to interrupt her friend's line of thought.

"You already told me what you think of Frank, remember?" Angela said. "Cole took you to dinner at the Cliffhouse," she repeated slowly, as though reviewing a vital clue in a murder mystery.

"To be honest, I think his choice of restaurant had something to do with Frank," Robin inserted, tossing her sleuth friend a red herring.

"So Cole was jealous?"

"Not exactly," Robin said, leaning back in her chair. "Well, maybe a little," she amended, knowing Angela would never believe her if she denied it completely. "I mean, Cole did invite me to dinner as soon as he learned I was dining with Frank, so I guess you could say he was a *little* jealous. But not much. Cole's not the jealous type—he told me that himself."

"I see." Angela was frowning as she walked back to her desk. Her look remained thoughtful for the rest of the morning, although she didn't question Robin again.

But when they left for lunch, she showed a renewed interest in the subject of Cole.

"How's Jeff?" she began as they stood in line in the employees' cafeteria.

"Fine," Robin said as she reached for a plastic tray.

"That's all you're going to say?"

"What more do you want to know?"

"I ask about Jeff once a week or so, then sit back and listen for the next fifteen minutes while you tell me about the latest craziness," Angela said heatedly. "It never fails. You've told me about him running away with a frying pan and an atlas. You've bragged about what a fabulous pitcher he's turning out to be and you've given me a multitude of details about every game he's played. After you tell me all about his athletic ability, you generally mention how good he is with animals and all the tricks he's taught Blackie in the past week."

Robin tried to respond but Angela ignored her and kept talking. "Today I innocently ask how Jeff is, and what do I get? *Fine.* All right, Robin, tell me what happened with Cole Camden before I go crazy trying to figure it out."

"It's something I need to figure out myself," Robin said. She paused to study the salads before selecting a mound of cottage cheese and setting it on her tray.

"What are you doing now?" Angela cried, throwing her arms in the air. "You hate cottage cheese. You never eat it unless you're upset and looking for ways to punish yourself." She took the small bowl from Robin's tray and replaced it with a fresh fruit salad, shaking her head the entire time.

The problem with Angela was that she knew Robin all too well.

They progressed a little farther down the line. Robin stood in front of the entrées, but before she chose one, she glanced at her friend. "You want to pick one of these for me, too?" she asked dryly.

"Yes, I do, before you end up requesting liver and onions."

Angela picked the lasagne, thick with melted cheese and spicy tomato sauce. "If you're looking for ways to punish yourself, girl, there are tastier methods."

Despite her thoughtful mood, Robin smiled.

Once they'd paid for their lunches, Angela led her to a window table that offered a certain amount of privacy. Robin busied herself arranging her dishes and set the tray aside.

Angela sat directly across from her, elbows braced on either side of her lunch. "Are you sure there isn't anything else you'd care to tell me?"

"About what?"

"About you and Cole, of course. I can't remember the last time I saw you like this. It's as if…as if you're trapped in some kind of maze and can't find your way out."

The description was so apt that Robin felt a tingling sensation along her spine. She did feel hopelessly lost. Her mind was cluttered, her emotions confused. She had one foot in the present, one in the past, and didn't know which way to turn.

"I talked to Frank on Sunday afternoon," Angela continued, dipping her fork into a crisp green salad. "He said he enjoyed the evening you spent with him, but doubted you'd be seeing each other again because it's obvious to him that you're in love with Cole Camden. In fact, Frank said you talked about little else the entire evening."

"He said all that?"

Angela nodded. "He's right, isn't he? You are in love with Cole, aren't you?"

"I…I don't know."

"What do you mean you don't know?" Angela persisted. "It's written all over you. You've got that glazed look and you walk around in a trance, practically bumping into walls."

"You make it sound like I need an ambulance."

"Or a doctor," Angela whispered, leaning across the table. "Or maybe a lawyer… That's it!" she said loudly enough to attract the attention of several people at nearby tables. "Cole took you to bed, and now you're so confused you don't know what to do. I told you I'd stumble on the answer sooner or later." Her eyes flashed triumphantly.

"That's not it," Robin declared, half rising from the table. She could feel the color crowding into her cheeks as she glanced around the cafeteria. When she sat back down, she covered her face with both hands. "If you must know, Cole asked me to marry him."

A moment of shocked silence followed before Angela shrieked with pure delight. "That's fabulous! Wonderful! Good grief, what's wrong with you? You should be in seventh heaven. It isn't every day a handsome, wealthy, wonderful man proposes to you. I hope you leapt at the chance." She hesitated, suddenly still. "Robin? You *did* tell him you'd marry him, didn't you?"

Robin swallowed and shook her head. "No. I asked him for some time to think about things."

"Think about things?" Angela squealed. "What's

there to think about? He's rich. He's handsome. He's in love with you and crazy about Jeff. What more could you possibly want?"

Tears brimmed in Robin's eyes as she looked up to meet her friend's avid gaze. "I'm afraid he's more in love with the idea of having a family than he is with me."

"Is Cole coming?" Jeff asked, working the stiffness out of his baseball mitt by slamming his fist into the middle of it several times.

"I don't know," Robin said, glancing at their neighbor's house as they walked to the car. "I haven't talked to him in the last few days."

"You're not mad at him, are you?"

"Of course not," Robin said, sliding into the driver's seat of her compact. "We've both been busy."

Jeff fingered the bill of his baseball cap, then set the cap on his head. "I saw him yesterday and told him about the game, and he said he might come. I hope he does."

Secretly Robin hoped Cole would be there, too. Over the past five days, she'd missed talking to him. She hadn't come to any decision, but he hadn't pressed her to make one, willing to offer her all the time she needed. Robin hadn't realized how accustomed she'd grown to his presence. How much she needed to see him and talk to him. Exchange smiles and glances. Touch him...

When she was married to Lenny, they were two people very much in love, two people who'd linked their lives to form one whole. But Lenny had been taken from her, and for a long time afterward Robin had felt only half alive.

All week she'd swayed back and forth over Cole's proposal, wondering if she should ignore her doubts. Wondering if she *could* ignore them. Sleepless nights hadn't yielded the answer. Neither had long solitary walks in Balboa Park while Jeff practiced with his baseball team.

"Cole said—" Jeff started to say, then stopped abruptly as his hands flew to his head. A panicky look broke out on his face and he stared at Robin.

"What's wrong? Did you forget something?"

"My lucky hat!" Jeff cried. "It's on my dresser. We have to go back."

"For a baseball cap?" Robin didn't disguise how silly she considered that idea. "You're wearing a baseball cap. What's wrong with that one?"

"It won't work. You have to understand, Mom, it's my *lucky* hat. I've been wearing it ever since we played our first game. I had that very same hat on when I hit my first two home runs. I can't play without it," he explained frantically. "We have to go back. Hurry, or we'll be late for the game. Turn here," he insisted, pointing at the closest intersection.

"Jeff," she said, trying to reason with her son. "It isn't the hat that makes you play well."

"I knew you were going to say something like that," he muttered, "and even if it's true, I want to be on the safe side, just in case. We've got to go back and get that hat!"

Knowing it would only waste valuable time to argue, Robin did as he requested. After all, his whole career as a major-league pitcher hung in the balance!

She was smiling as she entered her driveway. Sitting in the car while Jeff ran inside for his lucky cap, Robin glanced over at Cole's place. His car was gone. It'd been gone since early that morning, and she suspected he was at the property, working on his house. Jeff would be disappointed about Cole missing his game, but he'd understand.

Jeff came barreling out of the house, slamming the front door. He leapt into the car and fastened his seat belt. "Come on, Mom," he said anxiously, "let's get this show on the road." As if *she'd* caused the delay, Robin thought to herself, amused by her son's sudden impatience.

By the time they arrived at Balboa Park, the car park was filled to overflowing. Robin was fortunate enough to find a space on the street, a minor miracle in itself. Perhaps there was something to this magic-cap business after all.

Jeff ran across the grass, hurrying toward his teammates, leaving Robin to fend for herself, which was fine. He had his precious cap and was content.

The bleachers were crowded with parents. Robin found a seat close to the top and had just settled in place when she saw Cole making his way toward her. Her heart did an immediate flip-flop and it wasn't until he sat next to her that she was able to speak.

"I thought you were working up on the property this weekend."

"And miss seeing Jeff pitch? Wild horses couldn't have kept me away." He was smiling at her with that cocky heart-stopping smile of his.

"How have you been?" she asked. She couldn't keep her eyes off him. He looked too good to be true, and his dark gaze was filled with warmth and tenderness.

How could she help getting lost in eyes that generous? It seemed impossible to resist him any longer.

"I've missed you like crazy," he whispered, and the humor seemed to drain out of him as his eyes searched hers. "I didn't think it was possible to feel this alone. Not anymore."

"I've missed you, too."

He seemed to relax once she'd said that. "Thank you," he said quietly. "Have you been thinking about what I said last weekend?"

She bowed her head. "I haven't thought of anything else."

"Then you've made up your mind?"

"No." She kept her face lowered, not wanting him to see her confusion.

He tilted her chin with one finger, forcing her to meet his eyes. "I promised myself I wouldn't ask you and then I couldn't seem to stop myself. I won't again."

She offered him a weak smile, and Cole looked around him, clearly wanting to kiss her, but not in front of such a large gathering. The funny part was, Robin didn't care about being seen. She was so hungry for the reassurance of his touch, it didn't matter to her that they were in the middle of a crowded park.

"I see Jeff's wearing his lucky hat," Cole said, clasping her hand and giving her fingers a comforting squeeze.

"You know about that?"

"Of course. Jeff tells me everything."

"He panicked when he realized he was wearing the wrong one, and I had to make a U-turn in the middle of the street because he'd left the guaranteed-to-pitch-well baseball cap on his dresser."

"You can't blame him. The luck has lasted through five games now."

"I wonder if it'll last until he reaches the pros," Robin said, sharing a smile with him.

"You're doing all right?" Cole asked unexpectedly.

She nodded, although it wasn't entirely true. Now that she was with Cole, every doubt she'd struggled with all week vanished like fog under an afternoon sun. Only when they were apart was she confronted by her fears.

"After Jeff's finished here, let's do something together," Cole suggested. "The three of us."

She nodded, unable to refuse him anything.

"Come to think of it, didn't I promise Jeff lunch? I seem to recall making a rash pledge to buy him fish and chips because we were leaving him with Heather and Kelly when we went to dinner last week."

Robin grinned. "It seems to me you're remembering that correctly," she said.

They went to a cheerful little fish-and-chip restaurant down by the Wharf. The weather had been chilly all morning, but the sun was out in full force by early afternoon. Jeff was excited about his team's latest win and attributed it to the luck brought to them by his cap.

After a leisurely lunch, the three of them strolled along the busy waterfront. Robin bought a loaf of fresh sourdough bread and a small bouquet of spring flowers. Jeff found a plastic snake he couldn't live without and paid for it with his allowance.

"Just wait till Jimmy Wallach sees this!" he crowed.

"I'm more curious to see how Kelly Lawrence reacts," Robin said.

"Oh, Kelly likes snakes," Jeff told them cheerfully. "Jimmy was over one day and I thought I'd scare Kelly with a live garden snake, but Jimmy was the one who started screaming. Kelly said snakes were just another of God's creatures and there was nothing to be afraid of. Isn't it just like a girl to get religious about a snake?"

Jeff raced down the sidewalk while Cole and Robin stood at the end of the pier, the bread and flowers at their feet.

"You look tired," Cole said, as his fingers gently touched her forehead.

"I'm fine," she insisted, gazing out at the cool green waters of San Francisco Bay. But Cole was right; she hadn't been sleeping well.

"I see so much of myself in you," Cole said softly.

His words surprised her. "How's that?"

"The pain mostly. How many years has Lenny been dead?"

"Ten. In some ways I'm still grieving him." She couldn't be less than honest with Cole.

"You're not sure if you can love another man, are you? At least not with the same intensity that you loved Jeff's father."

"That's not it at all. I…I just don't know if I can stop loving him."

Cole went very still. "I never intended to take Lenny away from you or Jeff. He's part of your past, an important part. Being married to Lenny, giving birth to Jeff, contributed to making you what you are." He paused, and they both remained silent.

"Bobby had been buried for six years before I had the courage to face the future. I hung on to my grief, carried it with me everywhere I went, dragging it like a heavy piece of luggage I couldn't travel without."

"I'm not that way about Lenny," she said, ready to

ın nodded. "Just don't get in anyone's w
won't. Promise. Here, Mom, hold my snak
rusted her with his precious package before rac
ack down the pier.

"He's a fine boy, Robin."

"He loves you already. You and Blackie."

"And how does his mother feel?"

The knot in her throat thickened. "She loves you, too."

Cole grinned. "She just isn't sure if she can let go of her dead husband to take on a live one. Am I right?"

His words hit their mark. "I don't know," she admitted. "Maybe it's because I'm afraid you want to marry me because Jeff reminds you of Bobby. Or because you've created a fantasy wife and think I'll fit the role."

Her words seemed to shock him. "No. You've got that all wrong. Jeff is a wonderful plus in this relationship, but it's *you* I fell in love with. It's you I want to grow old with. You, and you alone, not some ideal. If you want to know the truth, I think you're stirring up all this turmoil because you're afraid of ever marrying again. The little world you've made is tidy and safe. But is this what Lenny would've wanted for you?" He gripped her firmly by the shoulders. "If Lenny were standing beside you right now and you could ask him about marrying me, what would he say?"

"I…don't understand."

"If you could seek Lenny's advice, what would he tell you? Would he say, 'Robin, look at this guy. He's in love with you. He thinks the world of Jeff, and he's ready to embark on a new life. This is an opportunity too good to pass up. Don't be a fool. Marry him.'?"

"That sounds like something my friend Angela would say."

"I'm going to like this friend of yours—just as long as she doesn't try to set you up with any more of her divorced cousins," Cole said, laughing. His eyes grew warm as he gazed at her, and she suspected he was longing to take her in his arms and kiss her doubts away. But he didn't. Instead, he looked over his shoulder and sighed. "I think I'll go see what Jeff's up to. I'll leave you to yourself for a few minutes. I don't mean to pressure you, but I do want you to think about what I said."

"You aren't pressuring me," she whispered, staring out over the water.

Cole left her then, and her hands clutched the steel railing as she raised her eyes to the sky. "Oh, Lenny," she whispered. "What should I do?"

Chapter 10

"Cole wants me to ask your advice." Robin continued to look up at the cloudless blue sky. "Oh, Lenny, I honestly don't know what's right for Jeff and me anymore. I love Cole. I love you. But at the same time I can't help wondering about Cole's motives...."

Robin paused, waiting. Not that she expected an answer. Lenny couldn't give her one. He never did; he never would. But unlike the other times she'd spoken to him, she needed a response, even though expecting one was totally illogical.

With every breath she took, Robin knew that, but the futility of it hit her, anyway. Her frustration was so hard and unexpectedly powerful that it felt like a body blow. Robin closed her eyes, hoping the heat of the sun would take away this bitter ache, this dreadful loneliness.

She felt so empty. Hollow all the way through.

Her fists were clenched at her sides as tears fell from her eyes. Embarrassed, she glanced around, grateful that the film crew had attracted most of the sightseers. No one was around to witness her distress.

Anger, which for so many years had lain dormant inside her, gushed forth in an avalanche of grief and pain. The tears continued to spill down her cheeks. Her lips quivered. Her shoulders shook. Her hands trembled. It was as if the emotion was pounding against her chest and she was powerless to do anything but stand there and bear it.

Anger consumed her now. Consumed her because she hadn't allowed it to when Lenny was killed. It had been more important to put on a brave front. More important to hold herself together for Jeff and for Lenny's parents. More important to deal with the present than the past.

Lenny had died and Robin was furious with him for leaving her alone with a child to raise. Leaving her alone to deal with filing taxes and taking out the garbage and repairing leaking pipes. All these years she'd managed on her own. And she'd bottled the anger up inside, afraid of ever letting it go.

"Robin."

Cole's voice, soft and urgent, reached out from behind her. At the sound, she turned and walked into his arms, sobbing, needing his comfort and his love in equal measure. Needing him as she'd never needed anyone before.

She didn't know how long he held her. He was whispering soothing words to her. Gentle words. But she heard none of them over the sound of her own suffering.

Once she started crying, Robin couldn't seem to stop.

It was as if a dam had burst inside her and the anguish, stored for too many years, came pouring out.

Cole's arms were securely wrapped around her, shielding her. She longed to control this outburst, longed to explain, but every time she tried to speak her sobbing only grew worse.

"Let it out," he whispered. "You don't have to say anything. I understand."

"He doesn't answer," she sobbed. "I asked him... Lenny never answers me...because he can't. He left me..."

"He didn't want to die," Cole told her.

"But he did...he did."

Cole didn't argue with her. He simply held her, stroking the back of her head as though reassuring a small child.

It took several minutes for Robin to compose herself enough to go on. "Part of me realizes that Lenny didn't want to leave me, didn't want to die. But he did and I'm so angry at him."

"That anger is what makes us human," Cole said. He continued to comfort her and, gradually, bit by bit, Robin felt her composure slip back into place.

She sensed Jeff's presence even before he spoke.

"What wrong with my mom?" he asked Cole.

"She's dealing with some emotional pain," Cole explained, speaking as one adult to another.

"Is she going to be all right?"

Robin hadn't wanted her son to see her crying and made a concerted effort to break away from Cole, to reassure Jeff herself. Cole loosened his hold, but kept his arm around her shoulders.

"I'm fine, Jeff. Really."

"She doesn't look so good."

Her son had developed the irritating habit of talking to Cole and not to her when she was upset. They'd done it that day her son had run away to the fort. Jeff and Cole had carried on an entire conversation about her while she was in their midst then, too.

Cole led her to a bench and they all sat down.

Jeff plopped down next to her and reached for her hand, patting it several times. Leaning toward Cole, he said earnestly, "Chocolate might help. One time Mom told me there wasn't anything in this world chocolate couldn't cure."

She'd actually said that? Robin started to smile. Wrapping her arms around her son, she hugged him close, loving him so much her heart seemed about to burst.

Jeff wasn't all that keen on being cuddled, especially in public, but although he squirmed he put up with his mother's sudden need to hold him.

When she'd finished, Jeff rolled his eyes and once more directed his comments to Cole. "She gets weird like this every once in a while. Remember what happened that day I ran away?"

"I remember," Cole said, and Robin smiled at the trace of amusement she heard in his voice.

"Will you stop excluding me from this conversation? I'm going to be all right. I just had this…urge to cry, but don't worry, it's passed."

"See what I mean?" Jeff muttered to Cole.

"But Jeff's right," Robin said, ignoring her son's comment. "Something chocolaty would definitely help."

"You'll be okay by yourself for a couple of minutes?" Cole asked.

"I'll be fine. I…don't know exactly what came over me, but I'm going to be just fine."

"I know you are." He kissed her, his lips gentle against her cheek.

The two of them left and once more Robin was alone. She didn't really understand why the pain and anger had hit her so hard now, after all this time. Except that it had something to do with Cole. But the last place she would ever have expected to give in to her grief was on Fisherman's Wharf with half of San Francisco looking on.

Jeff returned less than a minute later, running to her side with a double-decker chocolate ice cream cone. "Cole's bringing two more for him and me," he explained. "I told the guy it was an emergency and he gave me this one right away."

"That was nice of you," Robin said, wondering what the vendor must have thought. Smiling, she ran her tongue over the ice cream, savoring the cold chocolate. As profoundly as she'd wept, she felt almost giddy with relief now, repressing the impulse to throw back her head and laugh.

Cole arrived, and with Jeff on her left and Cole on her right she sat on the concrete bench and ate her ice cream cone.

"I told you this would work," Jeff told Cole smugly.

"And to think I scoffed at your lucky baseball cap," she teased, feeling much better.

When they finished the cones, Cole gathered up their packages and led them back to where he'd parked his car.

Blackie was there to greet them the instant they returned to Orchard Street. Jeff ran into the backyard to play with the dog, and Cole walked Robin to her door. He accepted her offer of coffee.

"I'm probably going to be leaving soon for my property," he said, watching her closely. He sat down at the table, his hands cupping the mug as though to warm them. "Will you be all right?"

Robin nodded. She walked over and stood beside him and pressed a hand to his strong jaw. "I realize you delayed going up there today because of Jeff and his baseball game. We're both grateful."

Cole placed his hand over hers and harshly expelled his breath. "I feel responsible for what you went through there on the pier. I should never have said what I did. I'm sorry, Robin, it wasn't any of my business."

"You only said what I needed to hear."

He smiled. "If I did, it was because of what happened to me in Seattle. It's quite a coincidence that both of us would come to grips with our pain while standing on a pier—me in Seattle, you here in San Francisco. I went home with this incredible sense of release. For the first time since Bobby and Jennifer's deaths, I surrendered my grief. In a way it was as though I reached up and God reached down and together we came to an understanding."

That so completely described what Robin had been feeling that for a long moment she couldn't say anything. What Cole had said earlier about carrying the pain, dragging it everywhere, was right on the mark, too. He understood; he'd done the same thing himself. A surge of love swelled within her.

"I know you don't want to hear this," he was saying. "I honestly don't mean to pressure you. But once I returned from Seattle and realized I was falling in love with you I started thinking about having another baby." He hesitated and took a gulp of his coffee. Then he stood up abruptly, nearly knocking the chair backward. "I'd better go before I say or do something else I shouldn't."

Robin followed him into the entryway, not wanting him to leave, but not quite ready to give him what he needed.

He paused at the screen door and his eyes immediately found hers. He couldn't seem to keep himself from touching her, brushing an auburn curl from her cheek. His knuckles grazed her skin lightly, and Robin's eyes closed of their own accord at the sensation that shot through her. Her heart was full, and she seemed to have all the answers now—except to the one question that was the most important in her life. And Jeff's.

"I'll see you sometime next week," Cole said roughly, pulling his hand away. Without another word, he walked out the door, pausing at the top of the porch steps.

He called for his dog and in response both Blackie and Jeff came running.

"You're not leaving, are you?" Jeff asked breathlessly.

"I'm taking Blackie for the rest of the weekend. You think you can get along without him till Monday, sport?"

Jeff shrugged and stuck his fingers in the hip pockets of his blue jeans. "I suppose. Where are you taking him?"

"To my property." Cole didn't turn toward Robin. It was as if he had to ignore her in order to walk away from her.

"Oh, yeah!" Jeff said enthusiastically. "I remember

you said something about it once. You're building a house, aren't you?"

"Remodelling one. My grandfather lived there as a boy and he left it to me, only it's been a lot of years since anyone's cared for that old house properly and there's plenty of work that needs to be done."

"I'll work for you," Jeff piped up eagerly. He made a fist and flexed his arm, revealing the meager muscles. "I know it doesn't look like much, but I'm strong. Ask anyone."

Cole tested Jeff's muscles, pretending to be impressed. "Yes, I can tell you're strong, and I'm sure I couldn't ask for a harder worker." Jeff beamed until Cole added regretfully, "I'll take you up there another time, sport."

Jeff's face fell.

Before she even realized what she was doing, Robin moved onto the porch. "Cole."

He turned to face her, but the movement seemed reluctant.

Perhaps it was because she didn't want to be separated from him any more than he wanted to be away from her. Perhaps it was the thought of Jeff's disappointment when he'd already had so many other disappointments in his life. Perhaps it was this newborn sense of freedom she was just beginning to experience.

She stepped toward Cole. "Could Jeff and I go up to the property with you?"

Jeff didn't wait for Cole to answer before leaping excitedly into the air. "Hey, Mom, that's a great idea! Really great. Can we, Cole? Blackie and I can help you, and Mom can... Well, she can do things like make us some grub and bring us lemonade and other stuff women do when their men are working."

"I'll have you both know I pound a mean hammer," Robin felt obliged to inform them. If she was going to Cole's farm, she fully intended to do her share.

Cole looked perplexed for a moment, as if he wasn't sure he'd heard her correctly. "I'd love to have you come—if you're sure that's what you want."

Robin just nodded. All she knew was that she couldn't bear to be separated from him any longer.

"Be warned—the house is only half done. The plumbing isn't in yet."

"We'll manage, won't we, Jeff?"

"Yeah," Jeff said eagerly. "Anyway, boys got it easy."

Cole laughed. "How long will it take you to pack?"

"We're ready now, aren't we, Blackie?" Jeff almost jitterbugged across the front lawn in his enthusiasm.

"Give me a few minutes to throw some things together," Robin said, grinning. Jeff was smiling, too, from ear to ear, as he dashed past her into the house and up the stairs.

Cole's eyes held Robin's in silent communication—until Jeff came bursting out of the house, dragging his sheets and quilt with him, straight from his bed.

"Jeff," she cried, aghast, "what are you doing?"

"I took everything off my bed. I can go without plumbing, but I need my sleep." He piled the bedding at their feet. "You two can go back to looking at each other. I'll get everything else we need."

"Jeff," Robin groaned, casting Cole an apologetic glance. "I'll pack my own things, thank you."

"You want me to get your sheets, too?" he called from inside the house.

"No." She scooped up the bedding and hurried into the house, taking the stairs two at a time. She discovered Jeff sitting on the edge of her bed, his expression pensive.

"What's wrong?"

"Are you ever going to marry Cole?" her son asked.

At the unexpectedness of the question, Robin's heart flew to her throat, then slid back into place. Briefly she wondered if Cole had brought up the subject with her son, but instinctively knew he hadn't. "W-what makes you ask that?"

He shrugged. "Lots of things. Every time I turn around you two are staring at each other. Either that or kissing. I try to pretend I don't notice, but it's getting as bad as some of those movies you like. And when you were crying on the pier, I saw something. Cole had his arms around you and he was looking real sad. Like… like he wished he could do the crying for you. It's the same look Grandpa sometimes gives Grandma when he figures out that she's upset, and she doesn't even have to talk. Do you know what I mean?"

"I think so," Robin said, casually walking over to her dresser drawer and taking out a couple of old sweatshirts. "And what would you think if I said I was considering marrying Cole?"

Robin expected shouts of glee and wild shrieks, but instead her son crossed his arms over his chest and moved his mouth in odd ways, stretching it to one side and then the other. "You're serious, aren't you?"

"Yes." She folded and refolded one of the sweatshirts, her heart pounding in anticipation. "It would mean a lot of changes for all of us."

"How many other people are involved in this?"

Robin hesitated, not understanding Jeff's concern. "What do you mean?"

"Will I get an extra set of grandparents in this deal?"

"Uh...probably. I haven't talked to Cole about that yet, but I assume so."

"That means extra gifts on my birthday and at Christmas. I say we should go for it."

"Jeffrey Leonard Masterson, you shock me!"

He shrugged. "That's how a kid thinks."

Robin shook her head in dismay at her son's suddenly materialistic attitude toward her possible marriage. She was still frowning as she stepped outside.

Cole was in his garage, loading up the trunk of his SUV when Robin joined him. She handed him one small suitcase and a bag of groceries she'd packed at the last minute.

Cole stowed them away, carefully avoiding her eyes. "I guess you said something to Jeff about us?" She could hear amusement in his voice.

"Yes. How'd you know?"

"He brought down a paper bag full of clothes and asked what kind of presents he could expect from my parents at Christmas. He also asked if there were any aunts or uncles in the deal." Robin's embarrassment must have showed, because Cole started chuckling.

"That boy's got a mercenary streak in him I knew nothing about," she muttered.

Cole was still grinning. "You ready?"

She nodded, drawing an unsteady breath, eager for this adventure to begin. Jeff and Blackie were already in the backseat when Robin slipped into the front to wait for Cole.

"Are we going to sing camp songs?" Jeff asked, leaning forward. He didn't wait for a response, but immediately launched into the timeless ditty about bottles of beer on the wall. He sang ninety-nine verses of that, then performed a series of other songs until they left the freeway and wound up on a narrow country road with almost no traffic.

Jeff had tired of singing by then. "Knock knock," he called out.

"Who's there?" Robin said, falling in with his game.

"Eisenhower."

"Eisenhower who?"

Jeff snickered. "Eisenhower late, how about you?" With that, the ten-year-old broke into belly-gripping guffaws, as if he should be receiving awards for his ability to tell jokes.

Cole's mouth was twitching and Robin had to admit she was amused, too.

"The turnoff for the ranch is about a mile up the road," Cole explained. "Now remember, this is going to be a lot like camping. It's still pretty primitive."

"You don't need to worry," Robin said, smiling at him.

A couple of minutes later, Cole slowed, about to turn down the long driveway. It was then that Robin saw the sign. Her heart jumped into her throat and her hands started to shake.

"Stop!" she screamed. "Stop!"

Cole slammed on the brakes, catapulting them forward. "Robin, what is it?"

Robin threw open the front door and leapt out of the car, running to the middle of the road. She stared at the one word on the sign even as the tears filled her eyes.

Cole's farm was named *Paradise.*

Chapter 11

"Robin, I don't understand," Cole said for the third time, his dark eyes worried.

"I bet my allowance she's crying again," Jeff muttered, poking his head out the side window. "Something weird's going on with my mother. She's been acting goofy all day. Why do you think it is?"

"I'm not really sure," Cole said as he continued to study Robin.

For her part, Robin couldn't take her eyes off the sign. Jeff was right about her crying; the tears streamed unrestrained down her face. But these were tears of joy. Tears of gratitude. Tears of acknowledgment. It was exactly as Cole had described. She'd reached up and God had reached down and together they'd come to an understanding. She'd finally resolved her dilemma.

Unable to stop herself, Robin hurled her arms around

Cole's neck. Her hands roamed his face. His wonderful, wonderful face.

Because her eyes were blurred with emotion, she couldn't accurately read Cole's expression, but it didn't matter. Her heart spilled over with love for him.

"Robin..."

She didn't let him finish, but began spreading a long series of kisses across his face, starting with his eyelids. "I love you, I love you," she repeated between kisses, moving from his cheek to his nose and downward.

Cole put his arms around her waist and pulled her closer. Robin was half-aware of the car door slamming and Jeff marching up the road to join them.

"Are you two getting all mushy on me again?"

Robin barely heard her son. Her mouth had unerringly found Cole's.

The unexpected sharp sound of a hand clap brought her out of her dream world. The kiss ended, and her eyes immediately went to Jeff, who was looking very much like a pint-size adult. His face and eyes were stern.

"Do the two of you know where you're standing?" Jeff demanded as though he'd recently been hired by the state police to make sure this type of thing didn't happen. "There are proper places to kiss, but the middle of the road isn't one of them."

"He's right," Cole said, his eyes devouring Robin. He clearly didn't want to release her and did so with a reluctance that tugged at her heart.

"Come with me," Jeff said, taking his mother by the hand and leading her back to the car. He paused in front of the door and frowned. "Maybe she has a fever."

"Robin," Cole said, grasping her hand, "can you explain now?"

She nodded. "It's the sign—Paradise. Tell me about it. Tell me why your grandfather named his place Paradise."

"I'm not sure," Cole said, puzzled. "He lived here his whole life and always said this land was all he'd ever needed. From what I remember, he once told me he thought of this place as the Garden of Eden. I can only assume that's why he named it Paradise."

Robin nodded, unsurprised by his explanation. "When Lenny and I were first married, we talked... we dreamed about someday buying some land and raising animals. Enough land for Jeff to have a pony and for me to have a huge garden. We decided this land would be our own piece of heaven on earth and...from that we came up with the idea of naming it Paradise."

Cole shook his head slowly, and she could tell he didn't completely understand.

"This afternoon, when I was standing on Fisherman's Wharf, you suggested I talk over my feelings about our getting married with Lenny."

"What I suggested," Cole reminded her, "was that you *imagine* what he'd say to advise you. I certainly didn't expect you to really communicate with him."

"I know this won't make any sense to you, but I've talked to Lenny lots of times over the years. This afternoon, what hit me so hard was the fact that Lenny would never answer me. That realization was what finally forced me to deal with the pain. To forgive Lenny for dying."

Jeff was looking at her in confusion, his mouth open and eyes wide.

"Here you were wanting to marry me and I didn't know what to do. I had trouble believing your proposal was prompted by anything more than the desire to replace the family you'd lost. I do love you, and I desperately wanted to believe you loved me—and Jeff. But I wasn't sure...."

"And you're sure now?"

She nodded enthusiastically. "Yes. With all my heart, I'm confident that marrying you would be the right thing for all of us."

"Of course we're going to marry Cole!" Jeff cried. "Good grief, all you had to do was ask me and I would've told you. We belong together."

"Yes, we do, don't we?" Robin whispered. "Cole," she said, taking both his hands with her own. "I'd consider it a very great honor to become your wife."

"Jeff?" Cole said, tearing his eyes away from Robin.

The boy's face shone and his eyes sparkled. "I'd consider it a very great honor to become your son."

Cole brushed his lips across Robin's and then reached for Jeff, hauling him into his arms and squeezing him tight. Blackie started barking then, wanting out of the car. Robin quickly moved to open the passenger door, and the black Lab leapt out. She crouched down and wrapped her arms around his thick neck, hugging him. "You're going to have a whole family now, Blackie," she said happily.

Two hours later, just at dusk, Robin was standing in the middle of the yard. She'd loved everything about Paradise, just as she'd known she would. The house and property were nothing like the place she and Lenny had dreamed about, but she hadn't expected them to be. The four-bedroom house was much larger than anything they'd ever hoped to own. The land was covered with

Ponderosa pine, and the rocky ground was more suitable to grazing a few sheep or cattle than planting crops.

Cole was showing Jeff the barn, and Robin had intended to join them, but the evening was redolent with a sweet-smelling breeze and she'd stopped to breathe in the fresh cool air. She folded her arms and stood there, smiling into the clear sky. A multitude of twinkling stars were just beginning to reveal themselves.

Cole walked quietly up behind her, and slipped his arms around her waist, pulling her against him. "Have I told you how much I love you?"

"In the last fifteen minutes? No, you haven't."

"Then allow me to correct that situation." He nibbled the back of her neck gently. "I love you to distraction."

"I love you, too."

He sighed then and whispered hoarsely, "It was a difficult decision to marry me, wasn't it?"

Robin agreed with a nod.

"Had I given you so many reasons to doubt me?"

"No," she said quickly, turning in his arms. She pressed her palms against his jaw. "I had to be sure in my heart that you weren't trying to replace the son you'd lost with Jeff. And I had to be equally certain you loved me for myself and not because I was Jeff's mother and we came as a package deal."

He shook his head decisively. "Jeff's a great kid, don't get me wrong, but there's never been any question in my mind about how I felt. The first time we met, you hit me square between the eyes. I didn't mean to fall in love again. I didn't even want to."

"I don't think I did, either," Robin confessed.

"Past experience taught us both that loving someone only causes pain. I loved Jennifer, but I could never make her happy. When we divorced I accepted my role in the breakup."

"But she had a drinking problem, Cole. You can't blame yourself."

"I don't, not entirely, but I accept a portion of the blame for what went wrong. It tore me apart to see Bobby caught in the middle, and in an effort to minimize the pain I didn't fight for custody. He was an innocent victim of the divorce, and I didn't want him to suffer any further distress. I was willing to do anything I could to spare him. Later, when I realized how serious Jennifer's problem with alcohol had become, I tried to obtain custody, but before I could get the courts to move on it, the accident happened. Afterward, I was left facing the guilt of having waited too long.

"The thought of ever marrying again, having children again, terrified me. I couldn't imagine making myself vulnerable a second time." He paused, and a slow, gentle smile spread across his face, smoothing away the tension. "All of that changed when I met you. It was as if life was offering me another chance. And I knew I had to grab hold of it with both hands or live with regret forever."

"Oh, brother," Jeff said as he dashed into the yard. "Are you two at it again?"

"We're talking," Robin explained.

"Your mouths are too close together for talking." He strolled past them, Blackie trotting at his side. "I don't suppose you thought about making me anything to eat, did you, Mom?"

"I made sandwiches."

"Great. Are there enough for Blackie to have one?"

"I think so. There's juice and some corn chips in the kitchen, too."

"Great," Jeff repeated, hurrying into the house.

"Are you hungry?" Robin asked Cole.

"Yes," he stated emphatically, "but my appetite doesn't seem to be for food. How long will you keep me waiting to make you my wife?"

"I'll have to call my parents and my brother so we can arrange everything. It's important to me that we have a church wedding. It doesn't have to be fancy, but I'd like to invite a handful of good friends and—"

"How long?"

"To make the arrangements? I'm not sure. Three, possibly four months to do it properly."

"One month," Cole said.

"What do you mean, one month?"

"I'm giving you exactly thirty days to arrange whatever you want, but that's as long as I'm willing to wait."

"Cole—"

He swept her into his arms then and his mouth claimed hers in a fury of desire. Robin found herself trembling and she clutched his shirt, her fingers bunching the material as she strove to regain her equilibrium.

"Cole…" She felt chilled and feverish at the same time. Needy, yet wealthy beyond her wildest dreams.

"One month?" he repeated.

"One month," she agreed, pressing her face against his broad warm chest. They'd both loved, profoundly, and lost what they'd valued most. For years, in their own ways, they'd sealed themselves off from others, because no one else could understand their pain. Then they'd discovered each other, and nothing would ever be the same again. Their love was the mature love that came when one had suffered and lost and been left to rebuild a shattered life. A love that was stronger than either could have hoped for.

"Do you see what I was telling you?" Jeff muttered to Blackie, sitting on the back porch steps. "I suppose we're going to have to put up with this for a while."

Blackie munched on a corn chip, apparently more interested in sharing Jeff's meal than listening to his comments.

"I can deal with it, if you can," Jeff continued. "I suspect I'll be getting at least one brother out of this deal, and if we're lucky maybe two. A sister would be all right, too, I guess—" he sighed deeply "—but I'll have to think about that. Girls can be a real headache, if you know what I mean."

The dog wagged his tail as Jeff slipped him another corn chip. "And you know what, Blackie? It's gonna be Father's Day soon. My very first. And I've already got a card picked out. It's got a picture of a father, a mother and a boy with a baseball cap. And there's a dog on it that looks just like you!"

* * * * *

THE COURTSHIP OF CAROL SOMMARS

In loving memory of
David Adler, Doug Adler and Bill Stirwalt
Beloved Cousins
Beloved Friends

Special thanks to
Pat Kennedy and her endearing Italian mother,
and Ted Macomber and Bill Hall
for the contribution of their rap music
and all the lessons about living with
teenage boys

Chapter 1

Carol Sommars swore the entire house shook from her fifteen-year-old son's sound system, which was blasting out his favorite rap song.

I'm the Wizard MC and I'm on the mike
I'm gonna tell you a story that I know you'll like
'Cause my rhymes are kickin', and my beats do flash
When I go to the studio, they pay me cash

"Peter!" Carol screamed from the kitchen, covering her ears. She figured a squad of dive-bombers would've made less of a racket.

Realizing that Peter would never be able to hear her above the din, she marched down the narrow hallway and pounded on his door.

Peter and his best friend, Jim Preston, were sitting

on Peter's bed, their heads bobbing in tempo with the music. They both looked shocked to see her.

Peter turned down the volume. "Did you want something, Mom?"

"Boys, please, that music is too loud."

Her son and his friend exchanged a knowing glance, no doubt commenting silently on her advancing age.

"Mom, it wasn't *that* bad, was it?"

Carol met her son's cynical look. "The walls and floors were vibrating."

"Sorry, Mrs. Sommars."

"It's okay, Jim. I just thought I'd save the stemware while I had a chance." Not to mention warding off further hearing loss…

"Mom, can Jim stay for dinner? His dad's got a hot date."

"Not tonight, I'm afraid," Carol said, casting her son's friend an apologetic smile. "I'm teaching my birthing class, but Jim can stay some other evening."

Peter nodded. Then, in an apparent effort not to be outdone by his friend, he added, "My mom goes out on hot dates almost every weekend herself."

Carol did an admirable job of disguising her laugh behind a cough. Oh, sure! The last time she'd gone out had been…she had to think about it…two months ago. And that had been as a favor to a friend. She wasn't interested in remarrying. Bruce had died nearly thirteen years earlier, and if she hadn't found another man in that time, she wasn't going to now. Besides, there was a lot to be said for the benefits of living independently.

She closed Peter's bedroom door and braced her shoulder against the wall as she sighed. A jolt of deafening music brought her upright once more. It was immediately lowered to a respectable level, and she continued back to the kitchen.

At fifteen, Peter was moving into the most awkward teenage years. Jim, too. Both boys had recently obtained their learner's permits from the Department of Motor Vehicles and were in the same fifth-period driver training class at school.

Checking the time, Carol hurried into the kitchen and turned on the oven before popping two frozen meat pies inside.

"Hey, Mom, can we drive Jim home now?"

The operative word was *we,* which of course, meant Peter would be doing the driving. He was constantly reminding her how much practice he needed if he was going to pass the driving part of the test when he turned sixteen. The fact was, Peter used any excuse he could to get behind the wheel.

"Sure," she said, forcing a smile. These "practice" runs with Peter demanded nerves of steel.

Actually, his driving skill had improved considerably in the last few weeks, but the armrest on the passenger side of the car had permanent indentations. Their first times on the road together had been more hair-raising than a horror movie—another favorite pastime of her son's.

Thanks to Peter, Carol had been spiritually renewed when he'd run the stop sign at Jackson and Bethel. As if to make up for his mistake, he'd slammed on the brakes as soon as they'd cleared the intersection, catapulting them both forward. They'd been saved from injury by their seat belts.

They all clambered into her ten-year-old Ford.

"My dad's going to buy me a truck as soon as I get

my license," Jim said, fastening his seat belt. "A red four-by-four with flames painted along the sidewalls."

Peter tossed Carol an accusing glare. With their budget, they'd have to share her cantankerous old sedan for a while. The increase in the car insurance premiums with an additional driver—a male teenage driver—meant frozen meat pies every third night as it was. As far as Carol was concerned, nurses were overworked, underpaid and underappreciated.

"Mom—hide!"

Her heart vaulted into her throat at the panic in her son's voice. "What is it?"

"Melody Wohlford."

"Who?"

"Mom, please, just scoot down a little, would you?"

Still not understanding, she slid down until her eyes were level with the dashboard.

"More," Peter instructed from between clenched teeth. He placed his hand on her shoulder, pushing her down even farther. "I can't let Melody see me driving with my *mother!*"

Carol muttered under her breath and did her best to keep her cool. She exhaled slowly, reminding herself *this, too, shall pass.*

Peter's speed decreased to a mere crawl. He inadvertently poked her in the ribs as he clumsily lowered the window, then draped his left elbow outside. Carol bit her lower lip to prevent a yelp, which probably would've ruined everything for her son.

"Hey, Melody," he said casually, raising his hand.

The soft feminine greeting drifted back to them. "Hello, Peter."

"Melody," Jim said, leaning across the backseat. He spoke in a suave voice Carol hardly recognized.

"Hi, Jimmy," Melody called. "Where you guys off to?"

"I'm driving Jim home."

"Yeah," Jim added, half leaning over Carol, shoving her forward so that her head practically touched her knees. "My dad's ordered me a truck, but it hasn't come in yet."

"Boys," Carol said in a strangled voice. "I can't breathe."

"Just a minute, Mom," Peter muttered under his breath, pressing down on the accelerator and hurrying ahead.

Carol struggled into an upright position, dragging in several deep gulps of oxygen. She was about to deliver a much-needed lecture when Peter pulled into his friend's driveway. Seconds later, the front door banged open.

"James, where have you been? I told you to come directly home after school."

Carol blinked. Since this was the boys' first year of high school and they'd come from different middle schools, Carol had never met Jim's father. Now, however, didn't seem the appropriate moment to leap out and introduce herself.

Alex Preston was so angry with Jim that he barely glanced in their direction. When he did, he dismissed her and Peter without a word. His dark brows lifted derisively over gray eyes as he scowled at his son.

Carol suspected that if Jim hadn't gotten out of the car on his own, Alex would have pulled him through the window.

Carol couldn't help noting that Alex Preston was an imposing man; he had to be easily six-two. His forehead was high and his jaw well-defined. But his eyes were what immediately captured her attention. They held his son's with uncompromising authority.

There was an arrogant set to his mouth that Carol found herself disliking. Normally she didn't make snap judgments, but one look told her she wasn't going to get along with Jim's father, which was unfortunate since the boys had become such fast friends.

Not that it really mattered. Other than an occasional phone conversation, there'd be no reason for them to have any contact with each other.

She didn't know much about the man, other than his marital status (single—divorced, she assumed) and the fact that he ran some sort of construction company.

"I told you I was going out tonight," Alex was saying. "The least you could've done was have the consideration to let me know where you were. You're lucky I don't ground you for the next ten years."

Jim dropped his head, looking guilty. "Sorry, Dad."

"I'm sorry, Mr. Preston," Peter said.

"It's not your fault."

To his credit, Alex Preston glanced apologetically at Peter and Carol as if to say he regretted this scene.

"It might be a good idea if you hurried home yourself," Alex told her son.

Carol stiffened in the front seat. She felt like jumping out of the car and informing him that they had no intention of staying anyway. "We should leave now," she said to Peter with as much dignity as she could muster.

"Later," Peter called to his friend.

"Later," Jim called back, still looking chagrined.

Peter had reversed the car out of the driveway and was headed toward the house before either of them spoke.

"Did you know Jim was supposed to go home right after school?" Carol asked.

"How could I know something like that?" Peter flared. "I asked him over to listen to my new CD. I didn't know his dad was going to come unglued over it."

"He's just being a parent."

"Maybe, but at least you don't scream at me in front of my friends."

"I try not to."

"I've never seen Mr. Preston blow his cool before. He sure was mad."

"I don't think we should be so hard on him," she said, feeling generous despite her earlier annoyance. Adults needed to stick together. "He was obviously worried."

"But, Mom, Jim's fifteen! You shouldn't have to know where a kid is every minute of the day."

"Wanna bet?"

Peter was diplomatic enough not to respond to that.

By the time they'd arrived at the house and Carol had changed clothes for her class, their dinner was ready.

"Mom," Peter said thoughtfully as she brought a fresh green salad to the table. "You should think about going out more yourself."

"I'm going out tonight."

"I mean on dates and stuff."

"Stuff?" Carol repeated, swallowing a smile.

"You know what I mean." He sighed loudly. "You haven't lost it yet, you know."

Carol wasn't sure she did. But she was fairly certain he meant to compliment her, so she nodded solemnly. "Thanks."

"You don't even need to use Oil of Olay."

She nodded, although she didn't appreciate such close scrutiny of her skin.

"I was looking at your hair and I don't see any gray, and you don't have fat folds or anything."

Carol couldn't help it—she laughed.

"Mom, I'm serious. You could probably pass for thirty."

"Thanks…I think."

"I'm not kidding. Jim's dad is going out with someone who's twenty-one, and Jim told me she's tall and blond and pretty with great big…you know." He cupped his hands over his chest.

Carol sat down at the table. Leaning her elbows on it, she dangled her fork over her plate. "Are you suggesting I find myself a twenty-one-year-old guy with bulging muscles and compete with Jim's dad?"

"Of course not," Peter said scornfully. "Well, not exactly. I'm just saying you're not over the hill. You could be dating a whole lot more than you do. And you should before…well, before it's too late."

Carol pierced a fork full of lettuce and offered a convenient excuse. "I don't have time to get involved with anyone."

Peter took a bite of his own salad. "If the right guy came along, you'd make time."

"Perhaps."

"Mr. Preston does. Jim says his dad's always busy with work, but he finds time to date lots of women."

"Right, but most of the women he sees are too young to vote." Instantly feeling guilty for the catty remark, Carol shook her head. "That wasn't nice. I apologize."

"I understand," Peter said, sounding mature beyond his years. "The way I see it, though, you need a man."

That was news to her. "Why? I've got you."

"True, but I won't be around much longer, and I hate the thought of you getting old and gray all alone."

"I won't be alone. Grandma will move in with me and the two of us will sit side by side in our rocking chairs and crochet afghans. For entertainment we'll play bingo every Saturday afternoon." Even as she spoke, Carol realized how ridiculous that was.

"Grandma would drive you crazy in three days," Peter said with a know-it-all smile, waving his fork in her direction. "Besides, you'd get fat eating all her homemade pasta."

"Maybe so," Carol agreed, unwilling to argue the point. "But I have plenty of time before I have to worry about it. Anything can happen in the next few years."

"I'm worried *now,*" Peter said. "You're letting your life slip through your fingers like…like the sand in an hourglass."

Carol's eyes connected with her son's. "Have you been watching soap operas again?"

"Mom," Peter cried, "you're not taking me seriously."

"I'm sorry," she said, trying to hide the smile that raised the corners of her mouth. "It's just that my life is full. I'm simply too busy to spend time developing a relationship." One look from her son told her he didn't accept her explanation. "Sweetheart," she told him, setting her fork aside, "you don't need to worry about me. I'm a big girl. When and if I decide to see another man, I promise it'll be someone muscular so you can brag to your friends. Would a wrestler be all right?"

"The least you could've done was get married again," he muttered, his patience clearly strained. "Dad would've wanted that, don't you think?"

Any mention of Peter's father brought with it a feeling of terror and guilt. They'd both been far too young and foolish to get married. They were high school seniors when Carol learned she was pregnant. Given her very traditional Catholic family, marriage had seemed the only option. She'd also believed her love and their baby would change Bruce. For those reasons, Carol had agreed to marry him. But from that point to the moment Bruce had died in a terrible car accident three years later, Carol's life had been a living hell. She'd have to be crazy to even consider remarriage.

"Peter," she said, pointedly glancing at her watch and pushing her plate away. "I'm sorry to end this conversation so abruptly, but I've got to get to class."

"You're just being stubborn, but fine. It's your decision."

Carol didn't have time to argue. She dumped the remainder of her meal in the garbage, rinsed off her plate and stuck it in the dishwasher. She left Peter after giving him instructions to take care of his own dishes, then she hurried into the bathroom.

She refreshed her makeup and ran a brush though her shoulder-length dark hair, then examined her reflection in the mirror.

"Not bad," she muttered, eyeing herself critically. Thirty-four wasn't exactly retirement age.

Releasing her breath, Carol let her shoulders fall. "Who are you kidding?" she said with a depressed sigh. She faced the mirror and glared at her image again. Peter might not think she needed Oil of Olay, but the dew was definitely off the rose.

Tugging at the skin on her cheekbones until it was stretched taut, she squinted at her reflection, trying to remember what she'd looked like at eighteen. Young. Pretty. Stupid.

She wasn't any one of those now. And even if she'd had the opportunity, she wouldn't go back. She'd made plenty of mistakes, but there wasn't a single, solitary thing she'd change about her current life. Although after Peter got his driver's license, she might modify that thought.

No, the only option open to her was the future, and she'd face that, sagging skin and all.

"Hey, Mom." Peter's voice cut into her musings. "Can I invite a friend over tonight?"

Carol opened the bathroom door and frowned at her son. "I can't believe you'd even ask that. You know the rules. No one's allowed here when I'm not home."

"But, Mom," he whined.

"No exceptions."

"You don't trust me, do you?"

"We're not discussing this now. I have a class to teach, and I'm already five minutes behind schedule." She blamed Peter for that. If he hadn't tried to convince her how attractive she was, she wouldn't be late in the first place.

Class went well. They were into the third week of the eight-week course sponsored by Ford Hospital in a suburb of Portland, Oregon. The couples were generally first-time parents, and their eagerness and excitement for the adventure that lay before them filled each session with infectious enthusiasm.

If Carol had known when she was carrying Peter that he was to be her one and only pregnancy, she would've taken time to appreciate it more.

Since she was the last to leave the building, Carol turned off the lights and hauled her material out to her car. The parking lot was well lit, and she hurried through the rain, sliding inside the car. She drew in a deep breath and turned the ignition key. The Ford coughed and objected before roaring to life. Her car had been acting a little funny lately, but it was nothing she could pinpoint. Satisfied that there wasn't anything too terribly wrong, she eased into traffic on the busy street.

It wasn't until she'd stopped for the red light at the first intersection that her car released a series of short pathetic coughs, only this time it really sounded…sick.

"What's wrong?" she cried as the light turned green. Pushing down on the accelerator, she leaped ahead, but it was apparent that the problem, whatever it might be, was serious.

"All right, all right," she said, "I get the message. You need a mechanic and fast." A quick glance down the business-lined thoroughfare revealed there wasn't a single service station in sight.

"Great," she moaned. "How about if I promise not to let Peter behind the wheel for a while. Will that help?"

The ailing car belched loudly and a plume of black smoke engulfed the rear end.

"Okay, so you're not interested in a deal." Turning into the first driveway she happened upon, Carol found herself in a restaurant parking lot. The minute she entered an empty space, the car uttered one last groan and promptly died. And of course she'd left her cell phone charging—at home.

For a full minute Carol just sat here. "You can't do this to me!" Her car disagreed. Climbing out, she walked around it, as if she'd magically discover a cure lying on the ground. The rain was coming down in sheets, and within seconds, she was drenched.

In an act of angry frustration, she kicked a tire, then yelped when the heel of her pump broke off. She wanted to weep.

With no other alternative, she limped into the restaurant, intent on heading for the ladies' room. Once she composed herself, she'd deal with the car and call Peter to tell him she was going to be late.

Alex thought that if his date giggled one more time, he'd have to walk away from the table. Thanks to this woman, he was going slowly insane. He should know by now never to accept a blind date.

The first thing Bambi did when they were seated at the restaurant was to pick up the saltshaker and start discussing the "amazing" qualities of crystal.

It took Alex five minutes to make the connection. The saltshaker was made of crystal.

"I'm crazy about hot tubs," Bambi said, leaning forward to offer him a generous view of her ample breasts.

"They're...hot, all right," Alex murmured, examining the menu without much enthusiasm. His friend—at least someone he *used* to consider a friend—claimed Bambi was every man's dream. Her name should have been his first clue. Once they'd met, he'd learned her given name was Michelle, but she'd started calling herself Bambi because she loved forest animals so much. Animals like deer and chipmunks and hamsters.

Alex didn't have the heart to tell her that in all the years he'd been camping, he had yet to stumble upon a single family of hamsters grazing in a meadow.

When the waitress came to take their order, it took

Bambi five minutes to explain how she wanted her salad served. Okay, he was exaggerating. Four minutes. He ordered a steak and asked for it rare.

"I'm on a diet," Bambi said, once the waitress had left.

He smiled benignly.

"Do you think I'm fat, Alex?" she asked.

Her big brown eyes appealed to him to lie if he must. Once more she bunched her full breasts together and leaned toward him. It was more than obvious that she wasn't wearing a bra. He suspected that he was supposed to swoon at the sight.

"You do think I'm fat, don't you?" Bambi asked, pouting prettily.

"No," Alex told her.

"You're just saying that to be nice," she purred, and demurely lowered her lashes against the high arch of her cheek.

Alex smoothed out the linen napkin on his lap, thinking he was getting old. Far too old for someone like Bambi/Michelle. His teenage son might appreciate her finer qualities, but he suspected even James had better sense than that.

"Do you have a hot tub?"

Alex was so caught up in his thoughts, mentally calculating how long it would take to get through dinner so he could drive her home, that he didn't immediately realize she'd directed the question at him.

"I love hot tubs," she reminded him. "I even carry a swimsuit with me just in case my date has a tub. See?" She reached inside her purse and held up the skimpiest piece of material Alex had seen in his entire life. It was all he could do not to grab it out of her hand and shove it back in her purse.

"I don't have a hot tub," he said, making a strenuous effort to remain civil.

"Oh, that poor, pathetic thing," Bambi said, looking past him to the front of the restaurant.

"I beg your pardon?"

Bambi used this opportunity to lean as far forward as possible, drape her breasts over his arm and whisper, "A bag lady just came into the restaurant. She's drenched, and I think she might be hurt because she's limping pretty bad."

Although he really wasn't interested, Alex glanced over his shoulder. The instant his gaze connected with the woman Bambi was referring to, he twisted his chair around for a better view. "That's no bag lady," he said. "I know that girl."

"You do?"

"Yes, she was with my son and his best friend this afternoon. I think she's another friend of theirs." He paused. "She might be in some kind of trouble." He wasn't in the business of rescuing maidens in distress, but someone had to do something. "Will you excuse me a moment?"

"Alex," Bambi cried, reaching out for his arm, stopping him. Half the restaurant turned to stare at them—including the woman at the front. Even from halfway across the room, Alex could feel her eyes on him.

"You can't involve yourself in other people's problems," Bambi insisted.

"She's just a kid." He pulled his arm free.

"Honey, one look at her and I can tell you she's no kid."

Disregarding Bambi's unsought advice, Alex dropped his napkin on the table, stood and walked away.

"Hello, again," he said when he reached his son's

friend. Bambi was right about one thing. She looked terrible—nothing like the way she'd looked earlier. Her hair fell in wet tendrils that dripped on her jacket. Her mascara had left black streaks down her face, and she held the heel of her shoe in one hand. "I'm James's dad—we met briefly this afternoon." He held out his hand to her. "Do you remember me?"

"Of course I do," she said stiffly, clearly resenting this intrusion. She glanced longingly at the ladies' room.

"Is something wrong?"

"Wrong?" she echoed. "What could possibly be wrong?"

She thrust out her chin proudly, but he resisted the urge to shake some sense into her. Sarcasm always set his teeth on edge. "I'd like to help if I could."

"I appreciate the offer, but no thanks. Listen, I think you'd better get back to your date." She nodded toward Bambi, and a smile quivered at the corners of her mouth. She had difficulty meeting his eyes.

Briefly Alex wondered what she found so amusing. But then again…he knew.

"I thought she was supposed to be tall," she said next, and it sounded like she was trying not to laugh outright. Alex didn't appreciate her sense of humor, but he wasn't going to respond in kind. She was the one standing there looking like a drowned rat. Not him.

Her brows rose as she studied Bambi. "Actually two out of three isn't bad."

Alex had no idea what she was talking about. His expression must have said as much because she added, "Jim was telling Peter how your date for this evening was tall and blond and had big—"

She stopped abruptly, and Alex could swear she was blushing. A bright pink color started creeping up her neck and into her cheeks. "I'm sorry, that was uncalled for."

Bambi apparently wasn't about to be the center of their conversation while sitting down. She pushed back her chair, joined them near the hostess desk and slipped her arm through Alex's. "Perhaps you'd care to introduce us, Alex darling."

Alex wanted to roll his eyes at the way she referred to him as "darling." They'd barely met. He doubted Bambi knew his last name. He certainly didn't remember hers.

Since he wasn't sure of anyone's name, Alex gestured toward Carol and said, "This is a friend of my son's...."

"Carol Sommars," she supplied.

Alex was surprised. "I didn't know Peter had a sister."

Carol shot him a look. "I'm not his sister. I'm his mother."

Chapter 2

"His mother," Alex echoed, clearly distressed. "But I thought…I assumed when you were with the boys that…"

"She's got to be *way* over thirty!" the blonde with her arm wrapped around Alex's exclaimed, eyeing Carol as possible competition.

Unwilling to be subjected to any debate over her age, Carol politely excused herself and headed blindly toward the ladies' room. The way her luck had been going this evening, it shouldn't be any shock that she'd run into Alex Preston of all people—and his infamous "hot date."

As soon as Carol examined herself in the mirror, she groaned and reached for her purse, hoping to repair the worst of the damage. No wonder Alex had mistaken her for a teenager. She looked like Little Orphan Annie on a bad day.

To add to her consternation, he was waiting for her when she left the restroom.

"Listen," he said apologetically. "We got off to a bad start. Can I do something to help?"

Carol thanked him with a smile. "I appreciate that, but I don't want to ruin your evening. My car broke down and I don't have my cell. I'm just going to call the auto club from here and have them deal with it." She already had the phone number and a quarter in her hand. The pay phone was just outside the restrooms.

"All right." Carol was grateful when he left. She was horrified by the way she'd spoken to him earlier and wanted to apologize—later. Alex had caught her at a bad moment, but he'd made up for it by believing she was Peter's sister. That was almost laughable, but exceptionally flattering.

She finished her call and tried three frustrating times to get through to Peter, but the line was busy. Sitting in the restaurant foyer, she decided to give her son a few more minutes before calling again.

Alex strolled toward her. "Is the auto club coming?"

"They're on their way," she answered cheerfully, flashing him a smile.

"Did you get hold of Peter?"

Her facade melted away. "I tried three times and can't get through. He's probably talking to Melody Wohlford, the love of his life."

"I'll contact James on my cell and have him get in touch with Peter for you. That way, you won't have to worry about it."

"Thank you." She was more gracious this time. "Knowing Peter, he could be on the phone for hours."

Alex stepped away and returned a minute later. "Jim

was talking to Peter. Fortunately we have call waiting so I got through to him." He shook his head slightly. "They're doing their algebra homework together, which is probably good because Jim needs all the help he can get."

"In this case it's the blind leading the blind."

Alex grinned, and the mouth she'd found so arrogant and haughty earlier now seemed unusually appealing. His smile was sensual and affable at the same time and Carol liked it a whole lot. It had been a good many years since she'd caught herself staring at a man's mouth. Self-conscious, she dragged her gaze away and looked past him into the restaurant.

Alex glanced uncomfortably at his table, where the other woman was waiting impatiently. "Would you like to join us and have something to eat?" he asked eagerly.

"Oh, no," Carol said, "I couldn't do that."

Alex's gray eyes reached out to hers in blatant appeal. "*Please* join us."

Carol wasn't sure what was going on between Alex and his date, and she was even less sure about putting herself in the middle of it, but… Oh, well, why not?

"All right," she agreed in a tentative voice.

Alex immediately looked grateful. He glanced back at the woman who was glaring at him, clearly displeased that he was paying so much attention to Carol.

However, if her disapproval bothered him, he didn't show it. He led Carol back to the table and motioned for the waitress to bring a menu.

"I'll just have coffee."

As soon as the waitress was gone, Alex introduced the two women. "Bambi, Carol. Carol, Bambi."

"I'm pleased to make your acquaintance," Bambi

said formally, holding out her hand. Carol thought she'd never seen longer nails. They were painted a fire engine red and were a good inch in length.

"Alex and I have sons the same age," Carol explained. Her coffee arrived, and she quickly took a sip to disguise her uneasiness.

"Eat your dinner, Alex," Bambi instructed. "There's no need to let our evening be ruined by Carol's problems."

"Yes, please," Carol said hurriedly. "By all means, don't let me keep you from your meal."

Alex reached for the steak knife. "Is Peter trying out for track this year?"

"He wouldn't miss it. I'm positive that's the only reason he's managed to keep his grades up. He knows the minute he gets a D, he's off the team. Who knows what'll happen next year when he takes chemistry."

"Jim's decided to take chemistry his junior year, too."

"I took chemistry," Bambi told them. "They made us look inside a worm."

"That's biology," Carol said kindly.

"Oh, maybe it was."

"I need to apologize for the way I blew up this afternoon," Alex continued. "I felt bad about it afterward. Yelling at Jim in front of his friends was not the thing to do. It's just that there are times my son frustrates me no end."

"Don't worry about it. I feel the same way about Peter when he does something I've specifically asked him not to do." Feeling guilty for excluding Bambi from the conversation, Carol turned toward her and asked, "Do you have children?"

"Heavens, no. I'm not even married."

"Children can be extremely wonderful and extremely frustrating," Carol advised Bambi, who seemed far more interested in gazing lovingly at Alex.

"Jim only has one chore around the house during the week," Alex went on to say. "He's supposed to take out the garbage. Every week it's the same thing. Garbage starts stacking up against the side of the refrigerator until it's as high as the cabinets, and Jim doesn't even notice. I end up having to plead with him to take it out."

"And two days later he does it, right? Peter's the same."

Alex leaned forward and braced his forearms against the table, pushing his untouched steak aside. "Last week, I didn't say a word, wanting to see how long it would take him to notice. Only when something began to stink did he so much as—"

"Pass the salt," Bambi said, stretching her arm between Carol and Alex and reaching for it herself. She shook it over her salad with a vengeance, then slammed it down on the table.

Apparently Alex felt contrite for having ignored his date. He motioned toward her salad. "Bambi's on a diet."

"I am not fat!" Bambi cried. "You said so yourself."

"I…no, I didn't mean to imply that you *needed* to be on a diet, I was just…making small talk."

"Well, if you don't mind, I'd prefer it if you didn't discuss my eating habits."

"Where's the protein?" Carol asked, examining Bambi's plate of greens. "You should be having some protein—eggs, lean meat, that sort of thing."

"Who are you?" Bambi flared. "Jenny Craig?"

"You're right, I'm sorry. It's just that I'm a nurse, and

I work with pregnant women, and nutrition is such an important part of pregnancy that—"

"Are you suggesting I'm pregnant?"

"Oh, no, not in the least." Every time Carol opened her mouth, it seemed she made an even worse mess of the situation. "Look, I think the auto club might need some help finding me. If you'll both excuse me, I'll wait outside."

"You should," Bambi said pointedly. "You're over thirty, so you can take care of yourself."

Carol couldn't get away fast enough. The rain was coming down so hard it was jitterbugging across the asphalt parking lot. Standing just inside the restaurant doorway, Carol buried her hands in her pockets and shivered. She hadn't been there more than a few minutes when Alex joined her.

Before she could say anything, he thrust his hands in his own pockets, sighed and said, "I gave her money for a taxi home."

Carol wasn't sure how to respond. "I hope it wasn't on account of me."

"No." He gave her another of his warm, sensual smiles. "It was a blind date. I should've known better than to let myself get talked into it."

"I went out on one a while ago, and it was a disaster, too." It got worse the longer she was single. Her friends seemed to believe that since she'd been alone for so many years, she should be willing to lower her standards. "How long have you been single?" she asked Alex.

"Two years. What about you?"

"Thirteen."

He turned to face her. "That's a long time."

"So Peter keeps telling me. According to him, I'm about to lose it and need to act fast. I haven't figured out precisely what *it* is, but I have a good idea."

"Jim keeps telling me the same thing. Between him and Barney—that's the guy who arranged this date—they're driving me crazy."

"I know what you mean. My brother's wife calls me at least once a week and reads me ads from the personal columns. She's now progressed to the Internet, as well. The one she picked out last week really got me. It was something like—Male, thirty-five, dull and insecure, seeks exciting, wealthy female any age who's willing to love too much. Likes string cheese and popcorn. If you can do *Sudoku for Dummies,* I'm the man for you."

"Maybe we should introduce him to Bambi."

They laughed together, and it felt natural.

"Give me your car keys," Alex said suddenly. "I'll check it out and if it's something minor, I might be able to fix it."

"I don't think it is. When the engine died, it sounded pretty final." Nevertheless, she handed him her key ring and stood under the shelter while Alex ran across the parking lot to test her car. She stood on her tiptoes and watched him raise the hood, disappear under it for a few minutes and then close it and come running back to her.

"I think you're right," he said, rubbing the black grease from his hands with a white handkerchief.

"Excuse us, please," a soft feminine voice purred from behind Carol. Bambi slithered past them, her arm looped through that of a much older gentleman. She cast Carol a dirty look and smiled softly in Alex's direction before turning her attention to her most recent admirer. "Now, what were you saying about your hot tub?"

The two were barely out of earshot when Alex started to chuckle. “It didn’t take her long, did it?”

“I really am sorry,” Carol felt obliged to say. “I feel terrible…as though I personally ruined your evening.”

“No,” he countered. “On the contrary, you saved me. By the time you arrived, I was trying to figure out how long my patience was going to hold out. I had the distinct impression that before the evening was over I was going to be fighting her off.”

Carol laughed. It didn’t require much imagination to see Bambi in the role of aggressor. Come to think of it, Carol had dealt with a handful of Bambi’s male counterparts over the years.

The rain had diminished and it was drizzling when the auto club van arrived. Alex walked the driver to Carol’s car, and together the two men tried to determine what was wrong with her faithful Ford. They decided that whatever the problem was, it couldn’t be fixed then and there and that the best thing to do was call a tow truck.

Carol agreed and signed on the dotted line.

“I’ll give you a lift home,” Alex volunteered.

“Thanks.” She was already in his debt; one more thing wouldn’t matter.

Within minutes, they were sitting inside Alex’s car with the heater running full blast. Carol ran her hands up and down her arms to warm them.

“You’re cold.”

“I’ll be fine in a minute. If I wasn’t such a slave to fashion,” she said with self-deprecating humor, “I would’ve worn something heavier than this cotton jacket. But it’s the same pale green as my slacks and they go so well together.”

"You sound just like Jim. It was forty degrees yesterday morning, and he insisted on wearing a shirt from last summer."

They smiled at each other, and Carol was conscious of how close they were in the snug confines of Alex's sports car. Her dark eyes met his warm gray ones. Without warning, the laughter faded from Alex's lips, and he studied her face. After viewing the damage earlier, Carol knew her hair hung in springy ringlets that resembled a pad used to scrub pots and pans. She'd done the best she could, brushing it away from her face and securing it at the base of her neck with a wide barrette she'd found in the bottom of her purse. Now she was certain the tail that erupted from her nape must be sticking straight out.

A small lump lodged in her throat, as though she'd tried to swallow a pill without water. "You never did get your dinner, did you?" she asked hastily.

"Don't worry about it."

"Listen, I owe you. Please…stop somewhere and let me treat you. It's after nine—you must be starved." She glanced at her watch and felt a blush heat her cheeks. It'd been longer than she could recall since a man had unsettled her quite this much.

"Don't worry about it," he said again. "I'm a big boy. I'll make myself a sandwich once I get home."

"But—"

"If you insist, you can have me over to eat sometime. All right? When it comes to dinner, Jim and I share the duties. A good home-cooked meal would be welcome."

Carol didn't have any choice but to agree, and she did so by nodding her damp head briskly until she realized she was watering the inside of his car. "Oh, sure, I'd like that." She considered saying that she came from a large Italian family and was an excellent cook, but that would sound too much like the personal ads her sister-in-law, Paula, insisted on reading to her.

"You *do* cook?"

"Oh, yes." Once more she held her tongue. Whereas a few moments earlier she'd been cold, now she felt uncomfortably warm. Her hands were clammy and her stomach was filled with what seemed like a swarm of bees.

They chatted amicably on the rest of the drive to her house. When Alex pulled into her driveway, she turned and smiled at him, her hand on her door handle. "I'm really grateful for all your help."

"No problem."

"And…I'm sorry about what happened with Bambi."

"I'm not," he said, then chuckled. "I'll give you a call later, all right? To check on your car…"

The question seemed to hang between them, heavy with implication. It was the "all right" that told her he was referring to something beyond the state of her car.

"Okay," she said almost flippantly, feeling more than a little light-headed.

"So, tell me about this man who brings color back to my little girl's cheeks," Angelina Pasquale said to Carol as she carried a steaming plate of spaghetti to the table.

Carol's mother didn't know how to cook for three or four; it was twelve or fifteen servings for each and every Sunday dinner. Her two older sisters lived in California now, and only Tony and Carol and their families came religiously for Sunday dinner. Her mother, however, continued to cook as if two or three additional families might walk in unannounced for the evening meal.

"Mama, Alex Preston and I just met last week."

"That's not what Peter said." The older woman wiped her hands on the large apron tied around her thick waist. Her dark hair, streaked with gray, was tucked into a neat bun. She wore a small gold crucifix that had been given to her by Carol's father forty-two years earlier.

Carol brought the long loaves of hot bread from the oven. "Alex is Jim's father. You remember Peter's friend, don't you?"

"He's not Italian."

"I don't know what he is. Preston might be an English name."

"English," Angelina said as if she was spitting out dirty dishwater. "You gonna marry a non-Italian again?"

"Mama," Carol said, silently laughing, "Alex helped me when my car broke down. I owe him dinner, and I insisted on taking him out to repay him. We're not stopping off at the church to get married on the way."

"I bet he's not even Catholic."

"Mama," Carol cried. "I haven't the faintest clue where he attends church."

"You taking a man to dinner instead of cooking for him is bad enough. But not even knowing if he's Catholic is asking for trouble." She raised her eyes as if pleading for patience in dealing with her youngest daughter; when she lowered her gaze, they fell to Carol's feet. She folded her hands in prayerlike fashion. "You wear pointed-toe shoes for this man?"

"I didn't wear these for Alex. I happen to like them—they're in style."

"They're gonna deform your feet. One day, you'll

trip and end up facedown in the gutter like y
Celeste."

"Mama, I'm not going to end up in a gutter."

"Your cousin Celeste told her mother the same th
and we both know what happened to her. She had t
marry a foot doctor."

"Mama, please don't worry about my shoes."

"Okay, but don't let anyone say your mama didn't warn you."

Carol had to leave the room to keep from laughing. Her mother was the delight of her life. She drove Carol crazy with her loony advice, but Carol knew it was deeply rooted in love.

"Carol," Angelina said, surveying the table, "tell everyone dinner's ready."

Peter was in the living room with his younger cousins, who were watching the Dodgers play Kansas City in a hotly contested baseball game.

"Dinner's on the table, guys."

"Just a minute, Mom. It's the bottom of the eighth, with two out." Peter's intense gaze didn't waver from the screen. "Besides, Uncle Tony and Aunt Paula aren't back from shopping yet."

"They'll eat later." Carol's brother Tony and his wife had escaped for the afternoon to Clackamas Town Center, a large shopping mall south of Portland, and they weren't expected back until much later.

"Just a few more minutes," Peter pleaded.

"Mama made zabaglione," Carol said.

The television went off in a flash, and four children rushed into the dining room, taking their places at the table like a rampaging herd of buffalo. Peter was the

years, which gave him an air of superior-
is cousins.

ay dinner at her mother's was tradition. They
a close-knit family and helped one another with-
question. Her brother had lent her his second car
while hers was being repaired. Carol didn't know what
she'd do without him. She'd have her own car back in
a few days, but Tony's generosity had certainly made
her life easier.

Mama treasured these times with her children and grandchildren, generously offering her love, her support and her pasta. Being close to her family was what had gotten Carol through the difficult years following Bruce's death. Her parents had been wonderful, helping her while she worked her way through college and the nursing program, caring for Peter when she couldn't and introducing her to a long list of nice Italian men. But after three years of dealing with Bruce's mental and physical abuse, she wasn't interested. The scars from her marriage ran deep.

"I'll say grace now," Angelina said. They all bowed their heads and closed their eyes.

No one needed any encouragement to dig into the spaghetti drenched in a sauce that was like no other. Carol's mother was a fabulous cook. She insisted on making everything from scratch, and she'd personally trained each one of her three daughters.

"So, Peter," his grandmother said, tearing off a thick piece from the loaf of hot bread. "What do you think of your mother marrying this Englishman?"

"Aw, Grandma, it's not like that. Mr. Preston called and Mom's treating him to dinner 'cause he gave her a ride home. I don't think it's any big deal."

"That was what she said when she met your father. 'Ma,' she told me, 'it's just dinner.' The next thing I know, she's standing at the altar with this non-Italian and six months later the priest was baptizing you."

"Ma! Please," Carol cried, embarrassed at the way her mother spoke so freely—although by now she should be used to it.

"Preston." Her mother muttered the name again, chewing it along with her bread. "I could accept the man if he had a name like Prestoni. Carol Prestoni has a good Italian ring to it…but Preston. Bah."

Peter and Carol exchanged smiles.

"He's real nice, Grandma."

Angelina expertly wove the long strands of spaghetti around the tines of her fork. "Your mama deserves to meet a nice man. If you say he's okay, then I have to take your word for it."

"Mama, it's only one dinner." Carol wished she'd never said anything to her mother. Alex had called the night before, and although he sounded a little disappointed that she wouldn't be making the meal herself, he'd agreed to let her repay the favor with dinner at a local restaurant Monday night. Her big mistake was mentioning it to her mother. Carol usually didn't say anything to her family when she was going out on a date. But for some reason, unknown even to herself, she'd mentioned Alex as soon as she'd walked in the door after church Sunday morning.

"What color eyes does this man have?"

"Gray," Carol answered and poured herself a glass of ice water.

Peter turned to his mother. "How'd you remember that?"

"I…I just recall they were…that color." Carol felt her cheeks flush. She concentrated on her meal, but when she looked up, she saw her mother watching her closely. "His eyes are sort of striking," she said, mildly irritated by the attention her mother and her son were lavishing on her.

"I never noticed," Peter said.

"A boy wouldn't," Angelina told him, "but your mother, well, she looks at such things."

That wasn't entirely true, but Carol wasn't about to claim otherwise.

As soon as they were finished with the meal, Carol's mother brought out the zabaglione, a rich sherry-flavored Italian custard thick with eggs. Angelina promptly dished up six bowls.

"Mama, zabaglione's high in fat and filled with cholesterol." Since her father's death from a heart attack five years earlier, Carol worried about her mother's health, although she wasn't sure her concern was appreciated.

"So zabaglione's got cholesterol."

"But, Mama, cholesterol clogs the veins. It could kill you."

"If I can't eat zabaglione, then I might as well be dead."

Smiling wasn't what Carol should have done, but she couldn't help it.

When the dishes were washed and the kitchen counters cleaned, Carol and her mother sat in the living room. Angelina rocked in the chair her mother's mother had brought from Italy seventy years earlier. Never one for idle hands, she picked up her crocheting.

It was a rare treat to have these moments alone with

Chapter 3

Carol's hand remained closed around the telephone receiver as she heaved in a giant breath. She'd just completed the most cowardly act of her life.

Regretting her actions, she punched out Alex's phone number again, and listened to the recorded message a third time while tapping her foot. At the beep, she paused, then blurted out, "I hope you understand…I mean…oh…never mind." With that, she replaced the receiver, pressed her hand over her brow, more certain than ever that she'd just made a world-class idiot of herself.

Half an hour later, Carol was sorting through the dirty clothes in the laundry room when Peter came barreling into the house.

He paused in the doorway, watching her neatly organize several loads. "Hey, Mom, where's the TV guide?"

"By the television?" she suggested, more concerned about making sure his jeans' pockets were empty before putting them in the washer.

"Funny, Mom, real funny. Why would anyone put it there?"

Carol paused, holding a pair of dirty jeans to her chest. "Because that's where it belongs?" she said hopefully.

"Yeah, but when's the last time anyone found it there?"

Not bothering to answer, she dumped his jeans in the washing machine. "Did you look on the coffee table?"

"It's not there. It isn't by the chair, either."

"What are you so keen to watch, anyway? Shouldn't you be doing your homework?"

"I don't have any…well, I do, but it's a snap."

Carol threw another pair of jeans into the churning water. "If it's so easy, do it now."

"I can't until Jim gets home."

At the mention of Alex's son, Carol hesitated. "I… see."

"Besides, it's time for wrestling, but I don't know what channel it's on."

"Wrestling?" Carol cried. "When did you become interested in *that?*"

"Jim introduced me to it. I know it looks phony and stuff, but I get a kick out of those guys pounding on each other and the crazy things they say."

Carol turned and leaned against the washer, crossing her arms. "Personally I'd rather you did your homework first, and if there's any time left over you can watch television."

"Of course you'd prefer that," Peter said. "You're

a mom—you're supposed to think that way. But I'm a kid, and I'd much rather watch Mr. Muscles take on Jack Beanstalk."

Carol considered her son's argument for less than two seconds. "Do your homework."

Peter sighed, his shoulders sagging. "I was afraid you'd say that." Reluctantly he headed toward his bedroom.

It was still light out, and with the wash taken care of, Carol ventured into the backyard, surveying her neatly edged flower beds. Besides perennials, she grew Italian parsley, basil and thyme and a few other herbs in the ceramic pots that bordered her patio. One of these days she was going to dig up a section of her lawn and plant an honest-to-goodness garden.

"Mom..." Peter was shouting her name from inside the house.

She turned, prepared to answer her son, when she saw Alex walk out the back door toward her. Her heart did a somersault, then vaulted into her throat and stayed there for an uncomfortable moment.

"Hello, Alex," she managed to say, suspecting that her face had the look of a cornered mouse. She would gladly have given six months' mortgage payments to remove her messages from his voice mail. It wasn't easy to stand there calmly and not run for the fence.

"Hello, Carol." He walked toward her, his gaze holding hers.

He sounded so...relaxed, but his eyes were a different story. They were like the eyes of an eagle, sharp and intent. They'd zeroed in on her as though he was about to swoop down for the kill.

For her part, Carol was a wreck. Her hands were

clenched so tightly at her sides that her fingers ached. "What can I do for you?" she asked, embarrassed by the way her voice pitched and heaved with the simple question.

A brief smile flickered at the edges of Alex's mouth. "You mean you don't know?"

"No...well, I can guess, but I think it would be best if you just came out and said it." She took a couple of steps toward him, feeling extraordinarily brave for having done so.

"Will you offer me a cup of coffee?" Alex asked instead.

The man was full of surprises. Just when she was convinced he was about to berate her for behaving like an utter fool, he casually suggested she make coffee. Perhaps he often confronted emotionally insecure women who left him nonsensical messages.

"Coffee? Of course...come in." Pleased to have something to occupy her hands, Carol hurried into the kitchen. Once she'd added the grounds to the filter and filled the coffeemaker with water, she turned and leaned against the counter, hoping to look poised. She did an admirable job, if she did say so herself—at least for the first few minutes. After all, she'd spent the last thirteen years on her own. She wasn't a dimwit, although she'd gone out of her way to give him that impression, and she hadn't even been trying. That disconcerted her more than anything.

"No, I don't understand," Alex said. He opened her cupboard and took down two ceramic mugs.

"Understand what?" Carol decided playing dumb might help. It had worked with Bambi, and who was to say it wouldn't with her? However, she had the distinct notion that if she suggested they try out a hot tub, Alex would be more than willing.

"I want to know why you won't have dinner with me."

Carol was completely out of her element. She dealt with pregnancy and birth, soon-to-be mothers and terrified fathers, and she did so without a pause. But faced with one handsome single father, she was a worthless mass of frazzled nerves. Fearing her knees might give out on her, she walked over to the table, pulled out a chair and slumped into it. "I didn't exactly say I wouldn't go out with you."

"Then what did you say?"

She lowered her gaze, unable to meet his. "That… something came up."

"I see." He twisted the chair around and straddled it. The coffeemaker gurgled behind her. Normally she didn't even notice it, but now it seemed as loud as the roar of a jet plane.

"Then we'll reschedule. Tuesday evening at six?"

"I…I have a class… I teach a birthing class to expectant parents on Tuesday evenings." Now that was brilliant! Who else would attend those classes? But it was an honest excuse. "That's where I'd been when my car broke down in the parking lot of the restaurant where I met you…last Tuesday…remember?"

"The night I helped you," Alex reminded her. "As I recall, you claimed you wanted to repay me. Fact is, you insisted on it. You said I'd missed my dinner because of you and that you'd like to make it up to me. At first it was going to be a home-cooked meal, but that was quickly reduced to meeting at a restaurant in separate cars, and now you're canceling altogether."

"I…did appreciate your help."

"Is there something about me that bothers you? Do I have bad breath?"

"Of course not."

"Dandruff?"

"No."

"Then what is it?"

"Nothing," she cried. She couldn't very well explain that their one meeting had jolted to life a part of her that had lain dormant for years. To say Alex Preston unsettled her was an understatement. She hadn't stopped thinking about him from the moment he'd dropped her off at the house. Every thought that entered her mind was linked to those few minutes they'd spent alone in his car. She was an adult, a professional, but he made her forget everything—except him. In thinking about it, Carol supposed it was because she'd married so young and been widowed shortly afterward. It was as though she didn't know how to behave with a man, but that wasn't entirely true, either. For the past several years, she'd dated numerous times. Nothing serious of course, but friendly outings with "safe" men. One second with Alex, and she'd known instantly that an evening with him could send her secure, tranquil world into a tailspin.

"Wednesday then?"

Carol looked warily across the kitchen, wanting to weep with frustration. She might as well be a good sport about it and give in. Alex wasn't going to let her off the hook without a fuss.

"All right," she said, and for emphasis, nodded. "I'll see you Wednesday evening."

"Fine." Alex stood and twisted the chair back around.

"I'll pick you up at seven." He sent her one of his smiles and was gone before the coffee finished brewing.

Once she was alone, Carol placed her hands over her face, feeling the sudden urge to cry. Closing her eyes, however, was a mistake, because the minute she did, her mother's whispered words, reminding her of how good lovemaking could be, saturated her thoughts. That subject was the last thing Carol wanted to think about, especially when the man she wanted to be making love with was the one who had so recently left her kitchen.

Abruptly she stood and poured herself a cup of coffee. It didn't help to realize that her fingers were shaking. What was so terrific about men and sex, anyway? Nothing that *she* could remember. She'd been initiated in the backseat of a car at eighteen with the boy she was crazy in love with. Or the boy she *thought* she was in love with. More likely it had been hormones on the rampage for both of them.

After she'd learned she was pregnant, Carol was never convinced Bruce had truly wanted to marry her. Faced with her hotheaded father and older brother, he'd clearly regarded marriage as the more favorable option.

In the last of her three years with Bruce, he'd been drunk more than he was sober—abusive more than he was considerate. Lovemaking had become a nightmare for her. Feeling violated and vaguely sick to her stomach, she would curl up afterward and lie awake the rest of the night. Then Bruce had died, and mingled with the grief and horror had been an almost giddy sense of relief.

"I don't want a man in my life," she said forcefully.

Peter was strolling down the hallway to his room

and stuck his head around the doorway. "Did you say something?"

"Ah..." Carol wanted to swallow her tongue. "Nothing important."

"You look nice," Peter told Carol on Wednesday when she finished with her makeup.

"Thanks," she said, smiling at him. Her attitude toward this evening out with Alex had improved now that she'd had time to sort through her confused emotions. Jim's father was a nice guy, and to be honest, Carol didn't know what had made her react the way she did on Sunday. She was a mature adult, and there was nothing to fear. It wasn't as though she was going to fall into bed with the man simply because she was attracted to him. They'd have the dinner she owed him and that would be the end of it.

But, as much as she would've liked to deny it, Alex was special. For the first time since she could remember, she was physically attracted to a man. And what was wrong with that? It only went to prove that she was a normal, healthy woman. In fact, she should be grateful to Alex for helping her realize just how healthy she was.

"Where's Mr. Preston taking you?" Peter asked, plopping himself down on the edge of the tub.

"Actually I'm taking him, and I thought we'd go to Jake's." Jake's was a well-known and well-loved Portland restaurant renowned for its Cajun dishes.

"You're taking Mr. Preston to Jake's?" Peter cried, his voice shrill with envy. "Are you bringing me back anything?"

"No." As it was, she was stretching her budget for the meal.

"But, Mom—Jake's? You know that's my favorite restaurant in the whole world." He made it sound as though he were a global traveler and connoisseur of fine dining.

"I'll take you there on your birthday." The way she had every year since he was ten.

"But that's another five months," Peter grumbled.

She gave him what she referred to as her "Mother Look," which generally silenced him.

"All right, all right," he muttered. "I'll eat frozen pot pie for the third time in a week. Don't worry about me."

"I won't."

Peter sighed with feeling. "You go ahead and enjoy your *étouffée*."

"I'm sure I will." She generally ordered the shrimp dish, which was a popular item on the menu.

Peter continued to study her, his expression revealing mild surprise. "Gee, Mom, don't you have a heart anymore? I used to be able to get you with guilt, but you hardly bat an eyelash anymore."

"Of course I've got a heart. Unfortunately I don't have the wallet to support it."

Peter seemed about to speak again, but the doorbell chimed and he rushed out of the tiny bathroom to answer it as though something dire would happen if Alex was kept waiting more than a few seconds.

Expelling a sigh, Carol surveyed her appearance in the mirror one last time, confident that she looked her best. With a prepared smile on her face, she headed for the living room.

The instant she appeared, Alex's gaze rushed to hers. The impact of seeing him again was immediate. It was difficult to take her eyes off him. Instead, she found herself thinking that his build suggested finely honed muscles. He was tall, his shoulders were wide and his chest solid. Carol thought he was incredibly good-looking in his pin-striped suit. His face was weathered from working out of doors, his features bronzed by the sun.

So much for the best-laid plans, Carol mused, shaking from the inside out. She'd planned this evening down to the smallest detail. They would have dinner, during which Carol would subtly inform him that she wasn't interested in anything more than a casual friendship, then he'd take her home, and that would be the end of it. Five seconds after she'd walked into the living room, she was thinking about silk sheets and long, slow, heart-melting kisses.

Her mother was responsible for this. Her outrageous, wonderful mother and the softly murmured Italian words that reminded Carol she was still young and it was time to live and love again. She was alive, all right. From the top of her head to the bottom of her feet, she was *alive.*

"Hello, Carol."

"Alex."

"Mom's taking you to Jake's," Peter muttered, not bothering to hide his envy. "She can't afford to bring me anything, but that's okay."

"Peter," she chastised, doubting Alex had heard him.

"Are you ready?"

She nodded, taking an additional moment to gather her composure while she reached for her jacket and purse. Glancing at her son, she felt obliged to say, "You know the rules. I'll call you later."

"You don't need to phone," he said, making a show

of rolling his eyes as if to suggest she was going overboard on this parental thing.

"We'll be back early."

Alex cupped her elbow as he directed her to the door. "Not too early," he amended.

By the time they were outside, Carol had bridled her fears. Her years of medical training contributed to her skill at presenting a calm, composed front. And really, there wasn't a reason in the world she should panic....

They talked amicably on the drive into downtown Portland, commenting on such ordinary subjects as the weather, when her car would be fixed and the approach of summer, which they both dreaded because the boys would be constantly underfoot.

Alex managed to find parking on the street, which was a feat in its own right. He opened her car door and took her hand, which he didn't release.

Since Carol had made a reservation, they were immediately seated in a high-backed polished wood booth and greeted by their waiter, who brought them a wine list and recited the specials of the day.

"Jim tells me you're buying him a truck," Carol said conversationally when they'd placed their order.

"So he'd like to believe."

Carol hesitated. "You mean you aren't?"

"Not to the best of my knowledge," Alex admitted, grinning.

Once more, Carol found herself fascinated by his smile. She found herself wondering how his mouth would feel on hers. As quickly as the thought entered her mind, she discarded it.

"According to Jim it's going to be the latest model, red with flames decorating the sidewalls."

"The boy likes to dream," Alex said, leaning back. "If he drives any vehicle during the next two years, it'll be because he's impressed me with his grades and his maturity."

"Oh, Alex," Carol said with a sigh, "you don't know how relieved I am to hear that. For weeks, Peter's been making me feel as though I'm an abusive mother because I'm not buying him a car—or, better yet, a truck. Time and time again he's told me that *you're* buying one for Jim and how sharing the Ford with me could damage his self-esteem, which might result in long-term counseling."

Alex laughed outright. "By the way," he added, "Jim isn't Jim anymore, he's James."

"James?"

"Right. He noticed that his learner's permit listed his name as James Preston, and he's insisting everyone call him that. Actually, I think he came up with the idea after I spoke to him about driving and his level of maturity. Apparently, James is more mature-sounding than Jim."

"Apparently," Carol returned, smiling. "Well, at least if Peter does end up having to go to a counselor, he'll have company."

Their wine arrived and they both commented on its delicious flavor and talked about the quality of Walla Walla area wineries.

Their meal came soon after. The steaming *étouffée* was placed before her, and she didn't experience the slightest bit of guilt when she tasted the first bite. It was as delicious as she remembered.

"Have you been a nurse long?" Alex asked, when their conversation lagged.

"Eight years. I returned to school after my husband was killed, and nursing was a natural for me. I was forever putting Band-Aids on my dolls and treating everyone from my dog to my tolerant mother."

"Next time I have a cold, I'll know who to call," Alex teased.

"Oh, good. And when I'm ready to put the addition on the house, I'll contact you," Carol told him.

They both laughed.

The evening wasn't nearly as difficult as Carol had feared. Alex was easy to talk to, and with the boys as common ground, there was never a lack of subject matter. Before Carol was aware of it, it was nearly ten.

"Oh, dear," she said, sliding from the booth. "I told Peter I'd check in with him. Excuse me a minute."

"Sure," Alex said, standing himself.

Carol was in the foyer on her cell, waiting for Peter to answer when she looked over and saw that Alex was using his own cell phone.

"Hello."

"Peter, it's Mom."

"Mom, you said you were going to phone," he said, sounding offended. "Do you know what time it is? When you say you're going to phone you usually do. James is worried, too. Where have you guys been?"

"Jake's—you knew that."

"All this time?"

"Yes. I'm sorry, sweetheart, the evening got away from us."

"Uh-huh," Peter said and paused. "So you like Mr. Preston?"

Carol hedged. "He's very nice," she murmured.

"Do you think you'll go out with him again? What

did you guys talk about? Just how long does it take to eat dinner, anyway?"

"Peter, this isn't the time or place to be having this discussion."

"Were there any leftovers?"

"None."

Her son sighed as if he'd actually been counting on her to bring home her untouched dinner—a reward for the supreme sacrifice of having to eat chicken pot pie, which just happened to be one of his favorites.

"When will you be home? I mean, you don't have to rush on my account or anything, but you'd never let *me* stay out this late on a weeknight."

"I'll be back before eleven," she promised, ignoring his comment about the lateness of the hour. Sometimes Peter forgot who was the adult and who was the child.

"You *do* like Mr. Preston, don't you?" His tone was too smug for comfort.

"Peter," she moaned. "I'll talk to you later." She was about to replace the receiver when she heard him call her name. "What is it now?" she said sharply, impatiently.

He hesitated, apparently taken aback by her brusqueness. "Nothing, I just wanted to tell you to wake me up when you get home, all right?"

"All right," she said, feeling guilty.

She met Alex back at their table. "Everything okay at home?" he asked.

"Couldn't be better." There was no need to inform Alex of the inquisition Peter had attempted. "What about Jim—James?"

"He's surviving."

"I suppose we should think about getting home,"

Carol suggested, eager now to leave. The evening had flown by. At some point during dinner, her guard had slipped and she'd begun to enjoy his company. There'd been none of the terrible tension that had plagued her earlier.

"I suppose you're right," Alex said with enough reluctance to alarm her. He'd obviously enjoyed their time as much as she had.

They had a small disagreement over the check, which Alex refused to let her take. He silenced her protests by reminding her that she owed him a home-cooked meal and he wasn't accepting any substitutes. After a couple of glasses of wine and a good dinner, Carol was too mellow to put up much of an argument.

"Just don't let Peter know," she said as they walked toward the car. Alex held her hand, and it seemed far too natural, but she didn't object.

"Why?"

"If Peter discovers you paid, he'll want to know why I didn't bring anything home for him."

Alex grinned as he unlocked his car door and held it open. He rested his hand on the curve of her shoulder. "You *will* make me that dinner sometime, won't you?"

Before she realized what she was doing, Carol found herself nodding. She hadn't had a chance to compose herself by the time he'd walked around the front of the car and joined her.

Neither of them spoke on the drive back to her house. Carol's mind was filled with the things she'd planned to tell him. The things she'd carefully thought out beforehand—about what a nice time she'd had, and how she hoped they'd stay in touch and what a good boy Jim—James—was and how Alex was doing a wonderful job raising him. But the trite, rehearsed words refused to come.

Alex pulled into her driveway and turned off the engine. The living room was dark and the curtains drawn. The only illumination was the dim light on her front porch. When Alex turned to face her, Carol's heart exploded with dread and wonder. His look was warm, eager enough to make her blood run hot…and then immediately cold.

"I had a good time tonight." He spoke first.

"I did, too." How weak she sounded, how tentative…

"I'd like to see you again."

They were the words she'd feared—and longed for. The deep restlessness she'd experienced since the night her car had broken down reverberated within her, echoing through the empty years she'd spent alone.

"Carol?"

"I…don't know." She tried to remind herself of what her life had been like with Bruce. The tireless lies, the crazy brushes with danger as though he were courting death. The anger and impatience, the pain that gnawed at her soul. She thought of the wall she'd so meticulously constructed around her heart. A wall years thick and so high no man had ever been able to breach it. "I…don't think so."

"Why not? I don't understand."

Words could never explain her fear.

"Let me revise my statement," Alex said. "I *need* to see you again."

"Why?" she cried. "This was only supposed to be one night…to thank you for your help. I can't give you any more…I just can't and…" Her breath scattered, and her lungs burned within her chest. She couldn't deny the things he made her feel.

"Carol," he said softly. "There's no reason to be afraid."

But there was. Except he wouldn't understand.

He reached up and placed his calloused palm against her cheek.

Carol flinched and quickly shut her eyes. "No... please, I have to go inside...Peter's waiting for me." She grabbed the door handle, and it was all she could do not to escape from the car and rush into the house.

"Wait," he said huskily, removing his hand from her face. "I didn't mean to frighten you."

She nodded, opening her eyes, and her startled gaze collided with his. She watched as he slowly appraised her, taking in her flushed face and the rapid rise and fall of her breasts. He frowned.

"You're trembling."

"I'm fine...really. Thank you for tonight. I had a marvelous time."

His hand settled over hers. "You'll see me again."

It wasn't until she was safely inside her living room and her heart was back to normal that Carol realized his parting words had been a statement of fact.

Chapter 4

"So, Dad, how did dinner go with Mrs. Sommars?" James asked as he poured himself a huge bowl of cornflakes. He added enough sugar to make eating it worth his while, then for extra measure added a couple of teaspoons more.

Alex cupped his steaming mug of coffee as he considered his son's question. "Dinner went fine." It was afterward that stayed in his mind. Someone had hurt Carol and hurt her badly. He'd hardly touched her and she'd trembled. Her dark brown eyes had clouded, and she couldn't seem to get out of his car fast enough. The crazy part was, Alex felt convinced she was attracted to him. He knew something else—she didn't want to be.

They'd spent hours talking over dinner, and it had seemed as though only a few moments had passed. There was no need for pretense between them. She didn't pretend to be anything she wasn't, and he was free to be himself as well. They were simply two single parents who had a lot in common. After two years of dealing with the singles scene, Alex found Carol a refreshing change. He found her alluringly beautiful and at the same time shockingly innocent. During the course of their evening, she'd argued with him over politics, surprised him with her wit and challenged his opinions. In those few hours, Alex learned that this intriguing widow was a charming study in contrasts, and he couldn't wait to see her again.

"Mrs. Sommars is a neat lady," James said, claiming the kitchen chair across from his father. "She's a little weird, though."

Alex looked up from his coffee. "How's that?"

"She listens to opera," James explained between bites. "Sings it, too—" he planted his elbows on the tabletop, leaned forward and whispered "—in Italian."

"Whoa." Alex was impressed.

"At the top of her voice. Peter told me she won't let him play his rap CDs nearly as loud as she does her operas."

"The injustice of it all."

James ignored his sarcasm. "Peter was telling me his grandmother's a real kick, too. She says things like 'Eat your vegetables or I'm calling my uncle Vito in Jersey City.'"

Alex laughed, glanced at his watch and reluctantly got to his feet. He finished the last of his coffee, then set the mug in the sink. "Do you have your lunch money?"

"Dad, I'm not a kid anymore. You don't have to ask me stuff like that."

"Do you?" Alex pressed.

James stood and reached inside his hip pocket. His eyes widened. "I…guess I left it in my room."

"Don't forget your driver's permit, either."

"Dad!"

Alex held up both hands. "Sorry."

He was all the way to the front door when James's shout stopped him.

"Don't forget to pick me up from track practice, all right?"

Alex pointed his finger at his son and calmly said, "I'll be there."

"Hey, Dad."

"What now?" Alex complained.

James shrugged and leaned his shoulder against the door leading into the kitchen. "In case you're interested, Mrs. Sommars will be there, too."

Alex was interested. Very interested.

He left the house and climbed inside his work van, sitting in the driver's seat with his hands on the steering wheel. He mulled over the events of the night before. He'd dated several women recently. Beautiful women, intelligent women, wealthy women. A couple of them had come on hot and heavy. But not one had appealed to him as strongly as this widow with the dark, frightened eyes and the soft, delectable mouth.

A deep part of him yearned to stroke away the pain she held on to so tightly, whatever its source. He longed to watch the anxiety fade from her eyes when she settled into his arms. He wanted her to feel secure enough with him to relax. The urge to hold her and kiss her was strong, but he doubted Carol would let him.

"Okay, Peggy, bear down...push...as hard as you can," Carol urged the young mother-to-be, clutching her hand. Peggy did as Carol asked, gritting her teeth, arching forward and lifting her head off the hospital pillow. She gave it everything she had, whimpering softly with the intensity of the labor pain. When the contraction had passed, Peggy's head fell back and she took in several deep breaths.

"You're doing a good job," Carol said, patting her shoulder.

"How much longer before my baby's born?"

"Soon," Carol assured her. "The doctor's on his way now."

The woman's eyes drifted closed. "Where's Danny? I need Danny."

"He'll be back in a minute." Carol had sent her patient's husband out for a much-needed coffee.

"I'm so glad you're here."

Carol smiled. "I'm glad I'm here, too."

"Danny wants a son so much."

"I'm sure he'll be just as happy with a little girl."

Peggy smiled, but that quickly faded as another contraction started. She reached for Carol's hand, her face marked by the long hours she'd struggled to give birth. Carol had spent the past hour with her. She preferred it when they weren't so busy and she could dedicate herself to one patient. But for more days than she cared to remember, the hospital's five labor rooms had been full, and she spent her time racing from one to the other.

Peggy groaned, staring at a focal point on the wall. The technique was one Carol taught in her classes. Concentrating on a set object helped the mother remember and practice the breathing techniques.

"You're doing just fine," Carol said softly. "Take a deep breath now and let it out slowly."

"I can't do it anymore…I can't," Peggy cried. "Where's Danny? Why's he taking so long?"

"He'll be back any second." Now that her patient was in the final stages of labor, the pains were stronger and closer together.

Danny walked into the room, looking pale and anxious…and so very young. He moved to the side of the bed and reached for his wife's hand, holding it to his cheek. He seemed as relieved as Peggy when the contraction eased.

Dr. Adams, old and wise and a hospital institution, sauntered into the room, hands in his pockets, smiling. "So, Peggy, it looks like we're going to finally have that baby."

Peggy grinned sheepishly. "I told Dr. Adams yesterday I was sure I was going to be pregnant until Christmas. I didn't think this baby ever wanted to be born!"

Phil Adams gave his instructions to Carol, and within a few minutes the medical team had assembled. From that point on, everything happened exactly as it should. Before another hour had passed, a squalling Danny, Jr., was placed in his father's arms.

"Peggy…oh, Peggy, a son." Tears of joy rained down the young man's face as he sobbed unabashedly, holding his son close.

Although Carol witnessed scenes such as this day in and day out, the thrill of helping to bring a tiny being into the world never left her.

When her shift was over, she showered and changed clothes, conscious of the time. She had to pick Peter up from track practice on her way home, and she didn't want to keep him waiting, although she was the one likely to be twiddling her thumbs.

* * *

The first thing Carol noticed when she pulled into the school parking lot was a van with Preston Construction printed in large black letters on the side. Alex. She drew in a shaky breath, determined to be friendly but reserved. After the way she'd escaped from his car the night before, it was doubtful he'd want anything to do with her, anyway.

The fact was, she couldn't blame him. She wasn't sure what had come over her. Then again, she did know…and she didn't want to dwell on it.

She parked a safe distance away, praying that either Peter would be finished soon and they could leave or that Alex wouldn't notice her arrival. She lowered the window to let in the warm breeze, then turned off the ignition and reached for a magazine, burying her face in its pages. For five minutes nothing happened.

When the driver's side of the van opened, Carol realized her luck wasn't going to hold. She did her best to concentrate on a recipe for stuffed pork chops and pretend she hadn't seen Alex approach her. When she glanced up, he was standing beside her car. Their eyes met for what seemed the longest moment of her life.

"Hello again." He leaned forward and rested his hands on her window.

"Hello, Alex."

"Nice day, isn't it?"

"Lovely." It wasn't only his smile that intrigued her, but his eyes. Their color was like a cool mist rising off a pond. Would this attraction she felt never diminish, never stop? Three brief encounters, and she was already so tied up in knots she couldn't think clearly.

"How was your day?" His eyes were relentless,

searching for answers she couldn't give him to questions she didn't want him to ask.

She glanced away. "Good. How about yours?"

"Fine." He rubbed a hand along the back of his neck. "I was going to call you later."

"Oh?"

"To see if you'd like to attend the Home Show with me next Friday night. I thought we could have dinner afterward."

Carol opened her mouth to refuse, but he stopped her, laying his finger across her lips, silencing her. The instant his hand touched her, the warm, dizzy feeling began. As implausible, as preposterous as it seemed, a deep physical sensation flooded her body. And all he'd done was lightly press his finger to her lips!

"Don't say no," Alex said, his voice husky.

She couldn't, at least not then. "I…I'll have to check my schedule."

"You can tell me tomorrow."

She nodded, although it was an effort.

"Good…I'll talk to you then."

It wasn't until he'd removed his finger, sliding it across her moist lips, that Carol breathed again.

"What do you mean you can't pick me up from track?" Peter complained the next morning. "How else am I supposed to get home? Walk?"

"From track practice, of all things." She added an extra oatmeal cookie to his lunch because, despite everything, she felt guilty about asking him to find another way home. She was such a coward.

"Mom, coach works us hard—you know that. I was so stiff last night I could barely move. Remember?"

Regretfully, Carol did. A third cookie went into the brown-paper sack.

"What's more important than picking me up?"

Escaping a man. If only Alex hadn't been so gentle. Carol had lain awake half the night, not knowing what was wrong with her or how to deal with it. This thing with Alex, whatever it was, perplexed and bewildered her. For most of her life, Carol had given and received countless hugs and kisses—from relatives, from friends. Touching and being touched were a natural part of her personality. But all Alex had done was press his finger to her lips, and her response…her response still left her stunned.

As she lay in bed, recalling each detail of their brief exchange, her body had reacted again. He didn't even need to be in the same room with her! Alone, in the wee hours of the morning, she was consumed by the need to be loved by him.

She woke with the alarm, in a cold sweat, trembling and frightened, convinced that she'd be a fool to let a man have that kind of power a second time.

"Mom," Peter said impatiently. "I asked you a question."

"Sorry," she said. "What was it you wanted to know?"

"I asked why you aren't going to be at track this afternoon. It's a simple question."

Intuitively Carol knew she wouldn't be able to escape Alex, and she'd be a bigger fool than she already was even to try.

She sighed. "I'll be there," she said, and handed him his lunch.

Peter stood frozen, studying her. "Are you sure you're not coming down with a fever?"

If only he knew…

When Carol pulled into the school parking lot later that same day, she saw Alex's van in the same space as the day before. Only this time he was standing outside, one foot braced against it, fingers tucked in his pockets. His jeans hugged his hips and fit tight across his thighs. He wore a checked work shirt with the sleeves rolled up past his elbows.

When she appeared, he lowered his foot and straightened, his movement leisurely and confident.

It was all Carol could do to slow down and park her car next to his. To avoid being placed at a disadvantage, she opened her door and climbed out.

"Good afternoon," she said, smiling so brightly her mouth felt as though it would crack.

"Hello again."

A lock of his dark hair fell over his forehead, and he threaded his fingers through its thickness, pushing it away from his face.

His gaze tugged at hers until their eyes met briefly, intently.

"It's warmer today than it was yesterday," she said conversationally.

"Yes, it is."

Carol lowered her eyes to his chest, thinking she'd be safe if she practiced what she preached. Find a focal point and concentrate. Only it didn't work as well in situations like this. Instead of saying what had been on her mind most of the day, she became aware of the pattern of his breathing, and how the rhythm of her own had changed, grown faster and more erratic.

"Have you decided?"

Her eyes rushed to his. "About…"

"Going to the home show with me."

She wished it could be the way it had been in the restaurant. There was something about being with a crowd that relaxed her. She hadn't felt intimidated.

"I…don't think seeing each other is such a good idea. It'd be best if we…stayed friends. I can foresee all kinds of problems if we started dating, can't you?"

"The Home Show's going to cause problems?"

"No…our seeing each other will."

"Why?"

"The boys—"

"Couldn't care less. If anything, they approve. I don't understand why there'd be any problems. I like you and you like me—we've got a lot in common. We have fun together. Where's the problem in that?"

Carol couldn't very well explain that when he touched her, even lightly, tiny atoms exploded inside her. Whenever they were within ten feet of each other, the air crackled with sensuality that grew more intense with each encounter. Surely he could feel it, too. Surely he was aware of it.

Carol held a hand to her brow, not knowing how to answer him. If she pointed out the obvious, she'd sound like a fool, but she couldn't deny it, either.

"I…just don't think our seeing each other is a good idea," she repeated stubbornly.

"I do," he countered. "In fact, it appeals to me more every minute."

"Oh, Alex, please don't do this."

Other cars were filling the parking lot, and the two of them had quickly become the center of attention. Carol glanced around self-consciously, praying he'd accept her refusal and leave it at that. She should've known better.

"Come in here," Alex said, opening the side panel to his van. He stepped inside and offered her his hand. She joined him before she had time to determine the wisdom of doing so.

Alex closed the door. "Now, where were we...ah, yes. You'd decided you don't want to go out with me again."

That wasn't quite accurate, but she wasn't going to argue. She'd rarely wanted anything more than to continue seeing him, but she wasn't ready. Yet...Bruce had been dead for thirteen years. If she wasn't ready by now, she never would be. The knowledge hit her hard, like an unexpected blow, and her eyes flew to his.

"Carol?" He moved toward her. The walls of the van seemed to close in around her. She could smell the scent of his after-shave and the not unpleasant effects of the day's labor. She could feel the heat coming off his body.

Emotion thickened the air, and the need that washed through her was primitive.

She backed as far as she could against the orderly rows of tools and supplies stacked on the shelves. Alex towered above her, studying her with such tenderness and concern that she had to repress the urge to weep.

"Are you claustrophobic?"

She shook her head.

His eyes settled on her mouth, and Carol felt her body's reaction. She unconsciously held her breath so long that when she released it, it burned her chest. If she hadn't been so frightened, she would have marveled at what was happening between them, enjoyed the sensations.

Gently Alex whisked back a strand of hair from her face. At his touch, Carol took a deep breath, but he er ears shut out the sound, not wanting anything or yone to destroy this precious time.

Alex groaned, not to communicate pleasure but rustration. Carol didn't understand. Nor did she comrehend what was happening when he released her gradally, pushing himself away. He turned and called, "The oor's locked."

"The door?" she echoed. It wasn't until then that she realized Alex was talking to the boys. Peter and Jim were standing outside the van, wanting in. She'd been so involved with Alex that she hadn't even heard her own son calling her name.

"Please open that door," she said, astonished by how composed she sounded. The trembling hadn't started yet, but it would soon, and the faster she made her escape, the better.

"I will in just a m He turned back to her and placed his ha her shoulders. "You're going with me nex Frid night. Okay?"

"N

He

She

ging

n a

ding

issed

the

are y

I've b

n," P

seemed to gain confidence when she didn't
from him. He cupped her cheek.

Her eyes momentarily drifted shut, and
own hand over his.

"I'm going to kiss you."

She knew it and was unwilling to dredge
termination to stop him.

His hands slipped to her shoulders as he slo
her forward. She considered ending this no
least amount of resistance, he would have rele
she didn't doubt that for a second. But it was a
moment had been preordained.

At first all he did was press his lips to hers. T
enough, more than enough. Her fingers curled i
shirt as he swept his mouth over hers.

She whimpered when he paused.

He sighed.

Her breathing was shallow.

His was harsh.

He hesitated and lifted his head, eyes
cked, his brow creased with a frown. W
ecided, he didn't share, letting her dra
ns.
ds were braced again
uth again. This ti
ad as he fu
t to re

stan
He k
slid ope
"What
manded.
minutes."
"Hi, Mo

rowed eyes. "Everyone else has gone home. Did you know you left your keys in the ignition?"

"I...Mr. Preston was showing me his...van." She was sure her face was as red as a fire truck, and she dared not meet her son's eyes for fear he'd know she'd just been kissed. Good heavens, he probably already did.

"Are you all right?" Peter asked her.

"Sure. Why?" Stepping down onto the pavement she felt as graceful as a hippo. James climbed in when she'd climbed out, she and Peter walked over to her car.

"I think you might be coming down with something," Peter said as he automatically sat in the driver's seat, assuming he'd be doing the honors. He snapped the seat belt into place. "There were three cookies in my lunch, and no sandwich."

"There were?" Carol distinctly remembered spreading peanut butter on the bologna slices—Peter's favorite sandwich. She must have left it on the kitchen countertop.

"Not to worry, I traded off two of the cookies." He adjusted the rearview mirror and turned the key. He was about to pull out of the parking space when a huge smile erupted on his face. "I'm glad you and Mr. Preston are getting along so well," he said.

Alex sat at his cluttered desk with his hands clasped behind his head, staring aimlessly into space. He'd finally kissed her. He felt like a kid again. A slow, easy smile spread across his face, a smile so full, his cheeks ached. What a kiss it had been. Seductive enough to satisfy him until he could see her again. He was going to kiss her then, too. He could hardly wait.

The intercom buzzed. "Mr. Powers is here."

Alex's smile brightened. "Send him in." He stood and held out his hand to Barney, his best friend. They'd been in college together, roommates their senior year, and had been close ever since. Barney was a rare kind of friend, one who'd seen him through the bad times and the good times and been there for both in equal measure.

"Alex, great to see you." He helped himself to a butterscotch candy from the bowl on the edge of the desk and sat down. "How you doing?"

"Fine." It was on the tip of his tongue to tell Barney about Carol, but everything was so new, he didn't know if he could find the words to explain what he was feeling.

"I've decided to forgive you."

Alex arched his eyebrows. "For what?"

"Bambi. She said you dumped her at the restaurant."

"Oh, that. It wouldn't have worked, anyway."

"Why not?" Barney said, unwrapping the candy and popping it in his mouth.

"I don't have a hot tub."

"She claimed you left with another woman. A bag lady?"

Alex chuckled. "Not exactly."

"Well, you needn't worry, because ol' Barn has met Ms. Right and is willing to share the spoils."

"Barn, listen…"

Barney raised his hand, stopping him. "She's perfect. I swear to you she's bright, beautiful and buxom. The three *b*'s—who could ask for anything more?"

"As I recall, that's what you told me about Bambi," Alex countered, amused by his friend's attempts to find him a wife. It wouldn't be quite as humorous if Barney could stay married himself. In the past fifteen years, his friend had gone through three wives. Each of them bright, beautiful and buxom.

They might've been the best of friends, but when it came to women, their tastes were as dissimilar as could be. Barney went for breasts, whereas Alex was far more interested in brains.

"You're going to let me introduce her, aren't you? I mean, the least you can do is meet Babette."

"No, thanks." The guy had an obsession with *B*-words, Alex thought. The next woman would probably be named Brandy. Or Barbie.

"You won't even have a drink with her?"

"Sorry, not interested."

Barney leaned back and crossed his legs, sucking on the butterscotch candy for a few seconds before he spoke. "She was first runner-up for Miss Oregon several years back. Does that tell you anything?"

"Sure," Alex said, reaching for a candy himself. "She looks terrific in a swimsuit and is interested in world peace."

Barney slowly shook his head. "I don't understand it. I thought you were ready to get back into dating."

"I am."

"Listen, buddy, take a tip from me. Play the field, sample the riches available, then settle down. I'm happier when I'm married, and you will be, too. Frankly, with your looks and money, I don't think you'll have much of a problem. There are plenty of willing prospects out there. Only I notice you aren't doing anything to meet one."

"I don't have to, with you around. You're worse than a matchmaker."

Barney ignored that. “It’s time, Alex. You said so yourself. Just how long are you going to wait? Gloria’s been gone two years now. She wouldn’t have wanted this.”

“I know.” At the mention of his late wife, Alex felt a twinge of pain. Time had healed the worst of it, but he’d always remember the agony of watching the woman he loved die.

“You want me to give you Babette’s phone number?” his friend asked gently.

Alex shook his head. “Don’t bother to introduce me to any more of your women friends.”

Barney’s mouth sagged open. “But you just admitted I was right, that it’s time to get out there and—”

“Remember the bag lady Bambi was telling you about?” Alex asked, interrupting his friend before he could deliver the entire five-minute lecture.

“Yeah, what about her?”

“I’m going to marry her.”

Chapter 5

"You know, Mom, I like Mr. Preston," Peter announced over dinner as though this was a secret he'd been waiting to share.

"He seems very nice," Carol agreed, reaching for a slice of tomato. She didn't want to say anything more to encourage this topic, so she changed it. "How was school?"

"Fine. James was telling me about all the neat things him and his dad do together, like camping and fishing and stuff like that."

"Your uncle Tony takes you with him."

"Not camping or fishing and besides, it's not the same," Peter murmured. "Uncle Tony's my *uncle*."

Carol paused, her fork over the plump red tomato. "Now, that was profound."

"You don't know what I mean, do you?"

"I guess not," Carol said.

"Going camping with Mr. Preston would be like having a dad."

"How's that?" She took a bite of her roast, then braced her elbows on the tabletop.

"You know."

"No, I don't."

Peter lapsed into silence as he mulled over his thoughts. "I guess what I'm trying to say is that James and I talked it over and we decided we'd like it if the two of you got married."

Carol was so shocked by her son's statement that she stopped eating. Peter was staring at her intently, waiting for some sign or reaction.

"Well?" he pressed. "Is it going to happen? I can tell you like each other."

Chewing furiously, Carol waved her fork at her son, letting it speak for her. The meat, which had been so tender a moment before, took on the quality of leather. The faster she chewed, the more there seemed to be.

"You may think I'm still a kid and I don't know much," Peter continued, "but it didn't take James and me long to figure out what was going on inside his dad's van."

The piece of meat finally slid down Carol's throat. She blinked, uncertain if she could speak normally.

Peter was grinning from ear to ear. "I wish you could've seen your face when Mr. Preston opened the door of the van." Peter didn't bother to disguise his amusement. "If I hadn't been arguing with James, I would've started laughing right then."

"Arguing with James?" Those three words were all she could force past her lips. From the moment the two boys had met on the first day of high school, they'd been the best of friends. In all the months since September, Carol couldn't remember them disagreeing even once.

"We had an argument when we couldn't get his dad to open the van," Peter admitted, his mouth twitching. "Your face was so red, and you had this stunned look, like an alien had hauled you inside his spaceship." Peter's deepening voice vibrated with humor.

"Peter," she demanded, furiously spearing another piece of meat. "What did you argue about?"

"We argued over what his father was doing with you in that van. What kind of son would I be if I didn't defend your…honor?"

"What did James say?"

Peter shrugged. "That his dad wouldn't do anything you didn't want him to."

"*Those* were fighting words?"

Peter shrugged again. "It was the way he said them."

"I see."

Peter scooped himself a second helping of the scalloped potatoes. "Getting back to the marriage part. What do you think?"

"That you need to finish your peas and carrots."

Peter's eyes rushed to hers, but only for a moment. Then he grinned. "Oh, I get it—you want me to mind my own business. Right?"

"Exactly."

"But think about it, Mom. Promise me you'll at least do that much. Meeting Mr. Preston could be the greatest thing that's ever happened to us."

"And when you're finished with your dinner, I want you to stack the dirty dishes in the dishwasher," Carol said without a pause. She ate the last bite of her roast, although it tasted more like rubber.

"Every time I mention Mr. Preston, are you going to give me another job to do?"

Her son was a quick study, Carol would grant him that.

"But you *are* going to see him again, aren't you?" he asked hopefully.

"The garbage should be taken out, and I noticed that the front flower beds should be weeded. I know you worked out there last Saturday, but—"

"All right, all right," Peter cried, throwing his hands in the air. "Enough—I get the message."

"I certainly hope so," she said and got up to carry her plate to the sink.

Carol waited until Peter was busy with his homework and the dishes were done before she snuck into the kitchen and turned off the light. Then she called Alex. She wasn't sure what she'd do if James answered.

"Hello."

"Alex?" She cupped her hand over the receiver and kept her eye on the doorway in case Peter strolled past. "I can't talk long. Listen, did James happen to have a heart-to-heart discussion with you about…us?"

"Not exactly. He said something about the two of them having a talk about you and me. Why?"

"That's what I'm talking about," she whispered, ignoring his question. "Over dinner Peter threw a grenade at my feet."

"He did *what?*"

"It's a figure of speech—don't interrupt me. He said the two of them argued when you didn't open the van door and afterward decided it would be just great if the two of us…that's you and me…got *married*." She could barely get the words past the growing lump in her throat.

"Now that you mention it, James did say something along those lines."

Carol pressed her back to the kitchen wall, suddenly needing its support. "How can you be so casual about this?" she burst out.

"Casual?"

"My son announced that he knew what was going on inside the van and that I should've seen my face and that fishing and camping with you would be like having a father." She paused long enough to draw in a breath.

"Carol?"

"And then when I try to calmly warn you what these two are plotting, you make it sound like…I don't know…like we're discussing basketball or something."

"Carol, slow down, I can barely understand you."

"Of course you can't understand me—I'm upset!"

"Listen, this is clearly disturbing you. We need to talk about it. Can you meet me for lunch tomorrow?"

"I'm working tomorrow. And can't go out for lunch, for heaven's sake—I'm a nurse."

"Okay, I'll meet you in the hospital cafeteria at noon."

Just then Peter strolled nonchalantly into the kitchen. He stood in the doorway, turned on the light and stared curiously at his mother.

"Sure, Mama, whatever you say," Carol said brightly—too brightly.

"Mama?" Alex echoed chuckling. "Okay, I get the picture. I'll see you tomorrow at noon."

* * *

Agreeing to meet Alex at the hospital was a mistake. Carol should have realized it immediately, but she'd been so concerned with the shocking news Peter had delivered over dinner that she didn't stop to consider what could happen once she was spotted with Alex in the gossip-rich cafeteria at Ford Memorial.

"Sorry I'm late," Carol murmured as she joined him at a table for two, sliding her orange tray across from his. A couple of nurses from surgery walked past, glanced at Alex, then at Carol, and then back at Alex. Carol offered her peers a weak smile. Once she returned to the obstetrics ward, she was in for an inquisition that could teach the Spaniards a lesson.

"I haven't been here long." Alex grinned and reached for his ham sandwich. "How much time do you have?"

Carol checked her watch. "Forty-five minutes."

He opened a carton of milk. "All right. Do you want to tell me what upset you so much about last night?"

"I already did."

"Refresh my memory."

Carol released a slow sigh. Several more of her friends had seen her and Alex, including Janice Mandle, her partner in the birthing classes. By this time, the probing stares being sent their way were rattling Carol's shaky composure. "Apparently James and Peter have come to some sort of agreement…about you and me."

"I see." Humor flashed through his eyes like a distant light.

"Alex," she cried. "This is serious. We've gone out to dinner *once,* and our sons are talking about where the four of us are going to spend our honeymoon."

"And that bothers you?"

"Of course it does! And it should bother you, too. They already have expectations about how our relationship's going to develop. I don't think it's a healthy situation, and furthermore, they know about next Friday." She took a bite of her turkey sandwich and picked up her coffee.

"You mean that we're going to the Home Show?"

Carol nodded. "Yes, but I think we should forget the whole thing. We're looking at potential trouble here, and I for one have enough problems in my life without dealing with the guilt of not giving my son a father to take him fishing." She breathed deeply, then added, "My brother doesn't camp or fish. Actually no one in our family does."

Alex held his sandwich in front of his mouth. He frowned, his eyes studying hers, before he lowered his hands to the plate. "I beg your pardon?"

Carol shook her head, losing patience. "Never mind."

"No," he said after a thoughtful pause. "Explain to me what taking Peter fishing has to do with us seeing each other Friday night and your brother Tony who doesn't camp and hunt."

"Fish," Carol corrected, "although he doesn't hunt, either."

"That part makes sense."

Curious stares seemed to come at Carol from every corner of the room. Alex had finished his sandwich, and Carol wasn't interested in eating any more of hers.

"Do you want to go outside?" she suggested.

"Sure."

Once they'd disposed of their trays, Carol led him onto the hospital grounds. The weather had been beautiful for April. It wouldn't last much longer. The rains would return soon, and the "Rose City" would blossom into the floral bouquet of the Pacific Northwest.

With her hands in the front pockets of her uniform, Carol strolled in the sunshine, leading them away from the building and toward the parking lot. She saw his van in the second row and turned abruptly in the opposite direction. That construction van would be nothing but a source of embarrassment to her now.

"There's a pond over this way." With its surrounding green lawns, it offered relative privacy.

An arched bridge stretched between its banks, and goldfish swam in the cold water. Sunlight rippled across the pond, illuminating half, while the other half remained in enigmatic shadow. In some ways, Carol felt her budding relationship with Alex was like sun and shadow. When she was with him, she felt as though she was stepping into the light, that he drew her away from the shade. But the light was brilliant and discomfiting, and it illuminated the darkest corners of her loneliness, revealing all the imperfections she hadn't noticed while standing numbly in the shadows.

Although gentle, Alex had taught her painful lessons. Until she met him, she hadn't realized how hungry she was to discover love in a man's arms. The emptiness inside her seemed to echo when she was with him. The years hadn't lessened the pain her marriage had brought into her life, but seemed to have intensified her self-doubts. She was more hesitant and uncertain now than she'd been the year following Bruce's death.

With his hand on her elbow, Alex guided her to a park bench. Once they were seated, he reached for her hand, lacing their fingers together.

"I don't want you to worry about the boys," he said.

She nodded and lowered her eyes. She couldn't help being worried, but Alex didn't understand her fears and revealed no distress of his own. That being the case, she couldn't dwell on the issue.

He raised her fingers to his mouth. "I suppose what I'm about to say is going to frighten you even more."

"Alex…no."

"Shh, it needs to be said." He placed his finger across her lips to silence her, and who could blame him, she mused. It had worked so well the first time. "The boys are going to come to their own conclusions," he continued, "and that's fine, they would anyway. For Peter to talk so openly with you about our relationship is a compliment. Apparently he felt comfortable enough to do so, and that reflects well on the kind of mother you are."

Carol hadn't considered it in those terms, but he was right. She and Peter were close.

"Now, about you and me," Alex went on, "we're both adults."

But Carol felt less mature than an adolescent when it came to Alex. She trembled every time she thought of him, and that was far more often than she would've liked. When he touched and kissed her, her hormones went berserk, and her heart seemed to go into spasms. No wonder she was frightened by the things Alex made her experience.

"I like you, and I'm fairly confident you like me."

She agreed with a sharp nod, knowing it wouldn't do any good to deny it.

"The fact is, I like everything about you, and that feeling increases whenever we're together. Now, if it happens that this attraction between us continues, then so be it. Wonderful. Great. It would be a big mistake for us to allow two teenage boys to dictate our relationship. Agreed?"

Once more, Carol nodded.

"Good." He stood, bringing her with him. "Now we both have to get back to work." Tucking her hand in the crook of his arm, he strode back toward the parking lot, pausing when he came to his van. He opened the door, then turned to face her.

"It seems to me we should seal our agreement."

"Seal it? I don't understand." But she did.... His wonderful, mist-gray eyes were spelling out exactly what he meant.

He caressed her cheek, then traced the outline of her lips. Whatever it was about his touch that sent her heart into such chaos, Carol couldn't understand. She reacted by instinct, drawing his finger between her lips, touching it with the tip of her tongue. The impact of her action showed in his eyes with devastating clarity.

He leaned forward and slipped his finger aside, replacing it with his mouth. His kiss was exquisitely slow and wildly erotic.

When he broke away they were both shaking. Carol stared up at him, her breath ragged, her lips parted and eager.

"I've got to get back to work...." she whispered.

"I know," Alex said. But he didn't make any effort to leave.

Instead he angled his head and dropped tiny kisses on her neck, then her ear, taking the lobe in his mouth before trailing his lips in heart-stopping increments back to hers. She was ready for him this time, more than ready.

The sound of a car door slamming somewhere in the

distance abruptly returned them to the real world. Carol leaped back, her eyes startled, her breathing harsh and uneven. She smoothed her hands down the front of her uniform, as though whisking away wrinkles. She'd been kissing him like a lover and in broad daylight! To her chagrin, Alex didn't look at all dismayed by what had happened between them, just pleased.

"I wish you hadn't done that," she said, knowing he wasn't the only one to blame—but at the moment, the most convenient.

"Oh, baby, I don't regret a thing."

She folded her arms over her chest. "I've got to get back inside." But she had to wait until the flush of desire had left her face and her body had stopped trembling.

"It seems to me," Alex said with a smile of supreme confidence, "that if kissing you is this good, then when we finally make love it'll be downright dangerous." With that, he climbed into the driver's seat, closed the door and started the engine.

"You didn't call me," Carol's mother complained the following Friday evening. "All week I waited for you to phone and tell me about your date with the non-Italian."

"I'm sorry, Mama," Carol said, glancing at the kitchen clock. Alex was due to pick her up for the Home Show in ten minutes. Peter was staying overnight at a friend's, and she was running behind schedule as it was. The last thing she wanted to do was argue with her mother.

"You *should* be sorry. I could have died this week and you wouldn't have known. Your uncle in Jersey City would've had to call you and tell you your mother was dead."

"Mama, Peter started track this week, and we've gotten home late every single night."

"So don't keep me in suspense. Tell me."

Carol paused. "About what?"

"Your date with that Englishman. Did he take you to bed?"

"Mama!" Sometimes the things her mother said actually shocked Carol. "Of course not."

"It's a shame. Are you seeing him again? But don't wear those shoes with the pointed toes or he'll think you're a loose woman. And to be on the safe side, don't mention your cousin Celeste."

"Mama, I can't talk now. Alex will be here any minute—we're going to the Home Show. His company has a booth there, and it'd be impolite to keep him waiting."

"Do you think he'll convert?"

"Mama, I'm not marrying Alex."

"Maybe not," her mother said with a breathless sigh, "but then again, who knows?"

The doorbell chimed, and Carol, who'd been dreading this evening from the moment she'd agreed to it, was flooded with a sense of relief.

"Bye, Mama."

Angelina said her farewells and added something about bringing Alex over to try her pasta. Carol was putting down the receiver by the time her mother had finished issuing her advice.

The doorbell rang again as Carol hurried into the living room. She rushed to open the door. "I'm sorry it took me so long to answer. My mother was on the phone."

"Did she give you any advice?" Alex teased.

"Just a little. She said it might not be a good idea if I mentioned my cousin Celeste."

"Who?"

"Never mind." Carol laughed a little nervously. Alex looked too good to be true, and the warm, open appreciation in his eyes did wonders for her self-esteem.

"You were worth the wait."

Carol could feel the blush in her cheeks. She wasn't used to having men compliment her, although her family was free with praise and always had been. This was different, however. Alex wasn't family.

His eyes compelled her forward, and she stepped toward him without question, then halted abruptly, realizing she'd very nearly walked into his arms.

"I'll…get my purse." She turned away, but his hand at her shoulder turned her back.

"Not yet."

"Alex…I don't think we should—"

But that was all the protest she was allowed. She closed her eyes as he ran his hand through her hair, then directed her mouth to his with tender restraint. He kissed her lightly at first, until she was pliant and willing in his arms….

When he pulled away from her, she slowly, languorously, opened her eyes to meet his.

"Don't look at me like that," he groaned. "Come on, let's get out of here before we end up doing something we're not ready to deal with yet."

"What?" Carol asked, blinking, still too dazed to think coherently.

"I think you know the answer to that."

They were in Alex's car before either of them spoke again. "If it's okay with you, I've got to stop at the office and pick up some more brochures," Alex said. "We're running low already."

"Of course it's okay," Carol told him. It was a good thing she was sitting down because her legs seemed too weak to support her. She was sure her face was flushed, and she'd rarely felt this shaky.

Her mind became her enemy as Alex headed toward the freeway. Try as she might, she couldn't stop thinking about how he'd felt against her. So strong and warm. A thin sheen of perspiration moistened her upper lip, and she swiped at it, eager to dispel the image that refused to leave her mind.

"How far is your office?" Carol asked after several strained minutes had passed. Alex seemed unusually quiet himself.

"Another quarter of an hour."

Not knowing how else to resume the conversation, she dropped it after that.

"Peter's staying with Dale tonight?" he finally asked.

"Yes. James, too?"

"Yes."

That was followed by ten more minutes of silence. Then Alex exited the freeway.

Carol curled her fingers around the armrest when he stopped at the first red light. The district was an industrial area and well lit.

As soon as he pulled into a side street, she saw his company sign. She'd never asked about his business and was impressed when she saw a small fleet of trucks and vans neatly parked in rows outside. He was apparently far more successful than she'd assumed.

Unlocking the door, Alex let her precede him inside. He flicked a switch, and light immediately flooded the office. One entire wall was lined with filing cabinets. Three desks, holding computers, divided the room. Carol didn't have time to give the room more than a fleeting glance as Alex directed her past the first desk and into another large office. She saw his name on the door.

The room was cluttered. The top of his desk looked as if a cyclone had hit it.

"The brochures are around here someplace," he muttered, picking up a file on a corner of the credenza. "Help yourself to a butterscotch candy."

"Thanks." As Carol reached for one, her gaze fell on the two framed photographs hidden behind a stack of computer printouts. The top of a woman's head showed on one of the photos, but that was all she could see. The second one was of James.

"I've got to get organized one of these days," Alex was saying.

Curious, Carol moved toward the credenza and the two photographs. "Who's this?" She asked, lifting the picture of the woman. She was beautiful. Blond. Blue-eyed. Wholesome. Judging by the hairstyle and clothes, the picture had been taken several years earlier.

Alex paused. "That's Gloria."

"She was your wife?"

Alex nodded, pulled out the high-backed cushioned chair and sank into it. "She died two years ago. Cancer."

It was all Carol could do to hold on to the picture. The pain in his voice stabbed through her.

"I…I thought you were divorced."

"No," Alex said quietly.

Carol continued to study the beautiful woman in the photo. "You loved her, didn't you?"

"So much that when the time came, I wanted to die with her. Yes, I loved her."

With shaking hands, Carol replaced the photograph. Her back was to Alex, and she briefly closed her eyes. She made a rigorous effort to smile when she turned to face him again.

He frowned. "What's wrong?"

"Nothing," she said breezily.

"You look pale all of a sudden. I thought you knew.... I assumed James or Peter had told you."

"No—neither of them mentioned it."

"I'm sorry if this comes as a shock."

"There's no reason to apologize."

Alex nodded, sighed and reached for her hand, pulling her down into his lap. "I figured you'd understand better than most what it is to lose someone you desperately love."

Chapter 6

"Gloria had problems when James was born," Alex began. His hold on Carol's waist tightened almost painfully, but she was sure he wasn't aware of it. "The doctors said there wouldn't be any more children."

"Alex, please, there's no need to tell me this."

"There is," he said. "I want you to know. It's important to me...."

Carol closed her eyes and pressed her forehead against the side of his head. She knew intuitively that he didn't often speak of his late wife, and that he found it difficult to do so now.

Alex wove his fingers into her hair. "In the years after Jim's birth, Gloria's health was never good, but the doctors couldn't put their finger on what was wrong. She was weak and tired a lot of the time. It wasn't until Jim was in junior high that we learned she had leukemia—myelocytic leukemia, one of the most difficult forms to treat." He paused and drew in an unsteady breath.

"Alex," she pleaded, her hands framing his face. "Don't, please—this is obviously so painful for you." But the moment her eyes met his, she knew nothing she said or did would stop him. She sensed that only sharing it now, with her, would lessen the trauma of his memories.

"We did all the usual things—the chemotherapy, the other drugs—but none of it helped, and she grew steadily worse. Later, when it was clear that nothing else could be done, we opted for a bone-marrow transplant. Her sister and mother flew in from New York, and her sister was the better match. But…that didn't work, either."

Carol stroked his cheek, yearning to do anything she could to lessen the pain.

He hesitated and drew in a quavering breath. "She suffered so much. That was the worst for me to deal with. I was her husband, and I'd sworn to love and protect her, and there wasn't a thing I could do…not a single, solitary thing."

Tears moistened Carol's eyes, and she struggled to keep them at bay.

Alex's voice remained firm and controlled, but Carol recognized the pain he was experiencing. "I didn't know what courage was until I watched Gloria die," he whispered. He closed his eyes. "The last three weeks of her life, it was obvious she wasn't going to make it. Finally she fell into a coma and was put on a respirator. The doctors knew she'd never come out of it and so did the nurses. I could see them emotionally removing themselves, and I couldn't bear it. I became a crazy man, refusing to leave her side, letting no one care for her but me. I held on to her hand and silently willed her to live with every breath I took. I honestly believe I kept her alive by the sheer force of my will. I was afraid to leave her, afraid that when I did, she'd slip silently into death. Eventually that was exactly what happened. I left her because Jim needed me and because I knew that at some point I'd have to leave. I sat in the hospital waiting room with my son, telling him about his mother, and suddenly a pain, an intense stabbing pain, shot through me—" he hesitated and gave a ragged sigh "—and in that instant, I knew she was gone. I've never felt anything like it. A few minutes later, a nurse came for me. I can remember that scene so vividly—my mind's played it back so many times.

"I stood up and Jim stood with me, and I brought my son as close to my side as I could, looked the nurse in the eye and said, 'She's gone, isn't she?' The nurse nodded and Jim started to cry and I just stood there, dazed and numb. I don't remember walking back to Gloria's room, but somehow I found myself there. I lifted her into my arms and held her and told her how sorry I was that I'd been so stubborn and selfish, keeping her with me those three weeks, refusing to let her die. I told her how I would much rather have been with her, how I'd wanted to hold her hand as she stepped from one life into the next."

By now Carol was weeping softly, unabashedly.

Alex's fingers stroked her hair. "I didn't mean for you to cry," he whispered, and his regret seemed genuine. "You would have liked her."

Carol had felt the same way from the first moment

she'd seen Gloria's photograph. Nodding, she hid her face in the strong curve of his neck.

"Carol," he whispered, caressing her back, "look at me."

She sniffled and shook her head, unwilling to let him witness the strength of her emotion. It was one thing to sit on his lap, and entirely another to look him in the eye after he'd shared such a deep and personal part of himself.

His lips grazed the line of her jaw.

"No," she cried softly, her protest faint and nearly inaudible, "don't touch me...not now." He'd come through hell, suffered the torment of losing his wife, and he needed Carol. He was asking for her. But her comfort could only be second-best.

"Yes," he countered, lifting her head so he could look at her. Against her will, against her better judgment, her gaze met his. His eyes were filled with such hunger that she all but gasped. Again and again, they roamed her face, no doubt taking in the moisture that glistened on her cheeks, the way her lips trembled and the staggering need she felt to comfort him. Even if that comfort was brief, temporary, a momentary solace.

"I'm sorry I upset you." He wove his fingers into her hair and directed her lips to his. His mouth was warm and moist and gentle. No one had ever touched her with such tenderness and care. No kiss had ever affected her so deeply. No kiss had ever shown her such matchless beauty.

Tears rained down Carol's face. Sliding her fingers through his hair, she held him close. He was solid and muscular and full of strength. His touch had filled the hollowness of her life and, she prayed, had helped to ease his own terrible loneliness.

"Carol," he breathed, sounding both stunned and dismayed, "what is it? What's wrong?"

"Nothing," she whispered. "Everything."

"I'm sorry…so sorry," he said in a low voice.

Confused and uncertain, Carol turned to face him. "You are? Why?"

"For rushing you. For thinking of my own needs instead of yours."

"No…" She shook her head, incapable of expressing what she felt.

"Are you going to be all right?"

She nodded, still too shaken to speak.

He placed his hands on the curve of her shoulder and kissed the crown of her head. "Thank you."

"For what?" Reluctantly her eyes slid to his.

"For listening, for being here when I needed you."

All she could manage in response was a tremulous smile.

For the rest of the evening, Alex was a perfect gentleman. He escorted her to the Home Show, where they spent several hours wandering from one display to another, discussing the ideas and products represented. They strolled hand in hand, laughing, talking, debating ideas. Carol was more talkative than usual; it helped disguise her uneasiness. She told him about her plan to dig up a portion of her back lawn and turn it into an herb garden. At least when she was talking, her nerve endings weren't left uncovered and she didn't have to deal with what had happened a few hours before…

After they'd toured the Home Show, Alex took her out to eat at a local Greek restaurant. By that time of the evening, Carol should have been famished, since they were having dinner so late. But whatever appetite she'd had was long gone.

When Alex dropped her off at the house, he kissed her good-night, but if he was expecting an invitation to come inside, he didn't receive one.

Hours later, she lay staring at the ceiling, while shadows of the trees outside her window frolicked around the light fixture like dancing harem girls. Glaring at the clock radio, Carol punched her pillow several times and twisted around so she lay on her stomach, her arms cradling her head. She *should* be sleepy. Exhausted. Drained after a long, trying week. Her job took its toll in energy, and normally by Friday night, Carol collapsed the moment she got into bed, waking refreshed Saturday morning.

She would've liked to convince herself that Alex had nothing to do with this restless, trapped feeling. She tried to analyze what was bothering her so much. It wasn't as though Alex had never kissed her before this evening. The impact he had on her senses shouldn't come as any surprise. She'd known from the first night they'd met that Alex had the power to expose a kaleidoscope of emotions within her. With him, she felt exhilarated, excited, frightened, reborn.

Perhaps it was the shock of passion he'd brought to life when he'd kissed her. No, she mused, frowning, she'd yearned for him to do exactly that even before they'd arrived at his office.

Squeezing her eyes closed, she tried to force her body to relax. She longed to snap her fingers and drift magically into the warm escape of slumber. It was what she wanted, what she needed. Maybe in the morning, she'd be able to put everything into perspective.

Closing her eyes, however, proved to be a mistake. Instead of being engulfed by peace, she was confronted with the image of Alex's tormented features as he told her about Gloria. *I figured you'd understand better than most what it is to lose someone you desperately love.*

Carol's eyes flew open. Fresh tears pooled at the edges as her sobs took control. She'd loved Bruce. She'd hated Bruce.

Her life ended with his death and her life had begun again.

It was the end; it was the beginning.

There hadn't been tears when he'd died—not at first but later. Plenty of tears, some of profound sadness, and others that spoke of regrets. But there was something more. A release. Bruce had died, and at the same moment, she and Peter had been set free from the prison of his sickness and his abuse.

The tears burned her face as she sobbed quietly, caught in the horror of those few short years of marriage.

Bruce shouldn't have died. He was too young to have wasted his life. Knowing he'd been drunk and with another woman hadn't helped her deal with the emotions surrounding his untimely death.

I figured you'd understand better than most what it is to lose someone you desperately love. Only Carol didn't know. Bruce had destroyed the love she'd felt for him long before his death. He'd ravaged all trust and violated any vestiges of respect. She'd never known love the way Alex had, never shared such a deep and personal commitment with anyone—not the kind Alex had shared with Gloria, not the kind her mother had with her father.

And Carol felt guilty. Guilty. Perhaps if she'd been a better wife, a better mother, Bruce would have stopped drinking. If she'd been more desirable, more inventive in the kitchen, a perfect housekeeper. Instead she felt guilty. It might not be rational or reasonable but it was how she felt.

"Well?" Peter asked as he let himself in the front door the next morning. He dumped his sleeping bag on the kitchen floor, walked over to Carol and dutifully kissed her cheek.

"Well, what?" Carol said, helping herself to a second cup of coffee. She didn't dare look in the mirror, suspecting there were dark smudges under her eyes. At most, she'd slept two hours all night.

"How did things go with Mr. Preston?"

Carol let the steam rising from her coffee mug revive her. "You never told me James's mother had died."

"I didn't? She had leukemia."

"So I heard," Carol muttered. She wasn't angry with her son, and Alex's being a widower shouldn't make a whole lot of difference, but for reasons she was only beginning to understand, it did.

"James said it took his dad a long time to get over his mother's death."

Carol felt her throat muscles tighten. He wasn't over her, not really.

"James keeps a picture of her in his room. She was real pretty."

Carol nodded, remembering the bright blue eyes smiling back at her from the framed photograph in Alex's office. Gloria's warmth and beauty were obvious.

"I thought we'd work in the backyard this morning," Carol said, as a means of changing the subject.

"Aw, Mom," Peter groaned. "You know I hate yard work."

"But if we tackle everything now, it won't overwhelm us next month."

"Are you going to plant a bunch of silly flowers again? I don't get it. Every year you spend a fortune on that stuff. If you added it all up, I bet you could buy a sports car with the money."

"Buy who a sports car?" she challenged, arms akimbo.

"All right, all right." Peter clearly didn't want to argue. "Just tell me what I have to do."

Peter's attitude could use an overhaul, but Carol wasn't in the best of moods herself. Working with the earth, thrusting her fingers deep into the rich soil, was basic to her nature and never more than now.

The sun was out when Carol, dressed in her oldest pair of jeans and a University of Oregon sweatshirt, knelt in front of her precious flower beds. She'd tied a red bandanna around her head, knotting it at the back.

Peter brought his portable CD player outside and plugged it into the electrical outlet on the patio. Next, he arranged an assortment of CDs in neat piles.

Carol glanced over her shoulder and groaned inwardly. She was about to be serenaded with music that came with words she found practically impossible to understand. Although maybe that was a blessing…

"Just a minute," Peter yelled and started running toward the kitchen.

That was funny. Carol hadn't even heard the phone ring. Ignoring her son, she knelt down, wiping her wrist under her nose. The heat was already making her perspire. Bending forward, she dug with the trowel, cultivating the soil and clearing away a winter's accumulation of weeds.

"Morning."

At the sound of Alex's voice, Carol twisted around to confront him. "Alex," she whispered. "What are you doing here?"

"I came to see you."

"Why?"

He joined her, kneeling beside her on the lush, green grass. His eyes were as eager as if it had been weeks since he'd seen her instead of a few hours.

"What are you doing here?" she demanded again, digging more vigorously than necessary. She didn't want to have this conversation. It was too soon. She hadn't fully recovered from their last encounter and was already facing another one.

"I couldn't stay away," he said, his voice harsh and husky at once, and tinged with a hint of anger as if the lack of control bothered him. "You were upset last night, and we both ignored it instead of talking about it the way we should have."

"You were imagining things," she said, offering him a false smile.

"No, I wasn't. I felt guilty, too."

"Guilty?" she cried. "Whatever for?"

"Because I told you about Gloria and didn't ask about your husband. It would've been the perfect time for you to tell me."

Carol's stomach lurched. "That was a long time ago…and best forgotten."

"But you loved him and were saddened by his death, and I should've realized that talking about Gloria would be especially painful for you. I should have been more sensitive."

She shut her eyes. "There's no reason to feel guilty. You talked openly and honestly, and I appreciated knowing about your wife."

"Maybe so," Alex conceded, "but I frightened you, and now you're feeling confused."

"Nothing could be further from the truth." She continued to work, dragging the trowel through the damp soil.

Alex chuckled softly. He gripped her shoulders and turned her toward him as he scanned her features. "You shouldn't lie, Carol Sommars. Because you blush every time you do."

"That's ridiculous." As if on cue, she felt her cheeks grow pink. Carol groaned inwardly, furious with Alex and even more so with herself.

"No, it isn't ridiculous." He paused, and his mouth quivered as he studied her. "You're doing it now."

"Where are the boys?"

Alex's chuckle deepened. "Don't try changing the subject—it isn't going to work."

"Alex, please."

"Hey, Mom, you'll never guess what!"

Grateful for the distraction, Carol dragged her eyes away from Alex and turned to her son, who stood on the patio, looking exceptionally pleased.

"What is it, Peter?"

"James and Mr. Preston brought over one of those fancy, heavy-duty tillers. They're going to dig up that garden space you've been talking about for the past two summers."

Carol's gaze flew back to Alex's, full of unspoken questions.

"You said something last night about wanting to grow an herb garden, didn't you?"

"Yes, but why…I mean, you don't have to do this." She felt flustered and surprised and overwhelmed that he'd take a casual comment seriously and go out of his way to see that her wish was fulfilled.

"Of course I don't have to, but I want to. Peter and James and I are your willing servants, isn't that right, boys?" Neither bothered to answer, being far more interested in sorting through the CDs Peter had set out.

Two hours later, Carol had been delegated to the kitchen by all three men, who claimed she was a world-class nuisance.

"Mom," Peter said, "do something constructive like make lunch. You're in the way here."

Slightly taken aback by her son's assessment of her role, Carol muttered under her breath and did as he asked. Her ego suffered further when James sent his friend a grateful glance. Even Alex seemed pleased to have her out from under their capable feet.

Twenty minutes later, Alex entered the kitchen. He paused when he saw her stacking sandwiches on a platter. He walked over to her, slipped his arms around her waist and nuzzled her neck.

"Alex," she protested in a fierce whisper, "the boys will see you."

"So?"

"So, what they're thinking is bad enough without you adding fuel to the fire."

"They're too busy to care."

"I care!"

His growl was low as he slid his hand from her navel up her midriff. "I know."

"If you don't stop I'll…I'll…I'm not sure what I'll do—but it won't be pleasant." Her threat was an empty one, and Alex knew it as well as she did. She was trembling the way she always did when he touched her. The more intimate the caress, the more she shivered.

"I told the boys I was coming inside to pester you, and I'm nothing if not a man of my word," Alex informed her, clearly relishing her shyness.

"Alex…"

"Don't say it," he murmured. "I already know—this isn't the time or the place. I agree, but I don't have to like it." Slowly and with great reluctance, he released her.

Carol was aware of every nuance of this man. He made the most innocent caress sweet with sensations. His touch only created a need for more. Much more.

Once he'd released her, Carol sighed with relief—or was it regret? She no longer had any idea. She carried the platter of sandwiches to the table and brought out a pitcher of fresh lemonade.

Alex pulled out a chair and sat down. "I like watching you move," he whispered. "I like touching you even more."

"Alex…please don't. You're making me blush."

He laughed lightly. "I like that, too. Being with you makes me feel alive again. I hadn't realized how…desensitized I'd become to life. The first time we kissed I discovered what I'd been missing. All those arranged dates, all those wasted evenings—and all that time you were right under my nose and I didn't even know it."

"I…I think I'll put out two kinds of chips," Carol

said, completely unsettled by the way he spoke so openly, so frankly.

"You're beautiful." His eyes were dark, filled with the promise of things to come. "So beautiful…"

"Alex, please." She leaned against the counter, overwhelmed by his words.

"I can't help it. I feel as though I've been granted a second chance at life. Tell me I'm not behaving like an idiot. Tell me you feel it, too."

She did feel everything he did, more profoundly than she dared let him know. "We've both been alone too long," she said. "People in situations like ours must think these kinds of thoughts all the time."

Her comment didn't please him. He frowned and slowly stood. "You may find this difficult to believe, Carol, but there hasn't been anyone since Gloria who made me feel the things you do. And trust me, there've been plenty who tried."

Gulping, Carol whirled around and made busy work opening a bag of potato chips.

Alex joined her, leaning against the counter and facing her so she couldn't ignore him. "You, on the other hand, don't even need to touch me to make me respond. You might not want to admit it, but it's the same for you."

"When you decide to pester someone, you don't do it by half measures, do you?" she muttered.

"Admit it, Carol."

"I…"

He slid his lips across hers. "Are you ready to admit it yet?"

"No, I—"

He bent forward and kissed her again.

Carol's knees buckled and she swayed toward him.

Alex instantly reached for her. Without question, without protest, Carol fell into his arms, so hungry for his touch, she felt as if she were on fire.

The sound of someone clearing his throat was followed by, "Hey, we're not interrupting anything, are we?" Peter was standing just inside the kitchen. "In case you two haven't noticed, it's lunchtime."

Chapter 7

Alex pressed one knee down on the green and stretched out his putter, judging the distance to the hole with a sharp eye. He'd been playing golf with Barney every Sunday afternoon for years.

"So when do I get to meet this female dynamo?" Barney asked after Alex had successfully completed the shot.

"I don't know yet," Alex said as he retrieved his golf ball. He inserted the putter back inside his bag before striding toward the cart.

"What do you mean, you don't know?" Barney echoed. "What's with you and this woman? I swear you've been a different man since you met her. You stare off into space with this goofy look on your face. I talk to you and you don't hear me, and when I ask you about her, you get defensive."

"I'm not defensive, I'm in love."

"Alex, buddy, listen to the voice of experience. You're not in love, you're in lust. I recognize that gleam in your eye. Ten to one you haven't slept with her yet. So I recommend that you get her in the sack and be done with it before you end up doing something foolish."

Alex's gaze fired briefly as he looked at his friend. How did Barney know the progress of his relationship with Carol?

"I have every intention of sleeping with her. Only I plan to be doing that every night for the rest of my life. Carol's not the type of woman to have a fling, and I refuse to insult her by suggesting one."

Barney stared at Alex as if seeing him for the first time. "I don't think I ever realized what an old-fashioned guy you are. Apparently you haven't noticed, but the world's become a lot more casual. Our clothes are casual, our conversations are casual and, yes, even our sex is casual. In case you hadn't heard, you don't have to marry a woman to take her to bed."

"Continue in this vein," Alex said, "and you're going to become a casual friend."

Barney rolled his eyes dramatically. "See what I mean?"

If three wives hadn't been able to change Barney's attitude, Alex doubted he could, either. "As I recall, the last time we had this conversation," Alex reminded him, "you said settling down was the thing to do. I'm only following your advice."

"But not yet," Barney said. "You haven't played the field enough. There are riches out there—" he gestured with his hands "—female gold nuggets just waiting to be picked up, then set gently back in place for the next treasure-hunter."

"You mean like Bambi and what was the name of the other one? Barbie?"

"Stop being clever," Barney snickered. "I have your best interests at heart, and frankly I'm concerned. Two years after Gloria's gone, you suddenly announce it's time to start dating again. Man, I was jumping up and down for joy. Then you go out with a grand total of ten different women—most of them only once—and calmly inform me you've met *the one.* You plan to marry her, just like that, and you haven't even slept with her yet. How are you going to find out if you're sexually compatible?"

"We're compatible, trust me."

"You may think so now, but *bingo*, once she's got a wedding band, it's a totally different story."

"Stop worrying, would you?" Alex eased his golf cart into his assigned space. From the day he'd decided to look for another wife, Barney had been a constant source of amusement. The problem was, his most hilarious moments had come in the form of women his friend had insisted he meet.

"But, Alex, I *am* worried about you," Barney muttered as he lifted his clubs from the back of the cart. "You don't know women the way I do. They're scheming, conniving, money-hungry, and how they get their clutches into you is by marriage. Don't be so eager to march up the aisle with Carol. I don't want you to go through what I have."

After three wives, three divorces and child support payments for two separate families, Barney was speaking from experience—of a particularly negative sort.

"Gloria was special," his longtime friend said. "You're not going to find another one like her. So if it's those qualities that attract you to Carol, look again. You may only be seeing what you want to see."

"You wanna yell?" Angelina Pasquale shouted from the doorway of the kitchen into the living room where her grandchildren were squabbling. "Then let's have a contest. But remember—I've been doing it longer. They can hear me all the way in Jersey City."

Peter and his younger cousins ceased their shouting match, and with a nod of her head, Angelina returned to the kitchen, satisfied that a single threat from her was enough to bring about peace that would last through the afternoon.

Carol was busy slicing tomatoes for the salad, and her sister-in-law, Paula, was spreading garlic butter on thick slices of French bread.

The sauce was warming on the stove, and the water for the long strands of fresh pasta was just starting to boil. The pungent scent of basil and thyme circled the kitchen like smoke from a campfire. From Carol's earliest memory, her mother had cooked a pot of spaghetti sauce every Saturday evening. The unused portion from Sunday's dinner was served in a variety of ways during the week. Leftover pot roast became something delectable with her mother's sauce over top. And chicken with Mama's sauce rivaled even the Cajun chicken at Jake's restaurant.

"So, Carol," her mother began, wiping her hands on the ever-present apron. She took a large wooden spoon and stirred the kettle of simmering sauce. "I suppose your English friend thinks good spaghetti sauce comes from a jar," she said disparagingly. This was her way of letting Carol know the time had come to invite Alex and his son to Sunday dinner.

"Mama, Alex plays golf on Sundays."

"Every Sunday?"

Carol nodded.

"That's because he's never tasted my sauce." Angelina shook her head as though to suggest Alex had wasted much of his life walking from green to green when he could've been having dinner at her house.

Adding serving utensils to the salad, Carol set the wooden bowl on the dining room table.

Tony, Carol's brother, sauntered into the kitchen and slipped his arms around Paula's waist. "How much longer until dinner? The natives are getting restless."

"Eleven minutes," Angelina answered promptly. She tasted the end of the wooden spoon and nodded in approval.

Carol returned to the kitchen and noticed that her mother was watching her under the guise of waiting for the water to boil. The question Carol had expected all day finally came.

"You gonna marry this non-Italian?" her mother asked, then added the noodles, stirring with enough energy to create a whirlpool in the large stainless-steel pot.

"Mama," Carol cried. "I barely know Alex. We've only gone out a handful of times."

"Ah, but your eyes are telling me something different."

"The only thing my eyes are interested in is some of that garlic bread Paula's making," Carol said, hoping to divert her mother's attention from the subject of Alex.

"Here." Her sister-in-law handed her a slice. "But it's

no substitute for a man." Paula turned her head to press a quick kiss on her husband's cheek.

Tony's hands slipped further around Paula's waist as he whispered in his wife's ear. From the way her sister-in-law's face flooded with warm color, Carol didn't need much of an imagination to guess what Tony had said.

Carol looked away. She wasn't embarrassed by the earthy exchange between her brother and his wife; instead, she felt a peculiar twinge of envy. The realization shocked her. In all the years she'd been alone, Carol had never once longed for a pair of arms to hold her or for a man to whisper suggestive comments in her ear. Those intimacies were reserved for the happily married members of her family.

Yet, here she was, standing in the middle of her mother's kitchen, yearning for Alex to stroll up behind her, circle her waist and whisper promises in her ear. The image was so vivid that she hurried into the living room to escape it.

It wasn't until later, when the dishes were washed, that Carol had a chance to sort through her thoughts. Tony and Peter were puttering around in the garage. Paula was playing a game of Yahtzee with the younger children. And Angelina was rocking in her chair, nimble fingers working delicate yarn into a sweater for her smallest grandchild.

"So are you gonna tell your mama what's troubling you?" she asked Carol out of the blue.

"Nothing's wrong," Carol fibbed. She couldn't discuss what she didn't understand. For the first time, she felt distanced from the love and laughter that was so much a part of Sunday dinner with her family. For years she'd clung to the life she'd built for herself and her son. These few, short weeks with Alex had changed everything.

Alex had discovered all her weaknesses and used them to his own advantage. Digging up the earth for her herb garden was a good example. She could've asked her brother to do it for her. Eventually she probably would have. But Tony did so much to help her already that she didn't want to burden him with another request. It wasn't as if tilling part of the backyard was essential. But one casual mention to Alex, and next thing she knew, there was freshly tilled earth waiting for basil and Italian parsley where before there'd been lawn.

"You like this man, don't you?"

Carol responded with a tiny nod of her head.

A slow, easy smile rose from her mother's mouth to her eyes. "I thought so. You got the look."

"The look?"

"Of a woman falling in love. Don't fight it so hard, my *bambina.* It's time you met a man who brings color to your cheeks and a smile to your lips."

But Carol wasn't smiling. She felt confused and ambivalent. She was crazy about Alex; she prayed she'd never see him again. She couldn't picture her life with him; she couldn't picture her life without him.

"I lit a candle in church for you," her mother whispered. "And said a special prayer to St. Rita."

"Mama…"

"God and I had a good talk, and He told me it's predestined."

"What's predestined?"

"You and this non-Italian," her mother replied calmly.

"Mama, that doesn't make the least bit of sense. For

years you've been telling me to marry a rich old man with one foot in the grave and the other on a banana peel. You said everyone loves a rich widow."

"Keep looking for the rich old man, but when you find him, introduce him to me. With any luck his first wife made spaghetti sauce with tomato soup and he'll worship at my feet."

Carol couldn't keep from smiling. She wasn't so sure about her mother lighting candles on her behalf or deciding that marrying Alex was predestined, but from experience she'd learned there wasn't any point in arguing.

Tony, Paula and their two children left around five. Usually Carol headed for home around the same time, but this afternoon she lingered. The 1940s war movie on television held Peter's attention, and her eyes drifted to it now and again.

It wasn't until she felt the moisture on her cheeks that she realized she was crying.

Doing what she could to wipe away the tears so as not to attract attention to herself, she focused on the television screen. Her mother was right; she was falling in love, head over heels in love, and it was frightening her to death.

Silently Angelina set her knitting aside and joined Carol on the sofa. Without a word, she thrust a tissue into Carol's hand. Then she wrapped her arm around her daughter's shoulders and pressed her head tenderly to her generous bosom. Gently patting Carol's back, Angelina whispered soothing words of love and encouragement in a language Carol could only partially understand.

Alex didn't see Carol again until Monday afternoon when he pulled into the high school parking lot. He angled his van in front of the track, four spaces down from her car. He waited a couple of minutes, hoping she'd come and see him of her own free will. He should've known better. The woman wasn't willing to give an inch.

Deciding to act just as nonchalant, Alex opened his door, walked over to the six-foot-high chain-link fence and pretended to be watching the various groups participate in field events. Neither James nor Peter was trying out for any of those positions on the team.

Then he walked casually toward Carol, who was determined, it seemed, to ignore him, hiding behind the pages of a women's magazine.

"Hello, Carol," he said after a decent interval.

"Oh—Alex." She held the magazine rigidly in place.

"Mind if I join you?"

"Not at all." The hesitation was long enough to imply that she would indeed mind. Regardless, he opened the passenger door and slid inside her car. Only then did Carol bother to close the magazine and set it down.

By now, Alex told himself, he should be accustomed to her aloof attitude toward him. It was like this nearly every time they were together. She'd never shown any real pleasure at seeing him. He had to break through those chilly barriers each and every encounter. The strangest part was that he knew she was as strongly attracted to him as he was to her. And not just in the physical sense. Their lives were like matching bookends, he thought.

"Did you have a good day?" he asked politely.

She nodded and glanced away, as though she thought that sharing even a small part of her life with him was akin to admitting she enjoyed his company.

"I suppose it would be too much to hope that you missed me the last couple of days?" he asked.

"Yes."

Alex was almost embarrassed by the way his heart raced. "You missed me," he repeated, feeling like a kid who'd been granted free rein in a candy store.

"No," Carol said, clearly disconcerted. "I meant it would be too much to hope I did."

"Oh." The woman sure knew how to deflate his pride.

"It really was thoughtful of you to dig up that area in my backyard on Saturday. I'm grateful, Alex."

Crossing his arms, Alex leaned against the back of the seat and tried to conceal his injured pride with a lazy shrug. "It was no trouble." Especially since the two boys had done most of the work, leaving him free to "pester" Carol in the kitchen. With everything in him, he wished they were back in that kitchen now. He wanted her in his arms the way she'd been on Saturday afternoon, her lips moist and swollen with his kisses, her eyes dark with passion.

"The boys will be out any minute," Carol said, studying the empty field.

Alex guessed this was his cue to leave her car, but he wasn't taking the hint. When it came to Carol Sommars, he was learning that his two greatest allies were James and Peter.

It was time to play his ace.

Alex waited until the last possible minute. Both boys had walked onto the parking lot, their hair damp from a recent shower. They were chatting and joking and in a good mood. Climbing out of Carol's car, Alex leaned against the fender in a relaxed pose.

"Peter, did you say something about wanting to go camping?" he said, casting Carol a defiant look. "James and I were thinking of heading for the Washington coastline this coming weekend and thought you and your mother might like to go with us."

"We are?" James asked, delighted and surprised.

Peter's eyes widened with excitement. "Camping? You're inviting Mom and me to go camping?"

At the mention of the word *camping,* Carol opened her car door and vaulted out. Her eyes narrowed on Alex as if to declare a foul and charge him a penalty.

"Are you two free this weekend?" Alex asked with a practiced look of innocence, formally extending the invitation. The ball was in her court, and he was interested in seeing how she volleyed this one.

"Yes," Peter shouted. "We're interested."

"No," Carol said at the same moment. "We already have plans."

"We do?" her son moaned. "Come on, Mom, Mr. Preston just offered to take us camping with him and James. What could possibly be more important than that?"

"I wanted to paint the living room."

"What? Paint the living room? I don't believe it." Peter slapped his hands against his thighs and threw back his head. "You know how I feel about camping," he whined.

"Give your mother time to think it over," Alex urged, confident that Carol would change her mind or that Peter would do it for her. "We can talk about it tomorrow evening."

James gave Peter the okay signal, and feeling extraordinarily proud of himself, Alex led the way to his van, handing his son the keys.

"You're going to let me drive?" James asked, sounding more than a little stunned. "Voluntarily?"

"Count your blessings, boy, and drive."

"Yes, sir!"

Carol was furious with Alex. He'd played a faultless game, and she had to congratulate him on his fine closing move. All day she'd primed herself for the way she was going to act when she saw him again. She'd allowed their relationship to progress much further than she'd ever intended, and it was time to cool things down.

With her mother lighting candles in church and having heart-to-heart talks with God, things had gotten completely out of hand. Angelina barely complained anymore that Alex wasn't Catholic, and worse, not Italian. It was as if those two prerequisites no longer mattered.

What Carol hadn't figured on was the rush of adrenaline she'd experienced when Alex pulled into the school parking lot. She swore her heart raced faster than any of the runners on the track. She'd needed every ounce of determination she possessed not to toss aside the magazine she'd planted in the car and run to him, bury her face in his chest and ask him to explain what was happening to her.

Apparently Alex had read her perfectly. He didn't appear at all concerned about her lack of welcome. That hadn't even fazed him. All the arguments she'd amassed had been for naught. Then at the last possible minute he'd introduced the subject of this camping trip, in what she had to admire was a brilliant move. Her chain of resistance was only as strong as the weakest link. And her weakest link was Peter.

Grudgingly she had to admire Alex.

"Mom," Peter cried, restless as a first grader in the seat beside her. "We're going to talk about it, aren't we?"

"About the camping trip?"

"It's the chance of a lifetime. The Washington coast—I've heard it's fabulous—"

"We've got plans."

"To paint the living room? We could do that any old time!"

"Peter, please."

He was silent for a minute or so. The he asked, "Do you remember when I was eleven?"

Here it comes, Carol mused darkly. "I remember," she muttered, knowing it would've been too much to expect him not to drag up the lowest point of her life as a mother.

"We were going camping then, too, remember?"

He said *remember* as though it was a dirty word, one that would get him into trouble.

"You promised me an overnight camping trip and signed us up for an outing through the Y? But when we went to the meeting you got cold feet."

"Peter, they gave us a list of stuff we were supposed to bring, and not only did I not have half the things on the list, I didn't even know what they were."

"You could have asked," Peter cried.

"It was more than that."

"Just because we were going to hike at our own pace? They said we'd get a map. We could've found the camp, Mom, I know we could have."

Carol had had visions of wandering through the woods for days on end with nothing more than a piece of paper that said she should head east—and she had the world's worst sense of direction. If she could get lost in a shopping mall, how would she ever find her way through dense forest?

"That wasn't the worst part," Peter murmured. "Right there in the middle of the meeting you leaned over and asked me what it would cost to buy your way out of the trip."

"You said you wouldn't leave for anything less than a laser tag set," Carol said, tormented by the unfairness of it all. The toy had been popular and expensive at the time and had cost her a pretty penny. But her son had conveniently forgotten that.

"I feel like I sold my soul that day," Peter said with a deep sigh.

"Peter, honestly!"

"It wasn't until then that I realized how much I was missing by not having a dad."

The kid was perfecting the art of guilt.

"Now, once again," he argued, "I have the rare opportunity to experience the great out-of-doors, and it's like a nightmare happening all over again. My own mother's going to pull the rug out from under my feet."

Carol stopped at a red light and pretended to play a violin. "This could warp your young mind for years to come."

"It just might," Peter said, completely serious.

"Twenty years from now, when they lock those prison doors behind you, you can cry out that it's all my fault. If only I'd taken you camping with Alex and James Preston, then the entire course of your life would have been different."

A short pause followed her statement.

"Sarcasm doesn't suit you, Mother."

Peter was right, of course, but Carol was getting desperate. At the rate this day was going, she'd end up spending Saturday night in front of a campfire, fighting off mosquitoes and the threat of wild beasts.

Because she felt guilty, despite every effort not to, Carol cooked Peter his favorite chicken-fried steak dinner, complete with gravy and mashed potatoes.

After the dishes had been cleared and Peter was supposed to be doing his homework, Carol found him talking on the phone, whispering frantically. It wasn't hard to guess that her son was discussing strategies with James. The three of them were clearly in cahoots against her.

Carol waited until Peter was in bed before she marched into the kitchen and righteously punched out Alex's phone number. She'd barely given him a chance to answer before she laid into him with both barrels.

"That was a rotten thing to do!"

"What?" he asked, feigning innocence.

"You know darn well what I'm talking about. Peter's pulled every trick in the book from the moment you mentioned this stupid camping trip."

"Are you going to come or is this war?"

"It's war right now, *Mister* Preston."

"Good. Does the victor get spoils? Because I'm telling you, Carol Sommars, I intend to win."

"Oh, Alex," she said with a sigh, leaning against the wall. She slid all the way down to the floor, wanting to weep with frustration. "How could you do this to me?"

"Easy. I got the idea when you told me it was too much to hope that you'd miss me."

"But I don't know anything about camping. To me, roughing it is going without valet service."

"It'll be fun, trust me."

Trusting Alex wasn't at the top of her priority list at the moment. He'd pulled a fast one on her, and she wasn't going to let him do it again.

"Is Peter sleeping?" Alex asked softly.

"If he isn't, he should be." She didn't understand where this conversation was heading.

"James is asleep, too," he said. "After the cold shoulder you gave me this afternoon, I need something to warm my blood."

"Try a hot water bottle."

"It won't work. Keep the door unlocked and I'll be right over."

"Absolutely not. Alex Preston, listen to me, I'm not dressed for company and—"

It was too late. He'd already disconnected.

Chapter 8

Standing in front of her locked screen door, Carol had no intention of letting Alex inside her home. It was nearly eleven, and they both had to work in the morning. When his car pulled into the driveway, she braced her feet apart and stiffened her back. She should be furious with him. Should be nothing; she *was* furious!

But when Alex climbed out of his car, he stood in her driveway for a moment, facing the house. Facing her. The porch light was dim, just bright enough to outline his handsome features.

With his hands in his pockets, he continued to stand there, staring at her. But that seemed such an inadequate way to describe the intensity of his gaze as his eyes locked with her own. Not a muscle moved in the hard, chiseled line of his jaw, and his eyes feasted on her with undisguised hunger. Even from the distance that separated them, Carol saw that his wonderful gray eyes had darkened with need.

He wanted her.

Heaven help her, despite all her arguments to the contrary, she wanted him, too.

Before he'd marched two steps toward her, Carol had unlocked the screen door and held it open for him.

"I'm not going camping," she announced, her voice scarcely audible. Her lips felt dry and her hands moist. Once she'd stated her position, her breath escaped with a ragged sigh. She thought of ranting at him, calling him a coward and a cheat to use her own son against her the way he had, but not a word made it from her mind to her lips.

Alex turned and shut the front door.

The only light was a single lamp on the other side of the room.

They didn't move, didn't breathe.

"I'm not going to force you to go camping," Alex whispered. "In fact, I..." He paused as he lowered his eyes to her lips, and whatever he intended to say trailed into nothingness.

Carol felt his eyes on her as keenly as she had his mouth.

In an effort to break this unnatural spell, she closed her eyes.

"Carol?"

She couldn't have answered him had her life depended on it. Her back was pressed to the door, and she flattened her hands against it.

Not once during her marriage had Carol felt as she did at that moment. So...needy. So empty.

He came to her in a single, unbroken movement,

his mouth descending on hers. Carol wound her arms around him and leaned into his solid strength, craving it as never before. Again and again and again he kissed her.

"Alex." She tore her lips from his. "Alex," she breathed again, almost panting. "Something's wrong...."

She could feel his breath against her neck and his fingers in her hair, directing her mouth back to his, kissing her with such heat, Carol thought she'd disintegrate.

Her tears came in earnest then, a great profusion that had been building inside her for years. Long, lonely, barren years.

With the tears came pain, pain so intense she could hardly breathe. Agony spilled from her heart. The trauma that had been buried within her stormed out in a torrent of tears that she could no more stop than she could control.

Huge sobs shook her shoulders, giant hiccupping sobs that she felt all the way to her toes. Sobs that depleted her strength. Her breathing was ragged as she stumbled toward the edge of hysteria.

Alex was speaking to her in soft, reassuring whispers, but Carol couldn't hear him. It didn't matter what he said. Nothing mattered.

She clutched his shirt tighter and tighter. Soon there were no more tears to shed, no more emotion to be spent. Alex continued to hold her. He slid his arms all the way around her, and although she couldn't understand what he was saying, his voice was gentle.

Once the desperate crying had started to subside, Carol drew in giant gulps of air in a futile effort to gain control of herself.

Slowly Alex guided her to the sofa and sat her down, then gathered her in his arms and held her tenderly.

Time lost meaning to Carol until she heard the clock chime midnight. Until then she was satisfied with being held in Alex's arms. He asked no questions, demanded no explanations. He simply held her, offering comfort and consolation.

This newfound contentment in his arms was all too short-lived, however. Acute embarrassment stole through the stillness, and fresh tears stung Carol's eyes. Her mind, her thoughts, her memories were steeped in emotions too strong to bear.

"I…I'll make some coffee," she whispered, unwinding her arms from him, feeling she had to escape.

"Forget the coffee."

She broke away and got shakily to her feet. Before he could stop her, she hurried into the kitchen and supported herself against the counter, not sure if she could perform the uncomplicated task of making a pot of coffee.

Alex followed her into the darkened room. He placed one hand on her shoulder and gently turned her around, so she had no choice but to face him. "I want to talk about what happened."

"No…please." She leveled her eyes at the floor.

"We *need* to talk."

"No." She shook her head emphatically. "Not now. Please not now."

A long, desperate moment passed before he gently kissed the crown of her head. "Fine," he whispered. "Not now. But soon. Very soon."

Carol doubted she could ever discuss what had happened between them, but she didn't have the strength or the courage to say so. That would only have invited argument.

"I…I think you should go."

His nod was reluctant. "Will you be all right?"

"Yes." A bold-faced lie if ever there was one. She would never be the same again. She was mortified to the very marrow of her bones by her behavior. How could she ever see him again? And then the pain, the memories came rushing back…

No, she wouldn't be all right, but she'd pretend she was, the same way she'd been pretending from the moment she married Bruce.

The message waiting for Alex when he returned to his office the following afternoon didn't come as any surprise. His secretary handed him the yellow slip, and the instant he saw Carol's name, he knew. She was working late that evening and asked if he could pick up Peter from track and drop him off at the house.

The little coward! He sat at his desk, leaned back in his chair and frowned. He hadn't wanted to leave her the night before. Hadn't wanted to walk out of her kitchen without being assured she was all right. Carol, however, had made it clear that she wanted him to leave. Equally apparent was the fact that his being there had only added to her distress. Whatever Carol was facing, whatever ghost she'd encountered, was ugly and traumatic.

So he'd left. But he hadn't stopped thinking about her all day. The thought of her had filled every waking minute.

Even now, hours later, he could remember in vivid

detail the way she'd started to unfold and blossom right before his eyes. Because of him. For him.

His frown deepened. She'd never talked about her marriage. Alex assumed it had to be the source of her anguish, but he didn't know why. He didn't even know her late husband's name. Questions bombarded him, and he cursed the lack of answers.

And now, his sweet coward had gone into hiding.

"Will you talk to her, Mr. Preston?" Peter begged as he climbed inside the van in the school parking lot. "Mom's never gone camping, and I think she'd probably like it if she gave it half a chance."

"I'll talk to her," Alex promised.

Peter sighed with relief. "Good."

Sounding both confident and proud, James said, "My dad can be persuasive when he wants to be."

Alex intended to be *very* persuasive.

"I tried to reason with Mom this morning, and you know what she said?" Peter's changing voice pitched between two octaves.

"What?"

"She said she didn't want to talk about it. Doesn't that sound just like a woman? And I thought Melody Wohlford was hard to understand."

Alex stifled a chuckle. "I'll tell you boys what I'm going to do. We'll pick up hamburgers on the way home, and I'll drop you both off at my house. Then I'll drive over to your place, Peter, and wait for your mother there."

"Great idea," James said, nodding his approval.

"But while I'm gone, I want you boys to do your homework."

"Sure."

"Yeah, sure," James echoed. "Just do whatever it takes to convince Mrs. Sommars to come on our camping trip."

"I'll do everything I can," Alex said.

Carol let herself in the front door, drained from a long, taxing day at the hospital and exhausted from the sleepless night that had preceded it. That morning, she'd been tempted to phone in sick, but with two nurses already out due to illness, there wasn't anyone to replace her. So she'd gone to work feeling emotionally and physically hungover.

"Peter, I'm home," she called. "Peter?"

Silence. Walking into the kitchen, she deposited her purse on the counter and hurried toward her son's bedroom. She'd contacted Alex and asked that he bring Peter home, with instructions to phone back if he couldn't. She hadn't heard from him, so she'd assumed he'd pick up her son and drop him off at the house.

Peter's room was empty, his bed unmade. An array of clean and dirty clothes littered his floor. Everything was normal there.

This was what she got for trying to avoid Alex, Carol mused, chastising herself. Peter was probably still waiting at the high school track, wondering where she could possibly be.

Sighing, she hurried back into the kitchen and reached for her purse. She had to get him his own cell phone, she decided—it would help in situations like this.

The doorbell rang as she walked through the living room. Impatiently she jerked open the door and her eyes collided with Alex's. She gasped.

"Hello again," he said in the warm, husky way that never failed to affect her. "I didn't mean to startle you."

"You didn't." He had, but she wasn't about to admit it. "Apparently you didn't get my message.... Peter must still be at the school."

"No. He's at my house with James."

"Oh." That hardly expressed the instant dread she felt. They were alone, and there was no escape, at least not by the most convenient means—Peter.

Alex stepped into the house and for the first time, she noticed he was carrying a white paper bag. Her gaze settled on it and she frowned.

"Two Big Macs, fries and shakes," he explained.

"For whom?"

Alex arched his eyebrows. "Us."

"Oh..." He honestly expected her to sit down and eat with him? It would be impossible. "I'm not hungry."

"I am—very hungry. If you don't want to eat, that's fine. I will, and while I'm downing my dinner, we can talk."

It wouldn't do any good to argue, and Carol knew it. Without another word, she turned and walked to the kitchen. Alex followed her, and his movements, as smooth and agile as always, sounded thunderous behind her. She was aware of everything about him. When he walked, when he breathed, when he moved.

His eyes seemed to bore holes in her back, but she ignored the impulse to turn and face him. She couldn't bear to look him in the eye. The memory of what had happened the night before made her cheeks flame.

"How are you?" he asked in that husky, caring way of his.

"Fine," she answered cheerfully. "And you?"

"Not so good."

"Oh." Her heart was pounding, clamoring in her ears. "I'm…sorry to hear that."

"You should be, since you're the cause."

"Me? I'm…sure you're mistaken." She got two plates from the cupboard and set them on the table.

As she stepped past him, Alex grabbed her hand. "I don't want to play word games with you. We've come too far for that…and we're going a lot further."

Unable to listen to his words, she closed her eyes.

"Look at me, Carol."

She couldn't do it. She lowered her head, eyes still shut.

"There's no need to be embarrassed."

Naturally he could afford to be generous. He wasn't the one who'd dissolved in a frenzy of violent tears and emotion. She was just grateful that Peter had slept through the whole episode.

"We need to talk."

"No…" she cried and broke away. "Couldn't you have ignored what happened? Why do you have to drag it up now?" she demanded. "Do you enjoy embarrassing me like this? Do you get a kick out of seeing me miserable?" She paused, breathless, her chest heaving. "Please, just go away and leave me alone."

Her fierce words gave birth to a brief, tense silence.

Grasping her chin between his thumb and forefinger, Alex lifted her head. Fresh emotion filled her chest, knotting in her throat as her eyes slid reluctantly to his.

"I don't know what happened last night," he said. "At least not entirely." His voice was gruff, angry, emotional. "All I know is that I've never felt closer to anyone than I did to you—and I've never felt more helpless.

But we've got something special, Carol, and I refuse to let you throw it away. Understand?"

She bit her lower lip, sniffled, then slowly nodded.

The tension eased from Alex, and he reached for her, gently taking her in his arms. She went without question, hiding her face against his neck.

Long, lazy moments passed before he spoke. "I want you to tell me about your marriage."

"No!" she cried and frantically shook her head.

He was silent again, and she could feel him withdrawing from her—or maybe she was the one withdrawing. She wanted to ask him to be patient with her, to give her breathing room, time to analyze what was happening between them.

Just when she was ready to speak, she felt him relax. He chuckled softly, his warm breath mussing her hair. "All right, I'll strike a bargain with you. If you go camping with me this weekend, I'll drop the subject—not forever, mind you, but until you're comfortable enough to talk about it."

Carol raised her head, her eyes meeting his. "You've got a black heart, Alex Preston."

He chuckled and kissed the tip of her nose. "When it comes to courting you, I've learned I need one."

"I can't believe I'm doing this," Carol muttered as she headed up the steep trail into the trees. The surf pounded the Washington beach far below. But directly in front of her was a narrow path that led straight into the rain forest.

"We don't have to wait for you guys, do we?" James whined. He and Peter were obviously eager to do some exploring on their own.

Carol was about to launch into a long list of cautions when Alex spoke. "Feel free," he told the two boys. "Carol and I will be back at camp in time for dinner. We'll expect you to be there then."

"Great!"

"All *right*."

Within minutes both boys were out of sight, and Carol resumed the increasingly difficult climb. A mountain goat would've had trouble maneuvering this path, she told herself.

"You're doing fine," Alex said behind her. Breathless from the physical exertion required by the steep incline, Carol paused and took a couple of minutes to breathe deeply.

"I love it when you get all hot and sweaty for me."

"Will you stop," she cried, embarrassed and yet amused by his words.

"Never."

To complicate things, Alex moved with grace and skill, even while carrying a backpack. So far, he hadn't even worked up a sweat. Carol, on the other hand, was panting. She hadn't realized how out of shape she was until now.

"The view had better be worth all this effort," she said with a moan five minutes later. The muscles in her calves were beginning to protest, and her heart was pounding so hard it echoed in her ears.

To make matters worse, she'd worn the worst possible combination of clothes. Not knowing what to expect weatherwise, she'd donned heavy boots, jeans and a thick sweatshirt, plus a jacket. Her head was covered with a bright pink cap her mother had knitted for her last Christmas. Should they happen upon a snowstorm, Carol was prepared.

"It's worth the climb," Alex promised. "Do you want me to lead?"

"No way," she said, dismissing his offer. "I'd never be able to keep up with you."

A little while later, Carol staggered into a clearing. She stopped abruptly, astonished by the beauty that surrounded her. The forest she'd just left was dense with a variety of evergreens. Huge limbs were draped with mossy green blankets that hung down so far they touched the spongy ground. Moss-coated stumps dotted the area, some sprouting large white mushroom caps. Wildflowers carpeted the earth and a gentle breeze drifted through the meadow and, catching her breath, Carol removed her hat in a form of worship.

"You're right," she murmured. "This is wonderful... I feel like I'm standing in a cathedral...this makes me want to pray."

"This isn't what I wanted you to see," Alex said, resting his hand on the curve of her shoulder.

"It isn't?" she whispered in disbelief. "You mean there's something better than this?"

"Follow me."

Carol pulled off her jacket, stuffed her hat into one of the pockets and tied the sleeves around her waist. Eagerly she trailed Alex along the winding narrow pathway.

"There's a freshwater cove about a mile from here," he explained, turning back to look at her. "Are you up to the trek?"

"I think so." She felt invigorated. More than that, she felt elated. *Alive.*

"You're being a good sport about all this," Alex said, smiling at her.

"I knew I was going to be okay when I saw that you'd pitched the tents close to the public restrooms. I'm not comfortable unless I'm near something that goes flush in the night."

Alex laughed. They hiked for another twenty minutes and eventually came to the edge of a cliff that fell sharply into the water. The view of bright green waves, contrasted by brilliant blue skies, was beautiful enough to bring tears to Carol's eyes. The park department had set up a chain-link fence along the edge, as well as a rough-hewn bench that had been carved out of an old tree trunk.

Alex gestured for her to sit down. Spreading her coat on the bench, Carol sat down and gazed out at the vista before her.

"You hungry?"

"Starving."

"I thought you would be." He slipped off his pack and set it in front of them. Then he unfastened the zipper and removed a folded plastic bag that resembled the ones Carol used to line her garbage cans.

"What's that?" she asked.

"A garbage bag."

"Oh." Well, that was what it looked like.

Next, he took out a whistle, which he held up for her inspection. "A whistle," he announced unnecessarily. Finally he found what he was searching for and placed a thick chocolate bar and two apples on the bench.

"Without appearing completely stupid," Carol said, biting into her apple, "may I ask why you hauled a garbage bag all the way up here?"

"In case we get lost."

"What?" she cried in alarm. She'd assumed Alex knew his way back to their campsite. He'd certainly implied as much.

"Even the best of hikers have been known to get lost. This is just a precaution."

"When…I mean, I thought you were experienced."

He wiggled his eyebrows suggestively. "I am."

"Alex, this is no time to joke."

"I'm not joking. The garbage bag, the whistle and the chocolate are all part of the hug-a-tree program."

"Hug-a-tree?"

"It's a way of preparing children, or anyone else for that matter, in case they get lost in the woods. The idea is to stay in one place—to literally hug a tree. The garbage bag is for warmth. If you slip inside it, feet first, and crouch down, gathering the opening around your neck, you can keep warm in near-freezing temperatures. It weighs practically nothing. The whistle aids rescuers in locating whoever's lost, and the reason for the candy is obvious."

"Do you mean to tell me we're chowing down on our limited food rations?" Carol bit into her apple again before Alex could change his mind and take it away from her.

"Indeed we are, but then we're practically within sight of the campground, so I don't think we're in any danger of getting lost."

"Good." Too ravenous to care, Carol peeled the paper from the chocolate bar and took a generous bite.

"I was waiting for that," Alex murmured, setting aside his apple.

Carol paused, the candy bar in front of her mouth. "Why?"

"So I could kiss you and taste the chocolate on your lips." He reached for her, and his mouth found hers with such need, such hunger, that Carol groaned. Alex hadn't touched her in days, patiently giving her time to determine the boundaries of their relationship. Now she was starving for him, eager for his kiss, his touch.

His kiss was slow, so slow and deliberate. When he lifted his head Carol moaned and sagged against him.

"You taste sweet," he whispered, tugging at her lower lip with his teeth. "Even sweeter than I expected. Even sweeter than chocolate."

Chapter 9

Her sleeping bag and air mattress didn't look as comfortable as a bed at the Hilton, but they appeared adequate, Carol decided later that night. At least Alex had enough equipment for the four of them. All Carol and Peter owned was one GI Joe sleeping bag, decorated with little green army men, and Carol wasn't particularly excited about having to sleep in that.

They'd hiked and explored most of the afternoon. By the time everything was cleared away after dinner, dusk had settled over Salt Creek Park. Carol was out of energy, but Peter and James insisted they couldn't officially call it camping unless everyone sat around the campfire, toasted marshmallows and sang silly songs. And so a lengthy songfest had ensued.

Carol was yawning when she crawled inside the small tent she was sharing with Peter. Alex and James's larger tent was pitched next to theirs. By the dim light of the lantern hanging from the middle of the tent, Carol undressed, cleaned her face and then slipped into the sleeping bag.

"Is it safe yet?" Peter yelled impatiently from outside the tent.

"Safe and sound," Carol returned. She'd just finished zipping up the bag when Peter pulled back the flap and stuck his head in.

Smiling, he withdrew, and she heard him whisper something to James about how unreasonable women could be. Carol didn't know what she'd done that could be considered unreasonable, and she was too drained to ask.

"Good night, everyone," Carol called out when Peter dimmed the lantern.

There was a mixed chorus of "good nights." Content, she rolled onto her stomach and closed her eyes.

Within minutes Carol was fast asleep.

"Carol."

She woke sometime later as her name was whispered close to her ear. Jerking her head up, she saw Alex kneeling just inside the tent, fully dressed. A shaft of moonlight showed her that he'd pressed his finger to his lips, indicating she should be quiet.

"What is it?"

"I want to show you something."

"Now?"

He grinned at her lack of enthusiasm and nodded.

"It can't wait until morning?" she said, yawning.

"It'll be gone by morning," he whispered. "Get dressed and meet me in five minutes."

She couldn't understand what was so important that she couldn't see it by the light of day.

"If you're not out here in five minutes," he warned in a husky voice from outside her tent, "I'm coming in after you."

Carol grumbled as she scurried around looking for her clothes. It was difficult to pull on her jeans in the cramped space, but with a few acrobatic moves, she managed. Before she crawled out, she tapped Peter's shoulder and told him she'd be back in a few minutes.

Peter didn't seem to care one way or the other.

Alex was waiting for her. His lazy smile wrapped its way around her heart and squeezed tight. For all her moaning and complaining about this camping trip, Carol was having a wonderful time.

"This had better be good," she warned and ingloriously yawned.

"It is," he promised. He held a flashlight and a blanket in one hand and reached for hers with the other. Then he led her toward the beach. Although she was wearing her jacket, the wind made her shiver. Alex must have noticed, because he slid his arm around her shoulder and drew her closer.

"Where are we going?" She found herself whispering, not sure why.

"To a rock."

"A rock," she repeated, incredulous. "You woke me from a sound sleep so I could see a *rock?*"

"Not see, sit on one."

"I couldn't do this at noon in the warm sun?" she muttered, laughing at him.

"Not if you're going to look at the stars."

Carol's step faltered. "Do you mean to tell me you

rousted me from a warm, cozy sleeping bag in the middle of the night to show me a few stars? The very same stars I could see from my own bedroom window?"

Alex chuckled. "Are you always this testy when you just wake up?"

"Always," she told him. Yawning again, she covered her mouth with one hand.

Although the campsite was only a few feet away, it was completely hidden behind a clump of trees. Carol could hear the ocean—presumably at the bottom of some nearby cliff—but she couldn't see it.

"I suppose I should choose a tree now. Which one looks the friendliest to you?" Carol asked.

"A tree? Whatever for?"

"To hug. Didn't you tell me this afternoon that if I ever get lost in the woods a tree is my friend? If we get separated, there's no way I'd ever find my way back to camp."

Alex dropped a kiss on her head. "I won't let you out of my sight for a minute, I promise."

"The last time I trusted a guy, I was eighteen and I was pregnant three weeks later." She meant it as a joke, but once the words were out they seemed to hang in the air between them.

"You were only eighteen when you got married?"

Carol nodded, pulled her hand free from his and shoved it in the pocket of her jacket. She could feel herself withdrawing from him. She drew inside herself a little more.

They walked in silence for several minutes.

Suddenly Alex aimed the flashlight at the ground and paused. "This way."

"Over there?" Carol asked. She squinted but couldn't see any rock.

"Just follow me," Alex said. "And no more wisecracks about what happened the last time you listened to a guy. I'm not your first husband, and it would serve us both well if you remembered that." His words were light, teasing, but they sent Carol reeling.

He reached for her hand, lacing his fingers through hers. She could almost hear the litany of questions in Alex's mind. He wanted her to tell him about Bruce. But no one fully knew what a nightmare her marriage had been. Not even her mother. And Carol wasn't about to drag out all the pain for Alex to examine.

Within a couple of minutes, Alex had located "his" rock. At first Carol thought it looked like all the other rocks, silhouetted against the beach.

He climbed up the side, obviously familiar with its shape and size, then offered Carol his hand. Once they were perched on top, he spread out the blanket and motioned for her to sit down.

Carol did and pulled her knees under her chin.

Alex settled down beside her. "Now," he said, pointing toward the heavens, "can you see *that* outside your bedroom window?"

Having forgotten the purpose of this outing, Carol cast her gaze toward the dark sky, then straightened in wonder and surprise. The sky was so heavy with stars—hundreds, no, thousands of them—that it seemed to sag down and touch the earth. "Oh, Alex," she breathed.

"Worth waking up for?" he asked.

"Well worth it," she said, thanking him with a smile.

"I thought you'd think so." His returning smile flew straight into her heart.

She'd been struck by so much extraordinary beauty in such a short while that she felt almost overwhelmed. Turning her head slightly, she smiled again at this man who had opened her eyes to life, to beauty, to love and whispered fervently, "Thank you, Alex."

"For what?"

"For the hike in the rain forest, for the view of the cove, for ignoring my complaints and showing me the stars, for…everything." For coming into her life. For leading her by the hand. For being so patient with her.

"You're welcome."

Lost in the magic, Carol closed her eyes and inhaled the fragrant scent of the wind, the ocean and the night. Rarely had she experienced this kind of contentment and uncomplicated happiness.

When the breeze came, the trees whispered, and the sound combined with the crashing of the surf below. The scents of pine and sea drifted over her. Throwing back her head, Carol tried to take it all in.

"I don't think I appreciated how truly beautiful you are until now," Alex murmured. His face was carved in severe but sensual lines, and his eyes had darkened with emotion.

Carol turned, and when she did, he brushed back the curls from her cheek. His hand lingered on her face, and Carol covered it with her own, closing her eyes at all the sensations that accompanied his touch.

He brought his free hand to her hair, which he threaded through his fingers as though the texture was pure silk. He traced her lower lip with his finger. Unable to resist, Carol circled it with the tip of her tongue….

Time seemed to stand still as Alex's eyes sought and held hers.

He kissed her, and it was excruciatingly slow. Exquisitely slow.

He pressed warm kisses in the hollow of her neck and slipped his hands inside her jacket, circling her waist and bringing her closer. "The things you do to me," he said in a low voice.

"The things I do to *you?*" She rested her forehead against his own. "They can't compare to what you do—have always done—to me."

His lips twitched with the beginnings of a smile, and Carol leaned forward just enough to kiss him again.

Under her jacket Alex slid his hands up her back. He stopped abruptly, went still and tore his mouth from hers.

"What's wrong?" Carol asked, lifting her head. Her hands were on his shoulders.

"You're not wearing a bra, are you?"

"No. You said I had only five minutes to dress, so I hurried."

His eyes burned into hers, then moved lower to the snap of her jeans. "Did you…take any other shortcuts?"

"Wanna find out?"

He shook his head wildly. "I…I promised myself when you agreed to go camping that I'd do everything I could to keep my hands off you." Although she was still in his arms, Carol had to strain to hear him.

"I think that was a wise decision," she murmured, looking up at him. Alex's expression was filled with surprise. An inner happiness she'd banished from her life so long ago she hadn't known it was missing pulsed through her now.

When he finally released her, Carol was so weak with longing that she clung to him, breathing deeply.

"Carol," he said, watching her closely as she shifted positions. She climbed onto his lap, wrapped her legs around his waist and threw her arms around his neck.

"Oh…Carol." Alex moaned and closed his eyes.

"Shhh," she whispered, kissing him deeply. He didn't speak again for a long, long time. Neither did she…

Thursday afternoon, with a stethoscope around her neck, Carol walked down the hospital corridor to the nurses' station. Her steps were brisk and her heart heavy. She hadn't talked to Alex since late Sunday, when he'd dropped Peter and her at the house after their camping trip. There could be any number of excellent reasons why he hadn't called or stopped by. Maybe he was simply too busy; that made sense. Maybe he didn't want to see her again; perhaps he'd decided to start dating other women. Younger women. Prettier women. He was certainly handsome enough. Perhaps aliens had captured him, and he was trapped in some spaceship circling uncharted universes.

Whatever the reason, it translated into one glaring, inescapable fact. She hadn't seen or heard from Alex in four days. However, she reminded herself, she didn't need a man to make her happy. She didn't need a relationship.

"There's a call for you on line one," Betty Mills told her. "Want me to take a message?"

"Did the person give a name?"

"Alex Preston. He sounds sexy, too," Betty added in a succulent voice. "I don't suppose he's that handsome guy you were having lunch with a little while ago."

Carol's heart slammed against her ribs—first with alarm and then with relief. She'd done everything she could to ignore the gaping hole in her life without Alex there. All it would've taken was a phone call—she could have contacted him. She could've asked Peter to talk to James. She could've driven over to his house. But she'd done none of those things.

"Carol? Do you want me to take a message or not?" Betty asked.

"No, I'll get it."

Betty laughed. "I would, too, if I were you." With that, she turned and marched away.

Carol moved to the nurses' station and was grateful no one else was around to overhear her conversation. "This is Carol Sommars," she said as professionally as she could manage.

"Carol, it's Alex."

His words burned in her ears. "Hello, Alex," she said, hoping she didn't sound terribly stiff. Her pulse broke into a wild, absurd rhythm at his voice, and despite her best efforts, a warm sense of happiness settled over her.

"I'm sorry to call you at the hospital, but I haven't been able to reach you at home for the past few nights."

"I've been busy." Busy trying to escape the loneliness. Busy ignoring questions she didn't want to answer. Busy hiding.

"Yes, I know," Alex said impatiently. "Are you avoiding me?"

"I…I thought you…if you want the truth, I assumed you'd decided not to see me again."

"Not *see* you," he repeated loudly. "Are you crazy? I'm nuts about you."

"Oh." Her mouth trembled, but whether it was from irritation or sheer blessed relief, Carol didn't know. If he was nuts about her, why had he neglected her all week? Why hadn't he at least left her a message?

"You honestly haven't figured out how I feel about you yet?"

"You haven't been at the school in the past few days, and since I didn't hear from you it made sense—to me, anyway—that you wanted to cool things down, and I don't blame you. Things are getting much too hot and much too…well, fast, and personally I thought that… well, that it was for the best."

"You thought *what?*" he demanded, his voice exploding over the wire. "When I get home the first thing I'm going to do is kiss some sense into you."

"When you get home?"

"I'm in Houston."

"Texas?"

"Is there any other?"

Carol didn't know. "What are you doing there?"

"Wishing I was in Portland, mostly. A friend of mine, another contractor, is involved in a huge project here and ran into problems. There must've been five messages from him when we returned from the camping trip. He needed some help right away."

"What about James? He isn't with you, is he?"

"He's staying with another friend of mine. I've probably mentioned him before. His name is Barney."

Vaguely Carol *did* remember either Alex or James mentioning the man, but she couldn't remember where or when she'd heard it. "How…long will you be gone?" She hated the way her voice fell, the way it made her need for him all too evident.

"Another week at least."

Her heart catapulted to her feet, then gradually righted itself. "A *week?*"

"I don't like it any better than you do. I can't believe how much I miss you. How much I needed to hear your voice."

Carol felt that, too, only she hadn't been willing to admit it, even to herself.

There was a slight commotion on Alex's end of the line and when it cleared, he said, "I'll try to call you again, but we're working day and night and this is the first real break I've had in three days. I'm glad I got through to you."

Her grip tightened on the receiver. "I'm glad, too."

"I have to go. Bye, Carol. I'll see you Thursday or so of next week."

"Goodbye, Alex…and thanks for phoning." She was about to hang up when she realized there was something else she had to say. She cried his name, desperate to catch him before he hung up.

"I'm here. What is it?"

"Alex," she said, sighing with relief. "I've…I want you to know I…I've missed you, too."

The sound of his chuckle was as warm and melodious as a hundred-voice choir. "It's not much, but it's something. Keep next Thursday open for me, okay?"

"You've got yourself a date."

Tuesday evening of the following week, Carol was teaching her birthing class. Ten couples were sprawled on big pillows in front of her as she led them through a series of exercises. She enjoyed this work almost as much as she did her daytime job at the hospital. She and

Janice Mandle each taught part of the class, with Carol handling the first half.

"Everyone's doing exceptionally well tonight," Carol said, praising the teams. "Okay, partners, I have a question for you. I want you to tell me, in number of seconds, how long you think a typical labor pain lasts."

"Thirty seconds," one young man shouted out.

"Longer," Carol said.

"Sixty seconds," yelled another.

Carol shook her head.

"Ninety?"

"You don't sound too sure about that," Carol said, smiling. "Let's stick with ninety seconds. That's a nice round number, although in the final stages of labor it's not unusual for a contraction to last much longer."

The pregnant women eyed each other warily.

"All right, partners, I want you to show me your biceps. Tighten them as hard as you can. Good. Good," she said, surveying the room, watching as several of the men brought up their fists until the muscles of their upper arms bulged. "Make it as tight and as painful as you can," she continued. Most of the men were gritting their teeth.

"Very good," she went on to say. "Now, hold that until I tell you to relax." She walked to the other side of the room. "As far back as 1913, some doctors and midwives recognized that fear and tension could interfere with the birthing process. Even then they believed that deep breathing exercises and relaxation could aid labor." She paused to glance at her watch. "That's fifteen seconds."

The look of astonishment that crossed the men's faces was downright comical.

"Keep those muscles tightly clenched," Carol instructed. She strolled around the room, chatting amiably as the men held their arms as tight as possible. Some were already showing the strain.

"Thirty seconds," she announced.

Her words were followed by a low groan. Carol couldn't help smiling. She hated to admit how much she enjoyed their discomfort, but this exercise was an excellent illustration of the realities of labor, especially for the men. The smile remained on her lips as the door in the back of the room opened to admit a latecomer. Carol opened her mouth to welcome the person, but the words didn't reach her lips.

There, framed inside the door, stood Alex Preston.

Chapter 10

Carol stared at Alex. Alex stared at Carol.

The room went completely still; the air felt heavy, and the quiet seemed eerie, unnatural. It wasn't until Carol realized that several taut faces were gazing up at her anxiously that she pulled her attention away from Alex and back to her class.

"Now, where were we?" she asked, flustered and nervous.

"Ninety seconds," one of the men shouted.

"Oh. Right." She glanced at her watch and nodded. "Ninety seconds."

The relief could be felt all the way across the room.

A few minutes later Carol dismissed everyone for a fifteen-minute break. Janice strolled over to Carol and eyed the back of the room, where Alex was patiently waiting. He was leaning against the back wall, his ankles crossed and his thumbs hooked in the belt loop of his jeans.

"He's gorgeous."

Carol felt too distracted and tongue-tied to respond, although her thoughts had been traveling along those same lines. Alex was the sexiest man Carol had ever known. Unabashedly wonderful, too.

"He's…been out of town," she said, her eyes magnetically drawn to Alex's.

Janice draped her arm across Carol's shoulders. "Since your portion of tonight's class is finished, why don't you go ahead and leave?"

"I couldn't." Carol tore her eyes from Alex long enough to study her co-teacher. They were a team, and although they'd divided the class into two distinct sections, they stayed and lent each other emotional support.

"Yes, you can. I insist. Only…"

"Only what?" Carol pressed.

"Only promise me that if another gorgeous guy walks in off the street and looks at me like he's looking at you, you'll return the favor."

"Of course," Carol answered automatically.

Janice's voice fell to a whisper. "Good. Then we'll consider this our little secret."

Carol frowned. "I don't understand—what do you mean, our little secret?"

"Well, if my husband found out about this agreement, there could be problems."

Carol laughed. Janice was happily married and had been for fifteen years.

"If I were you I wouldn't be hanging around here talking," Janice murmured, giving Carol a small shove. "Don't keep him waiting any longer."

"Okay…thanks." Feeling unaccountably shy, Carol retrieved her purse and her briefcase and walked toward Alex. With each step that drew her nearer, her heart felt lighter. By the time she made her way to the back of the room, she felt nearly airborne.

He straightened, his eyes warm and caressing. "Hello."

"Hi."

"Peter told me you were teaching tonight and where. I hope you don't mind that I dropped in unexpectedly."

"I don't mind." *Mind?* Her heart was soaring with gladness. She could've flown without an airplane. No, she didn't mind that he'd dropped in—not in the least.

For the longest moment all they did was gaze at each other like starry-eyed lovers.

A noise at the front of the room distracted Carol. She glanced over her shoulder and saw several couples watching them with undisguised curiosity.

"Janice said she'd finish up here, and I could…should leave now."

Alex grinned, and with that, Carol could feel whole sections of the sturdy wall around her heart start to crumble. This man's smile was nothing short of lethal.

"Remind me to thank her later," Alex said. He removed the briefcase from her unresisting fingers and opened the door, letting her precede him outside.

They hadn't taken two steps out the door when Alex paused. Carol felt his hesitation and stopped, turning to face him. That was when she knew Alex was going to kiss her. It didn't matter that they were standing in front of a public building. It didn't matter that it was still light enough for any number of passersby to see them. It didn't matter that they were both respected professionals.

Alex scooped her into his arms and with a lavish sigh lowered his head and covered her lips in the sweetest, wildest kiss of her life.

"I've missed you," he whispered. "The hours felt like years, the days like decades."

Carol felt tears in the corners of her eyes. She hadn't thought about how empty her life had felt without him, how bleak and alone she was with him away. Now it poured out of her in a litany of sighs and kisses. "I…I missed you, too—so much."

For years she'd been content in her own secure world, the one she'd created for herself and her son. The borders had been narrow, confining, but she'd made peace with herself and found serenity. Then she'd met Alex, and he'd forced her to notice how cramped and limited her existence was. Not only that, he'd pointed toward the horizon, to a new land of shared dreams.

When Alex spoke again, his voice was heavy with need. "Come on, let's get out of here."

She nodded and followed him to his car, ready to abandon her own with little more than a second thought.

He unlocked the passenger door, then turned to face her. His eyes were dancing with excitement. "Let's dispense with formalities and elope. Now. Tonight. This minute."

The words hit her hard. She blinked at the unexpectedness of his suggestion, prepared to laugh it off as a joke.

But Alex was serious. He looked as shocked as Carol felt, but she noted that the idea had begun to gain momentum. The mischievous spark in his eyes was gone, replaced by a solemn look.

"I love you, Carol. I love you so much that my buddy in Texas practically threw me on the plane and told me to get home before I died of it. He said he'd never seen anyone more lovesick and made me promise we'd name one of our children after him."

The mention of a child was like a right cross to the jaw after his punch to her solar plexus, and she flinched involuntarily.

Alex set his hands on her shoulders, and a smile touched his eyes and then his mouth. He smiled so endearingly that all of Carol's arguments fled like dust in a whirlwind.

"Say something."

"Ah...my car's parked over there." She pointed in the general vicinity of her Ford. Her throat was so tight she could hardly speak.

He laughed and hugged her. "I know this is sudden for you. I'm a fool not to have done it properly. I swear I'll do it again over champagne and give you a diamond so large you'll sink in a swimming pool, but I can't keep the way I feel inside anymore."

"Alex..."

He silenced her with a swift kiss. "Believe me, blurting out a proposal like this is as much of a surprise to me as it is to you. I had no idea I was going to ask you tonight. The entire flight home I was trying to figure out how I could make it as romantic as possible. The last thing I expected to do was impulsively shout it out in a parking lot. But something happened tonight." He reached for her limp hands and brought them to his lips, then kissed her knuckles with reverence. "When I walked into your class and saw you with all those pregnant women, I was hit with the most powerful shock of my life." His voice grew quiet. "All of a sudden, my mind conjured up the image of you pregnant with our child, and I swear it was all I could do not to break down and weep." He paused long enough to run his fingers through his hair. "Children, Carol…our children." He closed his eyes and sighed deeply.

Carol felt frozen. The chill worked its way from her heart, the icy circles growing larger and more encompassing until the cold extended down her arms and legs and into her fingers and toes.

"I know this is abrupt, and I'm probably ruining the moment, but say something," Alex urged. "Anything."

Carol's mind refused to function properly. Panic was closing in, panic and a hundred misgivings. "I…don't know what to tell you."

Alex threw back his head and laughed. "I don't blame you. All right," he said, his eyes flashing, "repeat after me. I, Carol Sommars." He glanced expectantly at her.

"I…Carol Sommars…"

"Am crazy in love with Alex Preston." He waited for her to echo his words.

"Am crazy in love with Alex Preston."

"Good," he whispered and leaned forward just enough to brush his mouth over hers. His arms slipped around her, locking at the small of her back and dragging her unresistingly toward him. "You know, the best part about those babies is going to be making them."

A blush rose up her neck, coloring her cheeks with what she felt sure was a highly uncomplimentary shade of pink. Her eyes darted away from his.

"Now all you need to do is say *yes,*" Alex said.

"I can't. I…don't know." To her horror, she started to sob, not with the restrained tears of a confused woman, but the harsh mournful cries of one in anguish.

Alex had apparently expected anything but tears. "Carol? What's wrong? What did I say?" He wrapped his arms around her and brought her head to his shoulder.

Carol wanted to resist his touch, but she so desperately needed it that she buried her face in the curve of his neck and wept. Alex's arms were warm and safe, his hands gentle. She did love him. Somewhere between his rescue the night her car broke down and the camping trip, her well-guarded heart had succumbed to his appeal. But falling in love was one thing; marriage and children were something else entirely.

"Come on," Alex finally said. He opened the car door for her.

"Where are we going?" she asked, sniffling.

"My house. James won't be home yet, and we can talk without being disturbed."

Carol wasn't sure what more he could say, but she agreed with a nod of her head and climbed inside. He closed the door for her, then paused and ran a hand over his eyes, slumping wearily.

Neither of them said much during the ten-minute drive. He helped her out of his car, then unlocked the front door to his house. His suitcases had been haphazardly dumped on the living room carpet. When he saw Carol looking at them, he said simply, "I was in a hurry to find you." He led the way into the kitchen and started making a pot of coffee.

Carol pulled out a stool at the counter and seated herself. His kitchen—in fact, his home—wasn't at all what she expected. A woman's touch could be seen and felt in every room. The kitchen was yellow and cheery. What remained of the evening light shone through the window above the sink, sending warm shadows across the polished tile floor. Matching ceramic canisters lined the counter, along with a row of well-used cookbooks.

"Okay, Carol, tell me what's on your mind," Alex urged, facing her from behind the tile counter. Even then Carol wasn't safe from his magnetism.

"That's the problem," she said, swallowing hard. "I don't *know* what's on my mind. I'm so confused…."

"I realize my proposal came out of the blue, but once you think about it, you'll understand how perfect we are for each other. Surely you've thought about it yourself."

"No," she said quickly, and for emphasis, shook her head. "I hadn't…not once. Marriage hadn't occurred to me."

"I see." He raised his right hand to rub his eyes again.

Carol knew he must be exhausted and was immediately overcome with remorse. She *did* love Alex, although admitting it—to herself as much as to him—had sapped her strength.

"What do you want to do?" he asked softly.

"I'm not sure," she whispered, staring down at her hands, which were tightly clenched in her lap.

"Would some time help?"

She nodded eagerly.

"How long?"

"A year. Several months. At the very least, three or four weeks."

"How about two weeks?" Alex suggested.

"Two weeks," she echoed feebly. That wasn't nearly enough. She couldn't possibly reach such an important decision in so little time, especially when there were other factors to consider. Before she could voice a single excuse, Alex pressed his finger to her lips.

"If you can't decide in that length of time, then I doubt you ever will."

A protest came and went in a single breath. There were so many concerns he hadn't mentioned—like their sons!

She was about to bring this up when Alex said, "I don't think we should draw the boys into this until we know our own minds. The last thing we need is pressure from them."

Carol agreed completely.

The coffee had finished perking, and Alex poured them each a cup. "How about dinner Friday night? Just the two of us." At her hesitation, he added, "I'll give you the rest of this week to sort through your thoughts, and if you still have any questions or doubts by Friday, we can discuss them then."

"But not a final decision?" Carol murmured, uneasy with the time limitation. He'd said two weeks, and she was going to need every minute to make up her mind.

Carol woke around three with her stomach in painful knots. She lay on her side and at a breath-stopping cramp, she tucked her knees under her chin. A wave of nausea hit her hard, and she couldn't stifle a groan. Despite her flu shot last fall, maybe she'd caught one of the new strains that emerged every year.

She lay perfectly still in the fervent hope that this would ward off her growing need to vomit. It didn't work, and a moment later she was racing for the bathroom.

Afterward, sitting on the floor, her elbows on the edge of the toilet, she breathed deeply.

"Are you all right?" Peter asked from behind her.

"I will be. I just need a couple more minutes."

"What's wrong?" Peter asked. He handed her a warm washcloth, following that with a cup of water.

"The flu, I guess."

He helped her to her feet and walked her back to her bedroom. "I appreciate the help, Peter, but it would be better if you went back to bed. I'll be fine by morning."

"I'll call work for you and tell them you're too sick to come in."

She shook her head. "No...I'll need to talk to them myself." Her son dutifully arranged the blankets around her, giving her a worried look before he slipped out of her bedroom.

Peter must have turned off her alarm because the next thing Carol knew it was eight-thirty. The house was eerily silent.

Sitting up, she waited for an attack of nausea. It didn't come. She'd slept without waking even once. She was astonished that she hadn't heard Peter roaming about. He was usually as noisy as a herd of rampaging buffalo. Perhaps he'd overslept as well.

In case he had, she threw the sheets back, sat on the edge of the bed and shoved her feet into slippers before wandering into the kitchen. The minute she stepped inside, it was obvious that her son had been up and about. A box of cold cereal stood in the middle of the kitchen table, along with a bowl half-filled with milk and crusts from several pieces of toast.

Posted on the refrigerator door was a note from Peter, informing her that he'd phoned the hospital and talked to her supervisor, who'd said Carol didn't need to worry about coming in. He proudly added that he'd made his own lunch and that he'd find a ride home from track practice, so she should stay in bed and drink lots of fluids. In a brief postscript he casually mentioned that he'd also called Grandma Pasquale.

Carol's groan had little to do with the way she was feeling. All she needed was her mother, bless her heart, hovering over her and driving her slowly but surely crazy. No sooner had the thought formed in her mind than the doorbell chimed, followed by a key turning in the lock and the front door flying open. Her mother burst into the house as though Carol lay on her deathbed.

"Carol," she cried, walking through the living room. "What are you doing out of bed?"

"I'm feeling much better, Mama."

"You look terrible. Get back in bed before the undertaker gets wind of how you look."

"Ma, please, I'm just a little under the weather."

"That's what my uncle Giuseppe said when he had the flu, God rest his soul. His wife never even got the chicken stewed, he went that fast." She pressed her hands together, raised her eyes to the ceiling and murmured a silent prayer.

"Peter shouldn't have phoned you," Carol grumbled. She certainly didn't need her mother fussing at her bedside, spooning chicken soup down her throat every time she opened her mouth.

"Peter did the right thing. He's a good boy."

At the moment Carol considered that point debatable.

"Now back to bed before you get a dizzy spell." Her mother made a shooing motion with her hands.

Mumbling under her breath, Carol did as Angelina insisted. Not because she felt especially ill, but because arguing required too much energy. Carol might as well try to talk her mother into using canned spaghetti sauce as convince her she wasn't on her deathbed.

Once Carol was lying down, Angelina dragged the rocking chair into her bedroom and sat down. Before another minute had passed, she was busy with her knitting. Several balls of yarn were lying at her feet in case she wanted to start a second or third project in the next few hours.

"According to Peter you were sick in the middle of the night," Angelina said. Eyes narrowed, she studied Carol, as if staring would reveal the exact nature of her daughter's illness. She shook her head, then paused to count the neat row of stitches before glancing back at Carol, clearly expecting an answer.

"It must've been something I ate for dinner," she suggested lamely.

"Peter said you were looking at parts of a toilet no one should see that close up."

Her teenage son certainly had a way with words. "I'm feeling better," she said weakly.

"Your face is paler than bleached sheets. Uncle Giuseppe has more color than you, and he's been in his grave for thirty years."

Carol leaned back against the pillows and closed her eyes. She might be able to fool just about anyone else, but her mother knew her too well.

Several tense minutes passed. Angelina said not a word, patient to a fault. Yes, her mother knew; Carol was sure of it. She kept her eyes closed, afraid that another searching look would reveal everything. Oh, what the heck, Angelina would find out sooner or later.

"Alex asked me to marry him last night." Carol tried to keep her voice even, but it shook noticeably.

"Ah," her mother said, nodding. "That explains everything. From the time you were a little girl, you got an upset stomach whenever something troubled you, although why you should be troubled when this man tells you he loves you is a whole other question."

Carol didn't need to hear stories from her childhood to recognize the truth.

"So what did you say to him?"

"Nothing," she whispered.

"This man brings color to your cheeks and a smile to your eyes and you said *nothing?*"

"I…need time to think," Carol cried. "This is an important decision…. I've got more than myself and my own life to consider. Alex has a son and I have a son…. It isn't as simple as it sounds."

Her mother shook her head. Her rocker was going ninety miles an hour, and Carol was positive the older woman's thoughts were churning at equal speed.

"Don't be angry with me, Mama," she whispered. "I'm so frightened."

Angelina stopped abruptly and set her knitting aside. She reached for Carol's hands, holding them gently. A soft smile lit her eyes. "You'll make the right decision."

"How can you be so sure? I've been wrong about so many things—I've made so many mistakes in my life. I don't trust my own judgment anymore."

"Follow your heart," Angelina urged. "It won't lead you wrong."

But it would. She'd followed her heart when she

married Bruce, convinced their love would see them through every difficulty. The marriage had been a disaster from the honeymoon on, growing more painful and more difficult with each passing day. The horror of those years with Bruce had shredded her heart and drained away all her self-confidence. She'd offered her husband everything she had to give, relinquished her pride and self-respect—and to what end? Bruce hadn't appreciated her sacrifices. He hadn't cherished her love, but turned it into something cheap and expendable.

"Whatever you decide will be right," her mother said once again. "I know it will be."

Carol closed her eyes to mull over her mother's confidence in her, which she was sure was completely unfounded. Angelina seemed to trust Carol's judgment more than Carol did herself.

A few minutes later, her mother started to sing softly, and her sweet, melodious voice harmonized with the clicking of the needles.

The next thing Carol knew, it was early afternoon and she could smell chicken soup simmering in the kitchen.

Angelina had left a brief note for her that was filled with warmth and encouragement. Feeling much better, Carol helped herself to a bowl of the broth and noodles and leisurely enjoyed her first nourishment of the day.

By the time Peter slammed into the house several hours later, she was almost back to normal.

"Mom," he said rushing into the room. His face was flushed and his eyes bright. It looked as though he'd run all the way home. His chest was heaving as he dropped his books on the table, then tried to catch his breath, arms waving excitedly.

"What is it?" Carol asked, amused by the sight her son made.

"Why didn't you *say* anything?" he demanded, kissing both her cheeks the way her mother did whenever she was exceptionally pleased. "This is great, Mom, really great! Now we can go fishing and camping and hiking all the time."

"Say anything about what?" she asked in bewilderment. "And what's this about fishing?"

"Marrying Mr. Preston."

Carol was half out of her seat before she even realized she'd moved. "Who told you…who so much as mentioned it was a possibility?"

"A possibility?" Peter repeated. "I thought it was a done deal. At least that's what James said."

"James told you?"

Peter gave her a perplexed look. "Who else? He told me about it first thing when I got to school this morning." He studied her, his expression cautious. "Hey, Mom, don't look so upset—I'm sorry if you were keeping it a secret. Don't worry, James and I think it's a great idea. I've always wanted a brother, and having one who's my best friend is even better."

Carol was so outraged she could barely talk. "H-he had no business saying a word!" she stammered.

"Who? James?"

"Not James. Alex." If he thought he'd use the boys to influence her decision, he had another think coming.

Carol marched into her bedroom, throwing on a pair of jeans and an old sweatshirt. Then she hurried into the living room without bothering to run a brush through her tousled hair.

"Where are you going?" Peter demanded. He'd

ladeled himself a bowl of soup and was following her around the house like a puppy while she searched for her purse and car keys.

"Out," Carol stormed.

"Looking like that?" He sounded aghast.

Carol whirled around, hands on her hips, and glared at him.

Peter raised one hand. "Sorry. Only please don't let Mr. Preston see you, all right?"

"Why not?"

Peter raised his shoulder in a shrug. "If he gets a look at you, he might withdraw his proposal. Honestly, Mom, this is the best thing that's happened to us in years. Don't go ruining it."

Chapter 11

James answered the door, and a smile automatically came to his lips when he saw it was Carol. Then his eyes narrowed as though he wasn't sure it was her, after all. Carol realized he was probably taken aback by her appearance. Normally she was well-dressed and well-groomed, but what Alex had done—had tried to do—demanded swift and decisive action. She didn't feel it was necessary to wear makeup for this confrontation.

"Where is he?" Carol asked through gritted teeth.

"Who? Dad?" James frowned. "He's watching the news." The teenager pointed toward the family room, which was adjacent to the kitchen.

Without waiting for James to escort her inside, Carol burst past him, intent on giving Alex a piece of her mind. She was furious. More than furious. If he'd honestly believed that involving the boys would affect her decision, then he knew absolutely nothing about her. In fact, he knew so little, they had no business even considering marriage.

She refused to be pressured, tricked, cajoled or anything else, and before this day was over Alex would recognize that very clearly indeed.

"Carol?" Alex met her halfway into the kitchen. His eyes softened perceptibly as he reached for her.

Carol stopped just short of his embrace. "How dare you," she snapped.

"How dare I?" Alex repeated. His eyes widened with surprise, but he remained infuriatingly calm. "Would you elaborate, please, because I'm afraid I have no idea what you're talking about."

"Oh, yes, you do."

"Dad?" James ventured into the kitchen, giving Carol a wide berth. "Something must really be wrong," the boy said, and then his voice dropped to a whisper as he pointed to Carol's feet. "Mrs. Sommars is wearing two different shoes."

Carol's gaze shot downward, and she mentally groaned. But if either of the Preston men thought they'd throw her off her guard by pointing out that she'd worn a blue tennis shoe on her right foot and a hot-pink slipper on her left, then she had news for them both.

"I have the feeling Mrs. Sommars was in a hurry to talk to me," Alex explained. The smile that quivered at the corners of his mouth did little to quell her brewing temper.

James nodded. "Do you want me to get lost for a few minutes?"

"That might be a good plan," Alex replied.

James exchanged a knowing look with his father

before discreetly vacating the room. As soon as Carol heard James's bedroom door close, she put her hands on her hips, determined to confront Alex.

"How dare you bring the boys into this," she flared.

"Into what?" Alex walked over to the coffeepot and got two mugs. He held one up to her, but she refused the offer with a shake of her head. "I'm sorry, Carol, but I don't know what you're talking about."

Jabbing her index finger at him, she took several steps toward him. "Don't give me that, Alex Preston. You know very well what I mean. We agreed to wait, and you saw an advantage and without any compunction, you took it! Did you really think dragging Peter and James into this would help? How could you be so foolish?" Her voice shook, but her eyes were as steady as she could make them.

"I didn't mention the possibility of our getting married to James, and I certainly didn't say anything to Peter." He leaned against the kitchen counter and returned her disbelieving glare with maddening composure.

Angrily Carol threw back her head. "I don't believe you."

His eyes hardened but he didn't argue with her. "Ask James then. If he heard that I'd proposed to you, the information didn't come from me."

"You don't expect me to believe that, do you?" she cried, not nearly as confident as she'd been earlier. The aggression had gone out of her voice, and she lowered her hands to her sides, less certain with each minute. The ground that supported her outrage started to shift and crumble.

"I told you I wouldn't bring the boys into this," he

reminded her smoothly. "And I didn't." He looked over his shoulder and shouted for James, who opened his bedroom door immediately. Carol didn't doubt for an instant that he'd had his ear pressed to it the entire time they'd been talking.

With his hands in his jean pockets, James strolled casually into the room. "Yes, Dad?"

"Do you want to tell me about it?"

"About what?" James wore a look of complete innocence.

"Apparently you said something to Peter about the relationship between Mrs. Sommars and me. I want to know what it was and where you found out about it." Alex hadn't so much as raised his voice, but Carol recognized that he expected the truth and wouldn't let up until he got it.

"Oh…that," James muttered. "I sort of overheard you saying something to Uncle Barn."

"Uncle Barn?" Carol asked.

"A good friend of mine. He's the one I was telling you about who kept Jim while I was out of town."

"Call me *James,*" his son reminded him.

Alex lifted both hands. "Sorry."

"Anyway," James went on to say, "you were on the phone last night talking to him about the basketball game tonight, and I heard you say that you'd *asked* Carol—Mrs. Sommars. I'm not stupid, Dad. I knew you were talking about the two of you getting married, and I thought that Peter and I had a right to know. You should've said something to us first, don't you think?"

"For starters, this whole marriage business is up in the air—when and if anything's decided, you two boys will be the first to find out."

"What do you mean, the wedding's up in the air?" This piece of information obviously took James by surprise. "Why? What's the holdup? Peter and I think it's a great idea. We'd like it if you two got married. It'd be nice to have a woman around the house. For one thing, your cooking could use some help. But if you married Mrs. Sommars—"

"James," Alex broke in, "I think it's time for you to go back to your room before Carol decides she wants nothing more to do with the likes of us."

James looked affronted, but without further questions, he pivoted and marched back into his bedroom.

Alex waited until his son was out of sight. He sighed loudly and rammed his fingers through his hair. "I'm sorry, Carol. I had no idea James overheard my conversation with Barney. I thought he was asleep, but I should've been more careful."

"I...understand," Carol whispered, mollified.

"Contrary to what James just said," Alex continued, the line of his mouth tight and unyielding, "I don't want to marry you for your cooking skills. I couldn't care less if you never cooked again. I love you, and I'm hoping we can make a good life together."

James tossed open his bedroom door and stuck out his head. "Peter says she's as good a cook as his grandmother. She's—"

Alex sent his son a look hot enough to melt tar.

James quickly withdrew his head and just as quickly closed his door.

"I'll talk to Peter and explain the mix-up, if you'd like," Alex offered.

"No...I'll say something to him." Suddenly self-conscious, Carol swung her arms at her sides and retreated a couple of steps. "I suppose I should get home…."

"You were sick last night?" Alex asked, his expression concerned. "James told me when I picked him up after school. I would gladly have given Peter a ride, but he'd apparently found another way because he was gone before James could find him."

"Peter decided to run home."

"But you *had* been ill?"

She nodded. "I…must've caught a twenty-four-hour bug." Her eyes darted around the room. She felt so foolish, standing there with her hair a tangled mess, wearing the oldest clothes she owned, not to mention mismatched shoes.

"You're feeling better today?"

"A lot better. Thank you." She was slowly but surely edging toward the front door. The sooner she escaped, the better it would be for everyone involved. If Alex was merciful, he'd never mention this visit again.

She was all the way across the living room and had just reached the front door, when Alex appeared behind her. As she whirled around, he flattened his hands on either side of her head.

"Have you come to a decision?" he asked softly. His gaze dropped to her mouth. "Do you need any help?"

"The only thing I've managed to come up with is the flu," she murmured in a feeble attempt at humor. Alex wasn't amused, however, and she rushed to add, "Obviously you want to know which way I'm leaning, but I haven't had time to give your proposal much thought. I will, I promise I will…soon." She realized she was chattering, but couldn't seem to stop. "We're still on for Friday night, aren't we? We can discuss it then and—"

The doorbell chimed, frightening Carol out of her wits. She gasped and automatically catapulted herself into Alex's arms. He apparently didn't need an excuse to hold her close. When he released her several awkward seconds later, he smiled at her, then kissed the tip of her upturned nose.

"That'll be Barney now. It's time the two of you met."

"*That* was Carol Sommars?" Barney asked for the third time. He scratched his jaw and continued to frown. "No wonder Bambi mistook her for a bag lady. I'm sorry, man, you're my best friend and we've been buddies for a lot of years, but I've got to tell you, you can do better than that."

Chuckling, Alex dismissed his friend's statement and walked into the family room. If he lived to be a hundred, he'd never forget Carol's mortified look as she bolted from the house.

Barney certainly hadn't helped the situation any. Doing his best to keep a straight face, Alex had introduced the two. Barney's eyes had widened and his mouth had slowly dropped open in disbelief. It took a moment before he had the presence of mind to step forward and accept Carol's outstretched hand. Barney had mumbled that it was a pleasure to finally meet her, but his eyes had said something else entirely.

"Trust me," Alex felt obliged to explain, "she doesn't always look like that."

Barney stalked over to the refrigerator and opened it. He stared inside for a long time before he reached for a cold beer. "What time do the Trail Blazers play?"

Alex checked his watch. Both he and Barney were keen fans of Portland's professional basketball team.

The team had been doing well this year and were in the first round of the play-offs. "Seven."

"So," Barney said, making himself comfortable in the overstuffed chair. He crossed his legs and took a long swig of beer. "What happened to her foot?" he asked casually. "Did she sprain it?"

"Whose foot?"

"Carol's," Barney said, casting Alex a questioning glance. "She was wearing a slipper—you mean you didn't notice? Did she twist her ankle?"

"Nah," James answered for Alex, wandering into the family room holding a bag of pretzels. He plopped himself down on the sofa, resting his legs on the coffee table. "Peter says she does weird stuff like that all the time. Once she wore his swimming goggles in the shower."

Barney raised his eyebrows. "Should I ask why?"

"It made sense—sort of—when Peter explained it. His mother had gone to one of those cosmetics stores and they put some fancy makeup on her eyes, and she didn't want to ruin it when she took a shower, so she wore Peter's rubber goggles."

"Why didn't she just take a bath?" Barney asked. He threw Alex a look that suggested his friend have his head examined.

"She couldn't take a bath because the faucet was broken," James said, "and her brother hadn't gotten around to fixing it yet."

"That makes sense," Alex said in Carol's defense.

Barney rolled his eyes and tipped the beer bottle to his lips.

To his credit, Barney didn't say anything else about Carol until James was out of the room. "You're really serious about *this* woman?" His question implied that Alex had introduced Barney to the wrong one, and that the whole meeting was a setup to some kind of joke that was to follow.

"I'm totally serious. I told you I asked her to marry me—I can't get any more serious than that."

"And she's *thinking* about it?" Barney asked mockingly. Being the true friend he was, Barn clearly couldn't understand why Carol hadn't instantly leaped at Alex's offer.

To be honest, Alex wondered the same thing himself. True, he'd blurted out his proposal in a parking lot. He still had trouble believing he'd done anything so crazy. As a contractor, he'd sold himself and his company hundreds of times. He'd prepared bids and presented them with polish and professionalism. He always had solid arguments that made his proposals sound attractive and intelligent. Carol deserved nothing less.

But something had happened to him when he'd visited her birthing class. Something enigmatic and profound. Even now he had to struggle not to get choked up when he thought about it.

After nearly two weeks in Texas, Alex had been starved for the sight of her, and he'd barely noticed the others in the class. In retrospect, he was sure his reaction could be attributed to seeing all those soon-to-be mothers.

In fifteen years Alex hadn't given babies more than a passing thought. He had a son and was grateful for that. He might have suffered a twinge of regret when he learned there'd be no more children, but he'd been more concerned about his wife's well-being than the fact that they wouldn't be adding to their family.

Then he'd watched Carol with those pregnant couples, and the desire for another child, a daughter, had suddenly overwhelmed him. He'd decided while he was in Texas that he loved Carol and wanted to marry her, but the idea of starting a family of their own hadn't so much as crossed his mind. But why not? They were both young enough and healthy enough to raise a houseful of children.

He'd been standing at the back of her class, waiting for her, when it happened. Out of nowhere, yet as clear as anything he'd ever seen or felt, Alex saw Carol pregnant with a child. *His* child. He'd realized at the time that this—he used the word *vision* for lack of a better one—was probably due to physical and emotional exhaustion. Wanting to hold on to the image as long as he could, he'd closed his eyes. He'd pictured her.... Her breasts were full, and when she smiled at him, her eyes had a radiance that couldn't be described. She'd taken his hand and settled it on her protruding stomach. In his fantasy he'd felt their child move.

This fantasy was what had prompted the abrupt marriage proposal. He wanted to kick himself now. If he'd taken her in his arms, kissed her and said all the things she deserved to hear, things might have gone differently. He hadn't meant to rush her, hadn't meant to be so pushy, but once he'd realized how resistant she was to the idea, he'd panicked. The two-week ultimatum was unfair. He'd tell her that on Friday night when they went out for dinner.

Then again, maybe he wouldn't. He'd wait to hear what she was thinking, which way she was leaning, before he put his foot any farther down his throat.

Then he began to smile. Perhaps it wasn't too late for a proper proposal, after all.

"Alex?"

His name seemed to be coming from some distance away.

"What?" he asked, pulling himself out of his thoughts.

"The game's started," Barney said. "Don't you want to see it?" He peered closely at Alex. "Is something wrong with you?"

Yes, something *was* wrong, and there was only one cure. Carol Sommars.

Carol dressed carefully for her dinner date with Alex Friday evening. After going through her closet and laying half of everything she owned across the bed, she chose a demure, high-necked dress of soft pink that buttoned down the front. That seemed safe enough, especially with a shawl.

She'd hardly ever felt this awkward. Trying to make her decision, she'd swayed back and forth all week. One day she'd decide she would be a fool *not* to marry him, and the next, she'd been equally convinced she'd be crazy to trust a man a second time.

Marrying Alex meant relinquishing her independence. It meant placing herself and her son at the mercy of another human being. Memories of her marriage to Bruce swiped at her viciously, and whenever she contemplated sharing her well-ordered life with another man, she broke into a cold sweat.

Years ago, someone had told her it took a hell of a man to replace no man. It wasn't until Carol graduated from college with her nursing degree and was completely on her own that she fully understood that statement. Her life was good, too good to tamper with, and yet…

Her thoughts were more confused than ever when the doorbell chimed. She paused, took a calming breath and headed across the room.

"Hello, Alex," she said, smiling stiffly.

"Carol."

He looked gorgeous in a three-piece suit. Her eyes took him in, and she felt some of the tension leave her muscles. It was when she met his eyes that she realized he was chuckling.

"We're going to dinner," he said, nodding at her dress, "not a baptism."

She blinked, not sure she understood.

"If that collar went any higher up your neck, it'd reach your nose."

"I…I was removing temptation," she said, embarrassed by the blush that heated her face.

"Honey, at this rate, the only thing we'll be removing is that dress."

Carol decided the best thing to do was ignore his remark. "Did you say where we're going for dinner?"

"No," he answered cryptically, and his warm eyes caressed her with maddening purposefulness. "I didn't. It's a surprise."

"Oh." After all the time they'd been together, after all the moments she'd spent in his arms, after all the dreams she'd had about Alex, she shouldn't feel this uncomfortable. But her heart was galloping, her hands felt damp, her breath was coming in soft gasps—and they hadn't even left her house yet.

"Are you ready?"

It was a question he shouldn't have asked. *No*, her mind screamed. *Yes*, her heart insisted. "I guess so," her lips answered.

Alex led her outside and held open his car door.

"It was thoughtful of you to drop the boys at the theater. Personally I don't think they were that keen on seeing a Disney movie," she said, slipping inside his car.

"Too bad. I gave them a choice of things to do this evening."

"Attending a kids' movie on the other side of town or being set adrift in the Columbia River without paddles probably isn't their idea of a choice."

Alex chuckled. "I don't want anyone disturbing us tonight."

Their eyes met. Alex's were hot and hazy and so suggestive, Carol's heart skipped a beat. For sanity's sake, she looked away.

"I hope you like steak."

"I love it."

"The champagne's cooling."

"You must've ordered in advance," she murmured, having difficulty finding something to do with her hands. Her fingers itched to touch him…*needed* to touch him. A need that only confused her more.

"I…hope you explained to Barney—your friend—that I…that I don't normally look the way I did the evening we met. When I got home and saw myself in the mirror…well, I could just imagine what he must've thought." Carol cursed the madness that had sent her rushing out of her house that evening to confront Alex.

"Barney understood."

"Oh, good."

A couple of minutes later, Alex turned into his own

driveway. Carol looked at him, somewhat surprised. "Did you forget something?"

"No," he said.

A moment later, he let her into the house. She paused in the doorway, and her heart gave a sudden, sharp lurch. They weren't going to any restaurant. Alex had always planned to bring her back to his house.

The drapes were drawn, and the lights had been lowered. Carol saw that the dining room table was set with crystal and china. Two tapered candles stood in the middle of the table, waiting to be lit.

Alex went over to the stereo and pushed a single button. Immediately the room was drenched with the plaintive sound of violins.

Carol was still trying to assimilate what was happening when he walked over to the table and lit the candles. Tiny flames sent a golden glow shimmering across the pristine white cloth.

"Shall we?" Alex said, holding out his hands.

Carol was too numb to reply. He took the lacy shawl from her shoulders and draped it over the back of the sofa. Then he pulled her purse from her unresisting fingers and set it next to the shawl. When he'd finished, he turned and eased her into his arms.

Their bodies came gently together, and a shudder went through her. She wasn't a complete fool—she knew what Alex was planning. She lowered her eyelids. Despite her doubts and fears, she wanted this, too.

For a moment, she battled the feeling, then with a deep sigh, she surrendered.

Alex wrapped his arms around her. "Oh, baby," he whispered in her ear. "You feel so good."

She emptied her lungs of air as his hands slid down her back, to her waist.

There was music, such beautiful music, and then Carol realized they were supposed to be dancing. She rested her fingertips on his shoulders as his mouth moved toward hers. Carol sighed. Alex's breath was moist and warm, his hands gentle as they pressed her closer and closer.

When he kissed her, the moment of anticipation ended, and Carol felt a tremendous surge of relief. He groaned. She groaned. He leaned back and began to unfasten the buttons at her throat.

That all too brief pause helped Carol collect her scattered senses. "Alex," she whispered, "what are you doing?"

"Undressing you."

"Why?" she asked breathlessly, knowing what a stupid question it was.

"Why?" he repeated with amusement. "Because we're going to make love."

Her pulse went wild.

"I love you," he said. "You love me. Right?"

"Oh...yes."

"Good." He kissed her again, so passionately she could hardly resist—and yet she had to. She broke away from him with what little strength she still possessed.

"Alex...please don't."

"Tonight's a new beginning for us. I'm crazy in love with you. I need you so much I can't think straight anymore."

"You brought me here to make love to me, didn't you?"

"You mean it wasn't obvious?" he asked as he nibbled kisses along the side of her neck.

"Why now? Why not that night on the Washington coast…? Why tonight?"

"Carol, do we need to go through this evaluation?"

"I have to know," she cried, pushing herself away from him. Her hands trembled, and it was with some difficulty that she rebuttoned her dress. "The truth, Alex. I want the truth."

"All right," he murmured. "I thought…I believed that if we made love, it would help you decide you wanted to marry me."

Carol felt as though he'd tossed a bucket of ice water in her face. She raised her hand to her pounding heart. "Oh, no…" she whispered. "Not again."

"Carol? What's wrong?"

"Bruce did this to me, too…pressured me into giving in to him…then he hated me…punished me…." Blindly she reached for her purse and shawl, then headed for the front door.

Alex caught up with her before she made it outside. His hand clasped her shoulder as he turned her to face him. By then she was sobbing, her whole body trembling with terror. Stark terror—stark memories.

Alex took one look at her and hauled her into his arms. "Carol." He threaded his fingers through her hair. "It's all right, it's all right. I would *never* have forced you."

Chapter 12

All Carol could do was cry, and the pile of used tissues was mounting. Alex tried to comfort her, to help her, but everything he did seemed to make matters worse. One thing he'd immediately recognized—she didn't want him to touch her.

She'd curled herself up on his sofa and covered her face as she wept. She wouldn't talk to him. She wouldn't look at him. The only comprehensible statement she'd made in the last fifteen minutes had been a demand that he take her home.

Fear knotted his stomach. He had the inexplicable feeling that if he did as she asked, he'd never see her again. He had tonight and only tonight to repair the trust he'd unwittingly destroyed.

"Carol, I'm sorry." He must have told her that twenty times. It was true enough. Everything he tried to do with this woman was wrong. Tonight was the perfect example. For days he'd been searching for a way to prove to Carol how much he loved her and how right they were for each other.

This evening had seemed the perfect place and time. He'd planned it all—the music, champagne, the carefully worded proposal, the diamond ring.

He'd thought that if everything went well, they'd make love, and afterward, they could discuss the details of their wedding and their lives. He wanted her in his bed, and although it was more than a little arrogant of him, he didn't think he'd have any problem getting her there.

He'd also come to the conclusion that once they made love, she'd be convinced that they belonged together, and their marriage would naturally follow.

At first, his plan had worked flawlessly. Carol had walked into the house, seen that the table was set and the candles ready to light. She'd looked at him with those huge eyes of hers and given him a seductive smile. Then, with barely a pause, she'd waltzed into his arms.

From there everything had gone downhill.

One minute he was kissing her, marveling at the power she had over his body, and the next, she was cold and trembling, demanding answers that should've been obvious.

"Would you like some coffee?" he asked her gently for the second—or was it the third?—time. Although his arms ached with the need to hold her, he resisted.

"No," she whispered. "I want to go home."

"We need to talk first."

"Not now. I *need* to go home." She rubbed her face

and plucked a clean tissue from the nearby box. Apparently she'd regained her resolve because she stood, wrapped her shawl around her, and stumbled to the door. "If you won't drive me, then I'll walk."

Alex heard the desperation in her voice and was helpless to do anything other than what she asked. As he stood, the regret swept through him. If there was anything he could do to ease her pain, he would've done it. If there were any words he could have uttered to comfort her, he would've said them gladly. But all she wanted him to do was take her back to her own home. Back to her own bed. Her own life.

Who did he think he was? Some Don Juan who could sweep this beautiful, sensitive woman into his bed and make love to her? He felt sick to his stomach at the way he'd plotted, the way he'd planned to use her body against her, to exploit the attraction between them to serve his own ends.

Now he was losing her, and there wasn't anyone he could blame but himself. He'd known his chances weren't good the night he'd asked her to marry him. He'd hoped to see joy in her eyes when he suggested it. He'd longed to see happiness on her face. He'd wanted Carol to hurl herself into his arms, excited and overcome with emotion.

He should've known he'd been watching too many old movies.

He'd asked Carol to marry him, and none of the things he'd hoped for had happened. Instead, her eyes had reflected fear. And tonight…tonight he'd witnessed stark terror.

Alex was astute enough to realize the problem lay in Carol's brief marriage. Whatever had gone on had left deep emotional scars. Even when he'd felt the closest to her, Alex had learned very little about her relationship with her late husband. She'd let tidbits of information drop now and then, but every time she did, Alex had the feeling she'd regretted it.

On her way out the door, Carol grabbed a handful of fresh tissues, and with nothing more to say, Alex led the way to his car.

He opened the passenger door, noticing how she avoided any possibility of their accidentally touching as she climbed inside.

The tension inside the car made the air almost too thick to breathe. He could hardly stand it and he wondered how she could.

When he braked at a stop sign, he decided to make one last effort.

"Carol, please, how many times do I have to tell you how sorry I am? I made a mistake. I behaved like a jerk. Tell me what you want me to do, because I'll do it. Anything you say. I love you! You've got to believe I'd never intentionally do anything to hurt you."

His pleas were met with more of the same strained, intolerable silence.

In frustration he pressed his foot to the gas, and they shot ahead. The seat belts were all that kept them from slamming forward with the car.

The fiercest argument of their courtship now ensued, and the crazy part was, neither of them uttered a word. Every once in a while, Alex could hear Carol drag a breath through her lungs, and he knew she was doing everything in her power not to cry. Each tear she shed, each sob she inhaled, felt like a knife wound.

He was losing her, and there wasn't a thing he could

do about it. It wouldn't be so tragic if he didn't care for her so much. After Gloria's death, Alex had never truly believed he'd fall in love again. Even when he'd made the decision to remarry, he hadn't expected to find the depth of emotion he'd experienced with Carol.

And now it might be too late.

"Hey, Mom, did you and Mr. Preston have a fight or something?" Peter asked the following morning.

"W-why do you ask?"

Peter popped two frozen waffles in the toaster, then stood guard over them as though he expected Carol to snatch them out of his hands.

"I don't know. Mr. Preston was acting strange last night when he picked us up from the movie."

"Strange?"

"Sad. Mr. Preston's usually loads of fun. I like him, I mean, he's about the neatest adult I know. He doesn't treat me like I'm a kid, and he likes the same things I like and—I don't know—I just think he's an all-around great guy. Fact is, Mom, men don't come much better than James's dad."

"He is…nice, isn't he?" she agreed. She tightened her fingers around the handle of her coffee mug and looked anywhere but at her son.

Peter leaned toward her and squinted. "Have you been crying?"

"Don't be silly," she said lightly, trying to make a joke out of it.

"Your eyes are all puffy and red like you have an allergy or something."

"Pollen sometimes affects me that way." Which was

the truth. It just didn't happen to be affecting her eyes at that particular moment.

The waffles popped up, and Peter grabbed them, muttering under his breath when he burned his fingers. He spread a thin layer of butter on them and followed that with a puddle of syrup. Once that task was complete, he added two more waffles to the toaster, then sat across the table from Carol.

"I kind of thought you and Mr. Preston might've had a fight," Peter said, obviously feeling it was safe to probe some more. "That would've been too bad because on the way to the movie he was telling us that he wanted to make this dinner the most romantic night of your life. Was it?"

"He...tried."

"How did the Baked Alaska taste?"

"The Baked Alaska?" Carol made a nondescript gesture. "Oh...it was great."

"Mr. Preston made everything himself. Right down to the salad dressing. James told me he'd been shopping for days. It would've been terrible if you'd had a fight and ruined it.... You love Mr. Preston, don't you?" Peter asked earnestly.

Carol closed her eyes to the emotion assaulting her from all sides. She would be lying if she didn't admit it. And her heart refused to let her lie. But no one seemed to understand that love wasn't a cure-all. She'd loved Bruce, too—or thought she did—and look where that had gotten her.

"Yes," she whispered. She'd averted her gaze, but she could hear Peter's sigh of relief.

"I knew you did," he said cheerfully, slicing into his waffle. "I told James you were wild about his dad and that whatever happened at dinner would be okay in the morning."

"I'm sure you're right," Carol murmured.

An hour later, Carol was working in the garden space Alex had tilled for her several weeks earlier. She was cultivating the soil, preparing it to plant several different herbs that afternoon. She'd done her homework and discovered a wide variety that grew well in the moist climate of the Pacific Northwest.

Her back was to the kitchen, and she hadn't heard the doorbell. Nor was there the usual commotion that occurred whenever Peter let someone in.

Yet without a doubt, she knew Alex was standing in the doorway watching her. She felt his presence in the same way she experienced his absence.

Running her forearm across her damp brow, she leaned back and removed her gloves. "I know what you want to say," she said, "and I think it would be best if we just dropped the whole issue."

"Unfortunately that's a luxury neither of us can afford."

"I knew you were going to say that," she sighed, awkwardly struggling to an upright position. The knees of her jeans were caked with mud and the sweat was pouring down her flushed face.

There'd probably been only two other times in her life when she'd looked worse, and Alex had seen her on both occasions.

With the cultivator gripped tightly in her fist, she walked over to the patio and sank down on a deck chair. "All right, say what you have to say."

Alex grinned. "Such resignation!"

"I'd rather be working in my garden."

"I know." He flexed his hands a couple of times. "I suppose I should start at the beginning."

"Oh, Alex, this isn't necessary, it really isn't. I overreacted last night. So, you made a mistake—you're only human and I forgive you. Your intentions weren't exactly honorable, but given the circumstances they were understandable. You wanted to take me into your bed and afterward make an honest woman of me." She made quotation marks with her fingers around the words *honest woman.* "Right?"

"Something like that," he mumbled. Although of course the issue was much more complicated than that....

"The thing is, I've been made an honest woman once and it was the biggest mistake of my life. I'm not planning to repeat it."

"What was your husband's name?" Alex asked without preamble.

"Bruce...why?"

"Do you realize you've never told me?"

She shrugged; she never talked about Bruce if possible.

"Tell me about him, Carol," Alex pleaded, "tell me everything. Start with the minute you noticed each other and then lead me through your relationship to the day you buried him."

"I can't see how that would solve anything."

"Tell me, Carol."

"No." She jumped to her feet, her heart in a panic. "There's nothing to say."

"Then why do you close up tight anytime someone mentions him?"

"Because!" She paced the patio. Stopping abruptly, she whirled around and glared at him, angry all over again. "All right, you want to know? I'll tell you. We were teenagers—young, stupid, naive. We made out in the back seat of a car…and when I got pregnant with Peter we got married. Bruce died three years later in a car accident."

An eternity passed before Alex spoke again. "That's just a summary. Tell me what *really* happened in those three years you were married." His voice was soft and insistent.

Her chest constricted painfully. Would nothing satisfy him short of blood? How could she ever hope to describe three years of living in hell? She couldn't, and she didn't even want to try.

Alex wouldn't understand, and nothing she could ever say would help him. What purpose would it serve to dredge up all that misery? None that she could see.

Slowly she lowered herself onto the deck chair again, trying to still her churning thoughts, to nullify the agonizing memories. The pain was so distinct, so acute, that she opted for the only sane solution. She backed away.

Alex reached for her hand, holding it loosely. "I know this is difficult."

He didn't know *how* difficult.

"Bruce and I were married a long time ago. Suffice it to say that the marriage wasn't a good one. We were much too young…and Bruce had…problems." She bit her lip, not willing to continue. "I don't want to drag up the past. I don't see how it would do any good."

"Carol, please."

"No," she said sharply. "I'm not about to dissect a

marriage that ended thirteen years ago simply because *you're* curious."

"We *need* to talk about it," he insisted.

"Why? Because I get a little panicky when you start pressuring me into bed? Trust me, any woman who's gone through what I did would react the same way. You know the old saying—once burned, twice shy." She tried to make light of it and failed. Miserably.

For the longest time Alex said nothing. He did noth ing. He stared into the distance, and Carol couldn't tell where his thoughts were taking him.

"I never expected to fall in love again," he said.

Carol frowned at the self-derision in his words.

"Gloria knew I would, but then she always did know me better than I knew myself." He paused for a moment, and he gave a sad, bitter smile. "I'll never forget the last time we were able to talk. The next day she slipped into a coma, and soon afterward, she died. She knew she was dying and had accepted it. The hospital staff knew it was only a matter of time. But I couldn't let go of her. I had such faith that God would save her from this illness. Such unquestionable trust. He did, of course, but not the way I wanted."

"Alex..." Tears were beginning to blur her vision. She didn't want to hear about Gloria and the wonderful marriage he'd had with her. The contrast was too painful. Too bleak.

"Gloria took my hand and raised her eyes to mine and thanked me for staying at her side to the very end. She apologized because she'd been ill. Can you imagine anyone doing that?"

"No." Carol's voice was the faintest of whispers.

"Then she told me God would send another woman

into my life, someone healthy and whole who'd love me the way I deserved to be loved. Someone who'd share my success and who'd love our son as much as she did." He paused and smiled again, but it was the same sad smile. "Trust me, this was the last thing I wanted to hear from my wife. First of all, I was in denial, and I refused to believe she was dying, and second, nothing could have convinced me I'd ever love another woman as much as I loved Gloria."

Carol shut her eyes tightly and took deep breaths to keep from weeping openly.

"She told me that when I met this other woman and decided to marry her, I shouldn't feel guilty for having fallen in love again. She must've known that would be something powerful I'd be dealing with later. She squeezed my fingers—she was so weak, and yet, so strong. And wise, so very wise. Within a few hours she was gone from me forever." He rubbed his eyes and hesitated before continuing. "I didn't believe her. I didn't think it would be possible to love anyone as much as I loved her.

"Then I met you, and before I knew it, I was falling in love all over again." Once more he brought a weary hand to his face. His expression was blank, his eyes unrevealing. "And again I'm relinquishing the woman I love." He paused. "I'll give you the two weeks to make your decision, Carol. In fact, I'll make it easy for you. I won't call or contact you until the seventh—that's exactly two weeks from the day we talked about it. You can tell me your decision then. All right?"

"All right," she agreed, feeling numb.

Slowly he nodded, then stood and walked out of her house.

* * *

"The way I see it," Peter said, holding a red Delicious apple in one hand and staring at his mother, "James's dad can adopt me."

Carol felt the fleeting pain that tore through her every time Peter not-so-casually mentioned Alex's name. He seemed to plan these times with precision. Just when she least expected it. Just when she was sure she knew her own mind. Just when she was feeling overly confident. Then *pow*, right between the eyes, Peter would toss some remark carefully chosen for its effect. It was generally preceded by some bit of information about Alex or a comment about how wonderful life would be when they were one big, happy family.

"I'd have to marry Alex first, and I'm not sure that's going to happen," she said reproachfully. One challenging look defied him to contradict her.

"Well, it makes sense, doesn't it? *If* you marry him, naturally." Peter took a huge bite of the apple. Juice dribbled down his chin, and he wiped it away with the back of his hand. "I haven't heard from Dad's family in years, and they wouldn't even care if someone adopted me. That way we could all have the same last name. Peter Preston has a cool sound to it, don't you think?"

"Peter," she groaned, frustrated and angered by the way he turned a deaf ear to everything she said. "If this is another tactic to manipulate me into marrying Alex so you can go fishing, then I want you to know right now that I don't appreciate it."

She was under enough pressure—mainly from herself—and she didn't need her son applying any more.

"But, Mom, think about how good our lives would be if you married Mr. Preston. He's rich—"

"I've heard all of this conversation that I want to. Now sit down and eat your dinner." She dished up the crispy fried pork chop and a serving of rice and broccoli, and set the plate on the table.

"You're not eating?" Peter asked, looking mildly disappointed. "This is the third night you've skipped dinner this week."

Carol's appetite had been nil for the entire two weeks. "No time. I've got to get ready for class."

"When will these sessions be over?"

"Two more weeks," she said, walking into her bedroom. *Two weeks* seemed to be the magical time period of late. Alex had given her two weeks to decide if she'd accept his proposal. Two weeks that were up today. He'd granted her the breathing space she needed to come to a sensible decision. Only "sensible" was the last thing Carol felt. It shouldn't be this difficult. She wondered why she had so many doubts if she loved Alex—which she did. But Carol knew the answer to that.

Alex's marriage had been wonderful.

Hers had been a disaster.

He was hoping to repeat what he'd shared with Gloria.

She wanted to avoid the pain Bruce had brought into her life.

"Mom…phone."

Carol froze. She'd been on tenterhooks waiting for Alex to contact her. All day she'd felt a growing sense of dread. She'd expected Alex to come strolling out from behind every closed door, to suddenly appear when she least expected him.

The last thing she'd figured he'd do was phone.

With one shoe on, she hobbled over to her nightstand and picked up the phone, wondering what she was going to say.

"Hello."

"Carol, it's your mother."

"Hello, Ma, what can I do for you?" Relief must have been evident in her voice.

Angelina Pasquale said, "I was in church this morning, lighting a candle to St. Rita, when something happened to my heart."

"Did you see your doctor?" Carol's own heart abruptly switched gears. Her greatest fear was losing her mother to heart disease the way she'd lost her father.

"Why should I see a doctor?" her mother protested. "I was talking to God—in my heart—and God was telling me I should have a talk with my daughter Carol, who's deciding if she's going to marry this rich non-Italian or walk away from the best thing since the invention of padded insoles."

"Mama, I've got a class—I don't have time to talk."

"You've seen Alex?"

"Not...yet."

"What are you going to tell him?"

Her mother was being as difficult as Peter. Everyone wanted to make up her mind for her. Everyone knew what she should do. Everyone except Carol.

"You know he's not Catholic, don't you?" she told her mother, who had once considered that an all-important factor in choosing a husband. Religion and an equally vital question—whether her potential husband was allergic to tomatoes.

Her mother snickered. "I know he's not Catholic! But don't worry, I've got that all worked out with God."

"Mama, I'm sorry, but I have to leave now or I'll be late for my class."

"So be late for once in your life. Who's it gonna hurt? All day I waited, all day I said to myself, my *bambina's* going to call and tell me she's going to marry again. I want to do the cooking myself, you tell him that."

"Mama, what are you talking about?"

"At the wedding. No caterers, understand? I got the menu all planned. We'll serve—"

"Ma, please."

It took Carol another five minutes to extricate herself from the conversation. Glancing at her watch, she groaned. Rushing from room to room, she grabbed her purse, her other shoe and her briefcase. She paused on her way out the door to kiss Peter on the cheek and remind him to do his homework. Then she jumped in the car, still wearing only one shoe.

Her breathing was labored by the time she raced through traffic and pulled into the parking lot at the community center where the birthing classes were held.

She'd piled everything she needed in her arms, including her umbrella, when she realized she'd left her lecture notes at the house.

"Damn," she muttered. She took two steps before she remembered she was carrying her shoe.

"It might help if you put that on instead of holding it in your arms."

Carol froze. She whirled around, angry and upset, directing all her emotion at Alex. "This is *your* fault," she said, dropping her shoe to the ground and positioning it with her toe until she could slip her foot inside. "First, Peter's on my case, and now my mother's claiming she received a message directly from God and that He's worked out a deal with her, since you're not Catholic, and frankly, Alex—don't you dare laugh." She finished with a huge breath. "I swear, if you laugh I wouldn't marry you if you were the last living male in the state of Oregon."

"I'm sorry," he said, holding up both hands.

"I should hope so. You don't know what I've been through this past week."

"Your two weeks are up, Carol."

"You don't need to tell me that. I know."

"You've decided?"

Her eyes shut, and she nodded slowly. "I have," she whispered.

Chapter 13

"Before you tell me what you've decided," Alex said, moving toward Carol, his eyes a smoky gray, "let me hold you."

"Hold me?" she echoed meekly. Alex looked one-hundred-percent male, and the lazy smile he wore was potent enough to tear through her defenses.

"I'm going to do much more than simply hold you, my love," he whispered, inching his way toward her.

"Here? In a parking lot?"

Alex chuckled and slipped his arms around her waist, tugging her closer. Carol had no resistance left in her. She'd been so lonely, so lost, without him. So confused.

His mouth brushed hers. Much too briefly. Much too lightly.

Carol didn't want him to be gentle. Not when she was this hungry for his touch. Her lips parted in a firm and wanting kiss. Alex sighed his pleasure and she clung to him, needing him.

When they drew apart, she rested her forehead against his. "Okay," Alex said, his breath warm and heavy. "Tell me. I'm ready now."

"Oh, Alex," she murmured, and her throat constricted with ready tears. "I can't decide. I've tried and tried and tried, and the only thing I really know is I need more time."

"Time," he repeated. Briefly he closed his eyes. His shoulders sagged with defeat. "You need more time. How much? A week? A month? Six months? Would a year fit into your schedule?" He broke away from her and rubbed his hand along the back of his neck. "If you haven't made up your mind by now, my guess is you never will. I love you, Carol, but you're driving me insane with this waiting."

"Can't you see things from my point of view?" she protested.

"No, I can't," he said. "I'm grateful for this time we've had, because it's taught me something I hadn't been willing to recognize before. I'm lonely. I want someone in my life—someone permanent. I want you as my wife. I *need* you as my wife. But if you don't want what I'm offering, then I should cut my losses and look elsewhere."

A strangled cry erupted from her lips. He was being so unfair, pressuring her like this. Everything had to be decided in *his* time frame, without any allowance for doubts or questions. Something broke in Carol. Control. It was all about control. She couldn't—wouldn't—allow another man to control her the way Bruce had.

"I think you're right, Alex," she finally said. "Find yourself someone else."

The shock of her words hit him like a blow to the head. He actually flinched, but all the while his piercing eyes continued to hold hers. Carol saw the regret and the pain flash through his burning gaze. Then he buried his hands in his pockets, turned and marched away.

It was all Carol could do not to run after him, but she knew that if she did she'd be giving up her self-respect.

Janice Mandle stuck her head out the door and scanned the parking lot. She looked relieved when she saw Carol, and waved.

Carol waved back. Although she wanted nothing more than to be alone, she didn't have any choice but to teach her class.

Janice called, mentioning the time.

Still Carol couldn't seem to tear her gaze from Alex, holding on to him for as long as she could. He made her feel things she'd never known she was capable of experiencing. When he kissed her, she felt hot and quivery, as though she'd just awakened from a long, deep sleep. Spending time with him was fun and exciting. There'd been adventures waiting to happen with this man. Whole new worlds in the making. Yet something was holding her back. Something powerful. She wanted everything Alex was offering, and at the same time her freedom was too precious, too important.

Carol didn't see Alex again until the end of the week, when the boys were participating in the district track meet. James was running in the four-hundred- and eight-hundred-meter races, and Peter was scheduled for the 1500-meter. On their own, the two friends had decided to choose events in which they weren't competing together. Carol had been impressed with their insight into each other's competitive personalities.

Carol's mother had decided to attend the meet with her. Angelina was as excited as a kid at the circus. They'd just settled themselves in the bleachers when out of the corner of her eye, Carol saw Alex. Since they both had sons involved in track, she knew avoiding him would be nearly impossible, but she hadn't expected to see him quite so soon. Although, in retrospect, she should've realized he'd be attending this important meet.

Preparing herself, she sat stiffly on the bleachers as Alex strolled past. Instantly her heart started to thunder. His friend was with him, the one she'd met briefly—Barney or Bernie…Barney, she decided. Her hands were tightly clenched in her lap, and she was prepared to exchange polite greetings.

To her consternation, Alex didn't so much as look in her direction. Carol knew it would've been nearly impossible for him to have missed seeing her. If he'd wanted to hurt her, he'd done so—easily.

"So when does the man running with the torch come out?" Angelina asked.

"That's in the Olympics, Mama," Carol answered, her voice weak.

Her mother turned to look in Carol's direction, and her frown deepened. "What's the matter with you?" she demanded. "You look as white as bleached flour."

"It's nothing."

"What is it?" Angelina asked stubbornly.

"Alex…just walked past us."

"Not *the* Alex?"

Carol nodded. Before she could stop her mother, Angelina rose to her feet and reached for Carol's binoculars. "Where is he? I want to get a good look at this man who broke my daughter's heart."

"Ma, please, let's not get into that again." The way her mother had defended her had touched Carol's heart, although Angelina hadn't wasted any time berating her daughter's foolishness, either. She'd spent most of Sunday muttering at Carol in Italian. Carol wasn't fluent enough to understand everything, but she got the gist of it. Angelina thought Carol was a first-class fool to let a man like Alex slip through her fingers.

"I want one look at this Alex," Angelina insisted. She raised the binoculars to her face and twisted the dials until she had them focused correctly. "I'm gonna give this man the eye. Now tell me where he's sitting."

Carol knew it would be easier to bend a tire iron than persuade her mother to remove the binoculars and sit down before she made a scene.

"He's on your left, about halfway up the bleachers. He's wearing a pale blue sweater," she muttered. If he glanced in her direction, she'd be mortified. Heaven only knew what interpretation he'd put on her mother glaring at him through a set of field glasses, giving him what she so quaintly called "the eye."

Her mother had apparently found him, because she started speaking in Italian. Only this time her comments were perfectly understandable. She was using succulent, suggestive phrases about Alex's sexual talents and how he'd bring Carol pleasure in bed.

"Ma, *please,*" Carol wailed. "You're embarrassing me."

Angelina sat down and put the glasses on her lap.

She began muttering in Italian again, leaning her head close to Carol.

"Ma!" she cried, distressed by the vivid language her mother was using. "You should have your mouth washed out with soap."

Angelina folded her hands and stared at the sky. "Such beautiful *bambinos* you'd have with this man."

Carol closed her eyes at the image of more children—hers and Alex's. Emotion rocked through her.

Her mother took the opportunity to make a few more succinct remarks, but Carol did her best to ignore them. It seemed as if the track meet wasn't ever going to begin. Carol was convinced she'd have to spend the afternoon listening to her mother whispering in her ear. Just when she couldn't endure it any longer, the kids involved in the hurdle events walked over to the starting line. They shook their arms at their sides and did a couple of stretching exercises. Carol was so grateful to have her mother's attention on the field that it was all she could do not to rush out and kiss the coach.

The four-hundred-meter race followed several hurdle events. Carol watched James through the binoculars as he approached the starting line. He looked confident and eager. As they were taking their positions, he glanced into the stands and cocked his head just slightly, acknowledging his father's presence. When his gaze slid to Carol, his eyes sobered before he smiled.

At the gun, the eight boys leapt forward. Carol immediately vaulted to her feet and began shouting at the top of her lungs.

James crossed the finish line and placed second. Carol's heart felt as though it would burst with pride. Without conscious thought her gaze flew to Alex, and she saw that he looked equally pleased by his son's performance. He must have sensed her watching him because he turned his head slightly and their eyes met. He held on to hers for just a moment, and then with obvious reluctance looked away.

Carol sagged onto her seat.

"So who is this boy you scream for like a son?" her mother demanded.

"James Preston—the boy who finished second."

"So that was Alex's son?" Angelina asked slowly, as she took the binoculars and lifted them to her eyes once more. She was apparently satisfied with what she saw, because she grinned. "He's a fine-looking boy, but he's a little on the thin side. He needs my spaghetti to put some meat on those bones."

Carol didn't comment. She *did* love James like a son. That realization forced a lump into her throat. And her heart—her poor, unsuspecting heart—was fluttering hard enough to take flight and leave her body behind.

Feeling someone's eyes on her, she glanced over her shoulder. Instantly Alex turned away. Carol's hands began to tremble, and all he'd done was look in her direction....

James raced again shortly afterward, placing third in the eight-hundred-meter. For a high school sophomore, he was showing a lot of potential, Carol mused, feeling very proud of him.

When her own son approached the starting line for his race, Carol felt as nervous as she ever had in her life....

Since the 1500-meter meant almost four long turns around the track, it didn't have the immediacy of the previous races. By the time Peter was entering the final lap, Carol and her mother were on their feet, shouting their encouragement. Carol in English. Angelina in Italian. From a distance, Carol heard a loud male voice joining theirs. Alex.

When Peter crossed the finish line in a solid third position, Carol heaved a sigh of pride and relief. Tears dampened her lashes, and she raised her hands to her mouth. Both the first- and second-place winners were seniors. As a sophomore, Peter had done exceptionally well.

Again, without any conscious decision on her part, Carol found herself turning to look at Alex. This time he was waiting for her, and they exchanged the faintest of smiles. Sad smiles. Lonely smiles. Proud smiles.

Carol's shoulders drooped with defeat. It was as if the worlds of two fools were about to collide.

He was pushy. She was stubborn.

He wanted a wife. She wanted time.

He refused to wait. She refused to give in.

Still their eyes held, each unwilling to pull away. So many concerns weighed on Carol's heart. But memories, too—good memories. She remembered how they'd strolled through the lush green foliage of the Washington rain forest. Alex had linked his fingers with hers, and nothing had ever felt more right. That same night they'd sat by the campfire and sung with the boys, and fed each other roasted marshmallows.

The memories glided straight to Carol's heart.

"Carol?"

Dragging her gaze away from Alex, Carol turned to her mother.

"It's time to leave," Angelina said, glancing into the stands toward Alex and his friend. "Didn't you notice?

The stadium's almost empty, and weren't we supposed to meet Peter?"

"Yes..." Carol murmured, "we were...we are."

Peter and James strolled out of the locker room and onto the field together, each carrying a sports bag and a stack of school books. Judging by their damp hair, they'd just gotten out of the shower.

Carol and her mother were waiting where Peter had suggested. It seemed important to keep them as far away from the school building as possible for fear any of his friends would realize he had a family.

Alex didn't seem to be anywhere nearby, and for that Carol was grateful. And even if it made no sense, she was also regretful. She wanted to be as close to him as she could. And yet she'd happily move to the Arctic Circle to escape him. Her thoughts and desires were in direct contrast and growing more muddled every second.

Peter and James parted company about halfway across the field. Before they went their separate ways, they exchanged a brief nod, apparently having agreed or decided upon something. Whatever it was, Peter didn't mention it.

He seemed unusually quiet on the ride home. Carol didn't question her son until they'd dropped her mother off. "What's bothering you?"

"Nothing." But he kept his gaze focused straight ahead.

"You sure?"

His left shoulder rose and fell in an indecisive shrug.

"I see."

"Mr. Preston was at the meet today. Did you see him?"

"Ah..." Carol hedged. There was no reason to lie. "Yeah. He was sitting with his friend."

"Mr. Powers and Mr. Preston are good friends. They met in college."

Carol wasn't sure what significance, if any, that bit of information held.

"According to James, Mr. Powers's been single for the past couple years, and he dates beautiful women all the time. He's the one who arranged all those hot dates for James's dad...and he's doing it again."

"That's none of our business." Her heart reacted to that, but what else could she expect? She was in love with the man. However, it wasn't as if Alex hadn't warned her; he'd said that if she wasn't willing to accept what he was offering, it was time to cut his losses and look elsewhere. She just hadn't expected him to start so soon.

"James was telling me his dad's been going out every night this week."

"Peter," she said softly, "I think it would be best if we made it a rule not to discuss Alex or his dating practices. You know, and, I hope, have accepted, the fact that the relationship between James's dad and me is over...by mutual agreement."

"But, Mom, you really love this guy!"

She arched her eyebrows at that.

"You try to fool me, but I can see how miserable you've been all week. And Mr. Preston's been just as unhappy, James says, and we both think he's going to do something stupid on the rebound, like marry this Babette girl."

"Peter, I thought I just said I don't want to talk about this."

"Fine," he muttered, crossing his arms and beginning to sulk. Five minutes passed before he sighed heavily. "Babette's a singer. In a band. She's not like the run-of-the-mill bimbos Barney usually meets. Mom, you've got to *do* something. Fast. This woman is real competition."

"Peter!" she cried.

"All right. All right." He raised both hands in surrender. "I won't say another word."

That proved to be a slight exaggeration. Peter had ways of letting Carol know what was going on between Alex and his newfound friend without ever having to mention either name.

Saturday, after playing basketball with James in the local park, Peter returned home, hot and sweaty. He walked straight to the refrigerator and took out a cold can of soda, taking the first swallows while standing in front of the open refrigerator.

Carol had her sewing machine set up on the kitchen table. Pins pressed between her lips, she waved her hand, instructing her son to close the door.

"Oh, sorry," Peter muttered. He did as she asked, then wiped his face. "Ever hear of a thirty-six-year-old man falling head over heels in love with a twenty-three-year-old woman?" Peter asked disdainfully.

Stepping on a nail couldn't have been more painful—or more direct—than her son's question. "No. Can't say that I have," she said, so flustered she sewed a seam that was so crooked she'd have to immediately take it out. With disgust, she tossed the blouse aside, and when her son had left the room, she trembled and buried her face in her hands.

On Sunday morning, Peter had stayed in church a few extra minutes after Mass, walking up to the altar.

When he joined Carol in the vestibule, she placed her hand on his shoulder and studied him carefully. She'd never seen her son quite so serious.

"What's on your mind, honey?"

He gave her another of his one-shoulder rolls. "I thought if Grandma could talk to God, then I'd try it, too. While I was up there, I lit a candle to St. Rita."

Carol didn't respond.

After that, she and her son drove over to her mother's house. The tears started when she was in the kitchen helping Angelina with dinner. It surprised Carol, because she had nothing to cry about—not really. But that didn't seem to matter. Soon the tears were flowing from her eyes so hard and fast that they were dripping from her chin and running down her neck.

Standing at the sink washing vegetables helped hide the fact that she was weeping, but that wouldn't last long. Soon someone would see she was crying and want to know why. She tried desperately to stop, but to no avail. If anything, her efforts only made her cry more.

She must've made more noise than she realized, because when she turned to reach for a hand towel to wipe her face, she found her mother and her sister-in-law both staring at her.

Her mother was murmuring something to Paula in Italian, which was interesting since the other woman didn't understand a word of the language. But Carol understood each and every one. Her mother was telling Paula that Carol looked like a woman who was in danger of losing the man she loved.

With her arm around Carol's shoulders, Angelina led her into her bedroom. Whenever Carol was ill as a little girl, her mother had always brought her to her own bed and taken care of her there.

Without resistance, Carol let her mother lead her through the house. By now the tears had become soft sobs. Everyone in the living room stopped whatever they were doing and stared at her. Angelina fended off questions and directed Carol to her bed, pulling back the blankets. Sniffling, Carol lay down. The sheets felt cool against her cheeks, and she closed her eyes. Soon she was asleep.

She woke an hour later and sat bolt upright. Suddenly she knew what she had to do. Sitting on the edge of the bed, she held her hands to her face and breathed in deep, steadying breaths. This wasn't going to be easy.

Her family was still busy in the living room. The conversation came to an abrupt halt when Carol moved into the room. She picked up her purse, avoiding their curious eyes. "I…have to go out for a while. I don't know when I'll be back."

Angelina and Peter walked to the front door with her, both looking anxious.

"Where are you going?" her son asked.

She smiled softly, kissed his cheek and said, "St. Rita must have heard your prayers."

Her mother folded her hands and raised her eyes to heaven, her expression ecstatic. Peter, on the other hand, blinked, his gaze uncertain. Then understanding apparently dawned, and with a shout, he threw his arms around Carol's neck.

Chapter 14

Alex was in the kitchen fixing himself a sandwich when the doorbell chimed. From experience, he knew better than to answer it before James did. Leaning against the counter, Alex waited until his son had vaulted from the family room couch, passed him and raced toward the front door.

Alex supposed he should show some interest in his unannounced guest, but frankly he didn't care—unless it was one stubborn Italian woman, and the chances of that were more remote than his likelihood of winning the lottery.

"Dad," James yelled. "Come quick!"

Muttering under his breath, Alex dropped his turkey sandwich on the plate and headed toward the living room. He was halfway through the door when he jerked his head up in surprise. It was Carol. Through a fog of disbelief, he saw her, dressed in a navy skirt and white silk blouse under a rose-colored sweater.

At least the woman resembled Carol. His eyes must be playing tricks on him, because he was sure this woman standing inside his home was the very one who'd been occupying his thoughts every minute of every hour for days on end.

"Hello, Alex," she said softly.

It sounded like her. Or could it be that he needed her so badly that his troubled mind had conjured up her image?

"Aren't you going to say anything?" James demanded. "This is Carol, Dad, Carol! Are you just going to stand there?"

"Hello," he finally said, having some trouble getting his mouth and tongue to work simultaneously.

"*Hello?* That's it? You aren't saying anything more than that?" James asked, clearly distressed.

"How are you?" Carol asked him, and he noticed that her voice was husky and filled with emotion.

Someday he'd tell her how the best foreman he ever hoped to find had threatened to walk off the job if Alex's foul mood didn't improve. Someday he'd let her know he hadn't eaten a decent meal or slept through an entire night since they'd parted. Someday he'd tell her he would gladly have given a king's ransom to make her his wife. In time, he *would* tell her all that, but for now, all he wanted to do was enjoy the luxury of looking at her.

"Carol just asked you a question. You should answer her," James pointed out.

"I'm fine."

"I'm glad," she whispered.

"How are you?" He managed to dredge up the polite inquiry.

"Not so good."

"Not so good?" he echoed.

She straightened her shoulders, and her eyes held his as she seemed to be preparing herself to speak. "Do you…are you in love with her, because if you are, I'll… I'll understand and get out of your life right now, but I have to know that much before I say anything else."

"In love with her?" Alex felt like an echo. "With whom?"

"Babette…the singer you've been dating."

James cleared his throat, and, looking anxious, glanced at his father. "I…you two obviously need time alone. I'll leave now."

"James, *what* is Carol talking about?"

His son wore an injured look, as if to suggest Alex was doing him a terrible injustice by suspecting he had anything to do with Carol's belief that he was seeing Babette.

"James?" He made his son's name sound like a threat.

"Well," the boy admitted with some reluctance, "Mrs. Sommars might've gotten the impression that you were dating someone else, from…from something I said to Peter. But I'm sure whatever I said was very nebulous." When Alex glared at him, James continued. "All right, all right, Peter and I got to talking things over, and the two of us agreed you guys were wasting a whole lot of time arguing over nothing.

"Mrs. Sommars is way, way better than any of the other women you've dated. Sometimes she dresses a little funny, but I don't mind. I know Peter would really like a dad, and he says you're better than anyone his mom's ever dated. So when Uncle Barn started pressuring you to date that Babette, we…Peter and I, came up with the idea of…you know…"

"I don't know," Alex said sternly, lacing his words with steel. "Exactly what did you say to Carol?"

"I didn't," James was quick to inform him. "Peter did all the talking, and he just casually let it drop that you were dating again and…"

"And had fallen head over heels in love with someone else," Carol supplied.

"In the space of less than a week?" Alex demanded. Did she really think his love was so fickle he could forget her in a few short days? He'd only retreated to fortify himself with ideas before he approached her again.

"You said it was time to cut your losses and look elsewhere," she reminded him.

"You didn't believe that, did you?"

"Yes…I thought you must've done it, especially when Peter started telling me about you and…the singer. What else was I supposed to believe?"

"I'll just go to my room now," James inserted smoothly. "You two go ahead and talk without having to worry about a kid hanging around." He quickly disappeared, leaving only the two of them.

"I'm not in love with anyone else, Carol," Alex said, his eyes holding hers. "If you came because you were afraid I was seeing another woman, then rest assured it isn't true. I'll talk to James later and make sure this sort of thing doesn't ever happen again."

"It won't be necessary."

"It won't?" he asked, frowning. They stood across the room from each other, neither of them making any effort to bridge the distance. The way Alex felt, they might as well have been standing on opposite ends of a football field…playing for opposing teams.

Her eyes drifted shut, and she seemed to be gathering her courage. When she spoke, her voice was low and trembling. "Don't be angry with James…"

"He had no right to involve himself in our business."

"It worked, Alex. It…worked. When I believed I was losing you, when I thought of you with another woman in your arms, I…I wanted to die. I think maybe I did, just a little, because I realized how much I love you and what a fool I've been to think I could go on without you. I needed time, I *demanded* time, and you wouldn't give it to me…"

"I was wrong—I understood that later."

"No," she countered, "you were right. I would never have made up my mind because…because of what happened in my marriage. With Bruce."

The whole world seemed to go still as comprehension flooded Alex's soul. "Are you saying…does this mean you're willing to marry me?" he asked, barely able to believe what she was saying. Barely able to trust himself to stay where he was a second longer.

Alex didn't know who moved first, not that it mattered. All that did matter was Carol in his arms, kissing him with a hunger that seemed to consume them both.

"Yes…yes, I'll marry you," she cried between kisses. "When? Oh, Alex, I'm so anxious to be your wife."

Alex stifled the sudden urge to laugh, and the equally powerful urge to weep. He buried his face in the soft curve of her neck and swallowed hard before dragging several deep breaths through his lungs. He slid his hands into her hair as he brought his mouth to hers, exploring her lips in all the ways he'd dreamed of doing for so many sleepless nights.

Her purse fell to the floor, and she wound her arms around him, moved against him, whispering over and over how much she loved him.

"I missed you so much," he told her as he lifted her from the carpet and carried her across the room. He was so famished for her love that he doubted he'd ever be satisfied.

"I thought I'd never kiss you again," she moaned. "I couldn't bear the thought of not having you in my life."

Alex made his way to the sofa, throwing himself on the cushions, keeping her in his lap. He stroked her hair as he gazed into her beautiful dark eyes. Unable to resist, he kissed her again.

When they drew apart, Alex rested his forehead against hers and closed his eyes, luxuriating in the warm sensations inside him. He didn't want to talk, didn't want to do anything but hold her and love her.

"Alex," she whispered. "You asked me about Bruce, and I didn't tell you. I was wrong to hold back, wrong not to explain before."

"It's all right, my…"

She gently stroked his face. "For both our sakes, I need to tell you."

"You're sure?"

She didn't *look* sure, but she nodded, and when she started speaking, her voice trembled with pain. "I was incredibly young and naive when I met Bruce. He was the most fun-loving, daring boy I'd ever dated. The crazy things he did excited me, but deep in my heart I know I'd never have married him if I hadn't gotten pregnant with Peter."

Alex kissed her brow and continued to stroke her hair.

"Although Bruce seemed willing enough to marry me," she began, "I don't know how much pressure my father applied." Her voice was gaining strength as she spoke. "It was a bad situation that grew worse after Peter was born. That was when Bruce started drinking heavily and drifted from one job to another. Each month he seemed to be more depressed and more angry. He claimed I'd trapped him and he was going to make sure I paid for what I did." She closed her eyes and he heard her sigh. "I did pay, and so did Peter. My life became a nightmare."

Alex had suspected things were bad for her, but he'd no idea how ugly. "Did he beat you, Carol?"

Her eyes remained closed, and she nodded. "When Bruce drank, the demon inside him would give rise to fits of jealousy, fear, depression and hatred. The more he drank, the more the anger came out in violent episodes. There were times I thought that if I didn't escape, he'd kill me."

"Didn't your family know? Surely they guessed?"

"I hardly ever got to see them. Bruce didn't approve of me visiting my family. In retrospect, I realize he was afraid of my father. Had Dad or Tony known what was happening, they would've taken matters into their own hands. I must have realized it, too, because I never told them, never said a word for fear of involving them. It was more than that.... I was too humiliated. I didn't want anyone to know about the terrible problems we were having, so I didn't say anything—not even to my mother."

"But surely there was someone?"

"Once...once Bruce punched me so hard he dislocated my jaw, and I had to see a doctor. She refused to believe all my bruises were due to a fall. She tried to help me, tried to get me to press charges against him, but I didn't dare. I was terrified of what Bruce would do to Peter."

"Oh, Carol." The anger Alex was experiencing was so profound that he clenched his fists. The idea of someone beating this warm, vibrant woman filled him with impotent rage.

"I'd lost any respect I ever had for Bruce shortly after we were married. Over the next three years I lost respect for myself. What kind of woman allows a man to abuse her mentally and physically, day after day, week after week, year after year? There must've been something terribly wrong with me. In ways I can't even begin to understand, all the hurtful, hateful things Bruce accused me of began to seem valid."

"Oh, Carol..." Alex's chest heaved with the weight of her pain.

"Then Bruce didn't come home one night. It wasn't unusual. I knew he'd come back when he was ready, probably in a foul mood. That was what I'd braced myself for when the police officer came to tell me Bruce had been killed in an accident. I remember I stared up at the man and didn't say anything. I didn't feel anything.

"I was hanging clothes on the line, and I thanked him for letting me know and returned to the backyard. I didn't phone anyone, I didn't even cry."

"You were in shock."

"I suppose, but later when I was able to cry and grieve, mingled with all the pain was an overwhelming sense of relief."

"No one could blame you for that, my love," Alex said, wanting with everything in him to wipe away the memories of those years with her husband.

"Now…now do you understand why I couldn't tell you about Bruce?" she asked. "Your marriage to Gloria was so wonderful—it's what a marriage was meant to be. When she died, your love and James's love surrounded her. When Bruce died—" she hesitated, and her lips were trembling "—he was with another woman. It was the final rejection, the final humiliation." She drew in a ragged breath and turned, her eyes burning into his. "I don't know what kind of wife I'll be to you, Alex. Over the years I've thought about those three nightmarish years and I've wondered what would've happened had I done things differently. Maybe the fault *was* my own…maybe Bruce was right all along, and if I'd only been a better woman, he wouldn't have needed to drink. If I'd done things differently, he might've been happy."

"Carol, you don't truly believe that, do you?"

"I…I don't know anymore."

"Oh, love, my sweet, sweet love. You've got to realize that any problems Bruce had were of his own making. The reasons for his misery lay within himself. Nothing you could ever have done would've been enough." He cupped her face in his hands. "Do you understand what I'm saying?"

"I…I can't make myself fully believe that, and yet I know it's true. But Alex…this time I want everything to be right." Her eyes were clouded and uncertain, as if she suspected he'd be angry with her.

"It will be," he promised her, and there wasn't a single doubt in his heart.

Carol awoke when dawn silently slipped through the lush drapes of the honeymoon suite. She closed her eyes and sighed, replete, sated, unbelievably happy. Deliriously happy.

From the moment Carol had agreed to become Alex's wife to this very morning, exactly one month had passed. One month. It hardly seemed possible.

In one month, they'd planned, arranged and staged a large wedding, complete with reception, dinner and dance.

True to her word, Carol's mother had prepared a reception dinner that couldn't have been surpassed. Angelina had started dragging out her biggest pots and pans the Sunday afternoon she brought Alex back to the house to introduce him to the family.

Last week, Carol's sisters and their families had all arrived. The wedding became a celebration of love, a family reunion, a blending of families, all at once.

At the reception, Alex had surprised her with the honeymoon trip to Hawaii. The boys were mildly put out that they hadn't been included. Hawaii would have been the perfect place to "check out chicks," as Peter put it. To appease them, Alex promised a family vacation over the Thanksgiving holiday. Peter and James had promptly started talking about a Mexican cruise.

Carol smiled as she savored memories of her wedding day. Peter and James had circulated proudly among the guests, accepting full credit for getting their parents together.

Alex stirred and rolled onto his side, slipping his hand around her waist and tucking his body against hers as naturally as if they'd been married three years instead of three marvelous days.

Carol had been crazy in love with Alex before she married him, but the depth of emotion that filled her after the wedding ceremony made what she'd experienced earlier seem weak by comparison.

Never had she been more in love. Never had she felt so desirable. Just as she'd known it would be, Alex's lovemaking was gentle and unselfish while at the same time fierce and demanding. Thinking of how often and well he'd loved her in the last few days was enough to increase the tempo of her heart.

"Good morning," she whispered, as Alex turned to face her.

"Good morning."

Their eyes met and spoke in silent messages.

He was telling her he loved her. She was saying she loved him back. He was saying he needed her. She echoed that need.

Alex kissed her again, lightly, his lips as weightless as the creeping sunlight.

"Oh, love," he whispered reverently, spreading moist kisses over her face. "I don't think I'll ever get tired of making love with you."

"I certainly hope not." She smiled at him, brushing a stray curl from his brow. She fought back the ready tears that his love brought so easily to the surface. But it would've been impossible to restrain them. Alex didn't understand her tears, and Carol could find no way to explain.

He tenderly wiped the moisture from her face and kissed her eyes. "I can't bear to see you cry. Please tell me if there's anything I can do…."

"Oh, no…" After all the times they'd made love, learned and explored each other's bodies in the past three days, he still couldn't completely accept her tears, fearing he was the cause. Once again, Carol tried to make him understand. "I…I didn't realize making love could be so wonderful…so good."

Alex momentarily closed his eyes, his look full of chagrin and something else she couldn't name. "We didn't take any precautions last night."

His words triggered a slow easy smile. "I know, and I'm glad."

"Why? I thought we decided to wait a few months before we even considered starting a family.

"What do you think your chances of getting pregnant are?" he asked after several minutes of kissing and touching.

She smiled again. "About a hundred percent."

The room went quiet. When Alex spoke, his voice was strangled. "How would you feel about that?"

"Unbelievably happy. I want your child, Alex."

His mouth found hers again for a kiss that grew wilder and wilder. Nestling her head against his strong shoulder, Carol sighed. She felt happier than she'd ever imagined possible. Happy with her husband, her family, herself.

Epilogue

After all the years Carol had worked as an obstetrical nurse, after all the birthing classes she'd taught, she should be able to recognize a contraction. Still, she wasn't a hundred percent sure and had delayed contacting Alex until she was several hours into labor.

Resting her hands on her distended abdomen, she rubbed it gently, taking in several relaxing breaths. Twins! She and Alex were having *twins*. He felt as excited, as ecstatic, as she did. Maybe even more so... Everything was ready for their babies. The nursery was furnished with two cradles, each with a different mobile hanging above it, and Alex had painted a mural, a forest scene, on the wall for his daughters. All their little sweaters and sleepers were stacked in twin dressers he'd lovingly refinished.

Carol took another deep breath as the next pain

struck. Then, knowing she shouldn't delay much longer, she reached for the phone and called Alex at the office.

"Yes," he cried impatiently. This last week he'd been as nervous as…a father-to-be.

"It's Carol."

She heard his soft intake of breath. "Are you all right?"

"I'm fine."

"You wouldn't be calling me at the office if you were fine," he countered sharply. "Is something going on that I should know about?"

"Not really. At least not yet, but I think it might be a good idea if you took the rest of the afternoon off and came home."

"Now?"

"If you're in the middle of a project, I can wait," she assured him, but she hoped he'd be home soon, otherwise she was going to end up driving herself to the hospital.

"I'm not worried about *me*," he said. "Are the babies coming now? Oh, Carol, I don't know if I'm prepared for this."

"Don't worry. I am."

Alex expelled his breath forcefully. "I'll be there in ten minutes."

"Alex," she cried. "Don't speed."

She used the time before his arrival to make some phone calls, then collected her purse and her small suitcase—packed several weeks ago. Finally, she sank into her favorite chair, counting the minutes between contractions.

From a block away, Carol could hear the roar of his truck as he sped toward the house. The squealing of brakes was followed by the truck door slamming. Seconds afterward, Alex vaulted into the house, breathless and pale.

She didn't get up from her chair; instead, Carol held out both hands to him. "Settle down, big daddy."

He flew to her side and knelt in front of her, clasping her hands in his. It took him a moment to compose himself.

"This is it, isn't it? We're in labor?" he asked when he'd found his voice.

"We're in labor," Carol told him and stroked his hair.

"How can you be so calm about this?"

She smiled and bent forward to brush her lips over his. "One of us has to be."

"I know...I know...you need me to be strong for you now, but look at me," he said, holding out his hands for her inspection. "I'm shaking." Gently he laid those same shaking hands on Carol's abdomen, and when he glanced up at her, his eyes were bright with unshed tears. "I love these babies—our daughters—so much. I can't believe how lucky I am. And now that they're about to be born, I feel so humble, so unworthy."

"Oh, Alex..."

"I guess we'd better go. Is there anything we need to do first?"

"No. I've phoned my mother and the doctor, and my suitcase is by the door." She made an effort to disguise the intensity of her next contraction by closing her eyes and breathing slowly and deeply until it passed. When she opened her eyes, she discovered Alex watching her intently. If possible, he looked paler than he had before.

"Are you going to be all right?" she asked.

"I...I don't know. I love our babies, but I love you more than anything. I can't stand to see you in pain. I—"

His words were interrupted by the sound of another car pulling into the driveway and two doors slamming. James burst into the house first, followed by Peter, both looking as excited as if it were Christmas morning.

"What are you two doing home from school?" Carol demanded.

"We heard you were in labor. You don't think we'd miss this, do you?"

"You heard?" Carol echoed. "How? From whom?"

The two boys eyed each other. "We've got our sources," James said.

This wasn't the time or place to question them. "All right, we won't discuss it now. James, take care of your father. Peter, load up the car. I think it might be best if you drove me yourself. James, bring your father—he's in no condition to drive."

Their sons leaped into action. "Come on, Dad, we're going to have a couple of babies," James said, urging his father toward the late-model sedan the two boys shared.

By the time they got to Ford Memorial, Carol's pains had increased dramatically. She was wheeled to the labor room while James and Peter were left to fend for themselves in the waiting room.

Alex was more composed by now, more in control. He smiled shyly and took her hand, clutching it between both of his. "How are you doing?"

"Alex, I'm going to be fine and so are our daughters."

Janice Mandle came bustling in, looking pleased. "Okay, we all ready for this special delivery?" she asked.

"Ready," Carol said, nodding firmly.

"Ready," Alex echoed.

With Janice's help and Alex's love, Carol made it

through her next contractions. As she was being taken into the delivery room, Alex walked beside her. The pains were coming faster, but she managed to smile up at him.

"Don't worry," she whispered.

"I love you," he whispered back. He reached for her hand again and they met, palm to palm, heart to heart.

"Grandma, can I have seconds on the zabaglione?" James called from the large family kitchen.

Angelina Pasquale's smile widened and her eyes met those of her daughter. "I told you my cooking would put some meat on his bones."

"That you did, Mama," Carol said, exchanging a private smile with her husband. She and the babies had been home for a week. Royalty couldn't have been treated better. James and Peter were crazy about their sisters, and so far the only tasks allotted Carol had been diaper-changing and breastfeeding. She was well aware that the novelty would wear off, but she didn't expect it to be too soon. Angie and Alison had stolen two teenage hearts without even trying.

"I brought you some tea," Alex said, sliding onto the sofa beside her. His eyes were filled with love. From the moment Carol was brought to the delivery room, the light in Alex's eyes hadn't changed. It was filled with an indescribable tenderness. As she gave birth, his hand had gripped hers and when their two perfect identical daughters were born, there'd been tears in both parents' eyes. Tears of joy. Tears of gratitude. They'd each been granted so much more than they'd ever dreamed. New life. New love. A new appreciation for all the good things in store for them and their combined families.

The soft lilting words of an Italian lullaby drifted toward Carol and Alex. Eyes closed, Carol's mother rocked in her chair, a sleeping infant cradled in each arm. The words were familiar to Carol; she'd heard her mother sing them to her as a child.

When she'd finished, Angelina Pasquale murmured a soft, emotional prayer.

"What did she say?" Alex asked, leaning close to Carol.

A smile tugged at the edges of Carol's mouth. Her fingers were twined with Alex's and she raised his knuckles to her lips and kissed them gently. "She was thanking St. Rita for a job well done."

* * * * *